PRAISE FOR *SEASON OF MY ENEMY*

Season of my Enemy explores a fascina   a's
heartland during WWII. Author Na   lly
vivid detail one woman's struggle to w   n's
enemy—a German prisoner of war—   rs
fight overseas. Only with time in laboring together and sharing a mutual
faith can they finally strip away their differences and reveal one human
heart, in its desire to love and to long for peace and a future.
— Kate Breslin, bestselling author, *As Dawn Breaks*

Naomi Musch will transport you to wartime Wisconsin with her glimpse
into one of America's best-kept secrets. As the German Prisoners of War
help keep the country fed and the O'Brien family farm afloat, your senses
will come alive with the pungent aroma of freshly harvested produce, the
whirring and clacking of farm machinery, and the blistering heat of the
summer sun. Intrigue, faith, and budding relationships carry the story to
a satisfying and thoughtful conclusion. Don't miss this important piece of
history and the lessons it offers us all.
— Terrie Todd, author of *Rose Among Thornes* and
four other Historical Christian novels

Season of My Enemy is a well written story of survival on the home front
during WWII. Exploring raw and authentic topics like discrimination,
prejudice, and POW camps, Ms. Musch weaves a sensitive and beautiful
story that will satisfy fans of The Greatest Generation.
— Candice Sue Patterson, author of *Saving Mrs. Roosevelt*

Author Naomi Musch has crafted a poignant and heartwarming story
about the American WWII home front. Eloquent description immersed
me in the sights, sounds, and smells of harvest time on a farm. I was drawn
into the uncertainty, fear, and courage of people on both sides of the con-
flict as they tried to make sense of a world gone made. The characters have
stayed with me long after turning the last page.
— Linda Shenton Matchett, Amazon bestselling author
of *Spies & Sweethearts: A WWII Romance*

With exceptional skill, Musch weaves a tale about courage, resilience, and love on the home front during the Second World War. It's an intelligent and thoughtful read for history lovers.

— Patti Stockdale, author of the WWII romance, *Three Little Things*

Not all heroines wear capes. During the Second World War, many wore bib overalls as they plowed, planted, and harvested fields. Naomi Musch's courageous heroine faces grief, worry, prejudice, and longing in this tender story of a Wisconsin farm family determined to do their part for the war effort. Sometimes bowed but never broken, their quiet courage is a testament to all those who sacrificed so much during those troublesome years. *Season of My Enemy* belongs on the bookshelf of every fan of faith-based WWII fiction.

— Johnnie Alexander, bestselling and award-winning author of *Where Treasure Hides* and *The Cryptographer's Dilemma*

HEROINES OF WWII

Season
OF MY
Enemy

NAOMI MUSCH

BARBOUR
PUBLISHING

Season of My Enemy ©2022 by Naomi Musch

Print ISBN 978-1-63609-291-1

Adobe Digital Edition (.epub) 978-1-63609-293-5

All rights reserved. No part of this publication may be reproduced or transmitted in any form or by any means without written permission of the publisher. Reproduced text may not be used on the World Wide Web.

All scripture quotations, unless otherwise noted, are taken from the King James Version of the Bible.

This book is a work of fiction. Names, characters, places, and incidents are either products of the author's imagination or used fictitiously. Any similarity to actual people, organizations, and/or events is purely coincidental.

Cover image © Colin Thomas Photography Ltd

Published by Barbour Publishing, Inc., 1810 Barbour Drive, Uhrichsville, Ohio 44683, www.barbourbooks.com

Our mission is to inspire the world with the life-changing message of the Bible.

Member of the
Evangelical Christian
Publishers Association

Printed in the United States of America.

DEDICATION

First and always, this is for Jesus, "the author and finisher of our faith" who somehow never fails to teach me important truths through this process of imagining, crafting, writing, and editing a story. He even uses my characters to put themes into my heart and lessons in my life for which I hadn't had a clue. He's so good.

To my brothers and sisters in Christ who live Jesus all the time, who walk the walk and talk the talk, as they say. Especially for my dear friends who, when they say tell me they'll pray for me or someone I love, I know they truly will. That means the world to me. (I hope you know who you are. I'm afraid I'll forget someone if I start naming names.)

For my grandparents Elmer, Marie, Emil, and Dora who are no longer with me but left me a legacy. Maybe God will pass along my dedication: I think so often about each of you and what your younger lives might have been like, especially when I write in this era. I draw often upon images of daily life as I imagine it to have been for you. I'm glad I was able to grow up near you all. In this story particularly, I think of my heritage—German, Polish, Irish, Scottish, and the other mishmash of cultures my DNA tests inform me of. Somehow, they all came together here in Wisconsin—in me.

I also dedicate this story to my five grown children, Evan, Quinn, Cade, Beau, Jessamyn. When I decided that the O'Brien family in the story would have five siblings, I thought of each of you, two daughters, three sons, each with such individual strengths and talents in our family and with your own unique bonds to one another. My heart bursts with love for you.

Finally, but not lastly, for Jeff who doesn't read fiction, only nonfiction, nevertheless he always encourages me, prays for my writing, and gives me the time and space it takes me to pursue my passion. And he tells me stories. (Jeffrey Lee, I love doing the battle of Bedford Falls with you.)

⫢ CHAPTER I ⫢

Barron County, Wisconsin
June–July 1944

Fannie O'Brien stepped inside through the back porch screen door. It clattered shut against a sinking sun that cast long, dripping gold rays across the turned black earth in the western field. She headed straight to the kitchen sink. A platter of cold meat and bread sat on the table for supper, along with a bowl of steamed dandelion greens that Patsy picked that day, but Fannie was too thirsty and exhausted to care about eating just yet. She filled a glass with cold water and gulped it down without a breath. Then she wiped her wrist across her chin, closed her eyes, and breathed long and deep. Finally, she looked at Mom, who sat at the table sipping her chicory coffee, an odd, far-off expression on her face. Lately that was nothing new.

"You all right, Mom?"

Mom lowered her cup to its saucer. "Sit down, Fannie. We need to talk."

Fannie pulled out a straight-backed chair and seated herself with more of a plop than aplomb. "You didn't have to wait dinner. Where's Patsy?" She reached for a slice of bread and a thin piece of beef.

"We didn't wait. Patsy ate and is off somewhere."

Fannie scraped a little butter over the bread. "Jerry will be in soon."

Mom watched her for a long moment.

"What did you want to talk about?"

"I think it's time we ask for help."

Fannie froze, her hand poised in the air, a pinch of bread between her fingers. "Help?" She didn't mean for her voice to carry the tone that Mom's suggestion was ridiculously impossible.

Mom gave a single nod. "That's what I said."

Fannie nibbled the piece of crust, then set the rest on her plate and brushed crumbs from her dirty fingertips. She'd forgotten to wash before coming to the table, and the day's grit still clung head to toe. Who would ever have thought, just a few weeks ago, that she'd be sitting here with dry, cracked hands, grime embedded at the roots of her hair and in the pores of her knees, and every bone aching like she was sixty instead of twenty-two? She ushered out a weary sigh. "And who might we be getting that from? There's not a farmer in the county who isn't short-handed. Every family we know is struggling to find workers now that the migrants aren't coming like they used to." It was a bitter fact. The war had taken their men, her two older brothers included. Her dad in another way. Those who remained behind were either too young, too old, or stretched too thin with their own chores to help anyone else.

"There are other workers."

"Since when?" Fannie let out a huff and folded the bit of meat into her bread for a bite.

Mom watched her chew, then scooped up some greens. "I'm talking about those German prisoners. The ones the government is sending out to help at the farms and canneries."

Fannie nearly choked on a dandelion green. No wonder Mom let her swallow her meat first. "Uh-uh." She shook her head. "No. Don't even think about that. We're not going to have those Huns on this place." The very notion made her chest burn with indignation. "Dad would roll over in his grave." She lowered her eyes, ashamed for that last part, and let the dandelion work its way down. "I'm sorry, Mom," she said, when she could look her in the eye again.

"You're forgiven, but I think you're wrong. Your dad would tell you it's got to be done."

With grubby fingertips, Fannie stroked a circle on the dark oak tabletop, marked with years of bumps and scratches but as glossy and strong as ever. Every fiber of her body rebelled against Mom's insistence, but she didn't dare argue two split seconds after apologizing. She'd let Mom have her say, but Dad would never have allowed it. His farm, this property, would not be trampled on by those men whose every intention was to kill his boys. They maybe already had. For all Fannie knew, some of the very prisoners who had been shipped to Wisconsin could have been involved in Dale's capture or whatever had happened to Cal. Word locally was that the German prisoners were from General Rommel's Afrika Korps that surrendered last year.

Pure Nazis. Every last one.

"Your dad wouldn't have wanted you working your fingers to the bone, Fannie. That wasn't what he dreamed for you. You've already sacrificed too much."

"It's my decision."

"Your decision? It wasn't your decision for your brothers to get drafted. It wasn't your decision for your father to pass on." Her mom's voice choked with passion, but Fannie glanced up quick enough to notice she didn't shed her tears. "You've had to carry the load out there in the fields ever since, and I don't recall that ever being a decision you had in mind to make."

In a way, what Mom said was true. Fannie had sacrificed. She'd been so very close to earning her teacher's certificate from the county normal school. One more semester. That was all. Dad always spoke so proudly of her. *We'll have a teacher in the family soon,* he'd said. And her job. . . She loved her job. Yet she'd had to lay aside her education, and she could only manage working one day a week at the library now that the farm work had fallen on her shoulders. Still. . .

She wagged her head. "No, I know that. But think of it, Mom. *Germans.*" She hissed the word like she was talking about a crop full of corn borers.

The back door squeaked open and slammed shut, and Jerry tromped in.

"Wipe your feet," Mom said, just like she did every single time Fannie's sixteen-year-old brother came inside.

"I'm starving. What's for supper? I don't smell anything."

"Cold dinner tonight except for the dandelion greens." Mom prodded the bowl. "I suppose they're cold now too."

Jerry splashed his hands beneath the faucet sticking out of the tall backsplash and shook them off, showering water droplets. He swiped them over his filthy overalls and took a seat, grabbing for a short stack of bread and the meat.

Mom didn't say a word to reprimand him. Her gaze returned to Fannie. "They say it's safe. They send guards."

Fannie's stomach churned. Germans. . .here? While both her older brothers were over there fighting them? While Dale languished in a prison camp and who-knew-what had become of Calvin? They hadn't heard from him in weeks. Even after they sent him the terrible news about Dad's heart attack, they'd not gotten a single word back. There was no official notice he'd gone missing, but where could he be? Had he been involved in the recent D-Day invasion of Normandy? Was he safe? Alive even? Or would Fannie and her family find out that he too had been taken prisoner?

And now Mom suggested they bring Germans here to their own farm? It didn't matter if the army sent guards for the prisoners. No place was safe anymore. She looked hard at her mom. "It makes me sick to think about it. I don't like it. We'll manage."

"Think about what?" Jerry asked around a mouthful of bread and beef.

Mom picked up her cold cup and set it to her lips but didn't drink. Jerry chewed and stared, first at her mother and then at Fannie.

"Mom thinks we should get some of those Germans to work here."

He swallowed. "The PWs you mean? Those over there at that camp?" His brown eyes livened. Somehow he didn't seem nearly as tired out as Fannie was, even though he'd been working almost as long in the sun and wind as she had.

She nodded.

He took another bite. "Wow."

"Don't talk with your mouth full. You're not six," Fannie scolded. Mom was looking far away again.

Jerry swallowed and took a slurp of milk. Finally, his mouth was empty. "I could keep a gun handy and watch over 'em."

Mom jerked back to life. "You'll do no such thing. I said, they'll have a guard."

Fannie stiffened. "I don't like how you're talking like this is all settled."

"Far as I'm concerned, it is. I spoke to George Martinusen over at the co-op. They're planning to bring them in at their place too. It'll cost us less than what we paid the migrants."

Fannie's jaw dropped. "You mean we'd have to pay them too?"

"I wish I could get paid," Jerry said. "Hey, Fannie, how come you left the tractor out by the fence?"

"We can't just force them to work. It's an agreement of the Geneva Convention," Mom said.

Fannie rubbed her forehead as a pain lanced her thoughts. She shook her head. "I ran out of gas."

Jerry chuckled. "Forgot to watch the gauge again, huh?"

Fannie pinched her lips. Yes, so she'd forgotten. Not like she didn't have plenty on her mind. She'd wanted to finish getting that corner field disked before the sun went below the trees and the mosquitoes came out for their evening feast. As it was, she'd gotten half-eaten on the long walk back to the house.

Jerry chowed through some more of his meal. "I'll carry a can out for you in the morning. No big deal."

"Thanks, Jer."

Mom pushed up from her chair and took her cup to the sink. "I'll be writing a letter to petition the army for some of those workers first thing tomorrow. I've made up my mind."

The cold meat sat like a lump somewhere between Fannie's chest and stomach. She'd poured her heart and soul into the farm. How her mother could make such a big decision just like that, without caring what Fannie had to say about it, just about knocked the wind out of her.

Mom turned and leaned her backside against the sink. She folded her arms. "I know how this idea sits with you, Fannie. I know it seems like a disgrace. But do you know what's a bigger disgrace? It's the idea that our boys—your brothers—Calvin and Dale and all those others fighting in the mud over there—are depending on us. Not just to hold the farm together for when they get back, but because they'll go hungry if we don't. You've heard the government on the radio saying we need to get our farms in the fight. Well, I aim to keep ours in the fight. Just because your father isn't with us doesn't mean we can quit doing what needs—"

"I'm not quitting, Mom."

"I know you're not. You're killing yourself. Getting these crops in and harvesting them will help the cause, and it'll keep this family together, but I don't plan to sacrifice my daughter for my sons either. Still, we can't do it all alone. We need help, Fannie. I've got my hands full with the animals and the house. Patsy is doing the laundry and helping in the garden. That little girl may be only thirteen, but she's doing her share. Jerry. . ." She looked at him sitting there, and her eyes softened. "He's the man around here now, but he's still a boy too."

His chest momentarily puffed and just as instantly deflated. He swallowed down his last bite. "Just go ahead and agree with her, Fan. She's right."

Fannie didn't want to agree. She wanted the army to find her big brother Calvin and send him home. What right did they have to call a sixteen-year-old boy the man of their family when there was Cal? He

11

was the oldest. It was only proper that he should be the one to take over for Dad. Not her. Surely not Jerry.

But Fannie didn't have that choice. Mom *was* right. She even made sense. Fannie couldn't deny it, no matter how badly she wanted to.

Mom went on. "We have to do this. I'm not saying it'll be easy seeing those men here. It'll be a battle. Our own battle." She straightened away from the sink and lowered her arms to her sides. "But we have to let that be our flame. The thing that keeps us going until Cal and Dale are home. And pray, Fannie." Her voice caught. "Pray like never before." She turned away and cranked on the faucet, filling the dish tub with water. Probably now to hide her tears.

Fannie pushed her plate away. How could they do it? Bring those Nazis here?

Jerry rose and carried his empty plate and glass to the sink. "What are the prisoners going to do with the money they earn, anyway? Not like they got someplace to spend it."

"The army pays them in scrip." The passion had gone out of Mom's voice.

"What's scrip?"

"It's like coupons. They use them to buy things at the camp canteen. Razors and soap and such."

Fannie glanced again at her dirt-encrusted fingernails and rose. Her lower back complained. "I think I'll go take a bath."

Mom faced Fannie, and as her brow crinkled, she gave Fannie a wan smile. "I'm proud of you, Fannie. Real proud."

Fannie tried a smile, but her face felt stiff from sun and dirt.

"I'm proud of you too, Jerry." Mom's voice was tender. She laid a hand on Jerry's bony shoulder. Fannie was proud of him too.

But right now, she was going to stop thinking about the hard work they'd accomplished along with everything still to be done. She would forget the German PWs and anything other than a long soak in the tub. It might do her good to feel like a girl again, even for only an hour or two before she went to sleep and then got up to get dirty all over again. She turned and trudged up the stairs to her room.

Fannie put the German prisoners out of her mind. Over the coming days, she and Jerry got the western field disked, harrowed, and seeded with oats, and their routines settled into normalcy. Green shoots of corn and peas climbed taller. Fannie spent most of her days out in the field with a hoe. Jerry too. Mom handled slopping the hogs, milking their two cows, and raising her chickens. Mom hadn't mentioned the PW workers again, and after a couple more weeks, Fannie started wondering if she might have changed her mind.

On Friday morning, the last day of June, she donned a dress and left for her part-time job at the Rice Lake Public Library. Fannie had been working four days a week before her dad passed on. The job, which had been both an income and a sort of pleasant pastime for Fannie, was paying her way through normal school. Until quitting the program to take over the work of the farm. Maybe now she never would finish. Unless they really did get those PWs.

Sorting books and returning them to their correct locations on the shelves felt like coming home. She breathed in the scent of inked paper and binding and reveled in the quiet where the sounds of a chugging tractor and buzzing insects didn't invade. Before she finished for the day, she checked out a new stack of books for Patsy. That girl devoured reading material.

The next morning, Fannie slid back into her newly washed overalls and tied a kerchief over her hair, ready to face another day of outdoor work. The reprieve of the library refreshed her, and tomorrow after church they'd enjoy a potluck picnic following the service.

The library job and church services—those two small breaks each week—might get her through the summer and fall. Maybe by then the war would be over and Cal and Dale would both be home again.

Lord, let it be so.

She stepped onto the landing outside her bedroom door and met Patsy on her way to breakfast. Her sister wore one of Jerry's old checked shirts and rolled denim pants. Her hair was divided into pigtails only a shade lighter than Fannie's rich brown. Patsy cast big, chocolaty eyes and a smile at her.

"Good morning, Fan."

"Good morning." They started down the stairs.

"Thanks again for bringing me the books. I started *A Tree Grows in Brooklyn* last night. It's *sooo* good." Her words dripped with dramatics.

"I might have to read it sometime."

"You should." Patsy trotted on down ahead of her.

When would Fannie have time for pleasure reading again? She had no idea. The very thought seemed ludicrous. Maybe someday when life returned to normal, when she was finished with her education, when she became a teacher and could come home at night to grade her students' papers and tuck herself into bed with a good book.

Maybe not until I'm thirty.

Mom nodded at the table as Fannie strode into the kitchen. Pancakes and eggs waited. Fannie noted the maple syrup tin sitting on the table. Since the sugar rationing began, maple syrup was an even richer treasure for occasional use. Mom usually saved it for special days, but Fannie wasn't about to question it today. A minute later, Jerry came in, pulling up his suspenders and joining Fannie at the table. Mom set a pitcher of milk between them. "You two had better eat up. They'll be here soon."

"They? Who—" Suddenly Fannie knew who Mom meant. "How many are coming?"

"Could be half a dozen men or so. Depends." Mom shrugged without elaborating. "Patsy, when they come, you stay here at the house. I don't want to see you wandering out there acting curious."

"I don't want to go anywhere near those Germans. They probably have spies. But do I have to stay inside?" Patsy scrunched her nose.

Fannie and Jerry glanced at each other, an unspoken acknowledgment that they agreed with Patsy about the spies.

"Not inside, but right in the yard where I can see you. I've got work for you in the garden today."

Patsy nodded and turned to her breakfast.

Fortified with two eggs and a second pancake, Fannie dabbed the calico cloth napkin to her lips when the sound of a truck rumbling up the driveway captured all their attention. They rose and moved as a family toward the front door and stepped through to the porch.

The truck jerked to a halt, and an American soldier got out of the passenger door. He carried a rifle, and there was a pistol tucked into his belt holster besides. Another soldier stepped down from behind the wheel. Fannie's heart jerked when one of them flipped back a canvas covering the back and ordered the prisoners off the truck. She took only tiny breaths as she counted eight men climbing down. The enemy! Here on their soil! One by one she took note of them, especially of their youth. Why, they looked hardly older than she or Jerry. They wore tan and brown uniforms with the giant letters *PW* stamped on their backs. Their hair was cropped short, and they squinted into the morning sun as they took in their surroundings.

Fannie raised her chin, and a sigh of relief sat on the edge of her lips. Then the last two prisoners emerged, and she pressed her mouth into a line. They were older than the others. Not *old*, but definitely more mature or even in their prime. Probably not more than twenty-eight or thirty, they both had the same cropped haircuts as the younger men, but they had the solid bearing of a few extra years and experiences. Only about an inch separated the two in height, and both appeared taller than any of the men in Fannie's family. The face of the darker-haired man was narrower, and his eyes peered hawk-sharp toward them. The fair-haired man glanced toward her family and away with a set square jaw, taking in the barn, the sheds, and the fields. What was he doing? Calculating a way to escape or where to find a tool that would make a lethal weapon?

Fannie twitched when Jerry's boot scraped on the floorboard. His voice brushed her ear. "Well, this should be interesting," he said.

⋮ CHAPTER 2 ⋮

"Well." Mom might as well have grunted. It was as though her mind was so full, she couldn't sort through it all, and just that single word leaked out to make space. Was that all she was going to say?

Jerry moved to the steps.

"Jerry." Mom halted him.

"I'm just going down there. Somebody's got to."

He started down again, and this time Mom didn't stop him. He was too young for this. They would smirk at him, disrespect him. The Germans would smirk at all of them. *Kids and women ordering them around.* With a huff, Fannie started after Jerry. "I'll go too."

"Thank you, Fannie." Mom's words brushed over her in an almost-whisper as Fannie walked by.

She would not look at the prisoners. Not directly. She wouldn't give them an opportunity to catch her eye. She grazed them with only the most general glance as they lined up behind the truck. The guard called them to attention, and they straightened. Even so, with only that barest look, she could tell they stared. Not at Jerry but at her. Did one man lick his lips? Fannie's stomach cinched in on itself.

The guard dipped a nod at her. "Ma'am. I'm Corporal Taft. Where would you like the prisoners to begin?"

She blinked and drew herself taller as she scrambled for an answer. Then she pointed in a general direction toward the field west of the house. "The potatoes need hilling. Back there."

She turned to Jerry, who stood beside her, hands on his hips and feet braced apart. "Jerry, why don't you go get the hoes out of the shed. All of them. Looks like we'll be short. Bring the bug cans too." She faced the guard again. "You can have a couple of your men pick potato bugs." She glanced their way again.

One younger prisoner nudged the man next to him, and she tore her gaze away, berating herself for making eye contact as she turned to the field and shielded her eyes. She steeled her voice not to shake. "Follow me. I'll show them where to begin."

Corporal Taft shouted orders in English and then in German, and the men filed behind her. She forced a thick lump down her throat as they moved together like a hen leading her overgrown chicks to the field. There she stepped back as the American soldier told the prisoners what was expected. Jerry trotted up with hoes and handed them out. He gave her a grin, and she responded with a tiny shake of her head. She didn't need the prisoners thinking they were thrilled about having them here.

"You'll be right here then, Corporal Taft?" The thought of him turning his back on the prisoners unnerved her.

"Yes, ma'am. Right here. Or maybe in the shade over there by that tree." He nodded toward a cottonwood that edged the corner of the field nearest them. "You don't have to worry. These Germans are the safe ones. Most of them are glad their part in the war is over."

She took a more normal breath. Was that so? If the corporal was telling her so to ease her mind, it worked, if only slightly. She hoped it was the truth. "Thank you, Corporal. I'm glad to hear it."

"If they try anything, they'll lose working privileges permanently. They don't want that. They're willing to work. Not like the Japanese. The Japs would rather stand before a firing squad, some of 'em."

"Oh?"

"That's right. But not these Germans. They'd rather work than loaf around. And we've been careful not to let any of the real troublemakers out of Camp McCoy."

"Troublemakers?" Then there were problem prisoners after all, as she first suspected. Just like that, she was on edge again.

"The true Nazis. Captured SS and the like. Most of the PWs who are let out to the fields and canneries had no choice but to fight over there."

"These men?" She tucked a loose strand of hair into her scarf and glanced at the backs of the prisoners. Six of them were beginning to mound dirt along the rows of leafy green potato plants, while two others carried tin cans of old tractor oil, plucking voracious potato bug larvae from the leaves and stems and dropping them into the containers. She studied them for a prolonged moment, now that they had their backs to her.

"Must not be much of a country if your government has to force you to fight for it," Jerry said.

Corporal Taft snickered. "Oh, they gave it their best shot all right. And there are plenty of them over there willing to sock it to our boys."

Jerry sent a wad of spittle to the side. "Our brother Calvin will sock it right back. You can bet Dale is giving them what-for in that German prison camp too."

Fannie shrank at the thought of her brothers somewhere over there taking who-knew-what from the Nazis. She hoped they really were giving them—in her brother's words—*what for.*

"You've got kin who were captured?" the corporal asked.

"One of our brothers," Fannie said. "We think he's all right. Letters don't say a whole lot."

Corporal Taft looked solemn. He squinted out over the field of workers. "I'm sorry to hear it."

Jerry folded his arms and continued studying the prisoners also. "Wonder where they caught these ones."

"Most of them came from North Africa," the corporal said. "Some of Rommel's African Corp that our boys rooted out."

Fannie took a shuddering breath. Better to stop this talk about how dangerous the workers could be, supposedly safe or not. "My brother and I will be on the tractor over in the cornfield should you need us."

"I'm sure they'll do just fine. Once they finish here, if you want me to bring them over there to help, just let me know." Corporal Taft turned away. His attention fixed again on the men in the field.

Fannie nudged Jerry with an elbow and jerked her head for him to follow. "As if I want their help around the equipment," she muttered, once they'd gotten beyond the corporal's hearing.

Jerry's stride was long, inching past hers. "They look pretty harmless to me. Be nice to see if any of them knows how to run a tractor. You could use a break, and I wouldn't mind a swim."

She gave him a glare. "A swim. And while you're off swimming they're left alone here with Mama and Patsy. What'll you say next? That you'd like to invite them along for a dip?"

"Might be interesting."

Her temples throbbed at his nonchalant attitude, but when she glared again, he gave her a cockeyed grin. "I'm only fooling. Does me good to see them out there working in the sun. Must be scorching in those PW uniforms."

Fannie sniffed with a moment's satisfaction. "Sure must." Imagining them sweltering under those long-sleeved shirts was almost as satisfying as imagining them locked in a hole in the ground for what they'd done to the American soldiers. For all she knew, these very men might be responsible for Dale's capture or the fact that Calvin was missing.

She and Jerry arrived at the barnyard, where the tractor waited outside a three-sided shed with the cultivator hooked onto the back. "You want to drive or take the back seat?" she asked.

"I'll drive." Jerry leapt up to the tractor's seat. "Give the wheel a turn, will you, Fan?"

She brushed the wayward bangs that escaped her scarf and put her hands to the flywheel. "Ready?"

"Yep."

Fannie gave it a turn once, then once more. The tractor fired on the second try. Jerry adjusted the gas. "I'll walk alongside to the field," Fannie called out over the chug of the engine.

Jerry put the tractor into gear. At the edge of the cornfield, with the front tires lined up evenly between two rows of dark green, knee-high cornstalks, he stopped while Fannie climbed onto the low seat of the cultivator hooked behind. On either side of her were long handles that operated the disks and shovels.

"Ready?"

It was her turn to nod. Jerry took them forward. Deftly, Fannie operated the levers, keeping the blades carefully aligned to cut through the soil, ripping up weeds without harming the young corn plants as Jerry guided them through the field. The tractor chugged along, making enough noise to make it impossible to converse. Fannie was fine with that. It gave her time to consider the upheaval on the farm and in their lives. In *her* life.

At midmorning, she and Jerry switched places, and by noon the field was nearly finished. As they tilled down the last row of corn, Fannie raised her glance toward the farmyard and beyond it to the field where the PW workers had gathered in relaxed postures at the edge. A couple of the men were stretched out on the ground, leaning back on their elbows. If she squinted a little, she could see one man raising a canteen to his mouth. They must be taking their lunch break. Corporal Taft stood nearby, his gun resting casually across his arms.

Fannie licked her own parched lips. What right did they have to take a break until she said so?

"Hey, Fan," Jerry called from behind. "Slow up so I can jump off at the end."

She nodded to show she'd heard him and slowed to a near stop when she reached the edge of the corn. She looked back over her shoulder at Jerry as he dismounted the cultivator.

"Race you to the house," he said, egging her on with a jerk of his chin.

She gave him a weak smile then gunned the gas a little. He trotted off ahead. She let him lead the way, though she did give it a little push now and then, just to keep him running. A long, comfortable smile lifted her cheeks, making her feel for a moment like life wasn't insane. Like her dad hadn't died and she wasn't missing him like crazy. Like she didn't have to quit school and hours at the library to run the family farm. Like she didn't have Germans standing in her potato field.

With a sudden urge to be free of it all, she gave the tractor more gas and careened past her brother.

"Hey!" he yelled, laughing. She pulled up near the tractor shed, and not until she killed the engine and glanced up did she notice all those enemy soldiers watching her from where they lounged sixty yards off. She heard the distant vocal tones of their conversation, words she couldn't have understood even if they were closer, but their glances and gazes made her sure they were talking about her. She shouldn't have drawn attention by racing past Jerry. Or was it just because she was a woman and they hadn't seen many lately? Such a thought would make her flush if they weren't Germans, enemies responsible for her brothers' peril. The very kind who'd shot Alfie Swanson and Reginald Meyer, boys she'd grown up with. She thanked God Jerry wasn't old enough to go to war.

She turned her back on the prisoners and climbed down off the tractor. She ached to stretch her limbs, to shake them out after spending all morning bumping along through the cornfield, but it could wait. Tonight, sometime after supper, after the workers had all gone, she'd work the kinks out and maybe even join Jerry in a swim down at the creek. She'd take Patsy along too. They'd forget about this upheaval to their lives for a little while before the evening's mosquito crop came out looking for a feast.

"Miss O'Brien!" Corporal Taft hollered to her.

"Stay. I'll see what they want." Jerry moved past her, his breath still coming in shallow pants from his run.

She let him go. The way those prisoners looked at her got under her skin, and she couldn't deny it. This was something Jerry could probably handle. She strode toward the house with one eye peeled on Jerry and the PWs. The corporal was speaking, and Jerry nodded. Two men walked to the corporal at some command. Jerry turned around and headed back.

Fannie was almost to the porch steps when she saw the two PWs carrying water jugs toward the house. Jerry pointed past her toward the hand pump outside the barn.

She scored them with a glance as they passed by the house not thirty feet away, but one man's gaze caught hers. He was one of the older ones, her age or more. His hair was dark, his eyes gray in the distance. He wasn't at all the Aryan type she'd heard tell Hitler talked about as his perfect specimens of humankind, but then most of the others weren't either. His eyes narrowed, and then his face relaxed and his mouth lifted on one side. Whether she would call it a smile or a snarl, she didn't linger long enough to find out. She turned up the step and swung open the screen door. She'd watch the pump from the shadows on the inside.

The two Germans strode to the pump with empty pails, and Jerry waited outside a few yards away. She could hear the creak and slam of the pump handle each time one of them thrust it up and down. The farm had a water line that ran off a new electric pump into the barn, and another line went to the house, but her father had driven a shallow point for the old hand pump just for emergency use. Jerry was smart to have them use that now. No way would she want them going into the barn.

A voice called to them, *"Beeil dich!"* and they picked up their pace, careful not to slosh out too much of the water in the full pails they carried. Fannie leaned closer to the screen so she could see them heading back to the field. The older blond soldier waved them to hurry up. He'd been last man off the truck that morning. He'd rolled up the sleeves of his shirt over matured, hardened forearms, and even from this distance, she could see the sweat stains on his gray shirt. Fannie studied him top to bottom. What was his story? What malicious deeds had he done over there in Europe or Africa or wherever he'd been? He ran his tongue over his lips, then turned away as the men with the water drew near.

Jerry clomped up the steps, and she moved away from the screen door. He came inside.

Mom came into the kitchen. "Wipe your feet. How did it go out there?"

"Corn is tilled."

"I got a call from Dick Pearson today," Mom said. "He'll be over this afternoon to check the peas."

"They're ready when he is," Fannie said.

Mom raised her brow. "What about the prisoners? They look like they're going to work out for us?"

Fannie glanced at Jerry. He went to the sink and turned on the water, then reached for a glass. "Looks like they did okay on the potatoes. I didn't see any of the plants pulled out. Hills are nice and even."

"When did you see that?" Fannie moved alongside him to wash her hands. "Just now?"

"Yeah." He gulped down his water. "I told them they could fill their water jugs at the pump whenever they needed, so don't go sending Patsy out there without checking if they're around."

"I'll be sure not to." Mom swept a look toward the living room. "Patsy is asking a lot of questions. I don't want her curiosity causing any trouble."

Fannie shook water droplets from her hands and reached for a hand towel. "What kind of questions?"

"Nothing serious. She has the idea they're not quite human. 'Course, that's not too surprising given the talk she hears."

"I'll talk to her."

"Do that. My ears are about worn out with all her jibber-jabbering."

Fannie hung the towel on the wooden dowel in front of the sink, glad to share a smile with her mom and Jerry. Patsy could be a handful, smart as a whip and curious as a kitten. She couldn't get enough to read. "Maybe I'll take her with me to the library next Friday. It's been a few weeks, and I'm sure she'll need some more books by then."

"I'd appreciate that. Especially if those workers are here."

"You don't think I'll go off to the library if they're here." It wasn't a question. Fannie had no plan whatsoever of leaving her mother and Jerry alone with a bunch of Nazi soldiers. "I'm not leaving this farm if those Germans are within a mile. One lone guard is not enough to watch them, if you ask me. What if they circled him or something? He can't shoot them all. One guard," she said again with a shake of her head.

"Let's not have any talk about anyone getting shot," Mom said, just as Patsy came around the corner.

"Who's getting shot? Did the guard have to shoot one of those prisoners? I didn't hear anyone shoot."

"No one is getting shot," Mom said again.

"You'd know if someone got shot out there," Jerry said to his little sister.

Patsy shrugged like it didn't matter one way or another. "I'm hot. I'm going swimming."

"Not right now. You're going to go down to the cellar after lunch and sort the wash for tomorrow."

Patsy's shoulders slumped. "Why do I have to sort wash today? Why can't I do it in the morning?"

"It's nice and cool down there, so stop your complaining. You can help me set lunch on the table first."

"Oh, all right." Patsy's dramatic sigh followed Fannie as Fannie took her seat at the table. Soon they were all enjoying some leftovers from last night's dinner.

After their meal, as Fannie helped clear the table, another car motored up outside.

"I bet that's Mr. Pearson," Mom said.

"I'll go see to him, Mom."

"Are you sure? You've been doing everything."

"It's why I'm home." She pushed open the screen door and stepped outside. Right away she recognized the insignia of the cannery they contracted their peas to painted on the side of the car. Mr. Pearson, the cannery man, climbed out. She strode down the front steps to meet him.

"Hello, Mr. Pearson."

"Hi, there. You're Ellen's daughter. . . ." He stretched out the word, searching for her name.

"Fannie." She shook his hand.

"That's right. Fannie. I should remember. You've been helping your dad bring the peas in since you were that tall." He held a hand waist high. "So many youngsters, I forget everyone's name."

"That's all right. You're here to check the crop."

"That I am. Came as soon as I could. The viner has been pretty busy already. Figured your crop must be about ready."

"I think you're right. I checked them day before yesterday. Why don't you follow me out?"

He tugged the brim of his hat and strode alongside her toward the pea field. They passed by Jerry with his head under the hood of a beat-up old car that didn't run. He straightened to say hello. "You need me, Fan?"

"No, you keep on with what you're doing."

Dad had let him keep the old heap, saying it probably only needed some tuning and that it was a good project for a boy. Fannie figured it needed more than a tuning, but her father knew that if anyone was up to the task of figuring out the trouble, it was Jerry. He was clever with motors and gadgets. He didn't have a lot of time to call his own these days since Dad died, and she wouldn't steal this little bit from him now just to go check on the peas. Besides, since their father passed, that pile of tin held more significance to her brother than before.

The O'Briens marketed peas, snap beans, and potatoes, rotating them in the fields from year to year. They planted corn and oats too, some of it for their own livestock and the rest to sell. With the number of dairy farms in the state, there was always a market for corn, oats, and baled straw. Thankfully, beyond the livestock they raised for their own family, along with an occasional extra market beef and two or three hogs, they no longer had the demands of milking a dozen or more cows every day the way her parents had when she was a little girl. Now they only milked Mattie and Gertie, their two sweet-natured brown jerseys. Her dad and his father used to fill the silo with silage for the milk herd each year, but now it stood empty, a sentinel to the past as the fields were turned to cash crops.

"The fields look good this year," Mr. Pearson said. "We'll be working from sunup to nightfall for the next couple of weeks or longer. Been going strong all week."

"Glad to hear it. Even with so many men away?"

He grunted. "We've seen more kids and women bringing in the peas than ever before. And quite a few of those men like you've got out there in your front field." He nodded, indicating the PWs a long way off. "What are they doing? Hilling potatoes?"

Fannie nodded. They'd reached the edge of the pea crop, and she plucked a young pod. "Yes, sir. I suppose they'll be helping us bring in the peas too."

He stepped between rows of thick vines. "Well, I guess it would be a lot worse to lose the crops because they couldn't get brought in. I don't like admitting that we need the workers any more than anyone else around here, but it's a fact, now, isn't it?"

Fannie swallowed the gall she tasted. "I suppose it is, Mr. Pearson."

He stooped and raised a swath of drooping pea plants to have a look at the thickness of the long pods draping the ground beneath. He culled one here and there and cracked them open to have a look. He ran his thumb along the tender green insides, popping the young peas free until he had a handful. He rolled them over his palm, then poured them into his mouth. "I'd say they're about ready. Just another couple of days to fill out. Your family have plans for the Fourth?"

President Roosevelt had reminded the nation of the hardships their soldiers faced this holiday and that war employees would need to continue their work. As far as the O'Briens were concerned, he needn't have bothered. With their thoughts bent toward Calvin and Dale, as well as still mourning their father and husband, they would remain prayerful at home. "Not this year." There was no need to elaborate.

"Then I'll put you down for Tuesday and Wednesday. Can you manage it?" He looked her square in the eye. It was more than a casual question.

She reached for another pea pod. "We'll manage all right."

He gave her a smile, one that seemed to want to inspire confidence. "I'll see you then. Just come right away. We'll be ready first thing."

"We'll see you bright and early, Mr. Pearson."

They strolled at a thoughtful pace back toward his car. "You and your mother doing okay out here, Fannie? I felt real bad when I heard about your father and those brothers of yours."

"We're doing all right. My mom is a rock. Her faith, well. . ." Fannie shook her head. "I sometimes think she really could move mountains."

"Hearing that makes me glad. She isn't in this alone. Too many others facing loss with this war."

Fannie didn't like the idea that misery loved company. It was the same as wishing bad on somebody just so you didn't have to feel all the badness yourself. Yet she couldn't deny that knowing they weren't the only ones who understood how she and her family suffered was comforting. Convoluted comfort, but comfort all the same. "Yes. You're right. Awful as it is. We're praying that the army will be able to send Calvin home soon as they locate him."

Rather than turn toward his automobile, Mr. Pearson paused and glanced toward the potato field. Fannie had avoided looking in the PWs' direction, but now Mr. Pearson's gaze drew hers along with his. The men looked to be nearly three-quarters finished with their task.

"How about I go over there with you to talk to that soldier about those peas?"

"You don't have to do that. I can manage it all right."

"You sure? I don't mind helping."

She took a breath and let it out, and her burdens lifted just a little. "I can handle it. I've got Jerry here, and Mom's just inside."

"I'll leave you to it then." He looked at her one last time, as if he was a little reluctant to leave her with such a task. Mr. Pearson was a nice man. He had a wife and a couple of kids her age or thereabouts.

She didn't know them personally, as they'd grown up in a different town south of here, but she'd seen them working with their dad at the vinery off and on over the years.

Mr. Pearson got in his car and waved goodbye as he drove away. Fannie strode toward the field. She put a little more purpose into her step like she had that morning when she first marched down the steps to meet them. Like it or not, these prisoners were going to be sticking around, and if all went well, they were going to be responsible for getting the O'Briens' pea crop to market.

Corporal Taft was standing forty or fifty yards down the field's edge, right near that shady cottonwood he'd mentioned earlier. He pushed away from the tree trunk and walked toward her.

"Corporal Taft, how are things going?"

"Nearly done. The men did a good job, if I must say so myself. The truck will be back to pick them up by four."

The rows of potatoes that stretched out before her did look good. Healthy and green and nicely hilled with hardly a weed between them. "I appreciate the fact that they don't do shoddy work." She wasn't about to belabor the thanks. "That was the cannery man, Dick Pearson, who you just saw drive away. He's come by to check on the peas. Will you be able to bring the men back first thing Monday? It'll take us a day and a half to cut all the vines. Mr. Pearson will expect the first couple of loads Tuesday morning. We'll rotate cutting and hauling the rest of the day Tuesday and all day Wednesday."

"I'll have them here right on time."

"It'll be a long day. Once the viner is ready, we don't stop until we're done."

"I'll tell my sergeant so we can make arrangements."

Beyond him, one of the prisoners approached—the one she thought to be the oldest. The same man who'd waved the other two over with the water jugs. Fannie raised her chin to call attention to him, and the corporal turned around. "What do you need?"

The man spoke in German, and Corporal Taft answered, though the corporal's German didn't sound nearly as smooth. The man jerked his head with a nod, but his gaze wandered to Fannie as he said something else. Her shoulders tightened, but his expression was unreadable. Perhaps she only imagined that his remark had something to do with her. The planes of his face were smooth except for a day's white-gold beard stubble. Slight crow's feet appeared at the corners of his eyes when he

27

squinted against the sun. Her body remained taut as barbed wire as she considered how near this Nazi stood to her.

The corporal nodded and sent him on his way. The prisoner's glance flicked to her once more before he turned. She controlled her urge to say something not very clever.

"Captain Kloninger says they're about done," Corporal Taft said. "He wondered if there's anything else you want me to have them do until the transport truck arrives."

She hadn't had a chance to think ahead. "Just—just keep them picking potato bugs. They couldn't have gotten all those."

He chuckled. "No, I'm sure they haven't. I'll give them a water break and get them to it."

Her glance swept the workers and landed on the back of the PW the corporal had called Captain Kloninger. A captain. He'd no doubt killed his share of her countrymen. A man didn't become a captain in the German army unless he had certain skills and capabilities. And hadn't these men been captured under Rommel, a cunning and ruthless German fighter? A bitter taste rose in her mouth.

"They are impressed with the way you drive a tractor," Corporal Taft said, surprising her. "Most of these men are from some city over there. Not more than one or two natural-born farmers among them." A grin split his friendly, sun-browned face. "You drive better than my sister, that's for sure."

She gave him her attention. "Where are you from, Corporal?"

"I grew up in Iowa. My folks own a hog farm down there."

"Then you are a natural-born farmer."

"Yes, ma'am. I plan to be one again someday. This is pretty country you have around here."

"Yes, it sure is. My dad thought so. He was born and raised here too."

"Your family lost him a while back, so I hear."

Her heart clenched a little like it always did still when she allowed the reality to settle in. "Just this spring."

"I'm sorry for your loss. And that kid is your only brother still at home."

She nodded. Her gaze turned toward the prisoners who were making their way to the edge of the field, gathering the hoes. Her thoughts turned melancholy. "I wonder if my brother Dale is picking potato bugs in some German field."

Corporal Taft hitched his shoulders. "I doubt it. From what I hear, the German people don't have much left. Everything has gone to feed their army."

She didn't bother asking, *"Then what do they feed their prisoners?"* Surely those detained in prison camps weren't high on their priority list for issuing meat and potatoes.

Corporal Taft gave a command in German as the men approached. He turned to her with a smirk. "Those two years of German in high school paid off, I guess," he said. He spoke a few more words as they approached, all of them looking hot and tired.

The dark-haired man who'd come for the water earlier was carrying the hoes. He looked straight at her with those gray eyes of his. *"Es ist die Tochter des Bauern."* His grin broadened, and she immediately felt incensed.

The corporal replied briefly in German. Fannie wasn't sure what he said, but his voice was firm.

The man dipped his head at her in a show of respect, and the next words he said were gentle. He lifted the hoes and nodded toward the toolshed attached to the barn.

The corporal gave him leave to return them. He turned to Fannie. "I'll have him set them outside the door." He nodded at the man. "Go ahead." The man seemed to understand the English command. He smiled at Fannie as he passed her. Though she wanted to see something menacing in it, she didn't. It was just a smile.

She glanced toward the others who were dropping to the ground beneath the shade of the cottonwood. All except for Captain Kloninger, who stayed on his feet, uncapping one of the canteens. He watched her and the corporal, and she felt the need to draw her attention away. She didn't like him. Not one bit. The corporal could say all he wanted about how these men weren't dangerous. Maybe some of them weren't, but Fannie knew better.

This one was.

≡ CHAPTER 3 ≡

Shortly after sunup, Fannie tied a scarf over the hair knotted at her nape before heading out the back door. She met Patsy on the cobbled walk, returning from the barn with two pails of fresh, frothy milk.

She smiled at her little sister as they passed. "Glad to see you up and at 'em."

"Mom says I have to help you in the field today."

That halted Fannie. "Did she?"

"I always help with the peas."

"I was hoping we could get along with just me and Jer this time."

Patsy kept moving but called back. "I don't mind getting out of it, but I'm not gonna argue with Mama. She's determined."

Fannie would see about that. Mama had made it clear that Patsy was to stick close to the house with those Germans coming to work at the farm, so why would she want her out there with them today? They could manage without Pats, even though pea harvest had always been a family affair accomplished along with the hired migrant workers. Everyone chipped in, in some way. Fannie would have a quick chat with Mom about that at breakfast. First, she needed to check over the equipment and make sure everything was ready for the PWs' arrival.

The sun was just about to crest the treetops. They'd need to be in the field by seven if they were going to get the first loads to the vinery by noon. They had two flatbed wagons on standby ready to load. Jerry was out there now checking the tires and making sure everything else was shipshape.

Fannie hauled a gas can from the shed and filled the tractor's tank. Then she double-checked that the cutter was hitched all right.

Finally finished, she went back inside the house. Mama set a plate of pancakes on the table. "Eat plenty. Lunch is a long way off."

Fannie went to the sink to wash her hands. "Patsy said you're sending her out to help in the field today."

"You're going to need every hand."

"We'll do fine. Corporal Taft assures me the Germans are prepared to work hard. I'd rather you not let Patsy go out there."

Mom's glance shifted toward her younger daughter who was straining the milk with her ear turned toward them. "You know I don't want to," Mom said, "but I'll be out there too, and we can all keep an eye on her."

"I'm not going to do anything wrong," Patsy said, lowering the empty pail to the floor.

"Of course you won't." Mom opened the icebox for the nearly empty milk jar inside and poured out the remainder in a glass for each of them. "Here. You can use this after you wash it." She set the empty jar in the sink by Patsy. "I don't think you'll do anything wrong. We only worry about the Germans."

"You let Jerry and Fannie around them."

"Yes, because someone has to be in charge. That doesn't mean I like it."

"Won't the guard have a gun?"

Jerry burst through the back door and swiped his feet over the tattered rug. "What's everyone talking about guns?"

"Not guns," Fannie said, pouring syrup over her pancakes. "We're talking about the guard and the PWs and whether or not Patsy should help in the field today."

Jerry rolled his lips. "*Pfft*. As if her skinny arms can manage much anyway."

"Patsy, why don't you just stay here at the house and make sure we have a great big lunch," Fannie suggested.

Jerry jerked his chair up to the table and forked a stack of pancakes off the pile onto his plate. "Maybe Mom will let you bake us something sweet with that sugar she's been hiding."

Sometimes Jerry had good ideas. Maybe he was growing up. Fannie grinned at him.

Mom sighed. "That's probably not a bad idea. We're going to get thirsty out there. You can bring us out some water, Patsy. That won't cause any harm."

"That sounds okay with me. I don't feel like pitching peas anyway. I just want to see the prisoners up close." Her brow jumped with enthusiasm.

With that settled, they focused on stuffing themselves with pancakes. Then Fannie and Jerry rose from the table and headed outdoors to get the machinery lined up. They had just finished hooking up the pea wagon to the tractor when the rumble of a military truck came up their long driveway. Jerry watched it approach, but Fannie turned away and moved around the back of their own truck to load the pitchforks.

When she came around the truck again, Mom was leaving the house and the PWs were climbing out from the canvas back of the transport, all in their familiar gray uniforms stamped with the giant PW insignias.

Mom approached Fannie. "Want me to drive the truck?"

"That'll be best. I'll be on the tractor, and Jerry will operate the cutter."

The knot of German soldiers made their way toward them. Corporal Taft followed, his rifle in hand. Fannie climbed onto the tractor, and Jerry cranked the flywheel. The engine fired on the first try.

At the field, Fannie stopped so they could hand out pitchforks. Putting such a weapon into the hands of their enemy while they drove along with their backs turned seemed the height of stupidity to Fannie, but supposedly Corporal Taft wouldn't turn an eye away. A couple of men would need to toss the vines into a windrow so Mom wouldn't crush the tender peas with the truck, and the rest of the men would pitch the vines onto the wagon. Still, could the corporal watch them all at once? If her family survived the day, she'd ask for an extra guard next time. It stuck in her craw to have Jerry out on the back of the ensemble—within an arm's reach of those dagger-like pitchfork tines—and only one guard lagging somewhere beyond.

She parked and jumped down off the seat as the corporal approached. "Good morning, Corporal Taft."

"Good morning, Miss O'Brien. The men are ready. I've explained a little bit about the job. Do you have some details you'd like me to give them?"

She quickly explained the process, adding that after both the wagon and truck were full, they'd take their first load to the vinery.

As the corporal spoke in slower German, she watched the listening men. They waited patiently for his explanation, while the lead man—for so she thought of the blond captain—nodded in understanding and added a question or two. A couple of the men sent long glances the length of the pea field, probably trying to absorb the magnitude of the job awaiting them, but one man's glance caught hers. It was the darker-haired man with the probing gray eyes who'd smiled last night. He was a handsome man. Lean. Yet his gaze was keen and unnerving.

She jerked away, focusing again on the corporal. "I'll get started." She felt them watching her as she turned away.

Someone made a remark that brought a few chuckles, no doubt at her expense. Fannie gritted her teeth as she hiked herself up onto the metal seat. Never having been the overly sensitive type, she had learned to have a thick skin about a lot of things in life. The remark from the German wasn't probably the first she'd weather.

She'd forgotten the implements and glimpsed back long enough to see Jerry handing them out. Soon after, she put the tractor into gear, thankful that she was at the lead and didn't need to look at the workers. In fact, the field of tangled vines ahead took all her focus.

As she reached the end of the first row of cut peavines, Jerry gave a sharp whistle. She braked and turned on the seat. "What is it?" She had to holler above the racket of the tractor.

"I just want to give a check and make sure everyone is keeping up all right. I don't want Mom left too far behind in the truck."

Fannie nodded. She should have thought of that. Mom was back there in the middle of the work crew. "Maybe she should drive the tractor for a while and one of us can take the truck."

"I'm sure she's fine. Just let me go check." Jerry hopped off the mower seat and jogged past the workers turning the freshly cut windrow. He leaned up to Mom's truck window. Fannie watched the men. The peavines were a lot heavier than hay. She didn't envy them their part of the work in the long day ahead.

Fannie glanced back to the pickup again. The corporal stood alongside the wagon Mom pulled. That put her at ease. From that position, he could see the men ahead and behind and still be right there if Mom had any need. "Everything okay?" she hollered to Jerry as he trotted back. He waved her on.

Fannie cranked the steering wheel and turned to bring the tractor back in the opposite direction. Now she passed by the row of workers, a few who glanced at her but kept pitching peavines. Even though the day was young, the men already had sweat dripping down their brows. She waved at Mom as they passed each other, and Mom smiled. If they could just keep going like this, the crop would be harvested in a couple of days, and Fannie could relax.

Her thoughts turned to her dad for the next little while. How she missed him being out here doing the thing he loved. Farming was in his blood, and it was in Jerry's blood too. All her brothers really. Until the day Dale was captured, and even up to Cal's last letter back in March, they wrote how they missed the planting and the simple changing of the Wisconsin seasons. She sure hoped the army would find Cal soon and send him home. Once he got here, things would be all right again, or at least as all right as they'd ever be without Dad.

Her heart twisted. What if they never found Cal? What if he was gone too—not just captured like Dale but *gone*?

Fannie tightened her grip on the steering wheel. *No.* She would never believe that. The army didn't even say if he was missing. *Where are you, Cal? Why don't you write?*

Such thoughts pestered her the whole morning long. By ten o'clock they had the first wagon filled as high as they dared with vines full of plump pea pods. They decided Mom would drive the first load over to Pearson's viner and Corporal Taft would take the soldiers along to unload the vines. Every farmer was required to supply his own crew for that job. Another crew was contracted to pile the leftover vines into a mountainous stack nearby—after they'd been put through the enormous box-like machine and stripped of pods. The "stackers," those men and boys hired to build that pile of vines, would remove the vines coming out of the machine and keep piling them up. As the days went by and the mountain of green vines heaped to the warm sun, juices would flow out and ferment, and the men who held that task would go home stinking of the filth of it. Even those who weren't stacking managed to get pretty dirty and smelly, but it was worth it to the farmers. All those vines would turn to a sort of silage distributed to each farm that had contributed. As a by-product for their cattle and hogs, it would go a long way toward feeding their stock during the following months.

Fannie smirked. Stacking seemed like the sort of job those prisoners ought to be doing. While Mom was gone with the wagonload of peavines, Fannie and Jerry cut another row and then took turns at pitching them into a waiting windrow.

"I'm getting hungry," Jerry said when they reached the end of the row. "Since Mom isn't back with the truck yet, let's go see if Patsy has started any lunch."

They left things where they were and walked toward the house. "Sure would be nice if we had another truck to pull the second wagon," Fannie said.

"Be nice if we could keep a couple of those workers here instead of sending them all with the load. It doesn't take eight men to unload the vines. They'll just get in each other's way."

Fannie nodded. The problem was separating them with only one guard. If they could get another guard, maybe they could divide the crew. "I'll talk to Corporal Taft about that when they get back."

"I could always grab Dad's pistol and keep it on me."

Fannie shook her head. "I don't know if I like the idea of that. I doubt the army would approve."

"Oh, I don't know. They might."

Fannie didn't want them getting ahead of themselves. "Let's just go get something to nibble, and then we'll talk to the corporal about it."

Patsy met them at the door and held it open. "Just in time. I made up a batch of lemonade with honey to go with the cookies." The warm, sweet smell of baking goodness wafted out the open door. "Man, it's hot in there. Feels good to come outside." Her face was flushed from standing over a cookstove.

Fannie went in after her brother. He grabbed three oatmeal cookies off the platter and wasted no time popping half of one into his mouth. He spoke around the mouthful. "We could use a little lunch soon."

"I've just about got all the boiled eggs peeled."

Fannie poured a glass of lemonade and downed it. "That was good. Maybe you can bring us out a big jug of water. The PWs are probably parched."

"Okay!" Patsy spun around to look for the jug.

"Don't go smiling at them or anything when you bring it out." Fannie thought of the dark eyes of the soldier this morning. "In fact, try not to look directly at them. We don't want them getting any notions."

Patsy set the open jug under the faucet. "What kind of notions?"

Jerry laughed. He shook his head and stuffed another cookie in his mouth when Fannie glared at him.

"Some of them are just boys no older than Jerry. They haven't been around any girls in a long time."

"Oh. *Oh*," Patsy said again, her understanding taking hold.

Did Fannie imagine it, or was her sister's skin flushing an even deeper shade of pink than it had from the warm oven?

"Here comes Mom." Jerry pushed the screen door open and let it crack shut against the frame behind him.

Fannie stuck an extra cookie in her bib overalls pocket. "Thanks, Patsy."

The trucks, both Mom's and the army's, came to a halt in the barnyard. The men climbed out the back, and Mom strode toward the house. Fannie could smell the rancidness of the vinery, even though none of them likely went near the stack.

Mom brushed the back of her hand over her cheek. "If you have another load cut, why don't you take the truck and head out there, honey. I'll get cleaned up and help Patsy with lunch. After you get it loaded, have the men take a break. They have bag lunches."

"I'll bring the water," Patsy called.

"Take it out there now, Pats," Mom said. "But mind yourself. Don't get close to them. Just deliver the jug to Corporal Taft and get back to the house."

"I will. Fannie already told me."

Mom and Fannie shared a look. "You be careful too, Fannie. They'll be around the truck, and I saw the way a couple of them looked at you on that tractor."

"What do you think about Jerry taking Dad's pistol out there?"

Mom blinked, taken aback. Then she shook her head and turned away to the sink. "No. Not out there on the tractor. I don't want them to see us walking around with a firearm. It might prove as much of a temptation as a hindrance. 'Sides. . ." Mom set a pot under the faucet and turned it on. "There's enough violence in this world. We're safe. We have Corporal Taft handling things. Those men seem glad enough to be here doing something useful. Just forget about that gun."

"I'm going to ask Corporal Taft to bring another guard tomorrow. That way we can divide the crew and work faster."

Mom set the water pot aside. "I doubt we'll get another man. From what I hear, there's not a lot of guards to spare, especially with the crews sent to the canning factories. Mr. Pearson had a crew of them working there along with some local boys Jerry's age and even a few boys as young as ten or eleven."

Of course. Where would Mr. Pearson find able-bodied help otherwise?

Fannie adjusted the knot in her head scarf as a sigh escaped. "Guess we'll just keep doing what we can then."

Fannie went outside and climbed inside the truck. It smelled of the spent vines. The empty flatbed rattled behind as she drove out to the field. The men fell into pitching peavines as she drove alongside the windrow.

The corporal strolled alongside her for a bit. "Happy with the progress, Miss O'Brien?"

"Yes, thanks. I'm glad you asked. Corporal, is there any chance you can bring along another guard tomorrow so we can split the crew and keep loading while one of us takes the full load to the vinery?"

He shrugged. "It's a possibility. I'll have to see. We're stretched pretty thin now."

"I understand that, but we only have two days to get our peas in. The migrant workers used to keep up through the night, but you have to take the prisoners back at four o'clock, right?"

He nodded. "That's what I'm told. I'll see what I can figure out." He stepped off a ways and strolled toward the back of the truck and wagon.

Fannie looked into her mirror and could see some of the men tossing forkful after forkful of vines into the wagon. The corporal disappeared around the back, but she watched one of the prisoners on her side of the truck. It was the German captain. His blond hair fell down over his forehead as he jabbed his fork into a scoop of vines. He worked in a T-shirt, and his shoulders bunched as he pitched vines into the growing heap on the truck bed. He shouted something to one of the younger men a few yards back and then looked her way. As their glances caught in the side mirror, he gave a nod. That was all, just a nod. Then he turned back to his work.

Her nerves tingled as she gripped the wheel and watched her way ahead. She had done exactly what she told Patsy not to do. Twice now. Twice she'd caught the look of a German prisoner. Twice she'd felt the crawl of feelings she couldn't name. Regardless of what Mom said, from now on she was going to keep that pistol of her father's in the truck under the seat.

≡ CHAPTER 4 ≡

Wolfgang Kloninger was not the first to spot the girl with the long brown braids heading toward them carrying the jug. A remark from one of the other men brought his attention to the one who looked so much like her older sister that there was no mistaking the relationship, except that the younger girl was only just beginning to bloom, while the young woman who drove the truck and tractor—who seemed to be running this farm—was fully matured, or as some of his men said, ripe for plucking. There was a general chuckle about that comment, and Leo Friedrickson had made a ribald remark loud enough for her to hear, though she clearly didn't understand German. If she did, she might have at least stiffened her gait or given some indication that she'd heard. The American corporal had rebuked Leo, which was fine. Wolf didn't like having to rebuke his men over such things. They'd been through enough. Even though Leo was only an *Obergefreiter*, a noncommissioned officer of lower rank, he was closer in age to Wolf than any of the others in his command. Besides, the men deserved a bit of sport these days, even if it was only in admiring a woman they could never approach. They were harmless. Wolf did notice, however, that Otto Maltzahn gave Rudolf Ebner a discreet jab in the ribs at the younger girl's approach.

Rudy was the youngest of the bunch. Conscripted at seventeen, he'd yet to see his nineteenth birthday. Rudy hustled forward to relieve the girl of the heavy jug.

The girl's face turned a pretty shade of pink, though she made a clearly concerted effort not to look at Rudy. Then the older sister spoke curtly, and the younger one spun on her heels for the house. She was likely told to leave the jug and get away from them. It might not have come out just like that, but the tone of voice and expression on the woman's face made it clear. He reached for an apple in his lunch bag and discreetly let his study rove to the woman. She'd tied a handkerchief onto her head, but long chocolate-brown strands escaped the tangled knot of hair above her collar. Her eyes were brown as acorns and warm when she looked at one of her family members. Not so when she looked their way, which was seldom.

He polished the apple on his shirtsleeve. "Do not get ideas about these women." Wolf spoke just loudly enough to be heard by the seven other men. He glanced at the corporal who was also within hearing. The man nodded approval and walked a few feet away, giving them space to get comfortable on the grass with their sack lunches.

They stretched out on the ground with some murmurs and grunts. He couldn't blame them for having wayward thoughts. There was a time he welcomed such interests himself. At home. Not here in this foreign land where nothing could come of such things.

Leo nodded agreement. "They are not worth wasting your imagination." He unwrapped a thin sandwich from its waxed paper. The disdain in his voice made it clear Leo remembered that the Americans thought themselves superior. The man's gaze, nevertheless, rose from beneath his dark eyebrows to rest upon the pretty woman who directed them. Her mussed appearance with dirt smudging her chin couldn't hide the sun-kissed tone of her skin or the cocoa brown of her almond eyes. Her men's overalls and cotton blouse did little to camouflage enticing curves as she sat on the tractor or stepped into the truck. Now and again, she would walk ahead of them into the field or follow behind, bending to check the condition of the vines or pods.

Wolf occasionally found himself enjoying the sight as well. He had no one waiting for him in Germany. There had been several women he'd shared dinner with over the years or with whom he'd enjoyed a stroll in the park, but none of them struck his fancy for long. One young woman worked as a file clerk. Another served his coffee at the little shop he walked to for a breakfast roll each morning. Once his mother had invited a woman for dinner with hopes that Wolf might find her sweet and attractive. She was that. But most of her time was devoted to the Protestant Women's Auxiliary, and while they performed many honorable tasks, her work had little in common with Wolf's interests.

Looking at this American woman now stirred the same thoughts. She was pleasing to admire, but only for her looks and work ethic. He knew nothing else about her and never would.

He tossed away his apple core and finished his sandwich. Then he brushed bread crumbs off his shirt front, which seemed pointless when he looked down at the dirt and sweat stains covering him. With a sigh, he stretched back on the ground and clasped his hands beneath his head. Wisps of white clouds drifted beneath a sky as blue as any he'd ever seen. He nestled his head, imagining for a moment he was in the park a few blocks from his flat, listening to the chirp of birds and the fluttering pages of a book beside him. But instead of birds, he heard the murmur of his men commenting on the work and the farm, and instead of the fluttering of pages, he heard the squeak and smack of a screen door on the house. He closed his eyes and let his thoughts drift, only to find that the woman hadn't really left his mind. A few minutes later, her voice beckoned, and the corporal called them back to work.

Wolf sat up feeling unusually rested. He rose to his feet and glanced about. The younger girl had come back outdoors, this time with the mother beside her. They carried two more glass jugs of sparkling water, which they set on the ground a few feet away from his men.

There was an abundance of water. The years in Africa sometimes made him believe he would never have enough fresh water again. He got in line to fill his canteen.

The older woman spoke to the girl, who nodded and turned back to the house. A few of the boys looked on. That girl wouldn't stay young forever, but hopefully by the time she grew up, he and his boys would all be back home in Germany carrying on lives of their own.

Leo had water dribbling down his chin. He corked his canteen and strolled past the line of workers toward the tractor. The woman had gone around to the other side. Leo laid a hand on the big back wheel. Wolf couldn't hear what he said, but he was speaking to the woman. Then he patted the wheel and walked back, half a grin on his cocky face.

She climbed up, and her brother cranked the flywheel. The mother got into the truck and started the engine.

"Let's go." Corporal Taft thumbed to the transport truck. They all obeyed.

Once seated inside, Wolf turned his head toward Leo. "What did you say to her?"

"I pointed out that I was surprised at a woman driving such a piece of machinery so well. She could not understand, obviously. I admired the tractor. I wish I was the one driving it."

"We are not allowed."

Leo shrugged. "It is not as though we could use it to escape. Pursuers could run fast enough to catch us."

"If the corporal didn't shoot us before we got to the end of the field," Fritz Von Hecker said.

Wolf leaned back and closed his eyes. "We would be wise to remember that."

Fritz let out a sigh. He seemed the most likely to try such an attempt. While all of them were duty bound to escape if given the opportunity, Fritz had the strongest desire. He spoke frequently of missing his girl back home, and he worried constantly that harm might come to her and her family so close to the French border, should the Allies break through the line. He was a restless sort.

The truck hit a bump and lurched them all toward the ceiling. Wolf's eyes flew open, and he glanced again at Leo. "Did your family live on a farm?"

Leo shook his head. "No, but I've operated my share of machinery. This American-made tractor doesn't look much different to me than anything I've seen."

"You admire it though."

Leo shrugged. "I would enjoy anything other than riding in the back of this stifling truck smelling of the inside of a rotting pea pod."

Wolf grinned. "Tonight, even a shower under a cold hose would feel good."

The other men concurred.

"I wonder how many kilos of peas we've already loaded onto the wagons today." Hermann Claus spoke up from the farthest corner. He was a brilliant math student, one of Wolf's best back at the secondary school in Heidelberg.

"Why don't you figure it out?"

Hermann tilted his head and squinted one eye. His lips moved wordlessly. Otto finally threw his hat at him to confuse his concentration.

"Two thousand seven hundred kilograms, I estimate," Hermann announced with a smile at not having been disturbed by Otto at all. He shot Otto's hat back.

Horst Albrecht rolled his left shoulder and rubbed it. "I feel every gram."

A smile tugged on Wolf's lips. "Everyone will sleep well tonight."

Fritz sneered at Otto. "If you snore all night again, I'll suffocate you with my pillow."

"Try it, and Private Schorr will rescue me. He sleeps soundly but wakes up at anything unusual." Lanky and thin himself, Otto grinned at Schorr, the strongest of them all. He was built like a panzer, all muscle. For him, pitching peavines appeared to be all in a normal day's work. "He knows about farming. I bet he could drive that tractor."

Private Schorr shrugged noncommittally, but his slow smile agreed. He'd been raised on a farm in Germany. For all his size and strength, he was quiet and shy. He was quick to obey an order, and Wolf never had to issue him discipline. He'd been a student for a short time, just a year before going back to the farm with his father, only for the war to take him away from home again.

Unlike the rest of the men, Rudy, Otto, and Leo had never been Wolf's students at one time or another in Heidelberg. The others had been in his classes. They were the main reason Wolf had enlisted. He wanted to serve his country, naturally, but once the school began emptying of young men, he determined that the best way to serve was to go with them into the battles where he might continue to be an influence in their lives. They were his boys, after all. He'd come to know them and care about them and their families. Some would say he felt a calling to go with them. That might be the root of it, but he was always afraid to presume so. For if, indeed, he had a calling to go with his boys to lead and protect them, he had failed. Some of his students lay dead in the mud in France. Others were missing or killed in the Africa campaign. Still more were captured and imprisoned like these few who remained and felt almost like sons or younger brothers. His only comfort was that he had not let them go alone. He could still look out for these four—Horst, Richard, Fritz, and Hermann—and even Rudy, Otto, and Leo, if only slightly.

There were more like them back at Camp Barron. Men who'd been captured and needed a strong figure to look to for fortitude when they could not find their own within themselves. He would be that rod of iron for them if he could. Yet there were times when his own strength and courage felt depleted. Days he moved forward only out of some animalistic drive not born of any human instinct as grand as hope, but only the basest urge to survive. And that instinct had led each of them to this place.

As the wheels of the truck rumbled over the dirt road beneath them, and the canvas brushed against their backs in the darkened enclosure, he felt again the insides of a lorry groaning and roaring over the rocky desert ground. Weeks and months of flying from one place to another behind their indefatigable Field Marshal Rommel, only to end in *stelungskrieg*—static warfare—again and again, hunkered in trenches and rifle pits, crawling amid barbed wire and camouflaged machine gun nests. They had tricked the Allies many times but eventually stared defeat in the face by the sheer force of the numbers against them. Even so, they had not committed the atrocities of war he'd heard about. They had fought valiantly, and their surrendering troops walked out with their heads held high.

The truck jarred violently against another rut that sent them bouncing off their seats and reaching for something to hold on to, but just as quickly the ride veered and smoothed out. In another few minutes, gears downshifted and they arrived at the vinery.

Even the heat of the sun felt good as fresh air met them outside the canvas-covered vehicle. As some took pitchforks in hand to unload, Leo and Otto climbed to the top of the peas stacked on the wagon to push them free. The giant box-like machine that sorted the peas from the vines created a racket, and on the other end, the spent vines were already being hauled away to the rancid, growing mountain that oozed fermented green juice.

Before long, the job was finished. The men climbed into the waiting truck, except for Wolf, who walked up to the guard. "Perhaps tomorrow we can have another guard to ride with us and open up the sides."

"I already plan to look into it, Hauptmann Kloninger. Miss O'Brien has requested an extra guard as well."

"Danke." He nodded. "Corporal Taft," he said, stopping the man before he turned away. "O'Brien. . . I have heard you say this name. That is the name of the family for whom we are doing this work?"

Corporal Taft looked him over. They'd gotten along well these past days since arriving at Camp Barron. Wolf had tried to show himself compliant. He hoped that the guard had come to trust him enough to give out such a small piece of information. *"Ja."*

"Danke," he repeated, and hoisted himself into the truck.

The return drive was quieter. The long day and heat had caught up to all of them, and they mostly kept to their thoughts on the way back to the farm.

O'Brien. Fraülein O'Brien. Wolf tried a number of first names, but none would match. *Greta O'Brien. Susanne O'Brien. Perhaps. . .Clarice O'Brien. No. No German names.* What Irish names did he recall? Perhaps not Irish at all. She was American. *Elizabeth O'Brien. Mabel O'Brien.* She was definitely not a Mabel. Marian perhaps. *Lady Marian O'Brien.* That combination brought an inward smile as he conjured her into the Robin Hood tale.

"Hauptmann, you look content, like when you study," Hermann said.

Wolf glanced at him. "For now. I am restful. It has been a long time since we've been so."

"In body perhaps," said Leo. "Can our minds and souls ever be restful until we are home again?"

"We will be home again. Do not worry on that account. The Americans have kept to the rules of the Geneva Convention. When the war ends, we will all return to our families."

"And hopefully, they are waiting." Fritz stared at his hands clasped over his knees. He clearly was speaking of the family he hoped for and the girl he wished to wed.

"Have you heard from Emma?"

Fritz nodded. "Not often enough. And she forgets that I cannot tell her much of where we are. She begs for answers that are sure to be censored."

"But she is well?"

"For now. She and her family are close to the border, and they can hear the fighting at times. I fear that if the enemy pushes any farther, their home and village will be overrun. I do not like feeling afraid"—he cast a sharp glance over the other men— "but I do, and I admit it."

"It is no weakness to worry for those you love."

Fritz lifted grateful eyes toward Wolf, then lowered them to his hands again.

Another two rows of peas were cut by the time they returned, but only one had been pitched into a windrow. Fraülein O'Brien and her brother were walking toward them across the field, carrying pitchforks. Wolf jerked his head at Fritz and Horst, who hurried forward to relieve them of their implements and take over the job. As the others collected their own tools to work with, Wolf waited for the pair to draw close.

"Fraülein O'Brien." He dipped his head in greeting.

She startled. "Captain Kloninger." She cast an uneasy glance at her brother. "Captain, this is my brother Jerry."

This close, Wolf could see the flecks of dirt in her suntanned cheeks and make out the pupils of her dark brown eyes. Even that her lips were chapped. Her brother Jerry had the same skin tone and dark eyes. His nutty-brown hair parted to the side, but wispy bangs had difficulty staying off his brow. Jerry looked younger, but in height he'd shot ahead of his elder sister.

Wolf inclined his head again, wishing he could converse with them and ask about the work they might be expected to do in the days ahead. He also wanted to thank them for the job. They were still the enemy, but at least his men were allowed to breathe the fresh air and walk outside the barbed wire perimeter of their compound nearly every day. He could write to his parents, assuring them that he was healthy and able to remain active here, words certain to comfort them.

She moved on, but a backward glance his way showed her surprise at being addressed. What other thoughts did she harbor behind those dark, almond eyes? Wolf retrieved a pitchfork with an inward smile.

They ate supper an hour later, brought by a truck from the camp. It was a lukewarm gruel served by a camp cook and another guard. At least real meat swam in it, and it was filling and served with soft rolls. They were even offered a second helping. As a strand of beef caught between Wolf's teeth, he remembered the months of deprivation in Africa. While the Allies regularly ate tinned fruit, vegetables, and meat, his men suffered with dried vegetables and no fruit. The tins of meat the Italians provided were given much leery speculation as to its type. Now they never went hungry or thirsty.

As he took a long draught of water from his canteen, knowing it could easily be filled again, he recalled leading a convoy of lorries five hundred kilometers across the desert to bring back fresh water that had to then be rationed out, all while skirting air raids from encroaching Allied armies.

He took a second long drink.

Leo eyed him as he passed by, heading toward the already turned row. Wolf waved to the Obergefreiter—a rank close to the American Corporal Taft's—to join him. Putting a space between them, they waited beside the line of vines. A moment later, the O'Briens' truck drew up to the field with an empty wagon. Fraülein O'Brien was behind the wheel. She looked at Wolf as she pulled up beside the row. She glanced at Leo too, and he gave her a nod. Then, together, they started loading while she drove on slowly, keeping the wagon abreast of their progress.

The exertion felt good, even so late in the day with so much energy spent behind them. Wolf's meal had given him strength, and he felt its release like fuel burning with life. He huffed and tossed, huffed and tossed. Leo caught his energy, and the two worked in tandem while seeming almost to compete. Leo's quick grin indicated as much. As they neared the end of the row, they increased their speed even more, and every now and again Wolf glanced at Fraülein O'Brien's reflection in her side mirror, and she returned his glance.

By the time they finished and the back of the truck and both wagons were filled, the sun had almost fully set. Silence fell into twilight as the engines were cut. Fraülein O'Brien climbed stiffly out of the truck and walked past the men to speak to the corporal. Wolf heard their conversation clearly but understood only *vinery* and their nods.

He stepped closer, drawing their attention. "Will we work into the night, Corporal? The fact that we are out later than expected has not gone unnoticed by my men."

"We've received permission to work through the night if necessary. The vinery schedules farms for deliveries, and it must all be done within those parameters. Understand?"

Wolf nodded. "Ja, Corporal. I understand. I only wanted to know. If you do not mind, I also wanted to thank Fraülein O'Brien and her family for allowing us to work for her. Please tell her. And tell her we will continue to do our best as long as we are needed here." He punctuated his speech with a smile at her. She shifted her feet and folded her arms over her middle.

"I'll tell her." The corporal turned to Fraülein O'Brien, and with a few glances at Wolf during the speech, he passed along his message.

"There's more," she said to the corporal. Then she lowered her arms and finally looked at Wolf directly. "Thank you for saying so, Captain Kloninger." She paused so the corporal could translate, then continued. "I appreciate your willingness to be here despite. . .despite everything." She looked away nervously and back again. "You can be sure our family notices the hard work your men are doing." Her words sounded stiff and formal, but she waited for the corporal to finish translating and then nodded so the captain would know she was finished.

Wolf bowed slightly and turned away. He knew he hardly looked like the man of rank—the Hauptmann he was—in his filthy prison uniform, but his appearance was no cause to behave improperly. His men eyed the exchange momentarily before ignoring them altogether. Only Leo squinted, regarding the entire thing. Whether out of curiosity, suspicion, or simple weariness, Wolf couldn't tell, but he was certain that once they'd all rested, Leo would let him know.

⋮ CHAPTER 5 ⋮

At five o'clock in the morning, Fannie stepped once again into the rusty Ford and turned the engine over, breaking the lovely stillness of morning of a new day. Her body ached from head to toe, but she did her best to ignore the grip of weariness by telling herself that all she needed was another cup of coffee. She tucked her thermos beside her on the seat and pulled away from the yard. Once she got to the vinery, she could pour herself a cup and sip it while the crew took last night's load off the trailer. Then they'd all come back to the farm for the other wagon. Now that a second guard was coming, only four of the men would go to the vinery. The other four would stay and load the second trailer behind the tractor. At least she hoped Corporal Taft wouldn't be arriving alone today.

As the sun spread golden fronds over the edge of the eastern sky, her thoughts spread back to last evening when the prisoners returned to get the final load onto the wagon, and to the encounter with the German captain, Hauptmann Kloninger. He had caught her eye several times throughout the day, and though his expression was almost always unreadable, he'd seemed desirous of a smooth affiliation between them—between her family and his men. While part of her wanted to believe that he meant no disquiet to their lives, the other part remained suspicious. Hadn't she read of a German spy somewhere who tricked Americans he'd lived and worked with for years before the war—even graduating from an American university—only to cause them harm later on by subterfuge? How much more might these friendly appearing prisoners of war pretend compliance only to try to hurt them if given the chance? Weren't they secretly sworn to do so? Patsy read novels too old for her, and she claimed it was always the case. In the local newspapers Fannie scanned at the library, letters to the editor muttered the same concerns.

It still grated on her that her family was in the position of needing the Germans' help on the farm. Yet how would they have ever gotten so much done in the past twenty-four hours without it? The men had worked very hard. That much was true.

Fannie was grateful that she couldn't understand their talk, for maybe she would have to endure their complaints. Yet they didn't seem to complain. She heard their chuckles and light-sounding banter. Noticed their camaraderie. Jerry had too. She caught him grinning a time or two at some joking behavior he'd observed, even though he couldn't understand them either.

Of course, she was aware that some of them watched her with another kind of interest. They'd not acted out of line other than giving easily interpreted glances the first day they'd come to do the potatoes, when she'd thought one of them made an off-color remark. Still, she'd only assumed. After all, she'd been ogled by men before.

She wished she knew some of their names.

The notion took Fannie by surprise. What did it matter what their names were? *Kloninger.* That was the only one she knew, and it was interesting that he also had learned their last name. The curiosity must be mutual then. Or maybe it wasn't curiosity. Maybe it was something more sinister. But what?

What about that other one? The one with the dark hair and gray eyes who'd admired her tractor. Maybe she should let him try a turn on the mower just to offer an olive branch of trust. Of course, the prisoners weren't supposed to be allowed to operate machinery, but it wasn't like the mower was anything complicated, and she'd be right there running the tractor with a guard following along. The more she thought about it, the more the idea tickled her fancy. Maybe she was addled from lack of sleep.

Fannie pulled the heavy wagon into the vinery a few minutes later. The army transport was already there, and the prisoners were waiting beside it. The tarp had been removed so they could ride in the open air. She hadn't thought about how smothering it must have been inside yesterday, but she thought of it now.

She pulled her load alongside the viner, and the men took their places to unload while she uncorked her thermos and poured herself a cup of coffee. She took a sip and relaxed, resting an elbow on the open window. Captain Kloninger suddenly appeared beside her. Fannie jerked and nearly spilled on herself.

"*Guten Morgen*, Fraülein O'Brien." He offered a friendly smile, as bright as the morning.

"Good morning, Captain." His greeting was at least one phrase she knew in German, it surprised her to realize.

He expanded his chest with a deep breath, held it, and then expelled the air and smiled again as though to say it was a lovely day and good to be alive to enjoy it.

"Yes," was all she said, and her thoughts sprang to Dale and Cal, hoping they were well. Her smile fell away, and thankfully he walked away as she frowned. There was injustice in the entire thing. That Dale was imprisoned and they had no idea how he fared, and that Cal was someplace where they seemingly couldn't reach him. Did her brothers eat well? Rest well? Were they warm and safe? Did they enjoy a fresh breath of summery air and wear clean uniforms like Captain Kloninger did? Did the Germans or Japanese respect the Geneva Convention rules, or did Dale suffer? How was it fair that he might if these PWs did not?

She stiffened and tossed the grounds in her cup out the window. Then she got out of the truck and walked toward the viner to stretch her legs. Corporal Taft stood watching the men while he chatted with another soldier. She strolled over.

"Good morning, Corporal."

He bobbed his head. "Good morning, Miss O'Brien. This is Private Vicks. He'll be coming along out to your farm today. He can ride back and forth with the wagons, and I'll stay at the field so you can keep cutting your peas with some of the men."

"Nice to meet you, Private Vicks. Thank you. That will help tremendously. We can load much more quickly. Maybe we'll be finished by suppertime."

Private Vicks was young too, maybe only about twenty. As he moved, she noticed he had a slight limp. "Are you hurt, sir?"

"I took a little shrapnel, but I'm fine now. They sent me here." His brief explanation said much. He couldn't go back there, not with a wound to slow him down, but he could still serve by standing watch over prisoners. Again, she thought of Dale and Cal.

"I'm hoping my brother Cal will be home before long. We haven't heard from him in a while. The army is supposed to be locating him."

"I hope they send him to you soon." His lips pressed together in a grim line that made her uneasy.

"Thank you." She turned away again. Sometimes talking about it only made her nervous for Cal. She watched the men working down to the end of the load. They seemed vigorous and refreshed for the day. The coolness of the morning helped. The dark-haired PW with the gray eyes looked her way and lifted the corner of his mouth. She found herself returning a weak smile, but the moment after she did, she turned quickly away and uttered a prayer for Calvin's safe return.

She strode over to Mr. Pearson, who was supervising the viner. He glanced down from where he stood on a ladder, checking that nothing was binding on the conveyor. "Everything's right on schedule. Your loads are looking good."

"We should be done on time."

"Very good. I've got the Beillers' peas coming in today from over by Canton. You'll probably alternate loads."

She nodded and glanced toward her crew. "Looks like we're about finished. See you again in a little while, Mr. Pearson."

The men were in their truck and already pulling onto the road by the time she got her wagon turned around. She'd have to follow them. Now that the tarp was pulled back on the army truck, there was nothing else to do but watch the men riding in the back all the way home. And they could see her too.

She pretended not to pay them any mind, of course, but it couldn't be helped. Several of them seemed to be the talkers, keeping the other men listening or answering. One man, the young one built like a wrestler, barely spoke, but he smiled a lot. The two that most captured her curiosity were the captain and the dark-haired one. They both exhibited leadership, even though she didn't know if the duskier man held any rank. He turned his face aside to watch the country rolling by. His profile was angular and handsome, and she wondered what he thought of her beautiful America. Was Wisconsin anything at all like the place he'd come from?

Supposedly a lot of Germans came to Wisconsin because it reminded them of home in one way or another. Did he live on a farm, or was he from a city like so many of the immigrants around Milwaukee? Someplace like Hamburg or Berlin? Did he merely admire her tractor, or did he miss one of his own? His gaze turned back to the men with him and suddenly lifted to pin on her. This time she didn't pretend to look away but stared back.

His eyes appeared hooded, thoughtful, and neither smile nor frown expressed itself. He was entirely unreadable, but then maybe she was too. Then the transport hit a rut, and just as quickly his gaze moved on and so did

Fannie's. This time it was Captain Kloninger she saw looking at her, but only for a moment, and then he spoke to one of the young prisoners beside him.

Her driveway was just ahead, and she slowly loosened her jaw which, until then, she hadn't realized was tightly clenched. She felt needled and worn, as if she'd endured a long and uncomfortable conversation, when none had taken place. And yet the discussion did not feel ended.

As soon as the prisoners got out of the truck, Corporal Taft gave orders in German. Fannie headed off to the field where Mom and Jerry were already cutting the first row of the day. She could relieve her mother. They saw her approach and stalled the tractor. Mom climbed down. "I'll let you take over. I've got Patsy working on the bread. I want her to get a big jug of lemonade ready and brought out. Those men worked hard yesterday. I want them to have something special to show our appreciation."

Fannie moved past her to climb onto the seat. "What for? They're getting paid."

"I know, but I want to do this."

"Make sure you save us some," Jerry said from his place on the mower seat.

"This is no time to be selfish, Jerry," Mom said as she picked her way back over the cut peavines. "You'll have plenty."

"That's all that matters to me." Jerry grinned and hollered after her. "Other than that, give 'em all you want."

Fannie geared up the tractor and turned it at the end of the field. On the second row, they passed the Germans hustling along to catch up with the windrow.

Her brother whooped from behind her. "Faster! Faster! You can do it!"

She craned her neck to look behind. What was he yelling about? Two men were on each side of the windrow like teams in a race, laughing and pitching, but clearly trying to outdo one another to the end of the row. The other four PWs had gone down to the end of the row she'd just begun cutting.

They laughed and cast glances at Jerry, who continued to spur them on as she drove past, but they didn't slow down.

Finally clear of them, she turned and called to Jerry. He guffawed. At her. When she got to the end of the row and saw that the prisoners were some fifty yards back, she scrambled down off the tractor and marched back to him. Anger boiled inside her. "What are you doing?" she shouted. "Stop it. They aren't your high school football team. They're your enemy. Have you forgotten?"

Jerry drew back. "So what? I'm just having some fun. For crying out loud, Fannie, take it easy."

She leaned close to him. "Take it easy? They're here because Cal and Dale aren't. Have you forgotten that?"

His brown eyes dulled with a chill in them. "I didn't forget."

"You act like you have." She lowered her voice. The prisoners were getting close. "See to it you don't."

"They're not much older than me, Fan. Don't you forget that." He squared himself on his seat, and she climbed back up on the tractor. She refused to look at them as she rammed the tractor into gear and fed gasoline to the engine. She powered on, turning for another row.

Her heart pounded and her rib cage tightened like bands around her breaths. Poor Dale and Cal. She had to focus her thinking on them. Not on the fact that Jerry was right about these young men. They probably had families back home begging God for their sons' and brothers' return.

She passed them again as they neared the end of the windrow, some of them heaving for breath from exertion. Most of them so young.

Then the captain caught her looking and so did the gray-eyed man. She stopped and set the brake on the tractor. Climbing off, she took determined steps toward them. She walked directly up to the gray-eyed man. "What is your name?" She spoke demandingly. He glanced at his captain. "Name?" she asked again.

He blinked slowly and then said, "Obergefreiter Friedrickson."

"Oberge. . ." She frowned. "No, your name."

His brow leveled and the left side of his lips lifted slightly. "Leo Friedrickson."

"Come, Leo. I have a job for you." She ignored his near smirk and directed him to the mower. "Get down, Jerry. Show him how to operate the mower."

Jerry's eyes widened, preceding a grin. "Sure." He hopped down and pointed to the German to get on. Leo hesitated only a moment, then seated himself on the machine. Jerry pointed out the levers and offered explanation with lots of hand motions. He did a good job.

Fannie turned at Corporal Taft's approach. "We're not supposed to let them near the machinery, ma'am."

"Yes, I know, Corporal, but my brother needs a break. I'm not worried that they can cause any harm with you and me looking on. We have a full summer of work ahead. If I can train these men to do a few more tasks, it would help us tremendously."

He rubbed a hand over his jaw and glanced back at the other guard. "I have my orders, ma'am."

"Please, Corporal. You yourself promised me they'd be hard workers and that they weren't dangerous."

"I know. It's just—"

She gripped his arm but quickly let go. "I'm not going to mention it if you don't."

He removed his cap and scratched his forehead. Then he tugged his cap back on. "I guess there's no real harm in it as long as I can see what's going on. Go ahead."

"Thank you." An internal voice told her she was being defiant for no good reason, yet it was true that it would help if they could swap jobs now and then. If Jerry could take the tractor while a prisoner operated the mower, she could take a break from driving too. Maybe by summer's end, if they could be trusted enough, she'd give Leo a chance to drive the tractor he so admired.

She climbed aboard and glanced back. When Jerry gave her a thumbs-up, she started forward. She looked back a few times to see Jerry walking alongside and giving extra direction, but the man seemed to catch on pretty quickly. By the time she reached the end of the row, Jerry had gone off to ready the second wagon for loading, cheering on the crew on his way.

When she reached the end, she climbed down and met with the corporal again. Her mom was already standing beside him. "I'll take this load with the new guard, Fannie. You and Jerry stay here with the others. If we're not back by the time you get the wagon loaded, Patsy will have some fresh bread and apples to eat for a break. She'll bring them out. There'll be enough for everyone." She gave Fannie a meaningful look.

Had her mother and Jerry connived to make the prisoners feel at home today? Or was it the same feeling that was sweeping over her, that they were in this thing together and would just have to make the best of it as long as it lasted?

"Okay. Anything else?"

Mom smiled. "No. Just keep doing what you're doing. It's going well."

It was going well. There was no denying that. Even now, the men were pushing the empty wagon onto the field with their bare strength, no truck or tractor needed. To fill the load without a truck pulling the wagon was difficult. They had to detach the mower and hook up the wagon or else park the wagon midway up the field and haul the peas. That would be too tough a workout. Best start unhooking the mower.

Mom and the second guard headed off minutes later, the heavy load rumbling and bumping down the drive, and the army truck with four of their workers following. The remaining four included Captain Kloninger, Leo Friedrickson, the ox-like young man, and another young man with eyes almost as blue as the captain's but not quite. Jerry stood with them, trying to communicate as she and the corporal approached.

Jerry turned to them. "Fan, you've met Leo. This is Hermann and Richard," he said. Hermann reminded her of a young man from church. Light brown hair, smooth skin, an intelligent, straightforward look about him. Richard was the fellow with the thick arms and shoulders. "And this is Wolf, their captain. Wolfgang Kloninger."

She faced him yet again. "I have met their captain."

He said something, and the corporal translated. "Another good load."

With a nod at the other two men, she fidgeted and moved toward the tractor. "Let's get to work."

Wolf. How appropriate, she thought as she climbed aboard the tractor and waited for Jerry to crank it. She couldn't think of a more perfectly suited name for the leader of these enemy soldiers. *They are my enemies, no matter how many courtesies we share or how hard they work. I must never forget it.*

"Jump on the mower, Jerry."

"I think Leo was hoping to give it another go."

"I'd rather you cut this time."

"Whatever you say. You're the boss."

Her nerves sizzled at his smart-aleck tone. Yes, she was the boss. She put the tractor into gear and kept her eyes on the rows ahead. *The boss, indeed.*

They kept on cutting until the wagon was heaped as high as it could be, and even then they'd cut an extra row. As soon as Mom got back, they'd have enough ready for another load.

Patsy waved to them from the porch. Fannie waved back. Their mid-morning snack must be ready. The sun was already heating up the day to a low roast. She felt a softening toward the crew. They'd probably not had anything as nice as fresh-baked bread in months. Maybe even years.

Jerry leapt off the mower before she climbed down from the tractor seat. The men were still flipping peas but getting close to finishing as she left the field. Patsy held a tray heaped in still-warm, freshly baked bread slices slathered in melting, fresh butter. Another tray covered in sweating canning jars of cold lemonade sat on the edge of the porch. Jerry grabbed one up and slugged it down. He smacked his lips with a sigh and set the empty jar on the porch. "Fill that again for me, will you, Pats? I'll take the rest out to the workers."

"Thank you, Patsy. The bread looks and smells wonderful." Fannie gave her little sister an encouraging smile. "I'll take that for you."

Patsy gave up the bread tray. "There's more. I'll bring it out."

Fannie glanced at the men moving toward the shade of a big oak near the edge of the lawn. The guard was already standing there with a shoulder against the tree. "All right. You can join us."

"Thanks, Fannie." Patsy's eyes brightened.

Fannie's stomach growled at the aroma of the warm bread and butter. As she came near the group, the men's eyes lit up just like Patsy's. "My mother insists that you need some refreshment." She looked to Corporal Taft as she said it.

He must have smelled the bread too and didn't bother telling her they weren't allowed to feed the prisoners. He shifted toward the men. They all clamored together for a slice off the tray. Only their captain hung back. When they'd all begun gobbling down their snack, he finally approached.

She wished she knew what was going on behind his sky-blue eyes when he unhurriedly took a piece of bread and said, "Danke." Then he turned to Jerry for a jar of lemonade.

Patsy came out a minute later with the second tray, and she virtually glowed from the men's *oohs* and *aahs* at having another piece. They rubbed their stomachs, smiled, and nodded to show their appreciation. A couple of them took turns getting permission to go to the outhouse.

Jerry elbowed Fannie. "I suppose there isn't any trouble they can cause in there." He chuckled at his joke, and that dragged a grin out of her.

The rumble of the truck returning brought them to their feet. Fannie sent Patsy back to the house, and they all thanked her sister again. At least they didn't take the special treat for granted. Some of the younger of them might not be such bad men at heart.

The trailer bounced over the drive, and Mom jerked the truck to a halt. What was she in such a hurry for? Fannie frowned, and unease lurched through her when Mom burst out of the vehicle.

"Fannie! Jerry!" She waved a small paper. "A telegram!"

Fannie's pulse jumped. She and Jerry exchanged looks and jogged to meet her.

As they closed the distance, Mom cried out, "Cal's coming home!"

Fannie nearly tripped. She and Jerry exchanged glances. Her heart thundered so that she felt out of breath when they reached her mom. "Tell us what it says."

Mom's hands trembled as she opened the page. "Here, you read it, Fannie. I'm still shaking."

Fannie skimmed the page then read aloud. "Your son Calvin O'Brien recuperating in hospital in London. Will return to States as soon as able. Honorable discharge forthcoming." It was signed by a Captain Enger.

Fannie quivered and tears welled into her eyes. Patsy hollered from the porch. "What's going on?"

"Cal's coming home!" Jerry shouted. He whooped and hugged Mom. Then Fannie hugged her, and their sobs flowed. Patsy rushed into the fray.

They laughed and cried and hugged a few moments longer until reality came floating back. What a sight they looked. Fannie sniffed and smiled at Mom. "It doesn't say anything about his injury."

"No. But it does say he's recuperating. That's good news."

"They don't make it sound like it'll be long," Jerry said.

" 'As soon as able. . .' That could mean anything." Fannie looked for a hospital address where they could write, but none was given. "Maybe Cal will write soon."

"Yes. Maybe." Mom clasped her hands together. She'd stopped shaking, and now pure joy radiated from her face.

Fannie handed her the telegram. "I suppose we'd better not quit work today to celebrate."

"Tonight we will." Mom tucked the paper into her apron pocket.

Fannie glanced over her shoulder toward the waiting PWs. "They probably think the war ended."

Jerry shook his head. "Naw. They still think they're gonna win. They wouldn't expect us to be cheering."

"Let's go." Fannie pulled the askew blue handkerchief scarf off her head and used it to dab her eyes. Her bun hung loose. She must look an emotional mess, but it didn't matter. Nothing else mattered. Not how she looked. Not how much work still had to be finished today. Not what the PWs thought of them. All that mattered was that Cal was alive and coming home.

≣ CHAPTER 6 ≣

Leo Friedrickson knew right off it was a telegram in Frau O'Brien's hand. She'd received news of someone still in the war. Why else would they be cheering and bawling at once? Was it her husband? A son perhaps? Someone important to them, no doubt; someone who'd left these women and youngsters to run their farm alone, just as had happened with so many women, children, and old men in Germany. Except that in Germany they did not have the aid of Allied prisoners bringing in their crops for them. They should have forced them to work instead of locking them behind barbed-wire fences. Leo didn't believe the rumors that many prisoners, especially the Jews, were being executed. Though such tales of Nazi atrocities had reached them in North Africa, he gave them little credence.

He sipped slowly on his beverage, watching over the rim of his fruit jar as the family sauntered toward them. The eldest Fraülein had taken off her scarf. Loose strands of hair blew in the wind, free from the pins meant to hold it in place. Her face glowed with some news, even though her eyes were red with weeping.

Naturally, his glance shifted over the rest of her. She was a beauty, dark-eyed and tanned from the sun. Her body was meant for other things besides grubbing in the dirt. His mind drifted to feral thoughts momentarily, then he sloshed back the remainder of his lemonade. He puckered. Sugar was in short supply, he knew, so the flavor was tarter than he might like. Yet he detected a mild sweetener of some kind, honey possibly, and the beverage quenched his thirst.

She gave no explanation for what had taken place as she strode past, nor did Leo expect one. He turned along with the other workers to follow her and her brother into the field. She immediately headed for the pickup parked in front of the loaded wagon and bent to loosen the hitch. He hurried up to her.

"Lass mich dir helfen." He waved her hand away from the hitch to indicate his offer to help. She stepped back, and Richard Schorr came alongside to assist him. The others gathered around the front of the loaded wagon and muscled it into position to be hitched to the truck. Meanwhile, the boy called Jerry fired up the tractor and drove over to hook the empty wagon to that. As the crew strolled toward the task, Leo watched the woman and her mother converse until the mother headed back toward the house and Fraülein O'Brien strode toward them. With two fingers in the corners of her mouth, she gave a loud, sharp whistle. Her brother cranked his body around on the tractor. She waved him down and spoke to him.

The next thing Leo knew, the boy scampered into the truck and drove away with the extra guard and four of their crew.

Leo stepped forward. This presented an opportunity. The Fraülein was going to need help with the mowing. Just then, however, Wolf strode across in front of him, and the next thing Leo knew, his Hauptmann was the one climbing onto the mower's seat. Leo narrowed his gaze. Of course their Hauptmann would want to try such a job instead of laboring with the backbreaking work of pitching peas.

By all rights, Leo should have achieved a higher rank too, not merely have remained an Obergefreiter. The reminder tasted sourer than the lemon in his throat. He curled a lip. Let Hauptmann Kloninger have his ride on the pea mower. Next time Leo would plead a reason to run the tractor. He wanted a closer look at its operation from the seat above.

Leo came alongside his captain on the mower. The woman was pointing out levers and giving directions, just as her brother had done for Leo yesterday. Corporal Taft was explaining the process to Wolf in German.

Wolf nodded his understanding.

"So, you are going to give it a go," Leo said.

Wolf didn't acknowledge him. He was busily trying out the levers per Fraülein O'Brien's instructions. When she seemed satisfied, she marched back to the tractor, climbed up, and gave it gas.

Leo wished it were him on the mower, but he decided not to say anything about it. He took his place pitching peas onto the wagon alongside Hermann, the Hauptmann's former math student. Those who knew him said Hermann was brilliant—and only twenty-one years old. They said if he'd been able to graduate, he would have gone on to university and made something important of his life.

As they moved up one row of felled peavines and down the next, Leo and Hermann spoke only occasionally. Leo cast glances at the Hauptmann, who seemed to have gotten almost immediately used to handling the mower. More often than not, his glance toward the captain moved to the woman seated on the tractor, bouncing along on the spring seat, her hair coming more and more undone.

They had the load nearly full when she shut off the tractor and slid down again. With her forearm, she pushed her hair back, and after a quick remark to Wolf—a thanks or compliment perhaps—strode past them like a queen. Was Leo imagining it, or had her color heightened in the brief moment she'd addressed his Hauptmann? For just a flash, she'd seemed almost shy. She stopped and said something to the guard with much less diffidence than she had with Wolf, then walked toward the farmyard. The men all rested on the handles of their pitchforks as she disappeared inside the barn shed and came out a moment later lugging a gas can, clearly heavy for her.

Leo stabbed his pitchfork into the earth and called to the guard. "I'll help her."

He jogged across the end of the field and reached her before she'd gotten far. Her eyes refused to meet his as he said the same thing he'd said when he helped her with the hitch. "Let me help you."

She answered, "Ja. Danke."

He smiled, even though she didn't look at him to notice. That she would thank him in German was interesting. He tried something else to test her. "I am glad that you and your family received some happy news today."

Now her frown and the shrug of her shoulders showed she didn't understand. It didn't matter. He had discovered the depth of her knowledge. He forced a small laugh and smiled anyway. Was that the hint of upturned lips returned to him? He lingered over the possibility a second longer, and then he lugged the heavy can to the field, keeping one step ahead of her.

At the tractor, Richard helped Leo lift and pour the can of fuel into the tank. Fraülein O'Brien stood nearby, waiting to screw the cap back on. When the last drops emptied, Leo removed the can, shifting his stance suddenly so that his shoulder brushed hers. She took a hasty step away, but a satisfying sensation of touch lingered. She was flustered, and that pleased Leo too.

He lowered the can to the ground as she climbed back onto the tractor. Richard hustled to crank the flywheel for her. She didn't bother to thank him but turned her face to the rows of uncut peas.

After another hour's work, the boy returned with the empty wagon, and about the same time, an army truck brought their afternoon meal. The two guards stood their rifles against the shade tree in the yard and enjoyed a meal brought out by Frau O'Brien, while the shapely woman and her brother disappeared inside.

The guard gave the men further permission to refill their water at the pump, and Wolf dropped onto the grass beside Leo with his chicken sandwich and a potato boiled in its skin. "Sorry to take your job from you today, but I was intrigued to try the machine too."

Leo shrugged and swallowed a bite of cool potato. "It's of no consequence. You are the Hauptmann. I am only an Obergefreiter."

"You are experienced and have the respect of the younger men."

Leo gave a nod, accepting the compliment. "Perhaps I'll get some other opportunity later."

Wolf peered at him while breaking his sandwich in two. "Opportunity?"

Leo shrugged. "For some other interesting work, the same as you. Who knows where our service might lead?"

"What are you suggesting?"

"Nothing more than has been suggested since we began our training. The opportunity for advancement."

"Ah."

"It is a shame that our countrymen go with so little, while all this"— he spread his hand in a display of the crops before them—"will go to feed the enemy. They will send it to their armies in Europe and the Pacific."

"I am sure you are right, yet we are in a position to do little about it."

Leo looked at him steadily. Was the Hauptmann being serious? Or did he have ideas of his own that he would not speak aloud? They all had a directive, even if captured. He broached another topic. "Did you ever learn the Fräulein's first name?"

Hauptmann Kloninger glanced at the woman on the tractor and back to Leo. "I have heard her brother call her Fannie."

Fannie. Leo took a long sip of water, then lowered the canteen and wiped his mouth. Her name settled deep into his thoughts, giving her personality. Later, he would say it aloud. Practice it for when it might be useful to use. With a long, slow glance across the farm, the Hauptmann's remark followed into his thinking. *We are in a position to do little about it.* Leo capped his canteen. He could not agree with his Hauptmann.

The final load was ready to leave the farm late in the afternoon. The men would all go along in the transport lorry, and from there they'd return to Camp Barron. The young girl in braids stood outside with a jug, offering them each a refill of their canteens to drink on the way back. The two guards stood talking by the truck, and the rest of them waited wearily for a turn to get some fresh water. Fannie had just pulled the tractor and mower up to the shed and turned off the engine. She appeared as worn out as the men. Leo couldn't deny a sense of respect for her dedication. Corporal Taft walked over to speak to her. He was grinning like he'd accomplished their work for them. He probably had a thing for the woman, and being American, he could easily try to charm her with conversation. He didn't have to use his wits, if he had any.

Their conversation was brief. The corporal nodded and turned away. "Time to load up! Let's get this load going, and you can all get some rest."

Fannie O'Brien walked wearily toward them, passing them as they filed for the lorry. The boy climbed into the driver's seat of the farm truck. This final load was piled almost precariously high to finish off what remained of the crop. The boy had better drive slowly over those ruts, or he'd be bound to lose half the peas.

He turned over his truck's engine. The men found their seats in the back of the lorry. The farm truck whined. The boy turned the motor again.

Leo hiked himself into the lorry, watching the boy in the truck as he tried a third time. The truck sputtered and quit.

"The engine will not start," Horst murmured.

They all watched now. Even the two guards didn't get in but stood waiting for the pea truck to get going first.

After a fourth try, the boy got out of the truck and slammed the door. His sister had walked as far as the porch. Now she started back down the steps toward her brother. Her voice rose on a question.

He offered explanation, but the frustration in his voice, the shrug of his shoulders, and the lift of his hands said that he didn't know what was wrong. Leo didn't need to know much English to understand their trouble.

"Perhaps it is overheated," Richard said.

"The plugs could be fouled," Horst answered.

"Horst, do you know about engines?" Hauptmann Kloninger asked. Leo wanted to say that he could help, but the others knew it was right to ask Horst. Horst worked on their trucks often enough in the desert.

"Go and talk to the corporal. See if you can help."

Horst nodded at Wolf and got down off the truck. Wolf followed. He spoke to Corporal Taft, and Taft took Horst over to the O'Briens with Wolf following.

Jerry and Horst soon had their heads bent together under the hood while Wolf stood beside the corporal and Fraülein O'Brien talking things over. She planted her hands on her hips and waited.

Leo and the rest sat waiting, wishing to be out of there.

"If they don't get it started, they will lose the rest of the crop. It'll only be good for pigs." Otto said aloud what they were all coming to realize.

There were a couple of sighs, most for the waste of all their hard work, no doubt.

Leo spoke softly. "It is not the worst thing." At the blank looks, he added, "Every pea that leaves this farm goes to feed their soldiers or to sustain someone fighting against our countrymen."

Fritz's head moved slowly in the smallest nod of understanding.

Otto grinned. "Then we should be happy."

"Quiet."

Otto's grin fell away. "I was only joking. There is far too much to be serious about. It is not our problem. It is a malfunction of the truck and no concern."

Rudy nodded. "I agree with Otto. It's not our problem."

Leo turned his face from them to watch the goings-on at the pea truck again. Frau O'Brien had come out, and the youngest daughter stood on the porch watching too. Then Fannie O'Brien stormed off toward the barnyard. Wolf went with her.

A prickling sensation skittered up Leo's spine, and he narrowed his eyes. They disappeared into the shed together and came back a moment later with another can of fuel, only this one swung in Wolf's hand like it was light, more empty than full. Horst took it and disappeared beneath the hood. Jerry came around the side of the truck and got back in the cab again. He turned the engine. It fired, but after running only a few moments it sputtered.

Now Fannie O'Brien called to her brother, then went to the tractor by the shed.

Leo's stomach rumbled. It had been a long time since lunch, and they were all getting restless and hungry. He'd gone hours longer than this on less food in Africa, but that didn't mean it didn't pain him now to have to wait for a meal. Besides, he looked forward to a shower. Nevertheless, he was curious about what the O'Briens were going to do about their peas.

The tractor roared to life again, and in another minute, Fannie drove it over. Jerry was getting Wolf's help to unhitch the trailer. Leo studied them with a growing restlessness. Was she planning to pull the load all the way to the vinery with the tractor? It would take at least an hour to get there with that conveyance. Besides that, there was the load on the truck bed itself to deal with.

The corporal called Richard's name, and the brawny younger man climbed down to help Wolf and Jerry. In a few minutes, they had the loaded wagon switched to the tractor.

Sighs went up around the lorry as the crew realized the work they were in for. They'd have to follow the tractor slowly to the vinery, unload the trailer, and then in all likelihood, return to the farm—another hour's drive—and transfer the rest of the peas from the back of the dead truck to the trailer, and finally go back to the vinery behind the tractor again. They wouldn't be finished until well past dark. The corporal had made it very clear that this job must be completed today. The O'Briens' crops were scheduled at the vinery to take no longer.

Leo tamped down a groan. There was nothing to be done about it. He and the others got off the truck and retrieved pitchforks yet again. Over the next twenty minutes, they transferred the load.

Two hours later, covered in another layer of sweat and filth, they were on their way back to the farm, following the tractor and now-empty trailer that bobbed along behind. A few of the lads had fallen asleep, and their heads jerked about on their necks like the trailer on its hitch. They revived as the lorry turned into the O'Briens' drive.

To the welcome surprise of all, Frau O'Brien stood next to a picnic table loaded down with food. She waved them over. Plates were piled with beef sandwiches and mashed potatoes, all covered in thick gravy. She handed them each a plate and a fork. The youngest O'Brien, whom Leo heard the Frau call Patsy, set down a tray full of coffee in those small canning jars they'd used earlier along with a pitcher of cream. The hungry men nodded gratefully for the unexpected supper. They would have missed their meal at the camp by now and would likely only get bread and water or maybe a smear of peanut butter. Leo couldn't help noticing the generous portion of meat between the thick slices of bread as he cut into his dripping sandwich with his fork and crammed the bite into his mouth.

Pork. His jaw paused working only a moment. Not the beef he craved after all. He'd only assumed. Still, it didn't really matter. It was tender and went down willingly enough.

After the meal, Wolf turned to the men. "Head to the truck. We will leave momentarily."

"What about the load?"

"Herr O'Brien solved the problem. Fraülein O'Brien can now drive the truck. We will follow as before."

Leo turned away to set his empty plate on the picnic table. How had Jerry solved the problem? Was it really solved, or would the woman break down on the way to the vinery? He frowned into the dimming light of the distance. They might not lay their heads down for hours yet.

But the truck did not break down. Half an hour later, Fritz, Rudolf, and Hermann were shoving peas onto the conveyor while the rest of them waited in the lorry. Wolf spoke to the corporal, who again spoke to the woman, and she shook the corporal's hand. She turned to Wolf and said something to him, this time with much less hesitation than earlier in the day. Wolf bowed his head, his face genial.

Leo scowled, and he didn't care if it showed.

≡ CHAPTER 7 ≡

"Fannie, you all right?" Mama sat forward in her rocker, creases of the day's weariness lining her eyes.

Fannie halted at the bottom of the stairs. "I'm all right. Why are you still up?"

"I cleaned up the kitchen and sent Patsy out to do the milking after dinner. She's been so housebound these days."

"It won't hurt her any."

"I know. Something else bothering you?" Mom frowned.

Fannie wasn't very good at hiding her concerns. "Jerry says he thinks it's funny, the truck not starting before."

"The condensation in the lines you mean?"

Fannie let her head rest against the living room doorframe and folded her arms. She had asked Jerry how there could be condensation. They'd filled the tank with fuel during their lunch break, and it had been hot out all day. He'd shrugged and said they must've gotten some bad gasoline or something. Some kind of nonsense that didn't make sense to her. Then he said it was kind of funny, but he wouldn't elaborate.

Fannie didn't want to worry Mom. The main thing was that the peas were all harvested. "It's nothing, Mama. I just need to get some sleep. Patsy upstairs now?"

"She headed off to bed early too. Probably to read her book."

That brought a warmth to Fannie's heart. "I think I'll go on up and let her read me to sleep."

"I'll be right along behind you soon as Jerry comes in."

"He's just cleaning up outside."

"I'll wait."

Mom always waited. She'd probably be sitting in that rocker or standing by the cookstove waiting on the day Cal came home. Dale too. Just like she'd been waiting for Dad to come in from the barn on that day. He never did.

Lord, let Cal be home soon so maybe we won't have to bring those men back for any more work. Even if we do, God, let Cal be home to handle them. Fannie just wanted to go back to being a girl again, but it didn't seem fair to the rest of them to tell God that. It made her feel selfish and spoiled—which she wasn't. Fannie went into the bathroom and pulled the light chain, then looked at the back of her hand. She looked at the other one too. Dirt was part of her pores, showing every crease and line in hands she'd always thought would look smooth and young for many more years. At this rate they wouldn't.

She turned on the squeaky faucet handle and filled the basin with tepid water. It turned brown as soon as she began swishing her hands in it. She was too tired for a whole bath, bad as she needed one. She'd just have to wash her sheets extra well tomorrow if the weather was nice. They had missed their regular Monday washday except for laundering a few towels Mom had asked Patsy to do to keep her busy while the prisoners were here.

It felt good to scrub her arms and the back of her neck and face. In fact, Fannie had accomplished a pretty good sponge bath by the time she was ready to slip into her nightgown and poke her head into Patsy's bedroom to say good night.

As Mom predicted, Patsy was reading by the light of the pull-string lamp secured with flexible hooks to her metal headboard. Patsy waved her in. "Close the door and come here."

Fannie fought her desire to sigh and tell her "Not tonight," and crawled across her little sister's bed to sit beside her. "What's up?"

"This book is so good." Patsy widened her eyes with exaggerated wonderment. "I couldn't wait to finish chores so I could get back to it."

"What's it called?"

Patsy held it up to show Fannie the spine.

"You're reading *Rebecca*?"

"It's so creepy." Patsy shuddered with delight.

"Aren't you a little young for that story?"

Patsy gasped. "What do you want me to read—*Rabbit Hill*? I read that when I was ten." She dropped back onto her pillow. Fannie was about to tell her good night and happy reading when Patsy said, "Tell me about the prisoners."

Fannie expelled a breath. "It's late, Pats."

"No, it isn't. It's not even ten o'clock."

"It feels like midnight."

Patsy left her book lying on the nightgown draping her legs and clutched Fannie's arm. "Just tell me."

"What do you want to know?"

"They aren't very old, except for that one who sort of takes charge."

"Are you confusing Corporal Taft with one of the Germans?" Fannie knew she wasn't, but why would her thirteen-year-old sister notice such things?

Patsy shook her head. "No, not him. The German. He's handsome for somebody as old as he is."

"You mean just a few years older than I am?" Fannie raised her brow wryly.

"That other one isn't much younger. Just think. We have real Nazis right here on our farm."

"They're human beings, Patsy. You know that, don't you? And Corporal Taft says they aren't all Nazis. Some of them were just forced into service."

"I know." She plunged down into her pillow. "I think they both like you. The two older ones, I mean."

"Patsy, really." Fannie started to push off the bed, but Patsy sat up again and pulled her back.

"Don't go. Did you find out any of their names?"

Fannie pinched her lips, prepared to not let Patsy's inquisition go any further, but then she sighed. Her sister would just hound her later on. "I suppose you won't let it go. We *aren't* going to get to know them, so if I tell you their names, will you leave it be? And for heaven's sake, don't tell any of your friends about them. There are a lot of people who don't like some of the farmers and factories hiring the PWs."

"I won't tell." Her eyes shone.

"The *old* one is Wolfgang Kloninger, and the other one is Leo Friedrickson." She took a quick breath to continue, even while she was momentarily surprised at herself for remembering their names so easily. Their faces popped instantly to mind also. "And there's Richard and Hermann, and. . .oh, I forget the others. Jerry probably knows."

"Some of them are cute."

Fannie eyeballed her sister. "Like I said, I think you're a little young for *Rebecca*."

"Phooey." Patsy lay back on the pillow. She propped the book open on her chest.

"You know they made a movie about it just a couple years back."

The book fell flat. "They did?"

Fannie nodded as she rose and moved toward the door. "I saw it." She turned back and winked at her sister. "Sooo good." Then she slipped out, closing the door on Patsy's groan, and chuckled. Her little sister might turn into a writer someday. She had such an imagination. She might need a little reminding, however, that those PWs were the enemy.

The next couple of days felt almost normal, although stiff joints reminded Fannie of those long days of hard work earlier in the week. On Friday, gray skies blew in and it rained softly. Fannie offered Patsy a day at the library while she worked. She could hardly wait to return to her job. How she missed it!

She donned a tan, pleated skirt and a cream-colored blouse with a bow tie collar. She slipped on beige pumps that were practically like new, since she'd worn them so little in the past year. She crimped her hair and pulled it back to the side in a barrette, reminding herself to take along an umbrella since she didn't want to wear a hat. With a pinch to her cheeks and a couple of strokes of rose lipstick, Fannie almost felt like a woman again. She'd rubbed a little lanolin into her skin after a bath on Wednesday, so her hands didn't look quite so dry, even though she'd had to trim her nails to the quick, and she could do nothing about how brown her skin was.

Patsy was already downstairs finishing her breakfast and looking pretty in a checked skirt, light blue blouse, and saddle shoes. Her hair was parted neatly and woven into her usual pairing of braids.

"You clean up pretty well," Patsy said.

Fannie laughed. "Do I? So do you, my little milkmaid."

Patsy wrinkled her nose but smiled. "I'm ready when you are." She lifted a pile of books off the table.

"Let me sip my coffee and we'll go."

Mom handed them two sack lunches. "You might get caught in the rain, so drive carefully."

Only light sprinkles fell as the two dashed out of the house to the family car, a 1936 sedan Dad purchased when Fannie enrolled in the county teacher's college. It had served the family well for three years now, and Fannie never got behind the wheel without thinking of her dad and the many ways he'd unknowingly left them prepared for his homegoing.

Jerry had high hopes for getting the old Model A Ford parked beside the barn running too.

"At least it's a warm rain." As usual, Patsy sounded older than her thirteen years, as she shut the passenger door and settled her books in her lap.

"We need it." Fannie started the engine and headed down the drive. There was always a delicate dance that nature played for the farmers. The rain and sun to nurture and grow, bright weather to harvest, and times for the ground to dry up so they wouldn't get their equipment stuck in the fields. Sometimes the dance went out of step, and it became nearly impossible to till a field or bring in the hay. Then there were the occasional ravages of disease or insects to contend with. It had always been a concern, but now without Dad or Calvin to take charge, and the weight of the farm falling on her and her mother's shoulders, that dance became more nerve-racking. Nevertheless, for today at least, she would only have to think about sorting books and smiling at library patrons.

They arrived at the library and turned the corner to park alongside the stately brownstone building. After she opened the umbrella, she and Patsy scurried around the front of the building and up the wide concrete stairs, ducking under the columned portico as the pattering raindrops turned to a downpour.

"Made it just in time." Patsy followed Fannie inside, then disappeared in the aisles of books.

Fannie took their lunches to the staff break room and signed in on her time card.

"You're back." Mrs. Calloway, the head librarian, greeted Fannie with a smile. "And just in time. We have a stack of returned books to be processed."

"A number of them are my sister's, no doubt. She's reading *Rebecca* already." Fannie shook her head.

"At least she has good taste. I suppose it'll be *Gone with the Wind* next."

"I think I'll steer her to something else. Maybe *The Sword in the Stone*."

"I think that one just came back a few days ago."

"I'll check and see. Then again, she'll probably have ten others picked out before we go home today." Fannie moved to the return stack where books, magazines, and newspapers stood in small piles. She picked up the pile of papers first.

INVASION! one headline screamed. ALLIES LAND IN NORTHERN

France! Headlines on other papers were similar, all echoing the news from earlier in the month that Operation Overlord—D-Day—had been carried out and deemed a turning point in the war effort, even at the cost of nearly eleven thousand lives. It might have been Cal's among them, but thank heaven that wasn't the case. No one in the family spoke that fear aloud, but over the many passing days before they'd finally heard that he was coming home, the possibility taunted Fannie and no doubt her mother and Jerry too. They still didn't know which part of the world he was returning from.

She glanced at Patsy, who was intent behind the pages of a book in a chair across the room. Maybe Patsy was the exception in their family. She might never believe anything bad could happen to her stalwart eldest brother.

"And now we've been invaded too," Fannie murmured as she straightened the broadsheets. She'd read the articles and heard the daily radio reports. Yes, they were making strides in the war, but at such a cost. And now with having to pay for the help of Germans on their farm, it felt like their borders had been breached.

"Did you see the letters to the editor in the *Chronotype*?" Mrs. Calloway spoke over her shoulder, nearly startling her.

"No, I didn't."

"Folks are getting wind of the prisoner of war camp in Barron."

"And?" She set the papers aside and pulled out the file drawer of lending cards to begin checking in the returned books.

"Some are pretty upset. They claim that if we aren't careful, we'll be inviting Nazis to murder us in our beds." Her tone sounded dubious. "But there are some voices of reason out there, reminding everyone that the prisoners are human."

Fannie slid a book to the right and picked up another, moving slowly as she focused on Mrs. Calloway's remark. "What do you think?"

"I think caution is good, but they have to keep the prisoners someplace. And why not require their labor? We're missing too many of our own men. I hear they've been begging for workers at the canneries. Remember Faith Winkleman?"

Fannie nodded. Faith used to work summers at the library.

"She's working full-time at the cannery this summer, right along with both of her sisters."

"But Maryann is only sixteen." Faith's younger sister was in Jerry's class at school.

Mrs. Calloway took a chair behind her desk and settled her glasses on the bridge of her nose. "The girls are helping in every way they can while Mr. Winkleman does his part."

All three Winkleman girls working in the canning factory—Fannie could hardly imagine it, yet she already knew that the girls had all been hard workers long before the war. They must be working right alongside PWs too.

She turned to Mrs. Calloway. She kept her voice low in case there were any patrons besides Patsy somewhere amid the bookcases. "Have you heard what it's really like working with them? The PWs, I mean? Have you spoken to Faith or anyone else about it?"

Mrs. Calloway raised her head from her work and removed her glasses once more. "No, I haven't." She tented her fingers. "I've only heard what I've read. Oh, they worry about sabotage and things like that. But they're watched so closely I doubt there's anything to be afraid of. They seem more concerned about fraternization than anything else. I don't see the Winkleman girls as the kind to get caught in a flirtation with an enemy prisoner of war. Do you?"

"A flirtation? Oh. . .oh no. Certainly not." She turned back to her books and finished checking them in. Should she tell Mrs. Calloway about the PWs on their farm? She wanted to. Fannie had the highest regard for the head librarian. She was levelheaded and always kind. But would it be wise? Maybe later. Or maybe she should hold her tongue. After all, Cal would be home before they knew it. Then if they did need to hire the PWs back again, there'd be a man in the family to handle them. Fannie wouldn't even have to go near them again.

"We have good news." She scooped up the books and set them on a wooden cart. "My brother Calvin is coming home."

Mrs. Calloway gasped. "That's wonderful news, Fannie. I'm surprised you didn't say so right away. When do you expect him?"

"We don't know exactly. The army took their good-natured time locating him. Now we just have to pray that the war will end and Dale will be released too."

"Have you heard from Dale?"

"Only a couple of cards. There isn't much room on them to write, and he can't tell much or they blacken it out. We only know he's being held in a camp in Germany. We don't know much about his condition. He just says he's well enough. He tries to joke, but it doesn't read very funny."

"I'm so sorry, Fannie. Now that the Allies have invaded France, the war is sure to end soon."

"I hope so." Fannie pushed the cart away. She hoped so on so many counts.

By the end of the day, Patsy had finished reading *Rebecca* and returned it in exchange for three more novels. Fannie suggested she expand her reading to something factual or biographical, but Patsy wrinkled her nose and said she got enough of that kind of reading at school.

"When will the PWs be back?" Patsy asked abruptly as they reached the road leading home.

"In a few days, probably. Beans need cultivation and irrigating."

Her sister seemed satisfied with that answer, but now Fannie was curious. "Why do you ask?"

"Dorothy Jean came into the library today too. We were talking about them. She said her brothers drove over to that camp and spied on the prisoners."

Fannie flung her a look. "They what? Don't they know somebody could get hurt? People have been warned to stay away from the camps."

"The soldiers will shoot if a prisoner was to get out or come after them or something." The nonchalance of Patsy's response was even more shocking than her initial comment. Had they grown so used to the killing of their enemies that even a thirteen-year-old girl could become calloused?

"They are men. Young men like Jerry and Dale. They have families who want them to come home, Patsy. To talk about taking lives so casually is—is unbecoming. It's crass. Vulgar. Imm—"

"I get it." Patsy let out a deep sigh. "I didn't say *I* was going to go over there to spy on them. Jeepers."

"I wish you wouldn't talk about them in any way. It's no one's business that they come to the farm." Fannie pinched her lips and breathed out her nose. Patsy was only telling about her friend's foolish brothers. They were all young. Too young for war. Why weren't they busy working for the summer? "What's Dorothy Jean doing with her summer?" she asked to redirect the conversation as they turned into their drive.

"She doesn't have to do anything. Her dad's rich."

"Mr. Milton isn't rich."

"Could've fooled me."

Fannie glanced at Patsy again. "When did you become so aware of social standing?"

"I'm not so dumb. I can see that they live in a nicer house than ours, and they have two cars, and Dorothy Jean always has some new dress or other. She says her dad is going to buy her a car when she turns sixteen. The war will be over by then, and his stocks will be soaring. That's what she said. What are stocks anyway? They talk about them in books, but they never tell you what they are."

Fannie barely heard Patsy's question. She couldn't get past the notion that her little sister was already comparing them to other families. "Their house isn't that much nicer than ours, and they live on a city block. They don't have acres and acres to roam and call their own. Or a creek to swim in whenever they want. And besides, we have two cars too, and a truck and tractor besides." Fannie shut off the engine and got out.

"You can't count that old heap of Jerry's," Patsy said as she clambered out with her armload of books. "But speaking of swimming, I hope it's hot out on Sunday. I want a nice long swim before those PWs are back here ruining my week."

Fannie rolled her eyes, then caught Jerry coming out of the barn shed. His hands were black with grease that seemed also to have made its way onto his ripped T-shirt and his nose. "What are you working on?"

"Just been making sure the truck and tractor are tuned up for the next time we need them."

"Good idea."

"Got a minute?" He jerked his head and beckoned her toward the barn.

With a glance at Patsy disappearing into the house, Fannie followed, skirting a mud puddle from the half-day's rain. "What is it?"

"Remember I said that maybe we got some bad fuel?"

Fannie followed him inside, careful not to bump into anything with her good clothes on. "Yes, I remember."

"Have a look."

A glass jar sat on the workbench in front of the dusty window where light poured through the container, illuminating the contents. Clearly there was gasoline in there, but it sat on a half inch of something clear. "Is it water?"

"Yeah."

"So you were right. Which station did you buy the fuel from? I've heard some places will water it down."

"Fannie, I filled two cans at the same place, and the other is fine."

"Then there was condensation?"

"We haven't had enough temperature change from day to night to cause that much condensation. Besides, we filled up first thing, remember?"

"What are you saying, Jer?" Her head buzzed with the answer.

He folded his arms, and his brown eyes settled on her. "What do you think I'm saying?"

"Just tell me." She did know. She just couldn't say it.

"I'm saying there have been shenanigans."

"You mean somebody put that water in the truck?"

"You're pretty smart for a girl." Sarcasm laced his tone.

"Who would come along and do such a thing? And with the way things are? And how would they have done it?"

"Fannie, you're avoiding the obvious."

Yes, she was. She chewed on a hangnail and spat it out with a puff. "So, you really believe that somehow one or more of the PWs tried to sabotage the truck while we were all right there watching, and with a gun on them to boot."

"Thanks for not making me spell it out."

"That's impossible."

"Is it? They wandered to the pails to fill their canteens often enough. The guard couldn't walk on both sides of the truck at once. The tank is on the opposite side of the driver. They might have had another man watching or ready to distract Mom or whichever one of us was driving."

Fannie thought of the short time she drove the truck and that prisoner Wolf pitching peavines alongside, glancing up at her in her side mirror, nodding. Distracting her.

"You think it's really possible?"

"Think about it, Fan. And keep a close eye when they're back here next week." He slid the jar against the wall. "I think I can strain the gas off the top and make it usable again."

"Don't tell Mom."

" 'Course not. We'll handle it."

Fannie placed a hand on his shoulder. "Thanks, Jerry." She smiled encouragement. "Cal will be home soon."

⬚ CHAPTER 8 ⬚

VICTORY BEGINS ON THE FARM! OVERALLS ARE YOUR UNIFORM! Fannie recalled the words splashed across the posters meant to encourage the men and women who remained behind as the backbone of their war effort. Then she considered the Germans in her bean field. Sunlight blazed the sky, while across the ocean of green men in gray uniforms crouched, the giant letters *PW* stamped across their backs aimed at the heavens as if in silent supplication for their freedom. They too wore overalls instead of a soldier's uniform. Did they still long for Germany's triumph? Or would the assured well-being of their families offer victory enough?

Radio announcements told of the bombings and desecration of towns, villages, and even the major cities of Germany. Would the PWs have homes to return to?

Had Fannie only days ago told Patsy that they were simply men wanting to go home to their families?

Hurry home, Calvin.

She bent again alongside Patsy and Jerry. They hoed between the rows of beans on the east end of the field, while the PWs moved irrigation lines used to siphon water from the creek on the west. Far enough apart not to have to mingle. Corporal Taft and Private Vicks had bared their heads and rolled up their sleeves as they stood watch over the crew. Now and then, when their weeding got them close enough to the woods, one of the men would step away to do personal business, never far from sight of the guards.

"I'm so hot," Patsy groaned.

"We've only got another couple of rows. You'll have time for a swim before supper if you want."

77

"I don't know if I'll even have the energy."

"I'm sure you'll find some." Fannie chuckled, but she too wished for a long cool swim. "Maybe we'll go together."

"I think the swinging rope is getting ready to break." Jerry straightened and, with a hand to his lower back, bent backward in a stretch. "Me and my buddy Frank will have to fix it before you try swinging off it." He rolled his shoulders and bent to chop along the roots of encroaching weeds with his hoe.

"It won't break for me." Patsy stood and flung a handful of weeds into a wilting pile. "Maybe for Fannie."

Fannie threw a root ball at her back, hitting it square.

"Hey!"

"You just wait until we're in the creek."

"Speaking of water. . . Tonight I'd better check out the pipes they're moving. See to it they're laid out correctly."

"I'll go with you," Fannie said between short breaths as she chopped with her hoe.

Near the end of the day, the siblings finally walked to Meadows Creek. The PWs were only a few rows over from them, and they could finish hoeing the rest. They'd be gone by the time the O'Brien siblings emerged from the wooded ditch.

"My legs are so itchy from beans I can hardly wait to jump in." Patsy was already yanking off her shoes.

"I'll help you wash off." Jerry hoisted her over his shoulder and scuffled down the embankment while Patsy kicked and squealed. Her arguments were cut off the moment she went under the water with a splash. Jerry dove in beside her.

The creek wasn't deep. It only came waist high in the deepest places, except for one hole where the rope swing hung. But it ran clear and cool, and Fannie breathed a sigh of contentment as she waded in and sank down into the stream. A shiver ran through her, luscious and welcome. She faced the lazy current, pulled off her scarf, and held it while she dipped completely under. She came out with her face tilted to the sun, and when she stood again, she gave the scarf a good swishing.

Her work dress swam up around her thighs. That was getting a good rinsing too.

Patsy plunged out of the stream and up the bank to the rope swing, just as she said she would. With a holler, she pitched her body outward over the water and landed in the deepest hole, popping up like a cork an instant later.

Jerry shook his head. "You're lucky it didn't break before you jumped. No telling when it's going to give way."

"You're just chicken."

"I ain't chicken."

"Prove it."

"I don't have to."

Their banter continued, but Fannie stopped listening as she waded upstream, laid back in the water, and drifted down. She repeated the process again and again. After thirty minutes, feeling more refreshed than she had in a week, she stood up. "We'd better get going. Mom will be wondering where we are, and she'll probably need help with supper. Come on."

Patsy splashed past her and scrambled up the bank, pausing long enough to pop some wild blueberries into her mouth from the bushes scattered about.

Fannie pushed through the flow and leaned forward to find a foothold in the grassy overhang when movement atop the bank above drew her attention. She jerked back with an intake of breath at the sight of one of the Germans. Patsy lowered a blueberry-stained hand from her mouth as another man appeared and then another. Jerry stood silent in the water behind her. Soon the whole rank and file of German prisoners stood above them, spread out along the embankment. Fannie almost shrank back into the creek, but she held fast, her hands clinging to tufts of grass.

Then the guards appeared on either side of the line of prisoners, and Fannie nearly collapsed with relief. Yet all of their gazes were trained on the O'Briens, and not a few of them on Fannie in her wet, clinging work dress. She climbed over the bank with as much decorum as she could muster, then self-consciously reached for her wet hair at her back and pulled it forward to squeeze out the water, her elbows tight to her body as she did so. She spoke to her brother and sister. "Let's go."

The corporal gave her a nod. "Sorry, ma'am. We thought you'd gone to the house. We just wanted to give these men a chance to cool off. Save shower time back at camp."

Fannie raised her chin, ignoring their stares. "It's no trouble, Corporal. You go right ahead. I hope you get to cool off also."

His smile broadened. "We'll try."

One of the prisoners—Fritz, she thought his name was—had his shirt unbuttoned and couldn't struggle out of it fast enough. Other men followed suit.

Patsy gasped and Fannie frowned. "Hurry up, Patsy." She needed to get them out of here before the men were disrobed. She had the feeling they cared more about getting wet and cool than being modest right now. She marched along the edge of the creek bank with as much dignity as she could scavenge in her wet dress and bare feet, but she had to pass within two feet of Hauptmann Kloninger. He spoke a word, causing her to wheel.

"What?" She tossed a beseeching glance at the corporal, but he wasn't looking their way.

The handsome man spoke again, and his smile was. . .what? Apologetic?

She didn't know how to respond, so she turned away and waved her siblings along. They hurried down the short path back into the field, while behind them rose the shouts and splashes of the prisoners enjoying a reprieve in the O'Briens' swimming hole.

Fannie heated right back up again. The gall of them! Prisoners! Her enemies! *Enjoying our creek.* Fannie fumed silently the entire walk home, while Jerry and Patsy jabbered over the very thing between themselves.

They made it to the house just as Mom was setting their dinner on the table. Fannie apologized for not getting back sooner, but her mother waved off her explanations. "You children deserved some relaxation. I hope you do it often. Don't let these summer days get away from you completely. When you work hard, you should take some time to play hard too. Your dad always said so."

Fannie could almost hear her father telling them that. "That he did." She kissed her mom's cheek and hurried upstairs to get out of her wet clothes. She paused at the bedroom mirror, flushing again at what kind of coarse thoughts might've gone through those PWs' wicked minds. But now her anger quickly cooled. Was it really so bad that they had gone to swim in the creek, or was it merely her pride suffering humiliation at being caught unprepared and ogled so? Chagrined, she turned away from the mirror and hurriedly changed into a dry dress and brushed out her wet tangles. By the time she came back downstairs, her plate of chicken and rice was cool enough to dig into. Afterward Mom asked Patsy to help wash the dishes while Jerry went out to check the cow tank and throw scraps to the pigs.

"I'll get the clothes off the line," Fannie said.

"Would you do that? Thank you. I'll iron them tonight when it's cool."

"I don't know if it's going to cool down much." Fannie pushed her still-damp hair off her collar.

"Hopefully, the humidity will at least lift a bit."

Fannie plucked up the laundry basket and headed out the door. She took each garment off the line and folded it carefully before setting it in the basket, hoping to minimize the wrinkles. About halfway through, she unpinned a clean shirt of Jerry's to see the PWs strolling back across the field toward the yard. The guards flanked them, their weapons shouldered casually. Even from the distance, she could hear them talking amiably, clearly refreshed.

Her movements slowed down as she eyed them making their way closer. Some of them were still shirtless. Others had slipped their shirts on once again but left them open at the front. Some of their clothing was soaked through as it clung to wet skin.

They did a little laundry too.

A warm breeze lifted her drying hair and wrapped it in front of her eyes. She raised a hand to draw it back, and her gaze connected with Hauptmann Kloninger's. He said something to Corporal Taft, and she could hear Taft answer, "Ja."

Kloninger's head tilted as if in tentative question as he approached her. The corporal followed but stopped about fifteen feet away as the German approached. Fannie lowered her hands, clutching Patsy's clean gingham dress as the prisoner spoke to her. The only word she understood was *danke*. Thanks.

"You're welcome." She glanced at the corporal.

"He says he appreciates the chance to swim and rest. Thank you for allowing them the many privileges of working here on your farm."

"We appreciate the prisoners' hard work." She was drawn to his eyes, watching her response. She'd not liked their intrusion at the creek, but the fact that they understood it had been a privilege she could easily remove in the future pleased her. "They are welcome to avail themselves of the creek anytime. Under your watchful eye, of course, Corporal."

He gave her reply to the German, presumably without the addendum. The man smiled at her. He had a very genial smile that tilted his eyes at the corners and created fine lines. It seemed that each time they passed one another in a glance or a smile, his became less suspicious. And why should he be suspicious of her?

She looked at the corporal again. Would he allow her to ask a question? "Tell me, Mr. Kloninger, what do you and your men do when you return to camp at the end of such a day?"

The corporal considered a moment, then looked to the man and translated haltingly.

Captain Kloninger rattled off a long but rapid response, his face more animated than she had ever seen.

"The men eat their dinner, rest, write letters, and read books if they are lucky enough to have any in German." The corporal cleared his throat. "Mr. Kloninger is studying English."

"English? Why—" She clamped her lips shut for a moment then went on. "I am surprised Captain Kloninger would be interested in learning English. He will surely have little use for it once he returns to Germany."

The German captain spoke again.

"He would like his men to learn the language too. He believes it is important. He is a teacher."

A teacher. She straightened her posture, lowering her tight hold on Patsy's garment. "What kind of teacher?"

As the two men conversed back and forth, Fannie watched Wolfgang Kloninger with new interest. Why should she care if he was a teacher, and why did it matter to him that she knew it? And what concern was it to Fannie that his men enjoyed their use of a swim in her creek? Was it just because he suddenly appeared a little more human in her eyes?

Corporal Taft squared himself. "He says that some of these men were his students in the secondary school where he taught. Their education was cut short by the war, although some of them, Hermann Claus in particular, are quite intelligent and should have had the chance to study at university. Rudolf Ebner has missed most of his secondary schooling, and Captain Kloninger tries to help him as much as he can so that he'll not be so far behind when he returns. He's trying to learn English because he wants to be an example to the men, and he hopes that they'll learn it as well. It'll help them, for no one knows how long it will be before the war ends."

"It will end soon, I hope."

Taft repeated her words.

She looked directly at the German. "It's admirable that you wish to help your men. I hope you are successful. Do you know much English now?"

"Little." He held up his fingers in a narrow-gapped pinch, surprising her that he had understood at least some of her words.

She licked her lips and adjusted her stance. "I see. Well then, you are making headway." That last word brought a wrinkle to his forehead, but Corporal Taft explained.

The captain gave another smile.

"What resources do you use to study English with your men?"

The corporal answered for him. "They have use of a German-English translation book. Materials are limited. We allow them to read newspapers, though I don't think there are many men in the camp who are able."

Perhaps she could help. Yet the moment she thought of it, she also reprimanded herself for considering the notion. She should not get involved in even the most minor way. Besides, weren't there inherent dangers in the Germans learning English? They might use it to spy or. . .or something.

Get ahold of yourself, Fannie. They aren't your *students.*

The prisoners were here to work. That was all. She was fairly certain that it was against regulations for Mr. Kloninger to even speak with her like this. The corporal must know that. The memory of the water-tainted gasoline in their tractor flashed back. What were this man's true motives? He might only be saying he was a teacher as a ruse to harm them in some way.

"Well. . ." She laid the dress across the basket and hiked it to her hip. "Thank you again for your hard work today, Captain. And good luck on your studies."

The corporal translated, and she took a sideways step as if to go, but the German lifted a hand, palm up. She thought he was going to say something else, but instead he lowered his hand again and dipped his head. Then he turned and strode back to his men.

The other man, Leo, caught her gaze. His eyes remained on her, and when she turned her back and walked away, she felt them following her still.

⧉ CHAPTER 9 ⧉

On Sunday morning, Wolf moved through the breakfast line and carried his full tray to a nearby table in the mess tent. The mess was a larger version of the several dozen tents pitched at the work camp surrounded by fence and barbed wire and located on the east side of a village called Barron.

Throwing his long legs over a bench, he sat down and tried the biscuits and gravy flavored with pork sausage. Their situation could have been far worse. In fact, he'd already gained fifteen pounds since becoming a prisoner, weight he'd lost during his time in service. Last night he'd taken time to write a letter to his parents, wishing them well and assuring them that he and the boys with him were all healthy and safe. He used only spare words to speak of his work, careful not to name their location, as such information was certain to be censored. He imagined getting such a letter himself, full of spaces replaced with the word CENSORED in thick, black letters. His mother was not young, and seeing a page of such menacing dark words would only cause her undue worry.

He'd warned some of the others to avoid stating the obvious phrases that would be cut from their letters for the very same reasons, but he was sure some fellows paid no attention. Several men took ridiculous pleasure in making the job of the translator more difficult, and some simply wouldn't remember. Fritz Von Hecker would only be thinking about telling his girl how much he missed her, and Horst Albrecht would be asking after his sister's health. Leo Friedrickson was the only one who didn't use his evening to write a letter home. He'd lain back on his cot with his arms tucked beneath his dark head, staring at the ceiling and smoking in silence.

Wolf tilted his head once to see what Leo might be looking at. He smiled down at the fellow who was nearest his age, but Leo's gaze didn't falter, nor did he offer any notice of his captain. Wolf seldom recalled Leo ever writing to anyone, even when they were on the field in Africa. He was mostly a quiet sort, but when action came, he was as ready and explosive as a grenade. In all the months they'd served together, that was all Wolf really knew about him.

Wolf's glass of milk this morning was fresh and cold. The sun striking the roof didn't take long to heat up the inside of the packed structure like a kettle, so he enjoyed the long, chill draught.

Hermann Claus approached with his full tray. "Mind if I sit with you, Hauptmann?"

"Not at all." He indicated the empty seat beside him. Soft-spoken Hermann had dreams of becoming an architect. When he had been Wolf's student, his mathematical abilities had surpassed his teacher's, and he could grasp concepts faster than any of his classmates.

The two ate in companionable silence for a couple of minutes as the rest of the seats around the table quickly filled.

They'd been working at the O'Brien farm for two weeks now. Six months ago, Wolf and his men would have clamored for just one handful of peas or a single potato to satisfy their hunger. In North Africa, supplies had to travel hundreds of dangerous miles to reach them from Italy, and many never arrived. They'd surely not expected that their provisions would be improved as prisoners of war. Now, however, with their bellies full and warm, a safe place to lay their heads at night, and work to do to keep their hands busy, they didn't need to dig and pocket for later consumption the tubers they'd hilled, and they'd snacked on enough peas to grow tired of them. They were no longer desperate soldiers, dreaming of capturing an enemy convoy of tinned fruit and meat. Instead, while they plucked voracious aphids from beneath the leaves and built dirt around the stems of each potato plant, then went on to harvest mountains of peas, they knew that an adequate meal awaited them when they returned to the camp—and if they were lucky, Frau O'Brien would offer them some treat for which she'd scrounged enough flour to bake for them, even if it was only an oatmeal cookie to supplement their sack lunches. Slices of her fresh bread alone were like cake.

Wolf grinned at Hermann. "Did you work harder than the rest of us yesterday, Private Claus? You seem to have built your appetite while you slept."

The private devoured another bite. "The work was not so difficult. I am just glad to get outside this fence every day."

Leo swung his leg over a seat between Hermann and Otto and set down his tray. "There are better reasons to get outside the fence," he said, picking up a fork.

"It can't be for beer, since they give it to us here," Otto remarked. "It must be the women."

There was a murmur of assent across the table.

Wolf swept a quick glance over the room for the whereabouts of the guard. "Let us not talk of escaping fences," he said conversationally, not changing his tone.

Leo shrugged. "Why not speak of it? No one can hear us. There's not much better chance to consider the possibilities."

"There will be no such possibility." Wolf raised his glass to his lips to hide his irritation. Was this the sort of nonsense Leo dreamed up while he lay staring at the ceiling in his bunk? Could he not see how Otto hung on his words? Wolf did not want any of his men hurt or given stricter confinement because they developed some injudicious notion of escaping the compound for the momentary pleasure of meeting women. He tilted the glass back until it emptied. Then he set it down and wiped a napkin across his mouth. "Foolish behavior will only lead to loss of privilege. If one soldier among us gives the guards cause for distrust, we will all pay the price and be sent back to the main camp without any opportunities to work outside the gates, such as we now enjoy." He glanced around the table, lingering his glance a split-second longer on Otto. "We must count on one another to guard our privilege. There is little we can do for our country if we are locked in isolation for the duration of the war." He changed his tone as he picked up his tray and rose. "The harvest season is only beginning. From what I am told, we have many weeks ahead of us."

"Do you think the war will continue so long?" Rudolf Ebner asked. One so young as he must feel like his youth was completely stolen.

Not to mention the prisoners were uncertain what to make of American reports, whether they were propaganda or not. "We should all pray it ends soon," Wolf said. He gave them a departing nod and turned.

"Heil Hitler." The declaration behind him was soft but firm.

Wolf swung back around. "Who said that?" His gaze raked over them, demanding an answer.

Leo's chin rose, his expression resolute. "I did, Hauptmann."

Tension hardened Wolf's jaw. "You will not say it again."

Leo's chin lifted farther. "Why are you so compliant, Hauptmann

Kloninger? Is it really because you enjoy the luxury of a full plate of food and a bed for your head? I thought it was our duty to"—he cast a surreptitious glance across the hall—"do more than bend over backward to serve these Americans as though they are our masters."

Wolf darted a glance to the left and right, then narrowed his gaze on Leo. "I am a German, Obergefreiter Friedrickson." His voice was low with intensity. "My allegiance is to my country. If you doubt it, perhaps you would like to examine my record compared to yours."

Leo flinched. Everyone speculated in whispers as to why Leo had not achieved a higher rank, having been in service for almost as long as their captain. Whenever Wolf heard their conjectures, he squelched the gossip. It was surely nonsense. Leo gave the merest shake of his head, returning his attention to his breakfast. "*Nein*, Hauptmann. I believe your word."

Wolf squared his shoulders and gave a sharp nod. "Then see to it you do not question my motives again." He didn't wait for Leo's affirmation but assumed it as he spun on his heel.

Leo was normally a quiet man. Though he was clearly intelligent, he kept most of his opinions to himself. Lately, however, he seemed more restive. Or had Wolf only imagined it? Today's rebellious talk certainly sounded like a man tired and bored with his circumstances. While they all had their own way of showing their allegiance to the fatherland, there were some ways that led only to trouble. It would prove disastrous for those who simply wanted to do their work and get safely home again, should one troublemaker stir the pot and cause them all to suffer.

Wolf left the mess tent and strolled across the commons toward a group of other officers and men. One of them was a chaplain. He had shared briefly, from memory, some of God's Word to them this morning. He spoke about patience born of suffering. Apparently, his message had fallen on some deaf ears. Then again, Wolf hadn't noticed Leo in the crowd of listeners. He never did attend services.

What about the O'Briens? Did they worship on this Sunday morning? Did Frau O'Brien take them to a house of God to pray for their neighbors and loved ones overseas? Did Fannie O'Brien plead with God for someone special to come safely home? A fiancé perhaps? He wished he could ask her.

And why was that? Why did it matter if he knew the answer? Was it just his own boredom that made him want to acquaint himself with her? If he could step outside this fence, would he head to town to find a woman too, or would he walk the miles to the O'Brien farm with the hope that he could sit down with Fannie O'Brien over a cup of coffee and learn about her life? What did she do when she wasn't working on her farm?

This was why he mustn't let Leo or anyone else get ideas about what lay outside the compound. It stirred a man's blood in discontenting ways. They had only to wait out the war, and then they could go home to their families and the women who waited for them. In most of their cases, their mothers, but some of his boys had girls they'd met waiting, and a number of others had wives and sweethearts.

Unbidden, Fannie's face and figure lingered in his thoughts. Her smile, soft and understated at times, curved generously when she thought no one was looking. Satisfaction smoothed her brow over a job completed. Wisps of brown hair lifted in a breeze. His fingers tickled with the urge to tuck them back over her ear, even if only in his imagination. Her brown eyes swept into his gaze, and her mouth seemed waiting for—

"Hauptmann!" The shout jarred him, dissolving Fannie's image. Horst jogged up beside him. "Come join our crew in a soccer game against some of the cannery men."

Wolf grinned, forcing away the chimera aroused in his imagination. He nodded. "All right. I'll play."

More than two hundred men occupied the camp, and as the soccer game commenced, the majority of them gathered to watch and cheer for one team or the other. Bets were placed on the sidelines in the form of scrip and beer rations. The afternoon sun beat down on their heads, and sweat streamed over their bodies as the teams pounded up and down the field.

Leo waved them into a huddle before the next play. "Fritz, you bring the ball down. Horst, you take the left wing. Otto, you go right, and I'll follow rear striker. Everyone else, fan out like before. If you get a shot, take it. Otherwise, I'll come in from behind on the left. Knock it back to me."

There was no denying that Leo was the strongest player among them. The younger men were faster, but Leo informed them he'd once played in a league. He acted as coach now. Wolf was happy to see him enjoying the sport. Wolf wasn't a bad player himself, but he hadn't the deft footwork the younger men had. Especially Leo.

"Look. There are more observers." Rudy nodded at the roadside fence where a few vehicles had pulled over and civilians had gotten out to watch the game.

Leo clapped his hands together. "Let's go."

Wolf glanced toward the fence again. Some unreasonable idea that the O'Briens might be among the onlookers crept into his head. Fannie didn't seem the type of woman to enjoy such a spectacle. Her brother might perhaps. He probably played soccer or American football in school. Wolf pulled his thoughts back to the game and took his place on the field as the play was called.

They worked the ball according to Leo's plan, and ultimately Horst sent it backward, giving Leo the kick and the score. The crowd of fellow prisoners cheered, and scrip was exchanged. Leo grinned and accepted his teammates' rousing pats on the back. Then his gaze went to the outer fence where the civilian spectators had multiplied. Some of the observers clapped. Others jeered, and one of the Americans sent a wad of spit over the fence.

"Never mind them," Fritz murmured. "Let them think they are accomplishing something."

Wolf gave him a nod. "They wouldn't watch if they didn't enjoy the game, eh?"

Leo's earlier joviality settled into a grim mask before he suddenly turned toward the fence and shouted at the people standing there. *"Dir gefällt, wie wir spielen? Weil wir wild sind! Und deshalb wirst du den Krieg verlieren!"* He spat on the ground too, but as he turned away, a satisfied sneer stretched across his lips.

Using their game to tell these gawking Americans that the players' fierceness was what would win Germany the war made the rest of his team laugh and nod as they jogged back into their positions on the field. Even the opposing team laughed at the remark. But the abrasive talk through the fence set Wolf's shoulders in a stiff line.

"Easy," he said casually to the men nearest him. "It is fun to rattle the opponents' mental composure, but *they*"—he gave a slight tip of the head to the Americans—"are not on the field."

"Then we should take our complaint outside." Otto looked at Leo for support.

Suddenly, a rock thudded the ground a few yards away. Two more quickly followed. Shouting went up, and the prisoners yelled back and moved as a body toward the fence.

"Get back!" a guard called out, and one of them fired a shot into the air.

"Zurückkehren! Back!" Wolf echoed the same command to his boys as the storm to the fence stopped, yet one of the guards fired again, this time sending a few men scattering toward their tents and others to skulk

toward the field. Some remained standing and staring, as even most of the American spectators backed away from the fence.

Wolf clenched his fist to slow the sudden pounding of his heart as he caught the eyes of each of his teammates in turn. "They are not who we are playing against, ja?" He spoke through gritted teeth. "We are only having fun today. It is the Lord's Day. The war is no longer ours to win or lose."

Leo spat, nearly at the captain's feet but not close enough to make it look like the insult it almost was. He drew his arm across his mouth. "Right. We are not in that war any longer." He repeated Wolf's words, but the glare he carried with them was full of resentment. "Let's play soccer. It is our only battlefield."

"The game is over." Wolf glanced toward the guards who shouted at the prisoners to clear the field. The spectators were the first to leave. As if in a last-minute thumbing of their noses, a few car horns beeped while they pulled off down the road, stirring up dust that settled on the players' sweaty skin.

They shuffled off the field with guards walking close behind, their guns in hand. Tonight the prisoners would all suffer the punishment of those who wanted to respond to the American taunts. Wolf wished the day could end in another swim—or at least a camp shower. Not in a forced retreat to their hot tents. Nevertheless, if they didn't watch themselves, there would be no more summer swims—nor freedom of any kind.

⌇ CHAPTER 10 ⌇

Fannie closed the shed door and brushed her hands on her overalls—or more specifically—on Dale's overalls. She'd learned all about greasing tractor parts and oiling or sharpening tools of late. She soon discovered it was one thing to dirty an old work dress or her one and only pair of overalls with mud and manure, and quite another to entirely ruin them with gear grease. Therefore, she'd succumbed to Mom's suggestion that she put on a pair of her brother's worn overalls already broken in for such work.

She'd hesitated at first, fighting the notion that she was treating Dale's things as if he'd never come back for them. He *would* come back. He'd wear them again, and he'd want her to use them in the meantime if she needed to. She couldn't leave all the dirtiest work up to Jerry. He was busy enough chopping wood for next winter and replacing the broken tines on the hay rake. This morning he'd taken the truck into town to get more fuel. They decided to make sure both spare cans were properly filled with good fuel, and they'd keep an extra close eye on the truck from here on out.

It still bothered Fannie that someone could have tampered with the gas in the truck without their noticing. What had Corporal Taft been doing when that happened? How had they all been distracted? Each of them had been nearby, she and Jerry and sometimes even Mom and Patsy. However such sabotage might have occurred—if indeed it really was sabotage—Fannie would make sure it couldn't happen again.

Cal would soon be home, and when he got here, she wanted him to be proud of the way they'd kept things running smoothly. Not just for Dad's sake, but for him and Dale, just as the family was so proud of them.

Fannie peered over the bean field growing thick with green beans.

The work crew would help pick as soon as they took in the crop of hay. Might Cal get here before then? It could happen, couldn't it?

As it was, Fannie was going to have to miss her Friday workday at the library to help with the hay. They'd intended to have cut it yesterday, but it rained all day, and they needed a day of warm sunshine and a nice breeze to dry up the ground in order to start cutting. Then they needed that weather to hold until the fresh cutting dried and could be brought into the loft.

She headed around the side of the house and to the pump where she could wash the grease off her hands without soiling Mom's sink. She hadn't gone far when her mother raised her head from where she knelt on the cobbled walk, wrestling with a fieldstone.

"Want some help?"

"If you wouldn't mind digging that edge a little wider while I hold this up."

Fannie picked up the shovel and sliced it into the soil along the edge of the hole. "What's this one about?"

"I'll let you guess." Her mom's voice sounded cheery.

"Must be for Cal."

Mom settled the stone in the hole so that only the very top of it cleared the edge. "That's right." She sounded a little breathless as she moved the earth around the stone, fixing it solidly into the cobbled path. Then she pushed herself to her feet and brushed her hands together. "For Cal coming home."

"He isn't home yet." Fannie felt sorry for her words the moment they left her mouth. "I don't mean to sound doubtful. I know he's coming. Maybe any day now."

A tiny crease formed between her mother's brows and disappeared again just as quickly. She brushed Fannie's arm with a quick caress and stepped down on the rock to settle it. "The next thing you know, we'll be putting in a stone for Dale."

"I pray you're right. Sooner rather than later."

Fannie's mom had been laying cobblestones on a growing path between the house and barn since Fannie was a little girl. Every time a big prayer was answered or a blessing or strength was poured upon them, her mother laid another stone. A good thirty yards stretched between the two buildings, so the path had lots of room to grow and widen, despite all the stonework over the years. Mom called it her "Cobblestones of Confidence" pathway. She said it gave her a solid reminder—no pun intended—of all the times God had shown His loving-kindness and care.

Fannie noticed a second soft spot of ground where a new rock had been added. "What's that one there? I don't recall seeing it before."

"That's for the PWs."

Fannie froze. "You're thanking God for them? You really want to remember them forever after they're gone? The men who are responsible for Calvin and Dale—"

"Fannie. Honey." Mom held up a hand. "It's not the men in particular. It's knowing this farm is going to survive the war and your father's death."

A breeze cooled the sweat on Fannie's neck, but it made her shudder even in the heat. Her mom hadn't ever referred to her dad's loss so bluntly before. She used softer words, not *death*. Fannie made to head toward the pump, moving past her mother. "I guess I know that. I shouldn't have said it like that."

"That's all right. I understand." Mom touched her shoulder with a pat, and then Fannie stepped away.

"I don't hate them."

"I'm glad to hear it. We aren't to hate anyone. Even during war."

"I just. . . I don't know that I want to remember them later on when all this is over."

"You don't have to remember them, Fannie. Just remember that God took care of what we needed at this time. 'Give thanks in *all* circumstances,' remember? That's the important thing."

"Is it?" She turned and looked at her mother, but Mom didn't reply, only sighed. In truth, Fannie wasn't sure she expected an answer. Was that what God expected? To thank Him for getting by, or did He expect more? Fannie worried that maybe He did.

The next day, Fannie and Jerry took turns running the tractor, getting all the hay cut so it could lie in the sun and dry. The raking was done on Thursday, which meant the men would return on Friday to handle the long, hot chore of pitching it into a wagon and bringing it into the barn in the scorching heat. Fannie's mother insisted she go to work anyway.

"Jerry and I will handle things, Fannie." Mom set a bowl of potatoes on the table beside a platter of fried chicken. "You need to go to your job at the library. I won't have you giving that up entirely."

"I don't feel right leaving you and Jerry to do all the work."

"I work!" Patsy said, smashing her potato with a fork.

"And Patsy." Fannie gave her sister a wink.

Jerry pulled apart a chicken leg from its thigh. "It's just forking hay, Fan. The men will be here to do it. I'll drive tractor."

"And make sure they get it in the barn like they should." Fannie met his glance with a meaningful look. *Don't take your eyes off them for a second,* is what she wanted to say, but she didn't want to alarm Mom or Patsy.

"I can manage, and Corporal Taft will be here." Jerry returned her look with equal intimation.

Her chest relaxed with a tiny sigh. "All right then. If you insist. Patsy, you mind yourself if you have to go out there."

"She can help me at the house, just like usual." Mom smiled at Patsy.

Patsy shrugged as she picked apart her piece of chicken. "I don't know what the big deal is. They don't care about me, and that guard has a gun with him all the time."

"Speaking of which, did you hear about the big stir at the prison camp the other day? The guards had to fire shots in the air to get everyone settled down. Dorothy Jean told me all about it. Her brothers were there." Patsy dished out the information with as much excitement as a bland potato.

"What?" Fannie and her mother asked together.

"It wasn't anything," Jerry said. "Just some people watching them play soccer by the fence got a little out of hand, and then some of the prisoners got bothered and headed for the fence, so the guards fired a shot or two to stop anything from happening. Ruined the game."

"How do you know?" Mom raised a brow at him.

"Frank and me were watching them play."

"I want you to stay away from that camp." Mom's voice became firm. "Dorothy Jean's brothers ought to stay away from there too," she added with a sharp eye on Patsy.

Jerry wiped a napkin over his lips and raised his chin. "Say, Fannie, you know that fellow with the curly hair? Leo, I think he's called? He's a really good player. You should see how he moves the ball with his feet. He kind of coached the other guys. They were some of the workers who came here. They're all pretty good."

"Did you hear me, Son?"

"Yeah, Mom, sure. We just pulled over and watched for a little bit. We didn't holler anything or throw rocks or any of that. It was fun to watch."

"Just stay away, like I said."

Jerry's nod was barely a twitch, and Fannie doubted he meant to stay away. He reached for the chicken again, but Mom stopped him.

"Eat some more bread. I'll use the rest of the chicken in a casserole tomorrow. It'll go further, and you'll be hungry as a bear after you get that hay in the mow."

He sighed and reached for another slab of bread. He swathed it in an extra-thick layer of butter. "Can I have some jam?"

"Go ahead. Don't go overboard."

He pushed back from the table and headed to a late 1930s model refrigerator that they still referred to as the icebox.

Mom rose and peeled off her apron. "Patsy, clear the table when you're done. I've got to go check on Gertie. She was off her feed a little bit this morning. It might just be the heat."

Patsy's shoulders slumped, but she knew better than to grouse about being left with dishes. "I'll help you, Pats," Fannie said when Mom went out the back door.

"Thanks. I'm getting dishpan hands washing dishes morning, noon, and night."

Fannie chuckled. "We all have a price to pay with the extra work around here."

"I wish I could go to the library with you again tomorrow."

"I wish you could too, but I want you to help Mom. Jerry's going to have his hands full watching those prisoners."

"What for? Isn't that why they have a guard?"

Fannie caught herself. "I didn't mean he had to guard them. I only meant he has to make sure they know what to do."

"Right. I believe you. That's why the two of you keep that gun of Daddy's under the truck seat."

Fannie stopped dead with a platter in each hand and stared at her little sister. "I don't know how you know that, but don't touch it, and don't you breathe a word to Mama about that gun, you hear?"

"As if I would. I think it's a good idea." Patsy went about pouring hot water into the dishpan as if such a discussion were completely normal and not at all like they were talking about protecting themselves and their home from the enemy in the middle of a war.

Fannie stared a moment longer, then carried the leftovers to the icebox. "All right then. What were you doing snooping in the truck anyway?"

"I wasn't snooping. I couldn't find one of my library books, and I thought maybe I left it in the truck and it got under the seat somehow."

"Don't lose those books. You'll get a fine."

"Blah, blah, blah. I know, I know. You think I just started checking out library books yesterday? Honestly, Fan. You're worse than Mom sometimes."

For that, Fannie reached around her and splashed her with the dishwater.

"Hey!" Patsy tried to reciprocate, but Fannie dodged out of the way.

"Better stop now if you want me to help dry."

"You started it."

Fannie chuckled and picked up the sack towel and a clean, wet plate. They fell into routine then, but Fannie thought about tomorrow. She'd be worrying all day that something could go wrong.

The hours at the library dragged by the next day. She had looked forward to being there, away from the sweat and grime of putting up hay, but knowing that the prisoners were at home with Mom, Patsy, and Jerry kept her watching the clock. She told herself it would be fine. With so many hands, they would have the hay up in no time. She was almost surprised to see them still there when she came home at five o'clock. Four men and Jerry rested in a patch of shade beneath the eaves of the barn. The guard stood over by the porch talking with Mom.

Fannie hadn't even shut off the car's motor before she was searching the area for the others. Where were they? Were they inside the barn without either Jerry or Corporal Taft? She turned off the ignition and left the stack of books on the seat beside her as she hurried out of the car. Forcing calm she didn't feel into her gait, she walked toward them.

Four sets of eyes followed her every step, and she realized then how they saw her in her town clothes. Not like a farmworker today, but more like a woman. Her skin felt scorched. They'd never seen her looking so—so tidied up before, in her nice dress and shoes, her hair curled and pinned back at the sides, and she was wearing lipstick besides. She fought down the urge to run her tongue over her lips. Had it worn off? Maybe. Hopefully. Fannie lifted her chin, ignoring their too-interested stares. "How did everything go today?"

Jerry leaned away from the side of the barn and took a few steps toward her. "Went real good. Just got the last load in a bit ago."

"Really? All of it?"

"We worked pretty steadily all day. Barely took time to eat lunch. Wanted to beat the evening dew."

"Looks like you did that pretty handily." She glanced toward the men again. They all still watched her, but Wolf was not among them. "Where are the rest?"

"Oh. They didn't come. We only got these four today."

"I see." Her breath eased out. "I wondered."

"Here you go." Patsy came toward them with a tray of sliced buttered bread. The men moved in unison, muttering their thanks as they lifted slices from the plate and shoved them in their mouths. One of them, the young strawberry blond with green eyes that turned shy at times, was last in line. He lingered at the plate that still held two slices of bread, as if he couldn't decide.

"Well just take them both then," Patsy said with an exasperated sigh. She waggled the plate in front of him.

With both hands reaching for the offering, he took a piece in each, and a smile broke out over his freckled face. "Danke, Fraülein O'Brien."

Patsy's eyes widened, then she stuck out her tongue and spun on her heel back toward the house. The other three Germans laughed, and the young man blushed, but his shoulders jiggled in a chuckle.

"What on earth?" Jerry mumbled.

Fannie rolled her eyes. "I'll talk to her later." Her gaze turned and caught the oldest man present. Leo. He'd come but not his captain. Was he in charge here?

"What's going on?" Corporal Taft came up from behind. "Did one of you say something to Miss O'Brien?"

Leo stepped forward and explained in German.

The corporal chuckled. He turned to Fannie. "I'm sure your sister didn't understand."

"Yes, I heard—and saw."

Leo spoke again, and this time he seemed to be speaking directly to her.

"He apologizes for Rudy's offensive freckles," the corporal said, grinning as he said it.

"I'm sure it's quite all right. She's very young," she said pointedly, and the corporal's smile fell away. He turned to the prisoners and issued a command for them to head to the truck.

Fannie remembered the books. Today she'd scrounged some discarded copies at the library, a few worn-out volumes of English literature—including a book of grammar—some old magazines, and one book written in German that appeared to be a collection of short stories. She wasn't sure what type of stories they were, but maybe some of the prisoners would enjoy them. She'd had to explain to Mrs. Calloway, finally confessing that her family had hired the PWs to work at their farm, but the older woman smiled without judgment and gave her permission to take them all as a donation to the camp.

"If you will wait just a moment, Corporal, I have some books for the prisoners. Something for the camp library. They're in my car."

He gave a sharp whistle, and the men who'd started walking toward the camp truck halted. "Friedrickson!" He jerked his head to urge the man back.

The dusky, curly-headed Leo started toward them. Fannie shifted her weight evenly and straightened her shoulders.

"Go with Miss O'Brien. She has some books to send with you."

Leo held out his hand, palm up, in a gesture for her to lead the way. With a nod, she turned and strode purposefully the thirty or so paces to the automobile, sensing him only a step or two behind.

She didn't know why it rankled her to have to deal with this man. He'd done nothing wrong. What else had she expected? Was it that there was something enigmatic about him that she couldn't explain? Or was it simply that she had imagined passing the books to his captain, Wolf Kloninger, and seeing his appreciative smile? The very entertainment of such foolishness irritated her. She jerked the car door open and scooped up the armful of books. She ladled them into his waiting arms, and her fingers brushed against the taut muscles of his forearms. She stepped back quickly. "There you are. Please enjoy them. You do not have to return them." Did he even understand a single word she said? Likely not. She waved him toward the truck. "You can go now."

Leo's gaze met hers once again, and even though he dipped his head slightly, there was something almost insolent in his posture as he did so. Or in her peevishness did she imagine it? The fact that she wasn't sure annoyed her further. Then that same gaze roved over her, from the top of her head to her ankles in their pumps, and she knew it was more than her imagination. She rested her hand on the top of the car door, but she didn't move to close it. She kept it between them like a shield as she stared him down, anger simmering through her veins as he studied her with a long, slow smile before he slowly backed away with the books. Then he turned and carried them toward the truck at a pace demanding everyone await his leisure.

⌿ CHAPTER II ⌿

Leo peeled off his shirt and slung it around his neck, but the sting of the fabric scraping his skin reminded him of the sunburn on his shoulders. He ignored the pain and hefted a gunnysack stuffed with green beans to the truck waiting at the end of the field.

Days of farm work broken intermittently with soccer games at the camp had left his skin burned and peeling. Part of him hated the mundaneness of the days, while the other part recognized that it was better than the days of heat, fighting, and exhaustion they'd left behind in Africa. He was in better shape than he'd been in since the start of the war. Still, shouldn't he desire to be back there on the front now, driving out the Allies?

Rather than fight with his conflicting thoughts, he played soccer whenever he wasn't working. Soccer helped burn memories away with the freedom of running himself to exhaustion. Some of the other men spent their time in books. A few even took courses from American universities, receiving course work in the mail.

Leo huffed for breath as he carried the stuffed bean sack. What did those studious boys think they were going to do? Transfer their college credits to a university in Germany once the Americans were defeated? The idea almost made him chuckle. Waste of time. That's what it was. Hauptmann Kloninger acted as though those men were accomplishing some noble task by studying English. *English.* Leo spat as he finally reached the end of the long row. He flung the tied sack, flipping it onto the truck bed with the others that would get sent to the cannery today.

He turned back to the field and peered over the knee-deep ocean of leafy plants. Here on the farm, while bent over rows of beans for hours on end, he could do nothing but think. That was both a problem and a good thing. If he didn't let his thoughts become filled with boredom but turned them toward the useful task of winning the war, it wasn't so bad.

Leo stretched away the pain in his lower back. At that moment, the guard blew a whistle signaling a break.

"Bring your canteens. We will fill them at the pump." The corporal made drinking motions and waved them toward the farmyard a few hundred meters away. "The camp is sending your lunch. The truck should be here soon."

Leo, along with the rest, picked a slow pace as they walked back in the intense heat. When they finally reached the barnyard, they formed a queue at the pump. Leo got in line behind Horst. "Any news about your sister?"

Horst shook his head. "Nothing."

"What illness does she suffer from?"

"She has weak lungs. Ever since a bad case of pneumonia when she was small."

"I'm sorry to hear it."

"She tries not to let it hold her back." He smiled. "She can't run fast, but her tongue is not slow."

"How old is she now?"

"Fifteen." His smile drifted away. "I imagine she is about like that one now."

Leo followed Horst's gaze to the shade of the oak tree where the youngest O'Brien sat on the ground with an open book in her lap. He took a step forward in the line as Rudy left the pump. Rudy took a long drink and wiped water from his lips as he lowered his canteen. His gaze too went to the girl beneath the bower of branches. He strolled in her direction.

Leo watched with interest as the two struck up some form of conversation, Rudy pointing to the book in her lap, and she holding it up for him to read the cover—or pretending to read it. Leo doubted he'd learned much working English yet.

By the time Leo made it to the front of the line, filled his canteen, and quenched his thirst, the young soldier was still standing by the tree, making friends with the girl. Rudy stood at a safe distance from her. At least the corporal hadn't gone over there to stop the conversation, though the rules demanded that he should.

Leo strode over to them. "She is a bit young for your lovemaking, isn't she, Ebner?"

Rudy turned his head sharply at Leo's intrusion, and his freckled face reddened. "I am not—"

Leo laughed, silencing him. "Aren't you?" He glanced between them pointedly. "Perhaps you both need instruction from someone with experience."

He doubted the girl understood a single word of German, but she must have been old enough to understand the tone of his jeer, for she blushed to the roots of her light brown hair, just like Rudy. She veered her eyes away. Maybe it was Leo's shirtless torso that made her redden.

"Do not embarrass her." Rudy gathered control in his voice. "She is just a child."

"Not too much of a child anymore." Leo took another swig from his canteen and grabbed his shirt from his shoulders, wiping it over his mouth. He stared hard at her, waiting for her to glance again, relishing the chance to humiliate her.

"Friedrickson!" Hauptmann Kloninger's voice called to him.

Leo turned. "Ja, what is it?"

"Put your shirt on."

He sneered. With jerking movements, he tugged the soiled garment over his head.

Wolf approached. "Get back with the others." He gave a friendly nod to the girl who got to her feet, smoothing her dress down around her legs. *Guten Tag, Fraülein.*" He spun on his heels, expecting his men to follow.

Leo jerked his head at Rudy to lead the way while he cast another grin at the girl. She was a pretty thing and growing into womanhood sooner than was good for girls to do. He winked at her, then turned away before he could watch her blush or scowl or both. He would enjoy harassing Rudy over the incident in the days to come.

He clapped a hand on the fellow's shoulder as the lunch truck rumbled up the drive. "You have to expect a little teasing. If you had an older brother here, that's what he'd do."

Rudy shrugged away his hand. "You are not my brother. You're—" He cut himself short and stared ahead, jaw set.

Leo halted in his tracks, fury crawling up his insides at what he expected Rudy to say, but Rudy just kept marching. "What, Ebner? What were you going to say?"

Rudy marched away. "Leave me alone, Friedrickson."

Leo slowed his pace, letting Rudy charge ahead. He would find no camaraderie with that one.

They ate their liverwurst and cheese sandwiches and munched on apples, and some of them refilled their canteens before it was time to head back to the field. Every time Leo looked Rudy's way the rest of the afternoon, the private didn't bother hiding his scorn. What had his intention been? To cast the despicable word that Leo knew all too well? *Mischlinge*. No. Rudy wouldn't know he'd been called that before. None of these men knew, he hoped.

"We'll need more gunnysacks," Wolf was saying to the O'Brien youth Jerry. "More sacks," he repeated in English, gesturing to the boy.

Leo was standing in the shade of the barn shed's eaves. He straightened and waved. "I will find them."

The boy nodded, and Wolf said, "Ja. Go ahead."

On several occasions now, they'd been in and out of the front of the barn where the shed attached, usually hauling tools. They'd been in the loft of the barn itself, storing hay. Trust had grown, and with it, leniency. The PWs never lingered long but went in for what they needed to do and hurried back out. Usually, the guard stood at the door anyway, watching.

This time he didn't. Leo swung open the door and entered the dim interior. The building smelled of the dust and oil typical of a farmer's workplace. A workbench stretched across the opposite wall, and tools hung neatly in their places. The grindstone that Leo sometimes saw Jerry working at outdoors was housed in the corner and beyond it some of the larger pieces of equipment. A doorway into a back room hinted at a small forge and more storage.

Leo turned his attention to the stack of gunnysacks piled neatly to the left of the workbench, but not before sweeping the room with a scrutinizing search such as he could manage in a few moments, familiarizing himself with anything that he might use for a purpose. He had seen Jerry carry a gas can inside more than once, but they weren't left sitting in the open. They must be in that back room.

With a quick glance over his shoulder, he hustled to the doorway in the back and peered inside. Yes, there was a forge as well as more heavy tools. Sledgehammers, a splitting maul, and the gas cans. Bags and cans of who knew what. A barrel of old oil.

It was enough to know. Hastily, he hurried back to the sacks and slung a stack of them over his shoulder.

When he stepped back into the sunlight, Wolf looked his way. "Do you want help?"

"No. I have them."

Leo was sweating harder by the time they got back to the field. Even empty, the woven bags weren't light. He dropped them onto the ground where the men were to continue working. This field would need picking again in two or three days. The full flush of the summer growth season was upon them, and they'd be hard-pressed to keep up. Between pickings, they'd probably get sent to another farm. Some men from other crews were working full-time hours in the local cannery.

It was well into the afternoon by the time they finished. They'd filled all but three of the bags. Leo scooped them up. "Should I take these back to the shed?" He directed his question at the guard.

"Put them in the truck. Just lay them on the seat or the floor."

Leo had hoped for one more look in the shed. He wanted to see if those gas cans still contained fuel. He'd also noticed a few pipes lying around. He might be able to do something with those. Next time he came, he'd find a way to get inside again.

He walked around the side of the truck and opened the passenger door to stow the bags inside. One fell on the floor and hung out the door, so he leaned over and pushed it back in. As he did so, his glance caught something out of the norm. He bent a little farther and squinted at what he must only be imagining. It couldn't be, could it? Leo peered over the window ledge at the men on the other side of the truck, talking and loading their beans. Then he stretched his body across the shifting rod and reached his fingers under the driver's seat. The contact of hard, gun-shaped metal sent adrenaline shrieking through Leo's body, accelerating the pounding of his heart.

☰ CHAPTER 12 ☰

When would Cal be home? It had been a month since they were told he was convalescing and would return to them soon. What did they mean by soon? When the war ended?

Fannie rustled through the clothes lying across her bed, clean but wrinkled. She'd have to give them extra attention with the iron for letting them lie. For now, she just needed her cotton slip. Her yellow dress was thin and comfortable but too thin to wear without the much-needed slip. There it was. She yanked it from the pile and shimmied into it.

They were going to church today, though Fannie could think of a million things they ought to be doing instead. Mom insisted, however. Maybe she hoped Cal would get home sooner if she went to God's house to pray in person.

Fannie tugged her dress on. "Ooh. . ." she growled when she heard a thread snap under her arm. She pulled the garment back off to have a look. Sure enough, she'd ripped it. The hole was tiny enough. She'd have to hurry to get it stitched up and still leave for church on time. She might have believed God was reprimanding her for her wayward thoughts a moment ago, but He didn't need to. She could reprimand herself well enough.

She didn't even know what Cal was recuperating from. Had he suffered a war injury, or was it just rest he needed? She'd heard of men suffering everything from amputations to burning mutilation from mustard gas. It wasn't any of those things, was it?

Worry threaded through her. No. It was just the army taking its time. "Stop fretting and just get ready for church."

"Who are you talking to in there?" Patsy hollered through the door.

"Never mind. Maybe I'm praying and you're interrupting."

"Humph. Right. And you think I'm Patsy, but I'm really Gabriel." Her sister's voice trailed away down the hall.

Fannie had to giggle. That Patsy.

By the time their family reached the church, the heat and humidity had climbed, and Fannie's cotton slip clung to her skin. Too many days had passed since that dip in the creek. As they bustled into a pew near the front, Fannie's mind wandered over the possibilities of repeating such enjoyment later in the day. Patsy fanned herself with her hand, and Jerry did the same with his hat, while both Fannie and her mother did their best to sit still and simply endure. She wished she could catch just a slight stirring of the breeze from her sister's hand. Across the room, papers fluttered. One young boy even waved a hymnal. The pastor seemed unfazed as he preached an especially lengthy sermon. The preaching was hard and fiery this morning too.

It wasn't until dismissal that Fannie realized why. When she rose and turned, she saw the PWs seated in the back row. *Their* PWs, along with a few others. Richard, Hermann, Rudy, Horst. . .and Wolf. Leo, Otto, and Fritz were not among them. Wolf caught her eye with a nearly imperceptible nod before filing out with the rest.

Was he a Christian then? Part of her wanted to believe he was not a murderer. The other part told her heart that he had been in Africa killing Americans. Perhaps even shooting at someone they knew. There was no lack of young men from the area like her brothers fighting and dying overseas.

Patsy and Jerry wasted no time in breaking free into the fresh air, while Fannie and her mother visited with friends and neighbors before finally leaving the church.

Jerry met them at the bottom of the church steps. His pal Frank said goodbye and strolled toward his car parked down the block. "Are you ready to go yet? I'm starving."

Fannie scanned the churchyard. "Your stomach can wait a few more minutes. I want to speak to Faith if I can catch her."

"She already left with her sister."

"She did?" Fannie was a little let down. She and Faith used to be close, but lately, with Fannie's many obligations and Faith working at the canning factory, they'd hardly seen each other. She'd heard that Faith intended to switch schools and was planning on being a nurse now. Fannie wanted to ask her why, even though she thought she already knew. Posters in town talked about free education to women who wanted to join the U.S. Cadet Nurse Corps. It was a noble pursuit but not for Fannie. She was a little surprised that Faith would go that route. Faith's family was able to afford her education, and Fannie never would have guessed that her friend was cut out for nursing. Then again, they'd all grown up since the war began. Fannie's future had changed, at least for now. Faith might be taking life more seriously too. "I suppose we can get going then. Where's Patsy gone off to?"

She glanced over the disassembling crowd for her sister before spotting her by a shady elm all alone. Her gaze was on the departing soldiers, piling into their canvas-covered truck.

"I'll go tell her we're leaving," Fannie said. She strolled toward her, startling her when she finally got close enough to say her name.

"Gee, Fannie, you scared me."

"How can you be surprised with a crowd around?" Fannie smiled.

"You sneaked up on me. Maryann just left."

"I know. I was hoping to talk with Faith."

"Their mom had a roast in the oven."

"On a hot day like this? I'm glad I'm not going to their house."

"Me too." Patsy turned toward Fannie and tucked something into her dress pocket.

"What do you have there?"

"Just a note from Maryann."

"Oh?"

Patsy brushed by her. "Come on. Let's go."

Patsy wasn't usually in such a hurry. Or so short on conversation. Fannie caught up to her, and they walked together to the car. "Want to go swimming later?"

"Sure."

"Maybe we can convince Mom to come."

"I doubt it, but we can try."

"Maryann have much to say?"

Patsy reached for the door handle of the automobile. "What?"

"In her note?"

"Not really." End of subject. Patsy climbed inside the backseat while Fannie went around to the driver's side.

The drive back to the farm was a quiet one except for Mom humming a hymn. Finally, Jerry piped up. "Kind of odd seeing the PWs at church today, huh?"

Mom shifted in the passenger seat. "I've heard they're allowed to visit church services in the area. I'm glad to know that some of them at least are Christians."

"Seems crazy to me."

"Why so?"

"They're fighting us."

"Well. . .some of them must think the same thing of your brothers."

Fannie glanced at her mom, a little stunned that she could think from the enemy's viewpoint. "But their cause is far from noble."

Patsy cleared her throat. "You know, a lot of them were forced to fight for that Hitler. They didn't *want* to."

Fannie glanced in her rearview mirror and stared at Patsy. Did her little sister just stick up for their enemy? "What makes you say that?"

Patsy shrugged. "I read it somewhere, I guess."

That much was probably true.

Jerry leaned away from the window. "I guess we can see it's true. They're pretty much glad to be out of the war and working on the farm."

"Corporal Taft said the same thing," Mom said.

Quiet filled the car again for several moments until Patsy spoke up again. "What do you think Cal will say when he meets the PWs?"

They shared glances. "He might not have to," Fannie said. "If it takes much longer, bean picking will be done. We can pick the corn ourselves if we have to."

Patsy groaned. "I hope not. I mean, I hope Cal is back before then, but I sure don't want to pick all that corn by ourselves. I think Cal will know we need their help."

Fannie caught her gaze in the mirror and smiled, wanting to agree, but she couldn't quite make herself do it.

She pulled into the driveway a moment later. The temperature had climbed to near ninety, and the humidity weighed her down so that she barely felt like hiking up the stairs to her muggy bedroom to change clothes. Patsy didn't seem to be under any such weight. She ran up the stairs past Fannie and swung her bedroom door shut behind her with a bang. Fannie tapped on it as she went by. "Want to jump in the creek after lunch?"

"Sure," Patsy said loudly from inside.

"Okay." Fannie strode into her own room and unbuttoned her dress, letting it fall to the floor. Her skin breathed. Oh, that was better. She dropped onto her bed and pushed her clean laundry aside before falling back across the sheets. She didn't lie there long, however. She had to take care of her clothes and see if Mom wanted some help with lunch before going to cool off in the creek.

How did the prisoners manage in this weather? Did they just sit around in their T-shirts and slacks, wishing for shade? Did they even have shade? She knew they spent a lot of free time playing soccer and writing letters or reading, but who could play soccer on a day like today? Did they work on their English or read from the German books she'd given them? What other things did they do?

And what about Dale? What were his days in a German prison camp like? She only hoped he was comfortable and allowed the things he needed. Food, clean clothes, rest. Medical care if that was necessary. According to treaties of war on the treatment of prisoners, he should be getting those things. She frowned and pushed herself off the bed. She didn't want to think that there was any chance he might be suffering. She pressed her eyelids together. "Please keep him safe, Jesus. Amen."

Opening her eyes, she reached for a handful of clothes and folded them neatly. The things that needed pressing she draped over a chair by the open window. A breeze stirred through the opening, but it was a hot and sticky one. She changed into her swimsuit and a wrap-over skirt and left her room to help Mom set out lunch. Patsy's door was open a few inches now. Fannie stuck her head inside.

"Ready to grab a bite and go?"

"What?" Patsy sat on her bed, holding a piece of paper. It looked like the same letter she'd been reading outside the church earlier. She quickly folded it in half in her lap.

"I asked if you're ready to go. You don't even have your suit on."

"I will. Shut the door."

"What have you been doing?"

"Never mind. Just go."

Fannie frowned. "What's going on?"

"Nothing." Patsy's tone was annoyed and anxious.

"Oh?" Fannie didn't give ground. Patsy was up to something. Or her friend was. But what could it be? "What's Maryann been up to?"

"I don't know. Nothing." Patsy shrugged, her hand crushing the note.

"How don't you know? You have a letter from her right in your hands."

Patsy's face flushed. Sure, it was warm in here, but the rose blooming her cheeks told on her, just like the way she averted her eyes, refusing to look directly at Fannie. Fannie frowned and came closer. Patsy drew the letter tighter in her fist.

"What's the matter, Pats?"

"Nothing is the matter. Let's go swimming." She jumped off the bed, but the letter slipped from her hand.

It took only a glance for Fannie to see that the writing was not all in English, or if it was, it wasn't written in a feminine hand.

Patsy lunged for it, but Fannie snatched it from her hand as soon as she stood up. "Hey!"

"I'm not trying to pry, Patsy, but—" Her glance took in the awkward phrases and the smattering of German spellings. "Who wrote this?"

"It's none of your business."

"Patsy! Who?"

She chewed her lip then turned her back with a huff. "Just that fellow. That young one. Rudy."

"You have a letter from a German prisoner? What are you thinking?"

"It's nothing, Fan."

"Nothing?" Fannie trembled. "You call this nothing? Patsy—" She reached for her sister's arm and turned her around. "He can get into a lot of trouble for giving you this, and you. . ." She looked her sister deep in the eye, taking in the set of her jaw, the youth combined with the growing womanliness of her pretty figure in the polka-dot dress. "You don't even know what kind of trouble you're asking for."

"I'm not asking for anything." Patsy spewed her words. "It's just a stupid note. I didn't tell him to write it. I didn't even know what it was when he stuck it in my hand on his way out of the church."

"Did anyone see him?"

"I don't think so." Her voice softened. "He was pretty quick about it."

Fannie grasped Patsy's hand and gave her fingers a gentle squeeze. "Boys will do that sort of thing, but this is one boy you have to ignore. Completely. You can't take letters or—or anything from him. Don't even look his way."

"But he's nice. He doesn't mean any harm. He just wants to practice his English. He said so the other day right outside, and he wants me to read it to see if it's right."

Fannie folded her arms. "So he says."

Patsy growled.

"Don't snarl at me. I know men better than you do."

"Is that right? Since when? You don't see anyone. Or are you talking about those PWs too? That man Wolf likes you. So does the other one. Leo. I can tell. I'm not blind. They all notice you. Don't lie to me, Fan, and say you haven't noticed."

Her little sister was getting more grown-up than she'd realized. "Well, I don't plan to notice them back. And you can bet I won't be accepting letters from any of them."

"You gave them books to read."

"That's different."

"How?"

Fannie turned to the door, and Patsy followed. "It just is."

"Humph."

This discussion was over. Hopefully, she'd said enough to Patsy to make her realize the dangerous game she played. Maybe it wouldn't hurt to tell Rudy the same thing. She marched out the door.

The next day, they were back to picking beans. Fannie helped Jerry move some of the irrigation lines while it was early and still somewhat cool. Then Jerry drove the truck out to the field and parked it at the end of the row closest to where he picked and could keep an eye on it. The men arrived at eight o'clock, just as the dew was lifting off the plants.

Fannie left them to handle the picking without her. She'd help Mom with the wash. It would feel good to be doing woman's work again, and she'd rather have her arms submerged in warm water than be bent over a row of beans for a change. Plus, it might be good to spend some time with Patsy. Her sister was too often alone with her thoughts. Who knew where those would take her?

After all the wash was strung out on the line to dry and Fannie had emptied the water on Mom's flower bed, she went inside to help get lunch on the table.

Her mom handed her a plate of sandwiches. "Set these on the table then go and fetch Jerry. I cooked up a big batch of pudding this morning while the stove was still hot from breakfast. We'll share it with the workers. Their lunch truck should be here soon."

"You cooked pudding in this heat?"

"It didn't take long. It was the best I could come up with without having to bake."

"We don't need treats, Mom."

"It's not a treat. We had a lot of extra milk to use up, and it'll keep everyone going in this weather. I hope we get some rain soon."

"I saw some clouds to the west."

"Rain clouds?"

Fannie grinned. "Just clouds."

Mom gave a ladylike grunt. "What we need is a good soaking."

Fannie agreed, and they chattered on while Mom sliced up cucumbers and set out the rest of their lunch. Then Fannie left the house to fetch Jerry.

As she stepped through the door, the heavy air hit her again like the damp blanket she'd hung up fifteen minutes ago. Perhaps there was hope that those clouds would turn into something and break the smothering atmosphere. Stepping across the yard, her ears perked at the sound of singing coming from the bean field. It wasn't just a single voice she heard but the combined voices of a male choir—a male choir singing in English but with a marked German accent.

Was she hearing right? Were the PWs singing about having lots of land and riding through the wide-open country?

A solo voice took flight, crooning about the evening breeze and cottonwood trees and concluding with the popular title line "*Don't fence me in.*"

Their voices rose again with another verse, and as Fannie made her way into the field, they became louder. No one seemed to notice her approach, but her curiosity jumped another notch when Jerry sang out a long line about straddling his saddle. And then Wolf Kloninger, standing straight and tall, belted out the next line. His voice was crisp and clear in its pronunciations, but his tenor was a little off-key. No one seemed to mind, but Fannie wondered if he knew what a *cayuse* was.

He bent back to his row of beans as all the men joined in the final lines of the verse, ending with another resounding, "*Don't fence me in.*"

Corporal Taft clapped, and a couple of the men took a bow. Jerry clapped too.

Fannie's steps swished faster between the rows of bushes, taking her closer to her brother. She was unable to quench her smile as he noticed her. "Hey, Fan, want to sing with us?"

She chuckled. "Mom sent me to tell you it's lunchtime." The men went on picking, but they cast furtive glances her way. When she caught Wolf's gaze, he plopped some beans into his gunnysack and scratched his neck, as though their connection was completely accidental, yet somehow she knew it wasn't. "Who taught them Bing Crosby and the Andrews Sisters?"

Jerry shrugged. "They learned it at the camp, I suppose. Some of them are trying to practice their English. The rest are just mimicking the lyrics."

The remark reminded her of Patsy's comment yesterday about the letter written by Rudy, supposedly to practice his English. She was tempted to find out what the letter actually said, but Patsy would never forgive that kind of prying. She'd probably hidden it good and well by now anyway.

The rumble of the camp lunch truck brought her around. "Ready to go?"

"Sure." Jerry hefted his nearly full sack of beans over his shoulder and lugged it toward the end of the row.

Fannie walked alongside in the next row. "It's going well out here? The picking, I mean?"

"No trouble at all." He gave her a sideways glance. "I keep my eye on them. I'm not leaving it all up to the guard."

"I heard you singing too. Do you talk with them?"

They reached the truck, and Jerry deposited his bag. "Now and then. I've gotten to know a couple of the ones closer to my age. Horst knows about cars, and Richard is a farmer back home. Rudy likes to hear me talk about football."

A bee buzzed around her, and a droning began in her brain too. Were they forgetting these men were the enemy? The very men their brothers and neighbors fought against and in some cases were killed by? "What else do you talk about?" She had to know. Did Rudy ply Jerry with questions about Patsy? The buzz inside grew louder as aggravating possibilities took hold.

Jerry brushed his hands together and they turned toward the house. "Not much." He chuckled. "Their regular English is pretty bad. I do most of the talking. About hunting and cars. I do know they want to go swimming again."

She glanced back at the field and saw that the crew was also making its way out of the field. "Did you know that Rudy wrote a letter to Patsy?"

Jerry's stride hitched. "No, I didn't know that." He smirked. "Figures. He probably has eyes for her."

"She's a child." Fannie spoke with indignation, letting the bee in her bonnet have its way. It felt good, like it was supposed to. *They're our enemies, not our friends.*

"She's not really that little anymore, Fan, but I know what you mean."

She cast him a long look. Her brother was growing up too. If the stupid war lasted much longer, the army might take him—except that they couldn't now that he was the only male left to run the farm.

They reached the yard, and Jerry veered away to douse his head at the pump before coming in for lunch.

Fannie strode onto the porch. Before opening the door, she glanced back at the workers approaching the yard. Wolf clapped a hand on another fellow's shoulder. The lines of his face stretched in a laugh, and she couldn't help noticing the overall handsomeness of his features. His skin had tanned to a deep gold, and his blond hair was bleached nearly white.

He glanced toward the house and caught her looking, and she could almost tell just how blue his eyes were. The bee in her head returned, only this time, instead of buzzing angrily, it hummed and sipped warm nectar. She stared. She didn't want to believe he was a bad man, but there was the fact that the gas had been tampered with, and there was the truth that he was a German captain. A man didn't attain such rank because he was incapable. There were just too many reasons to hate him. She had to remember that. In fact, maybe it was time to reestablish some lines.

She lifted her shoulders and strutted back down the porch steps. He watched her approach and smiled so that friendly lines appeared at the corners of his eyes.

"Herr Kloninger, a word, if you please."

His smile sagged, and he glanced at Corporal Taft, who had heard Fannie and nodded at them. She moved off into the middle of the lawn away from the others but still in plain sight.

"Something is wrong with our work?" His English was definitely improving, but he still made all his *w*'s into *v*'s." It bothered her that she liked the sound of his voice and accent.

She shook her head. "No. Your work is fine. It's something else."

He waited for her to continue.

"It has come to my attention that one of your men wrote a letter to my little sister, Patsy."

He sighed and pinched his lips together. This was not good news to him either. This brought at least some relief to Fannie.

"He passed it to her at church. I don't have to tell you what this means."

He shook his head. "*Nein.* You do not. Who was it?"

"Rudy."

Lowering his gaze to the ground, he nodded thoughtfully. "This does not surprise. He is. . .young."

"He is old enough," she said under her breath.

"Ja. I speak with him."

She expelled a deep breath. "I don't want trouble."

"You will tell to Corporal Taft?"

116

She allowed herself a glimpse into his eyes, and she couldn't help succumbing to the hope in them. A battle squared off inside her. Could she trust his motives? The balance tipped. "No. I won't. As long as I have your word nothing like this will happen again."

He blinked, and she appreciated the humility etched on his face and in the droop of his shoulders. "Danke. It will not."

She gave a nod, prepared to leave, but his lips curved up in a less exuberant smile than before. "I have something also to say. I have thanks. . .about the books you give us."

"You are very welcome."

"Ja. They are much help. My men are happy to have reading."

"I'm glad they want to learn English, as long as they don't practice it on Patsy." She paused and then offered a small smile back at him. "I heard you singing."

He rubbed the back of his neck, turning self-conscious. Then he sang softly and still off-key, "Don't fence me in. . . ."

Fannie chuckled softly. "You like Bing Crosby?"

"Ja. You?"

She nodded. "Of course." He didn't seem to want to get his lunch, and oddly, neither did she. "Do you like other music too?"

"Oh, ja. Much musics. All kinds. But my singing. . . Not good." He grimaced.

"Mine either."

"I would like to hear you singing," he said, suddenly sobering.

The bee inside her landed on a honeycomb, and sweetness oozed through her. She chuckled cynically. "Oh no, you wouldn't."

He cleared his throat. "Maybe at church."

"Yes. And you can practice your English there, with the songs I mean."

He gave a minute nod and continued studying her.

She pulled in a deep breath and let it out. "I am a student too." Almost as soon as she said it, she wished she'd kept her personal life to herself. He had no business knowing what she did beyond the farm work, and she had no reason to want to share that information with him. . .did she? She shifted, intending to drop the subject there and go inside, but he followed it up too quickly.

"What do you study?"

"I'm enrolled at the county normal school."

"Normal school. What is normal school?"

"Like college. For teachers."

"Ah. *Universität*."

"Not. . .university, exactly," she said.

He smiled without holding back. "You will be teacher? Like me?"

"I suppose so." She tugged at the hairs on the nape of her neck.

"Das ist gut, ja?"

"Yeah—I mean yes."

"You want to teach. . ." He held his hand at hip level, then higher at shoulder level. "Small or large?"

Fannie shrugged. "It doesn't matter, I suppose." She jerked her hand between her waist and chest. "Younger students perhaps." She laughed, embarrassed but enjoying his interest in her desire to become a teacher. "You teach only older students?" She pointed toward the men sprawled across the grass, eating their sandwiches.

"Older, ja. *Realgymnasium*."

"Well then. . .I had better let you eat your lunch." She gave a nod and moved away, aware how he watched her go.

Her pulse threaded a staccato beat, and sweat made her palms sticky. What was the matter with her? Who was she anyway—Patsy? A thirteen-year-old girl smitten by the obvious interest of a handsome man? A handsome *German* man?

A German man who aroused her interest in a way it never had been before.

⪦ CHAPTER 13 ⪧

Fannie schooled her features against the trembling of her body as she stood on the train platform. When her mother grasped her hand, Fannie welcomed the clutch of her fingers and the brushing of their arms. The train had already screeched to a halt and let off a final puff of steam. All they could make out through the windows was the clamor of passengers into the aisle. The minute stretched on, then the doors opened. One after another, men and women disembarked and either hastened off to collect their luggage or were collected by their loved ones.

"Do you see him? Where is he?" Patsy bounced to her tiptoes, jostling Fannie's other shoulder.

"Not yet."

"What if he isn't on this train?"

"He'll be on it," Mom said, her voice sounding simultaneously breathless yet sure.

"He'll be on it," Fannie softly repeated.

Fannie had come home from work yesterday to find her mom sitting at the table with an open telegram lying before her, her face flushed, and water boiling away on the stovetop. Fannie's heart had lunged into her throat, fearing the worst possible news. As it turned out, it was some of the best. Cal was coming home tomorrow on the six o'clock train.

Tomorrow was today, and in just another minute, maybe sooner, they'd see him. *Cal. Alive and home. Safe.*

"There he is! I see him!" Jerry shouted from Mom's other side.

Patsy lurched forward. "Where?"

"There."

"I see him!"

119

Mom's body shifted and her grip tightened. She was probably wondering the same things as Fannie. Was Calvin whole or missing a limb? Had tear gas blinded him? Had he suffered some other terrible wound? Or was it shell shock? They'd heard stories about the invisible agonies war could lay upon a man. They still didn't know what injury was sending him home. Was it something so terrible he couldn't write and tell them?

The minute Mom spotted him, her hand tore free from Fannie's, and she choked on a sob. Then Fannie saw him too. "Calvin." She wanted to shout out like Jerry and Patsy, but there was a crowd, and Mom was crying. People scattered as he stood there, staring back at them, his duffel bag hitched over his left shoulder and his right hand twitching at his side. All in one piece.

Mom rushed to him in her leather pumps with the worn-down heels, and he dropped his duffel bag. Then the two fell together with Mom sobbing into Cal's collar and Calvin holding her in his arms.

Fannie's heart thundered in her chest as they gathered round, and they all embraced him too.

"Cal. You're home. Look at you. Just look at you. I'm so glad you're back. How was the trip? Are you hungry?"

Questions coming from all of them at once, as though he could actually answer any of them. They just couldn't stop themselves from pouring inquiries over him like rain through a leaky roof.

"Did you travel alone all that way? When did you leave Chicago? Here, let me carry your bag."

Jerry offered that. He swept up Calvin's bag and lumbered behind them as they swarmed him toward the family car.

He looked at each of them in turn, not really answering but nodding and saying things like "I missed you too" and "It's good to be back home." General things, to all of them at once. He seemed to soak in the fact that Patsy wasn't the little child he remembered, nor Jerry either. Jerry had passed Calvin in height by a good two inches. Fannie hadn't thought before of how tall her younger brother had gotten. Calvin looked at Jerry like he could hardly believe who he was seeing. Fannie realized for the first time too just how much Jerry looked like Dale these days. He had Dale's and their father's dimpled chin. Neither Cal nor Fannie or Patsy had that. Jerry and Dale shared straighter brown hair too, while Calvin's had a bit of curl to it like Patsy's did, though you could hardly tell that now with it being cut so short. She noticed he had a scar on his scalp that hadn't been there before, but she wouldn't ask him about that now.

Cal was quiet as Jerry and Patsy climbed into the backseat with his bag tucked between them. Fannie got behind the wheel, and Mom sat in the middle between her and Calvin. They rode quietly, giving him a chance to get used to them again. Every now and then, Mom smiled at him and he smiled back. "I'm so happy to have you home, Son."

He didn't answer, but he patted her leg, and now she went to squeezing his hand instead of Fannie's.

"Wait until you see the farm," Jerry said. Fannie glanced at Jerry in the rearview mirror as he sat forward and laid a hand on Cal's shoulder. "It's doing really great, if I do say so. Beans are coming in like crazy. Picking every few days now. Got the hay in and the pea crop." He patted Cal's shoulder again and sat back.

Cal's glance turned to the view out the side window as Jerry rattled on about the work they'd been doing. He didn't respond. He just let Jerry go on. Every now and then Mom would offer another encouraging smile and he'd nod again. Fannie was just glad that no one mentioned the PWs. She wanted to break that news to him later. Mom must've been thinking the same thing.

"I cleaned your room for you," Patsy chimed in. "But don't worry. I didn't move anything important. I just washed up your bedding and dusted and swept things up real nice. You'll like it."

"Beans coming along?" Cal asked with a glance at Fannie.

She tightened her grip on the steering wheel. Hadn't he been listening to Jerry's prattle? Maybe being home was too distracting to have heard all of Jerry's detailed accounting. She nodded. "Yes. Very well. Like Jerry was saying."

He gave a nod too. "That's good. Your garden, Mom?"

"It's doing fine. Just fine. We could use some rain." They smiled at one another again. "I have a nice dinner waiting for you."

Patsy cleared her throat.

"I mean *we* have a nice dinner for you," Mom amended. "Patsy has become quite a good cook."

Fannie glanced over to catch Cal's response, but he was looking out the window at the passing fields and didn't offer any. Maybe it was best they just let him get used to being home. She could imagine how good it felt but how strange too, especially knowing Dale was still back there in some prison.

At last, the drive ended. When Fannie pulled to a stop in front of the house, Cal stared for a long moment before getting out. His eyes looked red. Tired. Emotional, it seemed.

Jerry lugged the duffel bag out. "I'll take your bag upstairs."

"Thanks," Cal said as Jerry passed by.

Mom paused and laid her hand on Cal's arm. "I guess I'll go put that dinner that I promised you on the table." Her eyes shone. "Welcome home, Son."

Cal watched her walk up the porch steps and into the house. "She'll probably say it a hundred times," Fannie said. He looked at her. "Want to take a walk?" She jerked her head toward the bean field, and he nodded.

They strolled casually and silently. The sun sat at their backs on the western horizon, casting lilac hues and long shadows. The air smelled of summer green. When they reached the field's edge, Cal bent and plucked a young bean, then snapped it in half in his teeth and munched. "Tastes like home."

Fannie didn't say anything, but she picked a bean and ate it too. Then she squared herself and looked at him. "It does."

Cal smiled. It was the first time he seemed to smile for real. Before, it seemed he was overwhelmed by their rushing at him, and his smiles showed unease. Now his shoulders relaxed. He took a deep breath and let it out slowly. He looked at her again. "Have you heard from Dale?"

She shook her head. "Not lately. Hopefully soon."

He studied her.

She chuckled at his perusal.

"You look different."

"I'm getting old." She looked out over the field as a breeze picked along the tops of the plants. It felt good rushing over her skin. Cooling and refreshing. "I'll be an old maid by the time the war ends."

He tapped her arm so that she looked at him again, and he frowned. "Don't you believe me?"

His face registered confusion. His eyebrows dipped and he blinked like something was wrong. "What did you say?"

"I said I'll probably be an old maid by the time this stupid war ends. All the men are gone fighting. Then again. . ." She sighed. "What does it matter? All I really care about now that you're home is that Dale comes home safely too."

He continued listening to her, but his expression was blank, as though he had no opinion on the subject.

"Cal. . . I probably shouldn't bring it up so soon. You haven't been home twenty minutes. But before everyone at once wants to know, can you tell me what happened? Not everything of course. But. . .you were hurt, weren't you? Wounded?"

They stared at one another for a long moment, until Fannie started to wonder if he was somewhere else.

Another breeze blew. This one raced gooseflesh up her arms. It was the strangest thing, for the evening was plenty warm. A whippoorwill trilled invisibly somewhere in the field. "Calvin? Are you all right?"

He pushed a hand through his short-cropped hair, across the raised scar. Finally, he looked at her again, working his jaw. After a long moment, he said, "I'm deaf, Fannie. I can't hear most anything you say."

Fannie jerked backward, unable to stem her shock. She had to open her mouth just to remind herself to breathe. She blinked several times. "I don't understand."

He chuckled, but for the first time, Fannie noticed how he watched her mouth move when she spoke to him. Like a violent storm when it blew branches and debris about the farmyard, recollections of meeting him at the station and driving home, and even this walk to the bean field came tumbling back. He had been unresponsive to their inquiries. Some of the answers he gave them could have been answers to anything and everything they'd asked. He'd said little of his own volition, and to much of their chatter he'd only nodded as if listening. Had he really not heard them? Was he only pretending up to now?

She stepped close and raised a hand to his arm. She studied his face, then shook her head slightly. "Nothing? You hear nothing?"

He lifted his hand with his forefinger and thumb only a small gap apart.

"A little bit?"

He shook his head. "Ringing a lot. Muffled sounds, like they're miles away."

She nodded and turned aside, still absorbing the news. So that's what it was. . .the reason the army sent him home. "I see." She glanced back, realizing he hadn't heard her. "I see," she said again. He acted like he could read at least some of the words she spoke on her lips, but maybe that's only because they knew each other so well.

Here she had been planning to tell him about the workers. How they'd managed with Cal being gone and that the PWs would be back again next week. But now. . . How could she possibly explain it all in a way he could understand? "Come on." She wagged her head toward the house. She'd have to write it out. In the meantime, she'd help him tell the family.

"I'm sorry, Fannie. I couldn't tell Mom in a letter."

She made sure to look at him directly and patted his shoulder. "It's all right. She'll understand." She slid her hand into his and gave it a reassuring squeeze.

When Cal went away to war, he'd given her reassurances that everything would be fine. He'd hugged her longer than he normally would. Now it was her turn. She reached an arm around his waist, and he draped his across her shoulder.

"The farm looks good." He cast her a small, acknowledging smile, but she didn't know how to answer, so she kept her explanations to herself as they walked back to the house to tell the news.

Mom stirred gravy on the stovetop. "There you are. Did you have a good look around?"

"Pretty good," Fannie said.

"Supper will be on the table in a minute."

"Is that a cake?" Cal said, giving a nod toward the obvious answer sitting on the sideboard.

"Sure is." Patsy strolled into the room and stood beside it. "I made it for you this morning."

Fannie watched. He must've understood her posture to know she was bragging.

"I can't wait to eat it. Haven't had much cake in a long time. Not since we were stationed in a little town in the north of France before the big push."

Fannie moved to their small secretary in the next room and pulled out a pad of paper and a pencil. She brought it into the kitchen and slipped it beside her plate casually, catching Cal with a glance before he lowered his eyes. "I'll go wash, if that's all right."

Jerry came in and flicked on a switch as the shadows of evening had begun to pervade the room. "Ta-da. Got the electricity hooked up after you and Dale left."

"Wow!" Cal gave an impressed nod before he left the room. Fannie could plainly see now that he reacted according to their actions. It was subtle. A trick he'd learned, no doubt.

"Get the milk, Patsy."

She pushed away from her masterpiece of confection and retrieved the milk pitcher.

"I'm surprised he didn't notice the electric appliances before I hit the switch," Jerry said. He shoved up his sleeves and pulled out his usual chair.

"He's got a lot to absorb." Mom set a platter on the table. "Fannie?"

"Yes?" Fannie pulled out the chair next to Cal's place.

"Everything all right?"

"Sure." She shrugged, but she was glad to busy herself taking her seat and not having to look her mother in the eye. She could tell them before he came back, but she thought it might be better to wait. He might want to tell them himself, or at least not have them all staring at him as he walked into the room. Mom would probably cry.

She didn't have any more time to think about their responses as Calvin returned to the kitchen and took his place beside Fannie.

"You could sit in Dad's chair," Patsy said, her voice solemn and serious.

Cal hadn't heard. Without any acknowledgment whatsoever, he reached for the pitcher and poured a glass of milk.

Patsy's brow curled as she looked at Cal. She cleared her throat. "Cal. . .I said you can have Dad's seat. We don't mind. It would be nice." When Cal proceeded to open his napkin without hearing, Patsy glanced at Fannie.

"I'm starved too, Mom." Fannie drew the attention to their mom, who carried a kettle and set it on the trivet in the center of the table.

"Whew. That was heavy."

"Smells heavenly," Fannie said.

Patsy ignored the food. "Tell Cal he can have Dad's place at the table. It's all right, isn't it, Mom?"

Mom cast a smile from Patsy to Calvin. "Sure, it is. Be nice to have a man at the head of the table again."

Calvin watched her speaking, but he clearly seemed confused.

"Unless you don't want to, Calvin. We understand." Mom must have taken his confusion for other kinds of uncertainties. He hadn't had the opportunity to become accustomed to home without Dad the way they all had. Suddenly, Dad's loss felt fresh again.

Fannie forced her shoulders to relax. She touched his arm with light fingertips, and when he flashed her a look, she mouthed, "*Tell them.*"

"Sorry." He pushed his plate back so he could rest his elbows on the table. He shrugged. "I thought maybe Fannie would tell you while I was upstairs."

"Tell us what?" Mom's face lost its joy as her lips fell into a small line.

He glanced at Fannie.

"It's okay, Mom," she said. "Cal didn't want to have to tell you. His

125

injury. It's his hearing."

"His—"

"I'm deaf." He looked around at all of them. "I can't hear." He bounced his foot and shifted. Then he shrugged. "Deaf as a rock."

Now everyone did stare.

"It's all right." Fannie forced a smile at them, encouraging them out of their shock. Hadn't he told her he could hear muffled sounds? Why did he exaggerate? "Everything will be all right."

Mom recovered but sat down slowly. "That's right." She waited for his attention and then nodded. "It's. All. Right." She enunciated each word.

They were all staring still, their earlier joy stifling completely.

"Sure." Calvin directed his eyes to his plate and focused on serving himself, effectively blocking out their further encouragements. Apparently, he did not feel the same.

☰ CHAPTER 14 ☰

After dinner, Calvin excused himself to his old room to settle in. It was just as well. They needed time to absorb the news, each in their own way. No one crowded him anymore. Jerry headed outdoors without comment. Mom chased Patsy off to do the evening milking, with an added stern warning not to pester Calvin about his condition. Fannie helped her mom with supper cleanup, but they worked silently for a while.

"How did you know?" Mom finally asked, while she scoured the heavy pot. "Did he tell you, or did you guess?"

"He told me. I'd no idea." She placed a plate on the shelf and lowered the dish towel in her hands as she turned to face her mother. "He said he wanted to tell you, but he was afraid to write it in a letter."

Mom's hands stilled in the sudsy water. Then she drew them out and wiped them on her apron, catching a sob. Fannie reached for her, and Mom sucked in a breath, stanching her tears. She shook her head and pushed away. "It's going to be fine. God brought him home to us, and that's the main thing. I just need to pray."

"Maybe his hearing will return."

Hope and doubt battled in Mom's red-eyed glimpse. "We will pray for it, but it'll be fine whether or not God heals him. Did Cal say it might be temporary?"

Fannie shook her head. She turned back to drying the rest of the dishes, removing herself into her own thoughts about Cal's condition. Was there a chance he might regain his hearing? How had he lost it? All the blasts probably. They would likely learn more in time.

They finished the dishes in time for Patsy to come in with the milk pail and set up the strainer in the sink. Once the milk was strained and refrigerated, Mom glanced toward the doorway and then to Fannie and Patsy. "We're not going to treat him like he's broken, but he will need time. You just act like yourself."

Fannie looked at Patsy. "He can understand a few things we say if it's short and we give him time to see our lips. If we speak loudly, maybe he can hear a little."

"Where did Jerry go?" Mom asked absently.

"I'm sure he's processing Cal's condition too."

"Poor Cal," Patsy whispered with a glance between them.

"You don't have to whisper, Pats." Fannie pushed away from the cupboard. "I'll go find Jerry."

"What about the workers? Did you mention them?" Mom's question halted Fannie.

She shook her head. "I'll tell him though, if you want me to. It's something I'll have to write down for him."

"Let me know when you do."

Fannie nodded and pushed out the door. She stood on the edge of the porch and glanced over the farmyard, searching for Jerry. Darkness edged the lawn. Shadows played around the buildings and bushes. She squinted across the field toward the outline of the woods. "Jer?" she called. "You out here?"

"Back here!" His voice called from behind the shed.

She strolled across the yard and walked around the back of the building. She found him standing there, his back to the wall, his gaze across the shadowy distant field while he picked at the bark of a short stick in his hands. He didn't acknowledge her but swatted a mosquito on his arm with the end of the stick.

"Just thinking about Cal?"

"Yep." He turned and pressed his shoulder into the shed wall. "I wonder if he really wants to be home. Maybe he'd rather be there fighting still."

"What makes you say that?"

Jerry shrugged his other shoulder. "That's what I'd want if it were me. Maybe he wishes he didn't get sent home."

Fannie leaned back against the shed. "Oh, I don't know. I think he's glad enough to be here. He's just worried about what it'll mean—not being able to hear."

"Won't matter none to running a tractor or doing just about anything else around here."

"I know, but I'm sure it makes him sad. Can you imagine not being able to hear a bird sing?"

Jerry waved at a mosquito trying to land on his forehead. "Nope."

"Mom said to treat him like normal. Not to push him, but to let him know that he hasn't changed as far as we're concerned."

"He is changed."

"Because he's deaf?"

"I mean he's different. I can tell. He's been out there"—he raised his chin—"in the world. It's made him different."

"I suppose you're right. I don't know if it's the world or the war, but he's bound to have been affected."

They fell silent then, and Fannie turned to the darkness. Stars popped out overhead but in patches. More clouds must be moving in. The mosquitoes soon developed a cloud of their own, biting and buzzing in her ears.

"I can't take it anymore. I'm going inside." She pushed away from the shed.

"I'll come too."

Inside the house, light spilled from the living room. Fannie wandered in to see that Calvin had come downstairs and was reading last Sunday's paper. Mom was sitting on the davenport across from him, her needlework in her hands. Patsy was buried in a book on the other end. Jerry strolled over to Cal and tapped his shoulder.

"Checkers?" He pointed at the side table by the window where a couple of board games and a deck of cards sat in their boxes.

Calvin hesitated but then nodded. "Why not?"

Fannie breathed deeply, happy that Jerry had taken the lead in pulling Calvin into their world. "I'm going to go wash my hair. Church tomorrow."

Mom kept at her needlework without looking up. "Fannie. . .if you don't mind, I think we might stay home tomorrow. Give Calvin a little longer to settle in. Of course, you can still go if you want."

"Oh. Well, not if everyone isn't going. I want to stay with you and Calvin too." Disappointment sank in, and it took her a long moment to realize she'd been hoping to see the prisoners in attendance.

No. Truth pricked at her consciousness. She'd hoped to see Wolf.

She lifted her chin and admonished herself. "I think I'll wash my hair anyway."

"Will you wash mine for me, Fannie?" Patsy spoke without raising her eyes from the pages of her book. "I love it when you wash my hair. It feels so good."

Fannie laughed. "Sure. If you heat up the water when I'm done."

"Holler when you're done heating yours."

An hour later, after they'd both gotten their hair washed and they'd tidied up the mess, their brothers were just finishing their game of checkers. Fannie noticed that Jerry had the pad and paper and had been writing notes to Calvin during the game.

Thank You for Jerry's help, Lord. She needed to be purposeful in praying for Cal. It was not the time to stop now, just because he was with them. She strolled over to them and bent to hug Calvin. "I'm going to brush my hair and get myself to bed early." She motioned putting her head on her hands, palms pressed together, and closing her eyes.

"See you at breakfast," Cal said.

She nodded. Once inside her room with the door closed, she turned and looked at the made-up bed. She wasn't really very tired. It was still early. She just wanted to be alone like Jerry had earlier. She still hadn't really processed Cal's arrival and condition herself. Jerry was right. Cal's deafness wouldn't affect the work he could do on the farm, but maybe he had other worries. He used to see a girl from time to time. Liza Brachman. He hadn't mentioned her in his letters home, and Fannie didn't know if they were waiting for each other or even if they had been serious. Yet maybe Cal wondered about her now—or wondered how any woman would receive his disability. Cal was handsome, and he'd never lacked for notice from girls, but maybe that would change.

She felt sorry for Cal to think of it, then just as quickly scolded herself. "Feeling sorry for him is exactly what he expects but doesn't want." She strode across the room and stripped out of her clothes. While she slipped a cotton nightgown over her head, she reminded herself that Cal's hearing loss might not be permanent. That was something she wouldn't hold off asking him about. She wanted to know what the doctors told him.

The next day, Calvin joined them late for breakfast. He looked well rested, yet there was something missing in his step. He moved with a kind of uncertainty, like this wasn't home anymore or at least not the home he remembered. Mom set a plate of eggs and toast in front of him before he was halfway seated. She followed it up with a cup of rich, black coffee.

"Wow!" Fannie couldn't hold back her surprise. Coffee rationing had kept them drinking their coffee weak for months.

"It's a special Sunday," Mom said with a smile. She served the rest of them and sat down with her own plate. "Let's pray."

They bowed their heads, and Mom led them in prayer. Was Fannie the only one thinking about how Cal couldn't hear the words being said? Mom thanked God for Calvin's return, for the good bean harvest, and for the food. She spoke in her normal voice, not raising it for Cal's benefit. She asked for rain and said "amen." The whole thing ended so abruptly that Fannie didn't doubt Mom had also belatedly thought of Calvin's separation from them in their prayer. Fannie tapped Cal's leg when Mom finished, letting him discreetly know the prayer had ended. He raised his head as though he had listened intently to every word.

Jerry reached over his plate for the pad of paper. "We each need to have one of these by our sides," he muttered. He scribbled a note in what Mom called his chicken scratching and held it up to Calvin. *Want to take a ride to town later?*

"You're driving?" Calvin said with a smirk.

"You bet I am. Better than you," Jerry said loudly. He held up his finger in a pause and proceeded to write down his remark.

"On a tractor maybe."

Jerry laughed.

Mom was writing on the paper now. She held it out to Cal. With a quick read, his shrug was noncommittal. Fannie leaned over to see what she'd written.

We'll be picking again in a few days. Think you remember what to do? Cal had helped Dad manage the workers in the past. He and Dale took turns driving the loads to the cannery. Sometimes they both went. Afterward, if the picking was done for the day, they might go fishing or stop at the grocer and bring back treats for the rest of them.

Cal chewed on a sausage and watched Mom like he was thinking about her question. Finally, he swallowed. "What do you mean? Where are the workers anyway? I didn't notice anyone around."

"They'll be here." Mom's voice sounded cryptic to Fannie's way of thinking. Did Cal notice?

"Hm." He went back to finishing his breakfast. "I probably shouldn't drive with people around."

"Why not?" Fannie grabbed the tablet and wrote down the words she'd blurted.

"Not safe."

"Pfft." She made sure he saw her disbelief, rolling her eyes with

131

disgust at the idea. She wrote again. Now was as good a time as any to ask her question. *What do the doctors say? Will your hearing come back?* She put the paper under his nose.

He looked at the words then shoveled the remainder of his eggs into his mouth. She waited, watching him. At last, he shook his head. "No. They say there's probably permanent damage to the nerves. Besides that, my brain took a pretty big concussion. It can't get the sound signals right anymore." He pushed his chair away from the table and picked up his plate, turning his back as he carried it to the sink.

She bored the family with a hard look. Patsy jumped up and carried her plate to the sink. When she got where Cal couldn't pass her, she deposited her plate and made swimming motions. "Want to go swimming in the creek later?"

He ruffled her hair. "We'll see."

"Hey!" She pulled away, wrinkling her nose in annoyance.

"I think I'll go out and have another look at the fields."

Jerry got up from the table. "Mind if I come along?" He gestured to himself and at Cal to make his question clear.

"Suit yourself." Cal pushed out the screen door, and Jerry hurried to catch up.

Fannie scraped some butter onto her toast. "You didn't mention who the workers are."

Her mother poured a second cup of dark coffee. "I didn't see the need."

"Don't you think he'll mind?"

Mom looked at Fannie over her cup. "Mind?"

Fannie sighed. "I guess it doesn't matter either way. We need the help." Cal not knowing about the PWs made her uneasy. What would he think of German soldiers here on their farm? Maybe even men he'd fought somewhere, for all she knew. She had loathed the idea of them coming here, and she hadn't even seen the ugly side of war that Cal had. She'd hated them for simply being Germans and for what the Germans were doing to their American boys over there. She despised the fact that some of the fellows whom she'd grown up alongside, gone to school with, or pitched peas beside were even now fighting and dying at German hands. Others like Dale were getting captured and put into prison camps. Yet she'd seen none of it firsthand. Cal had.

The reminder made her nervous. What was more, she no longer felt the strength of her own hatred like she had earlier. As much as she'd wanted to hang on to those feelings of wanting to get even with the Germans in some private way, she couldn't. The PWs worked hard for them. They never complained so that she heard. They were gracious, even thankful for the opportunity for good food and cool drinks—for an occasional dip in the creek. They didn't seem to take the leniency of their captors for granted.

Except in the case of the water in the gas cans, Fannie reminded herself. Maybe she'd let her guard down too far.

The kitchen door swung open with a crash. Fannie nearly jumped out of her skin. Mom sloshed her coffee on the tablecloth. Cal stood before them, his face a black cloud of fury. "I can't believe you've brought them here!"

There was no point asking who he meant. Fannie's surprise was only in that she hadn't expected to learn of his reaction to the news so quickly. "Cal."

"You expect me to work out there with them?" He ground his jaw so hard it bulged and his nostrils flared. "I'll shoot them all down dead before I work side by side with them."

"Calvin." Mom's jaw dropped as she stood to her feet. "You mustn't say such things." She spoke louder than they usually heard her speak, but Fannie doubted Calvin heard more than a muffle of thunder. It didn't matter. He must have understood her expression.

"Do you have any idea what I've seen them do, Mother? Any at all? Can you imagine what it's like to see your best friend blown to bits or a bullet tear through the brain of the man next to you?"

Mom teared up. "Son."

"Or watch a man get tangled up in barbed wire while machine gun fire riddles through him until he's nothing more than a—a rag?"

"Calvin. We need the workers." Mom's voice quavered.

Fannie stepped around the table and braced a hand on her mom's arm. She looked hard at her brother. She pointed at herself and her mother. "We can't do all the work alone, Cal. Dad's gone!" She shouted, not in anger but in hope he'd hear something. "Dad is dead!" she repeated, feeling like a knife blade slid into her chest when she said it. "Pats is young." She shook her head and felt the sting of tears but fought them back. "We can't do it all alone."

He knew they were arguing the point. She could see it mixed in his angry expression, but his fists didn't loosen at his sides.

Fannie scrambled for the paper and wrote down the words. *We can't do the work alone without you and Dad and Dale. We can't!!!* She handed him the pad, but he flung it away so that some pages tore free and fluttered across the floor.

"Go ahead and bring them then," he growled through gritted teeth. "But don't expect me to take charge. There's only one thing good for them, and if even *one* of them steps out of line, then that's when I'll handle things." He pushed past them, jostling Fannie's shoulder as he left the room.

Jerry came in, closing the door softly. "I heard," he said. "I'm sorry. I tried to tell him easy."

"It's not your fault." Mom shook her head wearily. "He's had a hard time. I'm sure he'll change his mind after he's had a chance to think it over."

Fannie looked beyond the kitchen door toward the living room and the stairway that stood between. The wake of Calvin's anger made her shudder. She ran a hand over her arm where he'd shoved by, as though she could brush off his fury, but she couldn't. Mom could be hopeful that Calvin would come around to see how desperately they needed the workers—and for him to take charge—but Fannie wasn't so sure he would. She wasn't so sure at all.

⫸ CHAPTER 15 ⫷

August 1944

Wolf rubbed the knuckles of his right hand as he fought to tamp down his restlessness. They were in the transport, heading to the O'Brien farm, and he was glad because he needed to work. The camp had gone on strike several days ago because prisoners hadn't gotten their scrip pay. The guards hadn't been paid either, and they sympathized. But a "no work, no eat" policy had halted the strike quickly enough. To Wolf, it didn't matter. He couldn't send scrip home to his parents, and he wasn't a smoker. He did like to purchase paper and extra pencils, however.

Hermann Claus had acquired a correspondence course from a college somewhere in the state, and Wolf had offered his guidance. He'd also been using some free time to school Rudy, Richard, and Fritz in higher mathematics. Despite his satisfaction on both fronts, he was anxious to return to some physical labor.

Or maybe he was anxious to see Fannie again.

Last Sunday, he'd attended church with some of the other men, but her family wasn't there. He wouldn't have been concerned if only one of them was missing, but none of the family was present. Had something happened at the farm? Was there work to be done that could not wait for the crew? Worse yet, was there sickness or had an accident of some sort occurred? As he bounced along in the bed of the truck, Wolf sat sedately, but his thumbs worked harder over his fingers laced in his lap. Fritz appeared antsy too. He tapped his knee.

"You are looking forward to working?" Wolf asked.

Fritz shrugged. "I am anxious but not for work. I want to go home."

Wolf frowned. The others looked at Fritz. "You have not heard from Emma lately?"

He shook his head and shifted his long legs. "Nein. It is unlike her."

"Perhaps she has been occupied with demands. She has brothers who are fighting?"

"Ja. Three brothers. Her mother is occasionally unwell. Her papa is fighting too."

"Then she is very busy."

"I am afraid they have been forced from their home."

"Ach!" Leo looked their way. "You have nothing to worry about. The Reich is winning."

"That is not what I have read," Hermann said in his soft voice.

"What *you* have read," Leo muttered. "I see you trying to read the American newspaper. It is propaganda."

Hermann lowered his head.

The conversation ended there as they turned into the O'Briens' long drive. Wolf was relieved to see things looking just the same as ever. The house still standing. The tasseled corn stirring in the breeze. Jerry stepped from the shed with gunnysacks slung over his shoulder.

The men jumped down from the truck and filed toward the bean field. Routine had set in over the days. Leo passed him, but like Wolf, he glanced toward the house when they heard the front door open, the squawk of the hinge carrying on the morning air.

Fannie stood on the porch, watching them without expression. Wolf wanted to wave, but not with Leo standing by. Then the door opened again and a man stepped out. The door slapped shut against the frame. What was more, the man carried a rifle. He stood it on its stock and stared at them.

Now Wolf did give a nod. A guarded sensation he recognized well skittered down his spine. It was like the first days of his capture, when he didn't know what would happen next and at every turn he expected the worst. That they might be lined up before a firing squad. Yet that's not what happened. While some of the Germans were shoved and threatened, not a finger of serious harm touched them. He and his men were ordered about, *ja, natürlich*. The American soldiers demanded obeisance, certainly. He had seen other men shot who were suspected of being S.S., even if they weren't, but Wolf's own troops had been spared such treatment. They were fed, howbeit reluctantly at times and with scraps. The Americans allowed them to pause and rest during the march toward their incarceration, though they'd been spit upon more than once. Then they were sent to England, and from England here, where their fortunes were vastly improved. It had been months since the last time he felt this unnerving unease slither through him.

He turned abruptly toward the field with the others. Leo moved behind him.

"I wonder who he is," Leo said. "Her man, perhaps."

Wolf didn't feel compelled to speculate aloud. Was the stranger her man? Had Fannie someone special? She was a beautiful girl, with her brunette waves and enticing figure. Eyes dark and sweet as chocolate. Hands slim and strong and made for holding. Surely she was admired by many men she'd known. Had this one always been nearby, or had he returned from war? He had the look of a soldier, with his short-cropped hair and that gun.

If he had recently come home, who was he? A close friend or another family member perhaps? Someone Fannie had been waiting for, just as Emma waited for Fritz and her brothers and father?

When they reached the end of the field, Wolf picked a waiting pail from a stack and moved to a place to begin. He kept to the left of the other pickers, where he could glimpse the house discreetly. Fannie stood speaking to the man on the porch. Finally, she marched down the steps and toward the truck. Yes, marched. The set of her shoulders and frown on her brow told him she was upset about something—or maybe only anxious to get to work.

Jerry stepped out the door then. Wolf tossed a handful of beans into his pail and spied him speaking to the gun-toting man. The fellow had taken a seat in the rocking chair with the rifle lying across his lap.

Jerry strode down from the porch. His attitude was unreadable. Wolf pushed thick, bushy plants gently to the side and reached for long, green clusters of beans, plopping them into his pail. The rumble of the truck reached the edge of the field behind him. With only half his attention on his task, Wolf kept a watchful eye on the O'Briens. Jerry followed the truck on foot. When it stopped, he tugged a stack of gunnysacks off the back. Fannie didn't get out of the truck right away. Wolf glimpsed her staring ahead at the woods, her arm resting on the window ledge. She was biting her thumbnail. He'd never seen her do that before.

As Jerry took a pail from the truck, Wolf lifted his own half-filled pail. He carried it to the end of the row and approached Jerry. "You have guest, ja?" He gave a curt nod toward the house.

"A guest?" Jerry shook his head. "That's our brother Calvin. Home from war."

Wolf picked up an empty gunnysack and focused on emptying his beans in order to hide the ocean of relief that swept through him. Not Fannie's man but her brother. "He is going hunting?"

Jerry's brow jerked up and he snorted. He turned to the truck. "Fannie, you going to sit in there until you cook?"

She jerked the door open and slid out. "I'll pick."

"You don't have to, you know. You can go sit with Cal."

"Cal ought to be joining us." The words sounded angry, and Wolf wondered what had happened to send their brother home from war. He appeared uninjured.

Even now a glance showed that he'd risen from the chair and stood watching them much the way Corporal Taft had done at first. These days the corporal usually rested off in the shade if any was near enough where he could keep a casual watch on the crew. He sometimes sat on the back of the truck talking with whoever drew closest, his rifle resting on his lap. Right now, the corporal stood amid the rows of beans, speaking with Leo and Horst.

Wolf shook the long gunnysack, settling his meager picking into the bottom. He turned his back to the house so he could comment to Fannie without her brother on the porch seeing. He searched for all the correct English words. "I am glad your brother has come home."

She didn't turn her head to look at him either, and her small "Thanks" made him wonder even more about the man.

Wolf moved on. Now was not the time to press for information, for that's what it would seem to her that he was doing. Pressing. She might become suspicious of his curiosity, and certainly her elder brother would.

He bent to fill his pail full this time. Rudy did the same only a few yards away. "Remember my warning, Rudy. Should the girl come out, you must not speak to her."

"Ja, I know."

"Have you noticed we have another guard today? Do not look his way."

"Ja. I saw him too."

"He is their brother Calvin, home from war."

"He reminds me of the guards at first."

Wolf gave a nod, though Rudy wasn't looking at him. "It is good you remember. We are not involved in a war of ideals. It is a war of hatred. We must mind ourselves to stay out of the path of strong feelings."

Rudy's hands worked quickly, beans *plunk-plunk-plunking* into his pail. Obviously, the boy suffered with his own kind of strong feelings. Still, he was young. When the war ended, he would stop thinking of Patsy O'Brien—if that's truly where his attentions lay. Wolf rubbed his thumb down the length of a long, slim green bean. *And will I no longer think of her sister?* He flipped the bean into the pail. Clearly, he should mind his own advice.

Rudy stood when the produce heaped the top of his pail.

Wolf straightened too. He laid a hand on Rudy's shoulder, pausing him as he was about to pass. "It would be wise if you guarded your eyes as well as you guard your tongue. Should Patsy come outside, keep them to the ground or elsewhere. Especially now."

He shifted his weight. "I will."

Wolf gave him a pat and let him move on.

"Back to work!" Wolf glanced at Corporal Taft who was directing his command at him. "Enough talking this morning."

Things had changed. The corporal had never spoken to Wolf in such a way since their first arrival at Camp Barron. Horst and Richard hitched eyebrows in surprise, but Wolf jerked his head in acquiescence and returned to picking. He would do best to set an example for them to follow.

Nevertheless, from time to time throughout the rest of the morning, he stole glances. Fannie remained aloof. She and Jerry picked in rows away from Wolf and the others.

And their brother Cal never left his post.

At noon, Taft blew a whistle for them to take a rest. "Kid's bringing the water to refill your canteens."

Wolf shifted his glance toward the farmyard again. Jerry made his way toward the field, hefting two sloshing pails of water. From a crate Taft had sent one of the men to haul off the back of the transport truck earlier, he handed them each a thin sandwich wrapped in brown butcher paper along with an apple.

"Eat as many beans as you want," Fannie shouted.

Wolf turned at her voice from where she stood in front of the truck. He collected his foodstuffs and wandered closer. "I think our stomachs will ache from all the beans we've already eaten." He charged his voice with humor.

She leaned back against the truck's hood and raised the heel of her foot to the bumper. The sun's rays touched her forehead, giving it a bronze sheen. "Well, it's the best I can offer today. Mom's busy cooking up a big dinner for Cal. She's so happy he's home, she's treating him like a king."

"Killing the—" He squinted in search of the English phrase.

"Fatted calf?"

"Ja. That is it. As she should. It is a good thing that he has returned to you safely." He unwrapped the sandwich, but he watched for her reaction. "Whole and sound," he added, as though it was an afterthought, though he sought to find out more about Cal.

"Whole. Not so sure about sound." She looked at him then but just as quickly turned her gaze as though she'd said more than she meant to.

Wolf bit off a third of his meager sandwich and wiped a forearm across his brow.

"He lost some of his hearing over there." She spoke quietly so that only Wolf heard.

"I am sorry."

She gave a quick glance, her eyes sheepish. "I probably shouldn't tell you that, but it might come back."

Wolf's own ears suffered ringing from time to time from the noise of continuous shelling and gunfire. It was a common ailment, so he'd discovered. He didn't know of anyone who'd been cured of it, much less after losing a lot of hearing. By her tone, he didn't think she really thought the chances were good either.

"But he has all his limbs." Her tone brightened forcedly. "He's well enough to pick the darn beans or drive the truck." She pushed away from the bumper and glanced toward the house. "Looks like he's finally taking a break too."

Wolf followed her gaze to where Cal was marching toward the outhouse, gun in hand.

A couple of the men headed toward the edge of the field for the same reason but with empty hands.

Wolf checked his posture as Jerry strode toward them. "Mom says to tell you to come and grab some lunch so she can get the kitchen cleaned up. She wants me to take Patsy to the store for a few things this afternoon."

"Did she ask Cal to do it?"

Jerry gave Wolf a wary glance. "You know she won't, Fan. Come on. Time to eat." He turned to leave the field, but Fannie shifted back to Wolf.

"Did you have that talk with Rudy that you promised me?"

"Ja. You have no cause for worry."

Fannie sighed and started away. "I've got more cause than you know," she muttered.

He let her pass by, and he strode to the water pail to fill his canteen, but he kept stealing glances at her as she slumped toward the house. He wasn't worried anymore about Rudy misbehaving. It was his own inability to keep his eyes on the ground that troubled him.

Minutes later, Taft blew his whistle again, and the men retrieved their empty pails.

"Twelve more rows today," Taft said. "Shouldn't take you more than a couple of hours longer."

Wolf scanned the waving green field, and he made an almost unconscious accounting of each of the men. He glanced across them again. "Where is Leo?" he asked Richard, who shuffled down the row beside him.

Richard swept a glance across the field. "He went to the woods a few minutes ago. He must not have finished his business and come back yet."

Wolf scanned again. "Perhaps not." He squatted into the greenery where he'd left off picking earlier, but he remained on the lookout for Leo. It wasn't good to be gone longer than the whistle. Taft must realize he hadn't returned. Wolf looked again over his shoulder, but the corporal was swigging on a canteen.

His sweat turned cold with relief when Leo's white shirt emerged from the edge of the tree line where the grassy lane ran between the beans and the cornfield.

Richard's glance went to Leo too, and he jerked his chin up. "Must have been the beans." He cast Wolf a grin and crunched down on a long, slender pod.

Wolf chuckled. "You're probably right. It's likely we'll all be taking advantage of the bushes or the privy for the next twenty-four hours."

Leo hiked toward them with purpose in his stride, like he couldn't wait to get back to work—or more like he didn't want to get into trouble for returning late after the whistle blew. Last week it might not have mattered so much. Corporal Taft was an understanding man, and he'd not been overly strict with them as long as they worked hard. But that had changed too. An air of soldierly purpose in Taft had emerged since Fannie's brother decided to take command of the front porch. He sat there now once again, like a general inspecting his ranks.

CHAPTER 16

Leo had to rein in his elation. Adrenaline screamed through his body as he climbed into the back of the transport and endured the jolting drive back to camp. All the other men looked beat. Leo had worked just as hard as they had, maybe harder to prove himself. Yet his blood spiked euphorically at his secret accomplishment, pushing fatigue away.

He had taken great risk in his spontaneous decision, yet no one had spied him lifting the gas can from the shade along the side of the truck that faced away from the bean field. Not even the man on the porch, who Rudy whispered was Fannie's brother Calvin. Nor had they spotted him as he quickly hid it behind some shady stalks on the edge of the cornfield on the other side of the lane, just a few feet away. Later on, when they were excused to relieve themselves, he'd moved it farther into the dense corn. There he spread splashes of fuel, then left the cap loose and tipped the can on its side, allowing a faint trickle into the patch of weeds growing around the thickening stalks. Should it be inadvertently discovered, it would look like an accidental spill of a can left out since the corn was last tilled. Then he'd hastened out the back of the field to return to the place he should appear from.

Tomorrow the patch should light easily enough. The green stalks might smoke first, but with the added fuel and no recent rain, they shouldn't take long to curl and burn.

The crew wouldn't pick beans again for a few days at least. Fannie informed them that they'd move on to harvesting the oats next and then storing the oat straw for animal fodder and bedding. With any luck, the field would become a raging inferno that would jump into the oats, destroying those too. Other than the beans that had already been harvested, Leo might single-handedly ruin the remaining crops of the O'Brien farm. It would be a small dent in this massive war his country engaged in, but a dent nonetheless. And it would be justified recompense for whatever destruction Fannie's soldier brother had wreaked while he was in Europe.

Perhaps when Leo returned to the fatherland, he would earn a medal.

He covered a smile with his hand, pretending to yawn. Then he leaned back and closed his eyes like some of the others, letting his vision play out secretly in his imagination. Wouldn't Fannie be shocked! How he would laugh then. They would try to stop the wreckage, but the water would be too far away. The brother on the porch would have to leave his gun behind to come out and help.

Leo would make a pretense of helping too. He would, perhaps, be the first to spy the fire. Wouldn't he?

No. He must let it work as much destruction as possible before someone else saw it. Then he would join in the shouting for help. No one would suspect mischief. It would appear to be a freak accident. He would nudge their thoughts with the idea that Fannie or Jerry O'Brien must have left the can out there on another day. He'd seen for himself that they kept several such cans in the shed. They could easily lose count.

"What is that I see? A smile on your face?" Otto nudged Leo's foot with his boot.

"I am resting contentedly."

"Dreaming of winning another game on Sunday?"

Leo smirked. "I don't have to dream about that. It's already decided."

Otto chuckled. Leo's fast footwork on the soccer field had become legendary around camp and, according to rumors, in the nearby communities as well. "I am getting better. You're lucky we almost always play on the same team."

He opened his eyes. "Maybe next time we can switch the teams up. I could use a challenge. Time for some new lessons for you perhaps." He winked.

"I am ready to throw down the gauntlet."

Richard grunted. "How can you talk of running on the field at the end of a day like this? I can only think of taking a nap."

"And of eating supper," Rudy added.

Leo jerked his chin at them. "What's the matter with you? I'm older than all of you except the captain. You don't see me complaining of stiff joints and weary muscles. You've all grown soft and weak." He glanced at

Wolf, who grinned in complicity but didn't add to the discussion.

Rudy scowled, his defenses ruffling. "I didn't say I wouldn't be up to a game. Just feed me with something more than those skinny sandwiches we had today."

There was a murmur of agreement. They wouldn't likely be treated to one of Frau O'Brien's picnics now that her son had returned.

"Fair enough," Leo said. "Tonight, after you've filled your gullet. Then you'll have no excuse. We'll go to the field for some training exercises. Will you join us, Fritz?" Leo looked down the line of men on his side of the truck to his friend who hadn't responded in any way.

Fritz rubbed his neck. "Not tonight. I am going to write to Emma."

"You've written already this week, haven't you?" Wolf asked quietly.

Fritz nodded. "But if my letters reach her, surely it is better to hear more from me than less."

Wolf nodded. "You must write to her as often as you are able. Tell us when you hear something."

Not *if* but *when*, Leo noted. Wolf might be feeding Fritz false hope. Something must have happened to Emma, or Fritz would have heard back by now. It made Leo glad he had no one to write to. At least no one who mattered. His parents must clearly understand that they would never hear from him again.

If they were alive.

A moment of chagrin nibbled at his conscience. Leo leaned back, his energy finally subdued.

After their evening meal at camp, Leo bought a package of cigarettes at the canteen with his scrip. He would be generous and share a few with Fritz. His comrade needed encouragement. But he'd make sure he had plenty with him tomorrow so that he could put his plan into action.

Thursday dawned warm and deliciously dry. The humidity had lifted, and a light breeze stirred the air. Conditions couldn't have been riper for Leo to carry out his plans.

When they marched on to the commons for roll call, Corporal Taft divided them out. "Only four of you for the O'Briens' place this morning. The rest are going to the canning factory to unload beans."

Leo momentarily panicked as Taft divided him over to the side of the factory workers. He scrambled for an idea. "Schorr, you trade." He quickly slid over into Richard's place, and the big fellow shrugged. He wouldn't argue since Leo held rank over him. Besides, the boys heading to the factory would probably be happy for a change.

He walked to the transport with Wolf, Fritz, and Rudy. He clapped Fritz on the back and offered him a cheerful smile. It was good that Fritz was there today. If anything went wrong, Leo could most likely depend on him. He'd decided he would put his action into play while they were all taking a respite to cast less suspicion. It would be easier with fewer men there to see him but also more difficult, as Taft would have fewer to guard.

When they stepped off the back of the truck, the first thing Leo noted was the vacant front porch of the house. He doubted they'd have to wait more than moments for the American soldier to step out onto the porch, gun in hand. Leo was surprised he wasn't already seated and waiting for them. But the door didn't open, and no one stirred about.

A clanking drew his attention to the tractor parked outside the shed. Fannie stood behind it at the hitch, where she and her younger brother were hooking up a big contraption with a wheel of wooden sickle bars that looked more windmill than tractor machinery. It was mounted above a piece of boxy equipment about a dozen feet long. As their crew drew closer, he could see that a canvas belt would feed cut stalks into the machine.

Wolf strode forward and ran his hand along one of the wooden bars. "This is what will cut your oats?"

Fannie's head came up, and she brushed her hands together. "Yes. It's called a binder. The belt will feed them into the machine here, and they'll come out in bundles over here." She spoke slowly so the Hauptmann could follow and pointed again. "Your men will stack them in shocks on the field to cure. Jerry will show you."

Leo paid attention too, watching as she described the action and discerning as many of the English words as he could catch—likely more than either she or the Hauptmann realized he grasped. Like the disk, there was a seat and handles for operating the machine.

Jerry climbed on. "Come on." He waved them to follow.

Now Leo understood why only four men were sent. This was probably a task the family might have been able to perform with only a couple of extra workers if the older brother Cal and sister Patsy were sent out to join them. He glanced back to the house, but the man had yet to put in an appearance.

It was another twenty minutes, when they were already well into the first round of cutting and stacking sheaves of grain, before Leo spied the family car heading down the drive away from the house. Calvin O'Brien stared at them from the front passenger window, then turned his face away.

A thrill raced through Leo. With luck, the rest of Fannie and Jerry's family would remain away from home until he could put his plan into action.

With one eye on the driveway and one on the task at hand, the morning passed slowly. It felt like midday before they reached a time to break, but it wasn't lunchtime yet. The other O'Briens had not returned.

The workers were near the far end of the field, close to the woods' edge, and not too far from the corn when given leave to take a latrine break. Rudy led the way. Leo nonchalantly pulled his smokes from his pocket and stretched out an arm, giving the pack a shake to offer one to Fritz. Fritz accepted. Wolf walked past.

Leo took his time smoking, letting his captain and Rudy finish their business and head back to the field. Even Fritz started back, but Leo gave him a soft whistle. "Walk slowly. Here."

Fritz didn't question, just accepted another cigarette and turned away. Leo smiled with satisfaction at Fritz's slow steps. Good ol' Fritz. He didn't need an explanation. He just followed Leo's orders. His head was probably so lost in worry about his girl that he didn't give Leo's remark a second thought.

Leo moved along the edge of the trees toward the stand of corn only a few yards off, then hustled up the row. He'd bent a stalk over at the end of the row where he'd put the can of gasoline so that he could find the place quickly, drop his smoke, and be on his way before the fire plumed.

He only had to go about ten yards in to find the can drained empty and a patch of stained ground around it. Those cornstalks had already yellowed two-thirds up the stalk, poisoned by the gas. They would catch fairly quickly, if he didn't miss his guess. He took care not to rub against those that were contaminated with fuel while he took his half-smoked cigarette and nestled the butt into the dry patch of weeds. They immediately burst into a small flame. He dared not wait around to see if they caught further.

"Come on, now. Burn."

He rubbed his hands in clean soil and wiped them on his pants as he hurried back to the tree line and the lane that led back to the oat field. Up ahead he could see that Fritz had reached the others. Leo took long strides, eating up the distance between them. A quick look over his shoulder told him nothing looked changed so far. There was not even a hint of smoke lifting above the corn.

He was torn between dismay that his plan might have failed and relief that he'd gotten back before a flame leapt into the sky.

He retrieved his canteen and dropped casually onto the ground, then unscrewed the cap for a long swig of tepid water. The day had warmed. Despite the drop in humidity, it was going to be another hot one. He gazed toward the oats they'd already shocked. If not for the fact that he was at war and this was his enemy's field, he could have appreciated the pretty sight of the golden oats with their fat heads. He'd even nibbled a few while he worked.

The hammering of his heart began to slow as he rested, and the feeling ebbed away that his plan was going to succeed. He'd nearly given it up when Rudy said, "What's that?"

He rose up slowly, like the others, and the throbbing in his chest started up again. "It looks like smoke," Jerry said.

Now. Now is the time. "*Brand!* Fire!" he shouted. "Quickly! *Feuerwehr!*" To be the one urging a fire brigade would look well for him. He hid a smile as he jumped into the lane and waved them to come along with him to fetch water. Others shouted and started running, but the most satisfactory sound was Fannie's cry and the rush of Jerry's feet pounding the earth to pass him. The boy would show promise on a soccer field.

Leo sped up. He would arrive at the pump first and fumble with the pails. He reached it steps ahead of the others and clattered the handle, but Jerry and Fannie had disappeared. Wolf was not there either.

Rudy and Fritz arrived a moment later and reached for the other two pails waiting there.

Two pails. Leo had to laugh inside. Yet where were Fannie and the others? Why hadn't they followed?

"Take them," Leo ordered. "I will search for more pails."

He headed toward the truck first. That's where they'd kept some water buckets before. But he slowed his steps as the other men rushed off. No sense being in too much of a hurry.

He looked back toward the corn where a dark plume billowed into the blue sky. The gas would be all burned up, leaving no trace. If they found the empty can later, negligence could still be blamed on the O'Briens.

He finally saw Fannie burst from the cornfield, run to the end of the field, and dip back in again. She and Wolf emerged a moment later carrying a long tube. *The irrigation tubes!* Of course! How long had it been since he'd last stepped over a pipe in the bean field? He'd not been deep enough into the patch yesterday to step over them.

He cursed under his breath. The fire would eat up a swath of corn, but it would never do the damage he'd hoped for once it touched the water's reach. Angrily, he glanced at Rudy and Fritz, bustling away with full water pails. He must do more.

He thought of the gun he'd stolen from under the truck seat and hidden. Had the O'Briens even realized it was gone? He didn't think so. He'd hidden the gun inside his pants and then stuffed it into a bush behind the outhouse. Perhaps he should take it with him now. He would take the gun back to camp and kill as many American soldiers as he could, beginning with their guards.

No. His thoughts were becoming erratic. *Too nervous.* Leo rubbed the back of his hand over his mouth as his gaze flitted between the buildings. Far away in the corn he could hear an occasional shout still. He must stick to the plan and bring the gun out only when necessary. If the fire was not successful, then he would perhaps use the pistol to kill the soldier brother or to shoot the O'Briens' livestock and escape. Fritz might come along.

Once again, he considered the place in which he'd frantically hidden the pistol. It was not a good hiding place. If the O'Briens searched, they would look where the prisoners had easy access. His gaze darted about at the house and barn and then to the unused silo and windmill, even as he moved to the barn shed in search of more pails. It wouldn't do to return to the field without trying. He nearly tripped on a loose cobblestone in Frau O'Brien's pathway just outside the barn.

A sneer lifted one side of his mouth as the answer made itself clear beneath his feet. Yes, he would put the gun beneath this rock. It would be easy to retrieve but difficult for anyone else to find. Within minutes he'd retrieved the gun, nestled it into the earth, and tucked it safely beneath the stone.

With another sharp glance toward the smoking field where he saw not a soul, he rose and brushed his hands together. Then he walked boldly into the barn where he found a spigot and two shiny new pails, which he filled promptly and hefted toward the now smoldering cornfield.

⋛ CHAPTER 17 ⋛

Fannie tore through the cornstalks, heedless of the leafy blades whipping her arms, now and then cutting her skin. Jerry along with Taft, and she with Wolf, grabbed the pipes and moved them closer to the fire's torch. So far, only a patch the size of their front yard looked ruined, and they could save the major portion if they could get the irrigation moved closer. Wolf's hands and feet worked with as much haste as her own. For the briefest moment, she glimpsed concern on his face that looked genuine. Was it?

How had the fire started? She could think of no way other than by human touch. The weather was too perfect, the crop too green, and the earth too rich. Other than the lack of any recent rains, there was no reason a fire would just erupt. Each of them had to be thinking—or knowing—the same thing. But who? When? The only reasonable cause was the men being allowed to smoke on their breaks. But was it by carelessness or intention? And if by intention, then how had it been managed? The entire crew had appeared shocked at the sight of the smoke. Just as shocked and concerned as Wolf did now.

She lugged her end of the heavy pipe with Wolf holding the other. On their break, he'd gone to the woods with the others. He was the first to return. Did that make him guilty? Who was last? She scrambled to recall. Fritz. No, Leo. Leo was last. But he was the first to shout *fire* and the first to rush to help.

It simply must have been an accident.

Her legs and shoulders burned from carrying the heavy pipe on the run. Except for Wolf, the prisoners had hurried off for pails of water, probably not realizing she and Jerry had moved the irrigation system into the corn last week. At least they'd been able to slow the fire's spread with a small gully of water while the rest of them moved the pipes closer.

Jerry was adjusting the tubes that would siphon the water up from the creek. Before long, water and mud soaked her feet as it trickled down between the rows. With the cooling effect, she let out a long pant of relief.

Wolf moved up to stand beside her. His men had begun refilling their pails in the creek a short way off, and they were adding to the irrigation by tossing their water directly onto the flames. She didn't see Leo among them, but when she looked back down the lane, she could see him hurrying toward them with two more pails he must have found somewhere. Right now, she didn't care where he'd gone in search of them, only that he'd made himself useful. When he reached them, Wolf took one of the pails and they hurried toward the blaze together.

In only another ten minutes, the fire fizzled out.

The workers, Taft, and Jerry all emerged into the lane with her. Her legs shook, and suddenly she couldn't deny the sob tightening her throat, making her long to gasp, so she turned away and trudged toward home. Jerry would know what to do. Taft would probably send them all back to work, or maybe he'd bring them up to the house for a well-deserved rest and something to eat. Yes, an early lunch maybe.

Her body quaked, and tears oozed out of her eyes. When she was far enough away to not be heard, the sobs left her, and her shoulders shook. Her anguish lasted only a few minutes, however; then she was angry. She sucked in air and rubbed her eyes. Why hadn't Cal been out there to help? With him, Mom, and Patsy, they could've cut the oats without any of the workers. They wouldn't need their help now if they all put their best effort into it. But Cal showed no compunction to see it her way, and lately he refused to even listen to her when she tried talking to him about it. He would literally turn a deaf ear to her when she stood in front of him, pleading and writing notes.

She sniffled and wiped her nose on her arm, then brushed her arm across her shirt. She was already covered with mud and smoke, so one more streak of filth didn't matter.

She tamed her thoughts. Even if Cal agreed to help, he wasn't here now, and for good reason. He had to see a doctor today, and Mom drove him so that she and Patsy could go to the grocery store. He would not have been able to help them even if he'd wanted to. At least they had saved the corn, and the fire had had no chance to damage the other crops.

Cal would be furious about the workers, for it was clearly a human act that had started the blaze, even if unintentionally. Later when they left, she and Jerry could have another look.

Fannie trudged into the house and to the bathroom where she looked into the mirror with disgust. Turning on the spigot, she scrubbed her face, hands, and arms. She'd lost her scarf somewhere, so after brushing out smoky mats and snarls and knotting up her hair, she went upstairs for another. All this busywork gave her time to clear her thoughts. Once she clomped downstairs again, she'd decided that the men needed something for her thanks in helping to put out the fire.

Mom was planning leftover pork for their supper, but she went into the kitchen and pulled it from the icebox for sandwiches. She'd seen the thin offerings they'd brought with them yesterday. Hardly enough to keep her little sister satisfied much less grown working men. She cut up all the bread they had along with the sliced pork and piled it on. She brought the offering outdoors where she found them waiting in the yard, taking turns at the pump for fresh draughts of water to quench their smoke-parched throats.

She held out the plate. "Thank you for helping us put out the fire." She didn't plan to say more than that. They'd understand.

The men accepted her offering with nods of thanks, then Wolf approached. "I am very sorry, Fannie," he said, his voice as regretful as if she'd lost her brother.

Her chest tightened. *Fannie.* Whether it was because of the gentle and natural way he'd spoken her given name or the fact that in the next instant she thought of Dale, tears threatened again. She cleared her throat, fighting them back. "Thank you."

She turned and handed the last sandwich to Corporal Taft. "Thank you for your quick help too, Corporal."

"Excuse?" Leo came forward. He'd already downed his sandwich. He glanced guilty eyes at both her and the corporal. He made a bit of a speech in German, looking mostly at Taft, but now and then at her. She caught the word *fire*, and he patted his pocket where a half-empty package of cigarettes poked out. It didn't take much to figure what he was getting at.

Corporal Taft was upset. His rebuke shot out in German along with a wave of his hand. He turned to her. "He's afraid the fire was his fault. He smoked a cigarette somewhere over there when he used the toilet." His words were curt and angry, and Fannie wondered if he even blamed himself. "I'll look into it further."

"There's no need, Corporal." She checked her anger. "He's apologized. It was an accident." She forced out the word. Was it? *Get hold of yourself, Fannie. Of course it was.* She stiffened her back. "In the future, we won't allow smoking here. They can smoke when they're back at camp."

"Yes, ma'am."

In this she had to agree with Cal. They'd been far too lenient with the prisoners. They were much too free here. *Even the good ones.*

The thought surprised her, assailing her with one of Wolf's smiles as he neared them. She needed to stop presuming he was a good one too.

"We are ready to go back to work if you wish." His blue eyes regarded her with that unnerving concern she'd seen earlier, and she only nodded, striding past him toward the oat field where the tractor stood waiting.

Another rush of relief washed over her. Thank God the fire hadn't gone farther. They might have lost everything. Their crops. The tractor. Perhaps even their home. She swallowed against the dangerous, frightening thought.

Mom and Cal came home an hour later. They hadn't seen any of the damage and couldn't without coming out to the field. Mom only wondered where her leftover pork went, and Fannie acknowledged that she fed it to the men without saying why except that they'd worked hard. Cal spent the afternoon in his usual chair on the front porch, a bottle of beer beside him—another habit he'd brought home that fueled his dark moods.

When the oats were cut and standing in neat tepees and the men had gone for the day, Fannie and Jerry headed for the field with a singleness of mind.

Jerry strode close beside her. "Are you going to tell Cal?"

"Eventually. I'll tell Mom. Maybe she can tell him. Not that he'll care."

"You don't think so?"

"I don't know if he gives two ounces for the farm anymore."

"He cares, Fan."

They turned the corner of the lane by the trees and moved along the edge of the scorched and ruined corn. She stopped and faced him, now far enough out of sight of the house. "You think so? I think Cal only cares about his hatred of the Germans. He just wants to sit there all day nurturing it."

"Because this is his home though, right?"

She shrugged. "I suppose. Come on. Let's see how it looks in there."

The muddy field sucked at her shoes. Jerry had disconnected the siphon earlier, but the corn had taken a good drenching to make sure the fire couldn't start again. It had needed watering at any rate.

They hadn't gone in far when a reddish-black lump caught her eye and she paused. It looked like. . . She slogged over to the can with most of the paint burned off it. Jerry followed her and pulled up short to see what she saw.

"Did you leave it out here?"

He shook his head. "Not that I remember."

"Neither did I."

"Are you sure?"

Was she? Had she left it behind weeks ago when they'd needed to fuel up? "Pretty sure."

"Pretty sure?" She looked up to see his brow arched at her. "Since when do you bring a can into the field? We always fuel up in the lane or at the shed. Dad's rules, remember?"

She nodded. Even so, she said, "I don't know, Jer."

"Now what'll you tell Mom?"

"We can't let Calvin know. He'll go off his head with hate. He'll shoot somebody. Remember what he said when he first found out about the workers? *'If even one of them steps out of line. . .'* I'm afraid he'll make good on his threats."

"We can't have someone out here sabotaging the farm."

"I know."

"Who do you think did it?"

She picked up the scorched can and gave it a shake. It was completely empty. What would have happened if it had been full? Would it have blown sky high? Had there been gasoline inside? Was that what made the fire spread? She shrugged. "I have no idea. Could have been any of them. Maybe they're all involved."

Jerry shoved his hands in his pockets. "They were all fast to help out today. Maybe it was one of the other PWs who put it out here. One of the ones not here today."

Fannie shook her head. "Sounds too coincidental. You're suggesting that someone in the crew who didn't even come today slipped the gas into the field, then Leo dropped his cigarette that not only caught fire on the weeds but also just happened to land near this gas can that might or might not have spilled a good seventy yards from the woods where they do their business."

"Something like that."

"Seems a stretch."

"Not if they planned it that way." Jerry shrugged. "Maybe someone intended to use the gas to make a bomb or something."

Fannie felt her blood drain at that idea.

"Or maybe it was that Fritz fellow who put the can in the field today," Jerry went on. "He's been pretty owlish lately."

"We would have seen him. Besides, we didn't even bring gas out of the shed today."

They stared at the scorched container in silence. Was it the work of a single saboteur, or could several be involved? Could the whole crew be planning to burn down their farm—or worse? The questions raced through Fannie's brain without answers.

Jerry reached for the can. "I'll carry that for you. I can take it out to the dump so Cal doesn't see it."

"I'll have to tell Mom." She relinquished the can. "She needs to know."

"You think it'll be the straw that sends them packing?"

"I don't know. She's very insistent that we can't do the work alone. But maybe she'll tell Cal that she's been worried about them, like he is, and that if Cal will put his boots on and help, she can send them away."

"Sounds like a good way to look at it to me."

They started toward home. The idea grew on Fannie. "Don't say anything about the fire tonight. Let's wait until tomorrow. We'll talk to Mom then."

"We smell."

He was right. They did smell. "You'd better clean off outside. I'll slip in the back and get upstairs without walking through the kitchen."

"Don't let Patsy catch you. She's got a nose like bird dog."

Fannie smiled for the first time that day. "I won't."

≣ CHAPTER 18 ≣

The following morning, Fannie followed Mom out to the chicken run. Mom had set Patsy to straining the fresh milk and had gone herself to feed the chickens. Fannie stepped on a cobblestone she knew to be loose, at the same moment noticing that it didn't wobble. Mom must've finally fixed that.

"Hey, Mom."

"Fannie, what are you doing out here? Don't you need to go to work today?"

"I'm just about ready to go. Mrs. Calloway won't mind my being a few minutes late. I wanted to grab a word with you." She stood on the outside of the fence, awaiting her mother's full attention. It wasn't long in coming.

"What is it? You look troubled."

"Do I?" Fannie touched a hand to her cheek. "I. . .I'm not troubled exactly."

A slight furrow dipped Mom's brow. She pushed open the wire door of the pen and stepped out, her apron drawn up to hold five eggs. Fannie stood near to not be overheard. She wasn't sure where Cal was off to this morning or if he was still in bed. "Something happened yesterday."

"What kind of something?"

"There was an accident."

"No one was hurt?" Mom didn't sound urgent. She saw herself that everyone was working and no one appeared injured.

"Nothing like that. There was a—a small fire."

"A fire!"

"Shh." Fannie glanced quickly toward the house. "I don't want Cal to

157

hear. It'll make him mad."

Mom looked at her with a twist in her lips, as though she were a peculiar girl, and then Fannie realized what she'd said. "I forgot."

"What do you mean, a fire?" Mom bunched her apron tighter.

"The corn caught fire on the south end. It didn't burn much," Fannie hastened to add. "But there was some damage."

Mom gasped. "I don't understand how—"

"We think a cigarette." Fannie's voice dropped to a whisper regardless that Cal wouldn't hear her. "It looks like it was an accident, but maybe not." Should she tell her about the gas can?

"A cigarette? Burning green corn and dirt?"

"It might have had some help."

"What do you mean?"

"Someone left a gas can in the field. I don't know if had any gas in it. It seemed to have been an empty can to begin with." She'd taken mental note of the loose cap, and her doubts that the can had been empty spurred on, but Mom didn't need to know that. "If there was any fuel involved, that might have contributed to the fire getting a start."

"Who on earth left a gas can in the field? Did Jerry—"

Fannie shook her head. "I don't think so. He knows the rules. I didn't either, that I recall. Still, someone put it out there."

"We don't know for sure." Her mother seemed as though she was about to defend the PWs but really couldn't. There was no proof one way or another. Fannie had puzzled all night long about how one of them could have managed it, but she couldn't see how. And yet. . .

"We keep a pretty tight accounting of the fuel." They all did. Her mom didn't really need reminding that they were rationed an amount for farm vehicles each week on their "R" card. They had to use it wisely. Why, just the loss of a can of fuel alone was a problem. Mom had to see that there was more to it than simple carelessness. "I'll take the blame though," Fannie said. "You can tell Cal it was my fault."

Mom turned toward the house, but she didn't hurry. "I know it wasn't your fault, Fannie, but I do see your point." She sighed. "No telling what Cal would do. He might march out there to the workers and—"

Fannie was glad she didn't finish her thought. She had her own worries about what Cal would do. She'd never known her brother to be so angry. . .so volatile. "What about the workers? What should we do?"

Mom shrugged a shoulder, while one hand supported the weight of the eggs in her apron. "I don't know. We need them here."

"Do you suppose we could suggest to Cal that his help might prevent us from needing so many of the workers? Would he see reason?"

"He might." She raised her eyes to Fannie. "But how do we know which workers are safe to keep around? If any of them do mean us harm, how will we know which ones? Maybe they'd all like to see the farm burn down."

Would they? Somehow, Fannie didn't believe that. She didn't want to think that someone like soft-spoken and intelligent Hermann or big but gracious Richard had nefarious motives. Surely not young Rudy. He couldn't mean any harm. *And Wolf.* Wolf had worked shoulder to shoulder with her to fight the blaze. He seemed to want to befriend her. If she was completely honest, she wanted to befriend him.

No, Fannie. She shook such thoughts away. She had to think clearly. Their whole family might be in danger. He was a captain trained in warfare. He'd been prepared for what to do in case of capture. Was she really no better than those simple-minded girls who flirted at the camp fence? Was it that she just did not want to see the truth right in front of her? And if not Wolf or Hermann or the others, then who? Leo Friedrickson came to mind. So did Otto and Fritz. And maybe Wolf directed them all how to act.

She put an arm around her mom in a gentle side hug so as not to upset the eggs. "It'll be all right, I'm sure. Corporal Taft was there and helped put out the fire. He's sure to keep an especially close eye open now."

"Yes, I'm sure he will. We won't borrow trouble." They reached the back step, and Mom paused with one foot on the stoop. "You just enjoy your day at the library. Maybe you can bring me home a magazine to look at. I could use something else to think about."

"Sure, Mom." She turned and, with a glance at Mom's cobblestones of confidence path, felt a moment's encouragement. "Before we know it, the season will end. We're going to get through it. Then we'll have another stone to lay, right, Mom?"

Mom's chin rose. "We sure will."

Fannie turned to leave. "I'm taking the truck today instead of the car. I'll need to refill a couple of cans. I think we can start digging potatoes next week."

"I'll tell Jerry to sharpen the shovels. Maybe Cal can help."

Fannie wouldn't hold her breath.

She had already carried the empty cans to the truck before getting into her good clothes for work. She brushed off the truck seat, hoping she wouldn't soil her skirt. She never liked having to drive the truck to the library. It usually smelled of grease, dirt, and sweat. Dust hung over the console and smudged the windows. She would park a block away at least.

She was almost to Rice Lake when she remembered the gun beneath the seat. It wasn't so unusual for anyone to keep a shotgun or other weapon in their vehicle, but she hadn't thought about it in a while. She would make sure it was tucked under the seat safely out of sight while she did her job. At least she hadn't needed it. Nevertheless, if there really was a saboteur among the PWs, would she need it in the future?

Traffic was nil downtown. Fannie drove up the main street, eyeing shop windows and noting what was playing at both the Majestic and the El Lago. *Since You Went Away* had Claudette Colbert, Jennifer Jones, Joseph Cotten, and Shirley Temple in a coming-of-age role. *The Seventh Cross* starred Spencer Tracy. War films. Probably very enthralling with such stars, but Fannie couldn't bring herself to be interested in anything more to do with peril and subterfuge. *The Adventures of Mark Twain.* Ah. There was one that sounded relaxing. Maybe she'd take Patsy. Jerry too, if he wanted to tag along with his sisters. They deserved a break. Something nice to celebrate all their accomplishments so far this season. Something to make them forget that so much more lay ahead and that Dale and all the other soldiers depended on them to do their part.

A service station was just ahead. She had a little time to spare. Should she fuel up the gas cans now or after work? Hm. . . After would be best. She trusted the folks around town, but with fuel in such short supply due to the need for rubber, she really shouldn't risk full cans of gasoline sitting in the back of the truck all day. She'd just pull in when her shift was over.

She sped on toward the library and soon arrived. She pulled to the curb a block away. As always, the feeling of calm descended over her. Here she was able to be the person she was meant to be, with thoughts of the farm tucked back into the recesses of her mind.

Yet not completely. Fannie killed the engine, but before climbing out of the truck, she bent and reached beneath the seat to assure herself that the pistol was still safely tucked away and wasn't about to slide out in broad daylight on the floorboards. Her fingers found dirt and grit aplenty, and even a few dry and crunchy bean leaves, but no gun. It must've slid farther back, or else Jerry had purposely stowed it out of reach.

She opened the door and stepped out of the truck, then tucked her skirt behind her legs while she bent to search again. Her chest tightened as she peered beneath the seat and ran her hand under, prodding the area beneath the springs.

Nothing.

Blood rushed to her temples. The gun had to be there. She glanced up and down the street before hurrying around to the other side of the truck. Cranking open the door, she bent so that her eyes were level with the floorboards. She shoved an arm under the seat as far as she could cram it and wiggled her fingers about, desperate for the feel of hard steel, to no avail.

She leaned out with a gasp. There was nothing more to it. The gun wasn't there. She glanced at her watch. It was time to start work.

A car drove by, and she used the moment to grasp her thoughts into order. *The gun is stolen. Right? No. No, it can't be. Jerry took the gun out. Or Cal. Cal might have found it and taken it. He prowls around at night. Who knows what he's doing?*

Her heart sagged with worry. She wanted to climb back behind the wheel and speed home, but to what end? To be told by Jerry that he removed the gun after the fire? That's probably what happened. He'd simply forgotten to mention it. She leaned against the truck door and breathed slowly. That was better. There was nothing she could do about it now.

Her fingers were filthy. She dared not use them to brush her dress or tidy her hair. She might have dirt streaked across her face. She reached for her purse and pulled out a compact. Once she was certain that she looked presentable, she crossed the street and headed up the sidewalk for the library. She'd go straight to the ladies' room and wash her hands. Then she'd sign in, and at the first spare moment she'd call home and speak to Jerry.

I can't worry Mom about this too. Not without a reason.

"Good morning, Fannie." Mrs. Calloway smiled from behind her desk as Fannie went to the stack of returned books waiting to be shelved.

"Good morning, Mrs. Calloway."

"Is it finally Friday? I swear, some weeks just seem longer. How's everything at the farm?"

Fannie turned her attention to the books for fear Mrs. Calloway could see how unnerved she felt. "All's well. We finished the oats this week. We'll start digging potatoes next."

"I don't know how you manage. How is Calvin? I heard he's home now."

Mrs. Calloway spoke naturally enough, but Fannie was sure there was an underlying curiosity in her tone that really wanted to know what injury sent him home. "He's doing all right for the most part. Making adjustments, you could say. He lost some of his hearing over there."

"I'm so sorry. That must be very hard for him."

"Yes, very. He didn't want to come home."

"No, I'm sure he didn't. Our boys want to stay in the fight and win this war."

Now Fannie did look up. "He's still in the fight, you could say. We all are. We're happy to have him home on the farm."

"I'm sure it's a big relief and a lot of help."

Fannie gave a wan smile rather than answer. She couldn't lie. Thankfully, Mrs. Calloway seemed content to let the conversation drop as she returned to the work on her desk. Fannie pushed the cart of books off to return them to the shelves. She passed the magazine rack. She mustn't forget to bring something home for Mom.

The morning dragged on, and Fannie was worried that if she called home during her first break, Jerry would be out somewhere and she'd miss him. She didn't want to make more than one call, or Mom would start to wonder. She would force herself to wait until lunchtime, when she'd likely catch Jerry at the house.

When the noon hour finally struck, she hurried to ask Mrs. Calloway if she could use the telephone. After the woman excused herself from the office to give Fannie privacy, she placed the call.

"Hello," Mom answered.

"Hi, Mom. Is Jerry around the house by chance?"

"Fannie. You never call from work. Is everything all right?"

"I just wanted to ask Jerry a question. It's kind of a surprise for him and Patsy," she said, grabbing at the excuse of mentioning the movies playing if necessary. "I don't want to mention it to Patsy until I come home, but I thought I'd better check with Jerry right away."

"He just came in for lunch. Let me get him for you." Mom must've pressed a hand over the receiver, for her voice calling Jerry to the phone was muffled.

"Hullo?"

"Jerry, I have a question, but you mustn't let on what I'm talking about."

"What is it?" he said after a moment.

"If Mom asks, I'm talking to you about going to the movies—*The Adventures of Mark Twain*. A surprise for Patsy."

SEASON OF MY ENEMY

"All right. Just spit it out."

She had to pose her question carefully in case an operator or anyone else was on the line. "Remember that handy tool we left in the truck? It isn't there. Did you put it away?"

A prolonged silence had her heart chugging its way down to the roots of her stomach. She heard Jerry exhale. "No. I didn't," he said at last. "I've never seen it." *Good boy.* But not the answer she'd hoped for.

"You didn't maybe put it back in the shed or even take it in the house?"

"No. Never did."

"You know what this means?"

"Maybe Cal wants to go too."

Was he suggesting that Cal took the gun? The idea had crossed Fannie's mind, so naturally Jerry wondered too.

"Okay. Well, you look around and see if you can find it. Don't mention it to anyone though. We'll talk when I get home."

"Of course, I won't. Sounds good."

She set the phone on its cradle and stood alone for a moment in the librarian's office. If she didn't take the gun, and Jerry hadn't taken the gun. . . And if it turned out Cal hadn't taken the gun either, then who had?

⊰ CHAPTER 19 ⊱

A breeze puffed out Wolf's shirt around his torso, but it was a heavy wind, hot and muggy with little cooling effect. There'd been a few distant rolls of thunder earlier, but nothing had come of the clouds scooting by north of them. Surely such oppressive heat portended rain, and with it, relief.

Wolf leaned against the barn shed and squinted at the sky as he awaited Private Vicks's distribution of their lunches. Corporal Taft stood speaking to Jerry O'Brien near the truckload of beans piled high in burlap bags nearly bursting from their seams. The other men lounged around the yard, some in the narrow shade of the roof like him, others filling their canteens at the pump or making their way to the privy.

The beans were played out. These later ones were thicker-skinned than those of the early pickings. Fannie said this would be their last big picking and that the family would handle any cleanup pickings to keep and can for their own larder.

He considered her again with surreptitious glances. She had taken full charge over recent weeks. Early on, she'd remained aloof, preferring Jerry to carry out many of her directives, but now she stepped fully into the lead role here on her farm. It was almost as though her brother over there on the porch didn't figure into things anymore.

"We'll begin digging potatoes after lunch," she announced, as Taft handed Wolf his sack of foodstuffs. She stood only a short way off, raising a metal cup to her lips after she'd spoken. He unwrapped another spam salad sandwich, just like they'd eaten every day this week, and watched her drink down the cup completely then wipe water from her lower lip with her fingertips. Her gaze caught his.

With a sidelong glance, she strolled over. A small smile slipped out. "Spam again, Captain?"

He pretended to give his sandwich a quick study, turning it sideways. "Mm. Good stuff." He took a huge bite, stuffing his cheeks and reveling in her light laughter.

"Soon as it cools down a little, Mom intends to cook a pot roast and shred it up for buns. I'm sure she's planning to share it."

Wolf couldn't help glancing toward Calvin in his usual place on the porch with both his gun and a bottle. Their gazes met. "And your brother? I suspect he would prefer our diets contain only this pink meat."

Her smile turned into a smirk. "I think you're right. But as Calvin isn't doing anything to help around here, he has no say in the matter." Her lips turned up again and her glance was coy, raising lightness in Wolf's chest.

An engine sputtered then roared to life over near the side of the barn, capturing their attention. A cheer among the workers followed. Fannie's brother Jerry clapped Horst on the shoulder where the two stood over the folded-back hood of a rusty Model A Ford that Wolf had never seen run. Both younger men were grinning and nodding as they congratulated one another in a mix of languages enough to make themselves understood.

"He finally did it," Fannie said as she watched the pair lean over the engine again. But her brilliant smile captivated Wolf. "He's been trying to get that thing running all year."

He studied her profile. "Horst is good with engines. They make a good team."

Her brow twitched, but there was a long pause before she acknowledged his remark. "They do at that," she said softly. "Your men have many talents, I'm certain." Then she glanced at him, and before he could respond, she shifted and walked away, leaving him to wonder at her cryptic reply.

An hour later, Wolf worked his way up a long row of potato plants. He pushed his booted foot against his shovel's blade, crunching it into the loosely mounded soil around the vegetation, but careful not to slice into any of the white flesh of the potatoes beneath the surface. Gently, he pried the plant from the earth, then quickly scooped up a half dozen big potatoes and put them in his gunnysack. He used the shovel again to sift the dirt, then raked it with his fingers, just to make sure he hadn't missed any stragglers. After collecting a few smaller potatoes, he moved on to the next plant. A few feet away, Leo worked through the same process.

Sweat streamed dirt streaks down the sides of Leo's neck, which Wolf noted when Leo lifted his chin with a sneer on his lips. "All this work for money that is useless outside of a prison. *Scrip.* Not even real money."

"At least it is something. More than what your family might have to see them through right now in Germany."

Leo seared him with a narrow look before tossing a potato into his sack with a thud. "Forgive me for not being grateful, Hauptmann. I find it ironic that we are here in a foreign country, prisoners forced to labor for our enemy, and you are content to do so. I do not know the condition of my family, but I do know that they are not eating from the hand of those who wish to destroy them."

"And who is it seeking to destroy them?" Horst piped up from the other side of Wolf. "I doubt it is the Americans."

Leo stopped digging and leaned on his shovel. He wiped a forearm across his jaw. "What are you talking about?"

Horst glanced toward Wolf and away, his eyes glinting with specu-lation that sent warning bells chiming in Wolf's brain. "They say you are Mischlinge." Horst jabbed his shovel into the dirt and spoke with a grunt.

Leo let go of his shovel and lunged, but he'd barely grasped Horst's dirty T-shirt when Wolf shouldered between them and grabbed hold of Leo's arm, straining to hold him back.

"You heard him," Leo said, his words seething between clenched teeth. "It is a dirty word."

"Shritt auseinander!" The distinct, heavy click of a rifle being bolted reached Wolf's ears even before the American corporal's command to step apart. Taft charged toward them, his gun at his shoulder. Wolf drew his hands back and stepped clear immediately, hoping that Leo had sense enough to respond in the same fashion. Leo lingered, his glare on Horst, who stared back, fists unfolding as he raised his hands at his side. "I said back! Now!" Corporal Taft centered the gun on Leo's chest from only three paces away.

Leo raised his hands and took a backward step with a shrug. "I am not the one causing the trouble."

"I'll decide that. Now get your shovel and get back to work. Any more problems and you'll all get sent back and put in lockdown. Under-stood? *Verstanden?*"

Leo rubbed his jaw with a half nod. "Verstanden." He gave another scowl at Horst.

"Ja, *Kapitän*," Horst said.

"I'll be watching you." Corporal Taft glanced at Wolf, and Wolf acquiesced with a nod, then bent to retrieve his shovel from where he'd let it fall. The corporal moved a dozen feet away, but his eyes remained narrowed on their activity.

"That was foolish," Wolf said in a low tone as he dug another potato plant. "I expect better self-control from my men, Obergefreiter Friedrickson. And you, Horst, would be wise to keep colorful remarks to yourself."

"When was I ever one of your men?"

Leo's remark grazed over Wolf, bringing him a brief pause, but he chose to ignore it and continued. "While I am the ranking officer here, you will not question my authority unless you wish to be sent back to the main camp."

"I do not wish it, Hauptmann, but if I am called by that name again, I will demand satisfaction."

Wolf tossed another potato into his sack with a cursory glance toward Leo. "And you will be given it, but not here. Do you not think it pleases the Americans to see us fighting among ourselves?"

Leo hefted his full sack of potatoes. "In truth, I do not care what the Americans think." He turned his back and moved down the long row toward the wagon parked at the end.

Wolf dug faster, bringing himself closer to Horst. "Why did you say such a thing?"

"Isn't it obvious?"

"You refer to rumors."

Horst tossed a potato into his bag along with a glance at Wolf. "Not a rumor, Hauptmann. Obergefreiter Friedrickson is a Jew. Everyone knows."

"Everyone? And how do *you* know?"

"Ask Otto. Fritz too. They will tell you. Leo claims that any Jewish blood ever to mingle in his veins was declared void by Hitler himself."

Wolf had heard of such things happening. Of Germany's need for soldiers forcing Hitler to accept Hebrews into the military and then declaring their Jewishness erased.

"Why would Leo do such a thing?"

"He abandoned his family when Germany declared war. He did not wish to be associated with them any longer."

Wolf stopped digging. "For self-preservation, you mean."

Horst dropped to his knees and rested in the black dirt. "He wished to fight for Germany. More than he wished to be a Jew."

Wolf turned toward the western sun, turning his hand around the end of the shovel's handle. *More than he wished to be a Jew.* Leo was willing to give up his own family? Wolf schooled his shock, though it took effort to do so. He scooped the dirt, this time shearing into a potato so that it stuck to the end of the blade. He pried it off. "Are you sure, Horst?"

"Ask him, Hauptmann. That is the only way to be certain."

He nodded absently. His student was right.

Later that evening, after they'd returned to camp and everyone had supped; after some had settled down to read, sleep, or find other recreation, Wolf waved Leo over to him. "I want to speak to you. Walk with me across the compound."

Leo sniffed. "If it is about today, Hauptmann Kloninger, I apologize for losing control."

"Come. Walk."

Wolf steered them toward the perimeter of the camp where they could stroll nonchalantly toward the soccer field. He didn't speak right away but was content to wait until they were clear of any listeners. Leo lit a cigarette and shook out the match. "So, what else is it you wish to say to me?"

"I wish to ask you if the rumors about you are true."

"You mean that I am what they say? A Jewish-German mongrel?"

"I wouldn't say that. But is there some part of your heritage you are ashamed of?"

Leo peered across the soccer field and flicked an ash. "I think Otto will become a very good player if he is given the opportunity to continue after the war." He nodded, keeping his thoughts to himself. Then he finally faced Wolf squarely. "My grandmother was a Jew. My father's mother. It is a fact I've worked hard to keep concealed." He took a drag of his cigarette and blew smoke out in a long stream. "Being of pure German blood yourself, you can understand why I would do that, can't you, Hauptmann? And now you will treat me differently because of it, I am sure."

Wolf shook his head. "No. You are wrong. I treat all the men under my command equally, unless they behave in such a way that forces me to act differently. Your lineage has no bearing on it whatsoever."

Leo laughed derisively. "Be careful, Hauptmann. The SS would disagree with you on that."

"How is it you have been able to serve in the army, Obergefreiter? Did you falsify your papers?"

He finished another long pull on the cigarette and ground it out beneath the toe of his shoe. "No. Our Führer declared my blood to be German, as he did for other Jews willing to fight for him." He gave Wolf a challenging gaze. "He was desperate for fighters. As I was second-degree Mischlinge, I was a good candidate."

Wolf considered Hitler's decree, comparing it to what Horst told him earlier about Leo's decision. The German ranks, once so full of proud, strong men, had depleted over the long years of fighting. Hitler had made many outlandish declarations, and few were brave enough to challenge him. So why not proclaim that he had power to wipe away the Jewish blood of a man and deem him Aryan, as long as such a decree fit with his designs?

"What of your family?"

A puff of air rushed out Leo's nostrils. "I am dead to them." His voice sounded as lifeless as the words he spoke. "My father refused to have anything to do with me after I enlisted. For all I know, they might all be dead."

The callousness of his tone sounded real. Did he truly not care anything for the fate of his family? "You have brothers and sisters?"

His gaze drifted to the field again. "A brother. He is older, married. He has three children. I haven't seen him in six years."

"What did he think of your joining the fight? Did he join also?"

Leo chuckled without humor. "He raged at me. Now?" He shrugged. "I do not know, nor do I care."

"I see."

Leo looked at Wolf. "I doubt that you do, but you'll say so." He lingered for a moment then reached into his pocket for another cigarette. "Is that it, Hauptmann? Or is there more you wish to ask me?"

"What will you do when the war is over?"

Leo lit a match and held it until it burned down to his fingertips, then dropped it without lighting the cigarette. "I will bask in the glory of victory like all good Germans." He lit another match, and this time his cigarette. He took a drag as he shook out his match, then let out a stream of smoke. "Truthfully, I don't think about it. There's no point. We don't know what we will return to." He swung a half smile at Wolf. "The war goes on and on. There is plenty of time to decide."

"I hope you are not right about that."

He flicked off an ash and smiled as though a wizened old man. "I am right, Hauptmann."

≡CHAPTER 20≡

The gun was still missing. Fannie and Jerry had searched everywhere. Jerry had even sneaked into Cal's room and looked for it there, and he'd watched for Cal to be carrying it, but there was no sign that their dad's pistol existed. After exhausting searches in every possible hiding place they could think of around the house, in and near the barn, sheds—and even the outhouse—they decided it must have been secreted somewhere in one of the fields or perhaps along the edge of the woods. Maybe even buried. There were hundreds of places it could have been hidden.

Or more likely, someone had taken it back to the internment camp.

"We have to tell Corporal Taft, Jerry." They were behind closed doors at the front of the barn in the toolshed. Fannie shook out a gunnysack and laid it neatly on the stack, then reached for another from the heap.

Jerry propped his hip against the workbench and folded his arms. "We don't even know how long it's been missing. Sure, it might have disappeared the day of the fire, but it could have been gone longer than that. I stopped thinking about Dad's gun weeks ago."

Fannie nodded. "I know."

"What point is there in telling the corporal now? Wouldn't the thief have done something with it already, especially if they've had it for weeks?"

"There's no telling. What if they use it to harm someone at the camp like Corporal Taft or Private Vicks? I'd feel awful. It could end up with someone at one of the canning factories and cause serious violence and sabotage."

"They're probably planning an escape. I doubt they intend to actually use it. They only want it as a prop. . .a threat." He peered past her out the dusty window, as though watching such a scene take place.

"A threat that could get somebody killed. What if it was Mom or Patsy? Jerry, we have to tell."

"You know what will happen." He turned from the window.

Yes, she knew. "We'll lose our workers." She thought of not seeing Wolf again. Maybe ever. Somehow, it had to come to that.

"We're not finished digging potatoes, and we've got a lot of corn, even with what we lost."

She shook out another bag. Dust clouded the already dim light in the room. "I guess we'll just have to handle the picking ourselves."

Jerry sighed. "That's a lot of work, Fan. I'm about farmed out."

She dropped the bag she held and stepped over the heap to place a hand on his shoulder. "It'll be sunup to sundown for a while, but we'll get it done. Then school will start up again, and you can have a well-deserved rest. Play some football with your friends."

"Sounds like a different life." His brows drew together. "Fan, do you think we should tell Mom? About the gun, I mean? Before we talk to Taft? Seems like she ought to know. She can help decide what to do."

"I don't know." Fannie shook her head. It felt heavy though she wasn't physically tired. She was weary of making the decisions. Worn out from being in charge.

"I think we should," Jerry said.

"I hate to load that kind of worry on her."

"She'll worry either way. It's what moms do. You shouldn't have to decide how to handle this alone."

"I have you." She gave him a weak grin.

"And we should tell Cal too. He still doesn't know about the fire. I think it's time to let the chips fall. Maybe he'll wake up a little bit, and maybe Taft will want his help guarding the prisoners out in the field. Might be the safer thing."

She shook her head. "No. If Mom decides to tell Cal about the fire, that's one thing, but unless he volunteers to help pick, we're keeping quiet about it. I don't trust him not to go wild."

"What about the Germans? Do you trust most of them? I mean, if they're going to keep coming here to work?"

As if beckoned, the familiar sound of the transport truck rumbled up the drive. Jerry moved toward the door but waited on her answer.

"Pray for me, Jerry. I want to believe the best—concerning most of them anyway. They seem like us. Just men stuck in a bad situation."

"I know what you mean. It's not what I expected to think about them."

"I want to do the right thing."

He nodded and went out to meet the truck.

The workers headed straight to the potato field, but Fannie made herself scarce by checking the corn. A heavy rain a few nights ago and a lot of hot weather the past few days meant the sweet corn would ripen fast. There was a smaller crop of field corn for the pigs and chickens. They would cut that and get it in the crib themselves in October after it had a lower moisture content. But the sweet corn was war corn, heading straight to the canning factory where more German workers would see it canned and sent off to Europe—to their American boys.

She strode into the thickest of the crop, glad to be sheltered by the tall stalks and tassels that rustled in the heat above her head. The air was cooler here, and her thoughts drew close, protected. She examined the cobs, felt their plumpness or lack thereof, yet her hands moved over them with only half her attention. Her thoughts still lingered over what to do about the missing gun. About Calvin. . .again. . .and the crops that still needed tending. About Mom and how badly they all missed Dad. And then about Dale. Was he well? Was he safe? When would they see him again—or wouldn't they?

"What should we do, God?" Fannie whispered. Then the gate of her heart broke open, and all her questions and needs poured out. She prayed for Dale first and then about all the rest. There was a good long time and a lot of pleading before she admitted her deepest longings. "I want to feel safe again, and I won't if we don't find Dad's missing gun. Yet. . ." She let out a shuddering breath as she fingered a long blade of corn. "I don't want the prisoners sent away. Not *all* of them. Just the bad ones. If there even are any bad ones, God."

She reached the edge of the corn that came out to the large burned section. She could still smell the char. "But if there are. . .if someone is intending to hurt us. . .please, don't let it be Rudy or. . ." She was about to go down a list of their names, all the boys who'd helped them this summer. But there was really only one she was thinking of, and she couldn't hide that from God. "Please don't let it be Wolf."

Wolfgang Kloninger. She mulled over what she knew about him. He was a teacher. A leader. A man who cared about those under his charge. Someone who seemed to love peace and education—or so he'd said and acted as if he did. Was it the honest truth? She prayed so again.

To her surprise, she felt better by the time she'd circled through the rest of the field. She kept a lookout for signs of the gun, to no avail.

Maybe she shouldn't be surprised at the new calm she felt. She'd been taught that prayer settled heart and mind, but she hadn't expected to feel anything like that, especially without having any answers. Yet, as she mulled over the dilemma, she realized she'd come to at least one conclusion. She would tell Mom about the missing gun. Jerry was right. Mom wasn't a flower. She'd buried a husband and watched her boys go off to war. One of them was in harm's way even now. Still Mom soldiered on. She would want to know. What's more, just like with the fire, she might know best how to handle the problem.

Fannie thanked God for the subtle direction and marched toward home. Cal was just stepping onto the porch with a cup of coffee in his hand. He leaned his gun against the side of the house and took a seat, then drew a slow sip from his cup.

Fannie waved and he raised a hand. She strode across the yard to the bottom step and faced him where he could see her and read her lips. "Nice out today. We'll finish the potatoes."

He shrugged. His gaze flicked toward the potato field. She wasn't sure if he understood her or not.

She pointed back at the corn. "It's almost ready. Soon."

"Some of it is ripe now."

Her pulse pricked. "You checked it?" Had he seen the site of the burn?

"Some."

He must not have gone in far enough. "You going to help us pick it?"

He took another sip of coffee.

"Cal!"

He jerked his gaze at her.

"You gonna help?"

He stared back blandly and slurped his coffee. He understood her question. His lack of answer was answer enough.

"You can't even see those PWs in the corn from here. What good will you do sitting here on the porch? They can't see you either. You don't even have the benefit of intimidation. You didn't even see the fire."

His features tightened. "What fire?" So, he'd understood that well enough.

She flipped a loose coil of hair off her cheek. "The fire that took out a section of the corn crop. But don't worry yourself now." She said it easily as a way to brush off the danger, then went on. "It was an accident, but the prisoners helped get it put out."

"Slow down. Why am I just learning about this now? When did it happen?"

She narrowed her eyes. "You didn't want to know. You never want to know. Why not make yourself truly useful? Don't you care?" It was a mouthful, and she doubted he caught much—not that he was always even looking at her speak—but he couldn't miss her aggravation. Especially when she spun on her heel and marched back toward the shed. "Some of us have to work." He would never hear that.

"I'll work when I need to. Right now, you have men at your beck and call to do that." His voice hit her like a board across the backside.

She wheeled back. "We need *you*, Cal." She pointed first toward the working men in the far field. "Yes, we need the PWs. We don't have any choice." Then she jabbed her finger at Cal. "But *you're* the man of the family now. How do you think I feel having to order around all these men? Is that what you want, Cal, for me to run this place? Dad expected more of you, and so did the rest of us."

He didn't move, but by his searing gaze and grinding jaw, she could see she'd struck a chord. Then he leaned back in his chair and ignored her.

She slumped her shoulders and turned away. She was through catering to Calvin's feelings about the prisoners. There might indeed be a saboteur among them. But just maybe they were only trying to make it through the roughest spot in their lives, just like she and her family were. She wasn't going to treat them all like criminals. If any of them was culpable, she'd just have to leave it in God's hands.

She took long strides down the cobbled path to the barn, grabbing up water pails by the hand pump and going to the water spigot inside. Cranking the knob, she filled the pails. It was going to be another cooker. The workers would need their canteens refilled well before a midday break. And another thing: she was going to ask Patsy to put together a tray of those biscuits she'd made yesterday to go with the sack lunches they'd brought, and to slather the biscuits with some fresh butter. Mom wouldn't mind.

Showing kindness might be the best way to keep them all safe. Let Cal have something to say about that if he wanted to. Taking Jerry's advice, she'd let the chips fall.

She plopped the water dipper into one of the buckets, her spent energy having burned away some of her anger at Cal. When she carried the pails past the front of the house toward the potato field—which suddenly looked a long way off—the barest glance informed her that Cal no longer sat on the porch. His rifle was gone too. When she was halfway to the field, the family car sped off down the drive, kicking up a wake of dust.

There went Cal, furious no doubt.

Otto was the first to come meet her, relieving her of the heavy pails. She'd lost only about an inch of water on the trek. "Danke," she said, even though she knew he understood *thank you* in English.

He smiled. "Not trouble."

If only you knew. She shaded her eyes to look over the field and almost immediately found Wolf plopping potatoes into his sack. He caught her gaze and offered her a nod and a smile.

She wanted to walk over to him and say hello, but she reined in the impulse. She went to Corporal Taft instead. "How is everything going today, Corporal?"

"Won't be long until they finish."

"My thoughts exactly. I checked the corn. Cal did too. We think some of it's ready to pick. Maybe we'll try a bit for supper tonight and get a go on it first thing Saturday."

Fritz came over for a drink. His wavy hair was wet. It looked like he'd used some of his canteen water to cool down on the outside.

"Patsy and I'll send out some biscuits at lunchtime," Fannie said. "Maybe by then the men would like to cool down at the pump."

"A good idea." Wolf's voice startled her from behind, but she recognized it before she saw him. She turned about with more pleasure than she meant to reveal. Yet she could not keep from smiling and being happy to speak to him.

"It's going to be terribly hot out today, I'm afraid. A day more suited to reading in the shade than digging potatoes. I'm sure that's what my sister will be doing."

"There will be other days for taking such pleasures again. Today we must finish with your potatoes. It is a good crop, ja?"

"Yes. Very good." She glanced at the bulging gunnysacks piled onto the wagon.

"And the corn will be next."

"Some of it is ready now." An idea sprang to mind. Something they'd done for the migrant workers in the past. "In fact, we'll plan on a big corn boil for lunch on Saturday. I'm sure Corporal Taft, being from Iowa, would enjoy that." She smiled at the corporal.

"That I would. Not sure your Wisconsin corn can measure up to corn from home, but I'm sure I wouldn't complain."

Fannie laughed. "We'll see about that. You'll be getting the first of the season. That'll be some mighty tender eating."

"With fresh butter?"

"The freshest."

Even Fritz smiled as he reached for a drink, and Fannie noted what a nice smile it was. She hadn't seen him smile since. . . Well, not in a very long time. She directed herself toward him. "You've been well? All of you?" she added.

He nodded, then dropped the dipper back into the pail and turned to go back to work. Wolf reached for the dipper. "He is. . .healthy." She could tell he was thinking of the right word. "He is most worried for his girl, Emma. Afraid of hardship for her family."

"I'm sorry. I guess we all have those we worry about." Who suffered the most need right now? The people of Europe? The soldiers? Dale?

"Ja." He drank down the dipperful and lowered it back into the pail without splashing. With another grateful nod, he took a step away, but Fannie wanted to stop him. To say. . .something.

"I'll pray for his family. And yours. For all of you."

He placed a hand on his chest. "Danke. Danke very much, Fannie."

She tried not to blush beneath the corporal's scrutiny but then decided she didn't care what he thought. She raised her chin. "I have work back at the house, but I won't forget to send out those biscuits later."

She returned with lighter steps. Mom was sweeping off the porch when Fannie arrived. Maybe now was the time to tell her about the missing gun. "Where did Cal go? I saw him taking off in the car."

"He didn't say."

"Maybe he's going to call on Liza." It was a stretch and just something to say. Since he returned, he hadn't mentioned the girl he used to squire around. Chances were, he wouldn't go to see her on a busy morning when she'd probably be at work.

"Something must've happened between them. Maybe with his injury. . ." Mom seemed to sweep away the rest of her thought with the dust.

"I wonder if he's afraid to tell her. Maybe she doesn't know."

Mom stalled with the broom and peered at Fannie. "I wonder if you're right."

Fannie shrugged. "Who knows what Cal thinks these days?"

"Be patient, Fannie. He'll come around eventually. It's a big change for him, and remember, he's faced the Germans over trenches with guns firing all around. He has a hard time seeing them as anything but the enemy."

"What about you, Mom? Do you still see them that way?"

She made slow, light sweeps. "In part. But in part, they're just boys."

"Men, you mean."

"Yes, men. Men caught up in this terrible war."

"Maybe they fought Cal and Dale. Maybe they're responsible for Dale's capture."

"I doubt it. Not with the millions of men fighting all over this earth. But even if they were, they had no choice. Just like Cal and Dale didn't have a choice. I pray for all of them. I pray for peace."

"That's how you manage, isn't it?"

Mom smiled tenderly at Fannie. "You've learned."

Fannie nodded. "Mom, I—"

The door swung open and Patsy stepped out. She plopped down in Cal's regular place, book in hand. "Can I go to work with you on Friday, Fannie? I'm almost done with my books. I need some new ones."

"Sure. If Mom doesn't need you here."

"It'll be fine," Mom said. "But don't get comfortable now, young lady. We're going to go down in the root cellar and clean it out. We've got potatoes going in there today."

Patsy groaned, but she perked up a moment later. "At least it'll be cool in there."

Mom chuckled. "That's right. A silver lining."

Fannie turned to go. "I'd take your chore any day, Patsy. I'm off to sort through bushel baskets. Oh—I promised the corporal and workers a corn boil on Saturday. Is that all right?"

"If the corn is ready, I'll be ready," Mom answered.

"Oh, yeah! Corn on the cob!" Patsy stood back up, apparently energized by the thought.

Fannie laughed as she strolled away. She would talk to Mom about the gun later. She slowed as she neared the end of the cobblestones, glancing for the hundredth time at the rock that Mom had resettled but skipping over it out of habit. Sometimes she forgot that it wasn't wobbly anymore. It had settled into the earth just like God's peace had settled into her heart while she prayed. Maybe she would lay a stone of her own in that path before long.

The stacks of bushel baskets were kept in the smaller storage room at the back of the barn shed. They'd need them to pick the corn, but they were full of dust and cobwebs from the previous year. Fannie drew them into the main room, then found a rag to wipe them out, making sure each one was sound for picking tomorrow. She'd only just finished when she heard Corporal Taft's whistle. Lunchtime already.

Minutes later, Jerry's voice sounded near the window. "I have to hit the privy. Wait for me here."

Fannie moved the baskets aside in two stacks. The men were going to need more gunnysacks this afternoon too. She might as well bring them out now. She went back into the smaller room and turned to the tidy pile lying in the semi-darkness when she heard a squeak. She sometimes thought of how the barn door sounded a lot like the squeak of their old windmill, but there was no breeze today.

"Hey, Jer, I—" She swallowed her words as she turned and saw a shadow standing just inside the doorway of the outer room. It was a man, but not Jerry, who jerked about at the sound of her voice, his hands going quickly behind his back.

⧗ CHAPTER 21 ⧗

Leo! She'd startled him, but her own heart jerked erratically. She couldn't make out his expression in the dim light that filtered through the dust-coated window, but she could see how his shoulders tensed and his arms moved from behind to stiffen at his sides. He stepped forward so that the light cast over him better. As she eased out her breath, he gave a chuckle that sounded forced. "You give me surprise."

She stared back stiffly, framed inside the doorway of the tiny back room. Leo stood beside the workbench where the larger tools, equipment, and several cans of gasoline were within reach. It shouldn't matter. He'd been in here before while collecting shovels and putting things away. *Was he told to come here now?* His shoulders relaxed, and then he pushed a hand through sweaty curls.

"What are you doing in here?" she demanded. She spoke to him with more force than she had in some time, but she saw no other way to keep her voice from shaking.

He shifted his stance casually and directed his glance beyond her. *"Säcke."*

Of course. She half-peered over her shoulder—crazily—she knew the sacks lay behind her right next to the old forge, but she didn't want to meet him eye to eye. His shadowed stare unnerved her, and her heartbeat only quickened. Her pulse sped faster than ever as he shuffled forward another step.

She moved aside, clearing the way to the stack of burlap bags. She could skirt past him and wait at the door. He paused, his features at once questioning and deciding. When he moved as if to angle his body away and come alongside her, so did Fannie, but she followed his movement

183

rather than look away toward the door—her means of escape. And then she spied it. The grip of her father's pistol jutted from the belt of his pants at the back of his waist where he'd concealed it when he came through the door. She only glimpsed it, yet she had no doubt.

And like lightning flashing through her brain, Fannie knew where it had been all this time.

Her intake of breath stopped him, and he stepped in front of her, preventing her flight. His gaze darkened, if that were even possible. He knew she'd seen.

"You took it. You stole it out of the truck."

"I don't know what you're talking about."

Fannie's lip quivered. "You hid it under the cobblestone." She should have known sooner! She should have at least remarked about the stone to Mom.

Fannie made to charge past him, but his hands shot out. He clutched the strap of her overalls and snaked an arm around her. The strength of his arm as he drew her back against him pushed her wind out, and he clapped his other hand over her mouth. With strength that surprised her, he forced her into the smaller room.

No! No! Fannie tried to yank her mouth free as she pushed against him, planting her feet on the floor and struggling, but he was too strong. His arms were like iron banded around her. With her free hand, she grabbed the doorframe between the rooms, but with a shove that made her fingers bleed, he pushed her through, never loosening his grip.

He breathed heavily, and she could feel the throb of his heart against her back. "Do not be foolish, Fannie. This does not have to end badly."

For whom? she wanted to ask, but she couldn't. She sucked hard for air, pulling back to free her nostrils, but he clenched his dirty hand tighter. She clawed at it, and finally he moved his fingers enough for her to pull in a breath.

"Be still," he growled again, but she promised him nothing.

No more did she feel his arm loosen around her than she recognized the steel end of the gun in her ribs. The gun gave Leo the desired effect. She fell very still. Only her breath panting out her nose and her heartbeat shattering her ribs sounded in her ears.

Now his lips touched her ear, and he whispered, "If you do not shout, I will let go."

Where is Jerry? Where are the others? Mama. . . Tears stung her eyes, but she swallowed against the flood pressing up inside. She wouldn't give

Leo the pleasure of knowing how frightened she was. She nodded.

With measured slowness, he drew back his hand and turned her to face him. She glanced down at the gun pointing at her stomach, its barrel the only thing separating them. Then he stroked her jaw from her ear to her chin and pushed back the tendrils of her hair. She clamped her lips together and breathed hard through her nostrils as he pushed her scarf back so that it fell from her hair.

"You look more Mischlinge than I do."

"I—I do not know that word." She strained to keep her voice at a whisper.

"Do you not? It means. . ." He squinted as if searching for an English word he knew to compare. "A dog of no breed. It is what it means to have your blood mixed with the Jews." His voice hardened on the word.

Shock spiraled deeper. *Leo. . . Jewish!* She'd read news stories and listened to the radio reports that spoke of Hitler's hatred of the Jews and how he deemed them subhuman. Such irrational thinking, the entire notion that some people still thought of others that way, made Fannie's skin crawl. Could Leo really mean that he himself was not as Aryan as his Führer dictated all Germany should be? She shot him a hard look, studied him with renewed curiosity that mingled with her fear. "Hitler called them a name."

"Untermenschen."

She didn't know that word either, but she could guess its meaning by the ugly way he said it.

He stroked her jaw again, and she jerked her head away. "Your eyes, your hair. . ." He let strands sift through his fingers. "Even your skin. . . You could pass for one of them. In Germany I could tell them you are Jewish and you would have to prove otherwise."

She'd not known he spoke so much English. She fought the trembling that threatened to collapse her knees. "Is that what you did? Proved otherwise?"

He tweaked her chin. Then he leaned close enough to breathe the scent of her skin, causing her to shudder. His breath tickled her ears. "I did not have to. My blood is no longer unclean." His lips brushed the fine hairs on her neck.

Her heart slammed against the gun still grinding her ribs. "Don't." She could hear the weeping in her own voice.

He chuckled and trailed his fingers around the back of her neck, then gripped it painfully, steering her farther into the room with their pressure while he pressed the gun barrel harder to move her forward.

When her toe caught on the pile of burlap and she nearly tripped into the heap, panic screamed through her. At the same moment, she heard Jerry's voice outside, calling Leo's name. Leo stepped back, releasing the gun from her rib cage as he glanced toward the door. Fannie gulped for breath. She didn't care anymore if Leo shot her. She was more afraid of what would happen to her brother. "Please. Don't hurt him."

Leo leered at her again, a look in his eyes that burned her with its loathing. "If you don't want him hurt, then do as I say."

Her throat tightened, but she nodded.

He aimed the gun at the door.

Should she charge him? Try to knock the gun away? What if it went off? Should she scream anyway? What did he intend to do if she didn't stop him? Now that she'd caught him with the gun, did he really have any intention of quietly leaving her here?

Someone is going to die.

Through the blood-pounding muffle of her thoughts, she heard others. The porch screen door squeaked. Had Mom and Patsy come up from the root cellar? *No! Stay!* And then men's voices. *Wolf.*

"He must be getting the bags." *Jerry!* "I'll check."

"Wolf!" His name tore from Fannie's lungs, and she tried to shove Leo, but he was immovable. "Wo—"

Leo spun so quickly she had no time to react. He cracked her sideways with the pistol across the skull, sending her toppling into the stack of burlap. Her head smacked against the wall, and a wave of dizziness turned the room on end.

The door burst open, and a shot fired.

Fannie screamed. Didn't she? Was it her voice that rang out after the gunshot, right before she descended into darkness?

She knew, as she came around, that only moments had passed. She was as dizzy as ever, and the haze before her was a combination of the strike to her head and the dust rising in the room. Bodies grappled, and she drew both feet back as they tumbled next to her.

"Jer. . ." She murmured, but she wasn't sure it was Jerry there. Was Jerry all right? Had he been shot? *Wolf. Leo.*

As her focus cleared, she made them out. Wolf and Leo, tumbling in the shadowy space, crashing against the cans of gas and then the workbench. Tools clattering to the floor. Blood on knuckles and cuts on faces. Rage on Wolf's as he glanced her way for a quarter second, his blue eyes blazing. Leo, with blood streaming from both nostrils, locked in battle against his captain. Wolf's fists beating him into submission.

And the gun spinning just out of her reach. She dragged herself forward on elbows and stretched fingers until she touched the metal then clasped it. She collapsed into a circle and pulled the gun under her body, hugging it where it could fall into no enemy's hands.

Then suddenly everything cleared. Other voices rushed in, and a bigger boom exploded just outside the door. Calvin shouldered in as the two men fell apart, both of them panting on the floor. He had his rifle pressed into his shoulder, and Fannie smelled the hot metal and gunpowder of its firing. Behind Cal came Corporal Taft with his pistol cocked also.

Wolf slid over closer to Fannie and raised both of his hands. Leo's hands came up slower.

Wolf peered at her, heedless of the weapon pointed at him. "Are you all right?"

She stared for a moment, taking him in. He'd saved her. She placed a hand on her head where a welt throbbed beneath her fingertips, but she nodded. "I think so."

"Get up, you scum." Cal spoke to both Germans at once. Did he not see what Wolf had done? "Get up off the ground and move."

Wolf rose. He glanced at Leo, who seemed nearly as dazed as Fannie. Wolf stretched out his hand to her.

Cal surged forward and shoved him with the butt of his rifle. "Get your hands off her."

Wolf's stomach convulsed at the jab, but he didn't resist or argue. He merely looked at her, then at Cal before he shuffled toward the door and into the sunlight with Calvin a pace behind, the gun still trained on Wolf's back.

"What happened?" Mom's voice, just outside, sounded frightened.

Fannie moved to get up, drawing the gun with her, but she ended up settling back onto the pile of gunnysacks. Nausea crept up her insides.

"Fan?" Jerry poked his head in the doorway as Corporal Taft hoisted Leo by the upper arm.

Taft gave Leo a shove toward the doorway. "I'm really sorry about this, Miss O'Brien," he said, his eyes glued to his prisoner.

"Fan?" Jerry rushed to her side. A moment later, Mom was inside too.

Fannie cradled her head. "Dad's gun, Jerry." She stretched out her legs, exposing the pistol lying on her lap. He reached for it and moved it out of harm's way.

"Fannie!" Mom gulped a sob and hurried to her. Together, Mom and Jerry raised her to her feet. "What did they do to you? What happened?"

"I'll be fine."

She limped with them past the window.

"You have a bruise!"

It felt like a lot more than a bruise. Her temple throbbed violently, and suddenly she knew she was going to throw up. "Mom. . ." She mumbled and turned her head.

Jerry stepped back, still holding her arm. "Don't worry. It'll make you feel better."

She would have laughed if she didn't want to cry so.

Stepping out of the hot, heavy air of the shed, Fannie stopped walking. She braced herself against Jerry and looked at the lot of prisoners standing at attention. Cal kept them under guard while Corporal Taft locked Leo in cuffs, Wolf standing beside him.

Fannie shook free from Mom and Jerry. She swiped the back of her hand over her mouth and trudged toward them. When she reached the cobblestone path, she gave the stone the barest glance, taking in its shifted position and the freshly loosened soil around it. She didn't have to step on it to know that it wobbled again.

She walked on. Without a word, she touched Cal's arm and brushed past.

"Fannie."

She ignored him and stopped before Wolf, whose wrists were being cuffed by Corporal Taft. Tears welled into her eyes anew as they looked at one another. "Danke."

His gaze held a depth of some emotion she couldn't begin to identify. Grief? Regret? Something. . .more? "I am sorry I could not stop him sooner."

"Climb up." Taft took him by the arm and steered him toward the back of the transport.

Fannie stepped back, and Wolf obeyed.

Leo sat inside in the far left corner of the truck, staring out but at no one in particular until his dark gaze clapped upon hers. Then he pursed his lips and silently kissed the air between them. His gray eyes went dull then, unrepentant as ever, though dirt smeared his face and blood stained his upper lip. A blue welt that matched her own swelled the temple above one eye.

Cal rushed forward and raised his weapon higher. "Try that again. I dare you."

Leo smirked then turned his face away.

Wolf sat in the near corner, as far removed from Leo as could be.

"He saved me," Fannie said to Corporal Taft and Cal together. "Wolf—Captain Kloninger saved me from Leo."

"I'll make a note of it," Taft said as he turned to the rest of the prisoners. "Get in."

They all filed past, some with eyes to the ground. Only Rudy and Richard Schorr took a glimpse of her. She wanted to offer them some thanks, some. . .thing. But why? Because she cared? And should she? Would any of them have done what Leo had done if given half a chance?

No. They had the same chance. The same opportunity.

Corporal Taft closed them in and strode back to her. "Do you have any idea where he got the gun, Miss O'Brien? I have to ask. Did you give it to him?"

She blanched. A new wave of dizziness assailed her. Thankfully, Calvin wasn't standing where he could read Corporal Taft's lips. She turned her back so that her brother couldn't see hers either. "Of course not, Corporal. It's my father's. Leo stole it out of the truck. We think during the fire. I was going to tell you."

"Were you?" He let the question hang there until she frowned.

"Of course. We—*I*—only just discovered it missing. The day of the fire—that's the only time that makes sense of when he might have taken it. We don't know for sure."

"I understand. Just doing my job. You won't have to worry about it happening again."

"The workers. . ." She stepped forward, urgency filling her tone as her gaze crossed the field of corn waving against the low-hanging sun.

"I'm sorry, miss. I don't foresee you getting them back."

"I see."

Jerry stood beside her. She hadn't even noticed him approach. "It's okay, Fannie. We'll manage." He turned to Calvin. "Won't we, Cal? We'll manage the corn picking." He nodded at the field.

Calvin lowered his weapon, cradling it in his arms. He cast a furtive glance at the prisoners in the back of the truck and then at his family, spread out like a wing before him. "Yeah. We'll pick the corn. I'll help."

A gush of relief and sorrow, a year of pent-up fears, all swept out of Fannie in a moment. And now she just needed to find a place to sit.

CHAPTER 22

October 1944

"It's very bad. Or very good, depending on how you look at it." Fritz held the letter in front of him. He'd not been so talkative in weeks. Months even. Hearing from Emma had changed him overnight. He'd been carrying her letter around for forty-eight hours and pulled it out of his pocket every chance he got to read it again.

"Oh?" Wolf tugged his woolen socks on and reached for a shoe. "Explain what you mean."

"It's either very bad—the way the war is going for Germany. Or it is very good, because if they surrender, we will be sent home soon."

"Do you think so?"

Fritz grinned ear to ear. "I can hope for anything now."

Wolf tied his shoes and stood. He gave Fritz a solid pat on the shoulder. "I'm glad she is well and her family too."

"I don't know how well. I think there is much she cannot tell me."

"Yes, I know what you mean." Wolf had gotten a letter recently from his own family. They'd sent supplies. Canned fish and vegetables. He was sorry they'd sent them, certain they needed it much more than he did. He would write again and thank them for their great sacrifice, but he'd tell them to keep future supplies for themselves or share them with someone in need there in Heidelberg. He would promise them that he was well fed. They wouldn't believe it if he did not promise it was so.

Wolf's mind tracked back over the summer months to the many picnics Frau O'Brien had spread for them. Even when things changed, when Fannie's brother returned and the offerings weren't as opulent, she'd still sent out the occasional roll and jam, or the offering of cold, fresh buttermilk, or a bowl of fresh-picked raspberries and jug of iced raspberry tea made from harvested leaves.

And he could still see Fannie's face glowing with the kiss of the sunshine, tendrils of her chocolaty hair escaping their banded scarf to blow across her cheeks.

"Horst's sister is better too," Fritz said.

"Is she? I didn't hear about that."

"He got a letter today. She is staying at a friend's home in the country."

"I suppose the air is better for her, and there might be more vegetables for her diet."

Fritz folded up his letter. "Do you think it's as bad as they say? That some of our people are starving?"

They'd all heard the sad stories, uncertain if they were true or American propaganda. "If the news is true, then it is not only our people who suffer."

"The Jews, certainly. I've read they're mostly in camps now or have been sent out of the country."

"So I've heard." Wolf made his way to the tent opening. Evening roll call would begin in a few minutes.

"Do you ever think about Leo?"

He opened the flap and paused for Fritz to go through. "All the time."

"Have you heard anything?"

"Not yet."

"Do you think they will execute him?"

"If he is found guilty of criminal acts, it is possible."

"Hauptmann Kloninger. . ." Fritz's voice dropped into a solemn note.

Wolf looked at him. The younger man's face had reddened and his gaze flitted away. "What is it, Fritz? You may speak freely."

"Nothing is wrong. I am only sorry. I suspected Leo was up to something. I even considered asking him to let me help."

Wolf frowned. Should he be concerned about Fritz's leanings now? "Why didn't you come to me? In what way did he arouse your suspicions?"

Fritz shrugged. "Leo hated the Americans more than anyone else did. More than I hated them. I cannot say I still do," Fritz admitted. "He was always looking for a way to harm or frighten them. Something that would bring him notice when he got back to Germany, I think. At least something that would bring him honor."

Wolf sighed. "I see. I am afraid that Leo didn't know who he was. Not really."

"I cannot say that I know who I am half the time. A German soldier. That's all."

Wolf pocketed his hands, and the pair strolled toward the parade ground. "And a student, and a worker. When you get home, you'll marry Emma, I presume? Then you will become a family man?"

"If I can find work enough to support her. And if she'll have me," he added sheepishly.

"I would be very surprised if she is not already planning her trousseau."

Fritz grinned fully. "I will have to think of a good way to propose."

"Talk to Otto about that. He's quite creative, and I suspect between him and the rest, you'll find some romantics among them."

"Not Otto!" Fritz laughed. "He likes women, but I wouldn't call him romantic. Maybe Horst."

Wolf glanced ahead where an American soldier was walking toward the men with a clipboard.

"What about you, Hauptmann? Will you go back to teaching after the war?"

Would he? That had been his plan. Since being sent from the farm to work in the canning factory over in Barron, however, Wolf wondered where the future would take him. At the moment, he couldn't imagine what his prospects looked like, though he acted like he did for the sake of the younger men.

"I will have to wait and see. My first thought will be toward my parents. I will look after their well-being, and then I will decide."

Fritz nodded, accepting his answer, just as the American called them to attention. The sergeant rattled off each prisoner's name and put a check after it on his chart as they responded.

The soldier lowered his clipboard and looked at them directly. "Tomorrow is Sunday, but no one will be leaving camp. As you know, two months ago one of your number was arrested and sent back to Fort McCoy where he was detained and awaited charges. Leo Friedrickson was charged for acts of sabotage against the United States and violating laws of war against civilians." The sergeant directed a severe look at Wolf, but Wolf remained unmoved. He'd been cleared of wrongdoing. Fräulein O'Brien's statement about the attack and Wolf's subsequent aid—backed further by the statements from her mother and brothers—gave him no reason to squirm under scrutiny now. He had only one regret, and that was that he had not been able to stop the attack before it could happen. If only he'd seen Leo's anger and resentment for what it was and could have been able to keep him from putting any plans into action that would result in Fannie's or her family's injuries. If only he could have stopped Leo from bringing destruction on himself.

"Herr Friedrickson. . ." the sergeant said with pause and emphasis, "has been given defense counsel and been tried by a military commission comprised of ranking U.S. Army officers."

Wolf's chest tightened, and he could not release his breath. He felt the tension of Horst and the others too, but he kept his gaze on the sergeant.

"He has been found guilty of acts of violence against American citizens, though it seems he worked alone. Therefore, he has not received a sentence of death but will remain imprisoned for the duration of the war plus twenty-five years."

"A life sentence," someone muttered as a collective release of breath passed down the line. Wolf suspected it was Otto who spoke.

The sergeant ignored the remark, or maybe he hadn't heard it. "Lest anyone else feel a need to recriminate, this camp will remain on lockdown for one week. After that time, you will return to your normal work." His glance connected with Wolf. "At the factory."

Since the incident at the O'Brien farm, the men were pulled from employment there and sent instead to one of the local canning factories where they learned to detest the smell of souring cobs of corn. From what Wolf had been able to surmise, no other group had been sent to the O'Briens' farm to finish out the season. They would do without the workers, probably to the blessed relief of Calvin O'Brien and Fannie's mother. Maybe to Fannie herself after what she'd been through.

Tonight, at lights out, when everyone else fell asleep or turned over with their own thoughts, he would pray for the O'Briens just as he always did. He would pray they had been able to bring in the remainder of their crops. Perhaps the sweetest of the corn at the factory had come from their field. He liked to imagine that it had.

What would Fannie do now, after the hard work of summer? Would she return to school or take more workdays at the library? Would she remain at home to help her mother in the kitchen, leaving the fall and winter chores to Calvin? Would her older brother have kept his word to help them now that the PWs were gone? Did they all rest easy, with the season coming to an end, and simply take the time to mourn their father's loss and their imprisoned brother?

Perhaps he would never know, though he liked to imagine that one day he would write to her and thank her for all she did for them while they were there—for all her family did.

"Dismissed!" the sergeant barked.

Wolf pushed a hand through his hair and turned to leave with the others, but the sergeant approached him unexpectedly. "Come to the office. There's someone to see you."

Wolf almost asked, *Me?* But it was best to nod and follow.

The main office was a small wooden building no more than ten feet square, thrown up in a hurry, with bare walls and a plank floor. The only pieces of furniture inside were a desk and chair, two file cabinets, and a spare wooden chair up against the wall. Wolf's glance fell to it immediately, taking in Fannie as she rose from the seat.

She was more beautiful than ever. Though the summer was spent, her skin still wore a bit of its bronzing. She wore a mid-length navy blue dress with blue-and-white buttons marching down the front. The dress was adorned with pockets and a lacy white V-neck collar, and her slimness was accentuated by a belted waist. Her waves of hair were left long and loose in the back, but she'd swept the front to the side and pinned it in place. She clutched a white pocketbook before her, and her eyes were wide and dark upon him. Was she as nervous and glad to see him?

The question was instantly crowded out by others. Was anything wrong? Was her family all right? Had she come alone?

"I'll wait outside, but the door will be open," the sergeant said. He stepped through, pushing the door wide. Wolf could see by the man's elbow he was barely out of sight and likely not out of earshot.

"Fannie." He reached up to remove a non-existent hat and pushed his hand through his hair again instead. He badly needed a trim. He offered a smile and indicated the chair. "Please, do not stand."

"It's all right." She waved away the offer. "This will only take a minute."

A minute was not nearly long enough. He wanted to drink her in. He also wanted to talk about all that had happened and tell her how horribly sorry he was. So much had been left unsaid.

"I heard he'll be locked up for a long time." She didn't need to mention Leo's name.

Wolf nodded. "Ja. So they have just told us."

"Oh. Well." She fidgeted. "I just wanted to—"

"Fannie, I am—"

They spoke at once. Wolf nodded to her.

"I just wanted to thank you for what you did that day. It shouldn't have taken me so long to come."

He held up his hand. "No thanks are needed. I regret I did not stop him sooner. I am sorry I did not know about the gun."

"Yes, well, we were all sorry about that."

He didn't know what to say. He wanted to say things that he'd let sift into his dreams, but they were foolishness by the light of day.

"The canning season will end soon. Do you know what you will do then?"

"They are sending us back to McCoy, and from there they will decide. It sounds as if we will be sent to the forests to cut trees." He'd never imagined himself a lumberjack, not in all his years of teaching and study. He'd never imagined any of the things he'd been doing this summer. "Is your family well?"

She brightened. "Yes, they are well. Calvin is doing better. He's working like crazy even." She chuckled, a sound he missed terribly. "He can hear a little bit more now than he could at first, but he says his ears never stop ringing. He says it was better before when he couldn't hear hardly a sound at all."

"Perhaps it is a good sign that he will hear better again soon."

She shrugged. "The doctor isn't as positive as you, but we are hopeful."

Wolf thought of Horst's recent letter from Emma. "And your other brother? You've heard from him?"

Her face fell and she shook her head. "Not for some time, but the war is bound to end soon."

His heart broke for her. "Ja."

The sergeant peered around the corner as if to remind them of his presence. Fannie licked her lips, and Wolf knew his time with her was fleeting.

She looked at him again and her step brought the space between them closer. Her gaze reflected his own feelings with a look of mild desperation. She held out her hand. With only a glimpse at the doorway where the sergeant waited, he shook it, lingering in the touch of her fingers as long as he dared.

"Thank you, Wolf. Thank you for all your hard work. Tell the others for me, won't you?"

Brazenness engulfed him. "Ja. I will write your family a letter from the woods camp if I am allowed and if you will not mind."

"Yes. Yes, please, write to us. We would like to know that you and Rudy and the rest are faring well in our Wisconsin winter." Her shoulders relaxed and she smiled. "You must be a good teacher, Wolf, for I have learned much from you this summer."

"And you will be a fine teacher too, Fannie. Do not quit on your dream."

"That's enough." The sergeant stepped aside, making way for him to depart.

"Ja. Danke, Sergeant." He gave a clipped bow. "Danke for coming, Fraülein O'Brien. I am very glad you did."

She nodded as he turned to go, his feet wanting only to remain glued to the wooden floor where he could breathe in her presence a little longer.

CHAPTER 23

Winter 1944–45

Fannie smiled as she held out the woman's book. "There you go. Not due for three weeks."

"That will give me plenty of time. Once Thanksgiving is over, we'll be settling in for winter. Don't expect it'll be much of a Christmas this year. Thank you." Without waiting for Fannie's reply, she took her book and turned away.

"Goodbye now."

As the woman departed, Fannie reached beneath the desktop for the cards that needed filing. Mrs. Calloway approached her. "You can leave those for me. You ought to be heading home. It looks like the snow is coming down a little heavier."

"Are you sure? I don't mind staying."

"No, go ahead. I only walk home. You have a drive. I don't want you sliding into a ditch."

"All right. Thank you, Mrs. Calloway."

"I'll see you on Monday."

Fannie nodded. She was happy to be getting more hours at work now that the harvest season was over and Calvin was taking up the task of managing things at home. Jerry and Patsy were back in school too. She wished she was. *Be content, Fannie. You'll get your old dreams back on track eventually.* Hadn't Wolf urged her not to give up on them? *It's just going to take a little longer. Think of Dale. He sure didn't plan to be stuck in a prison camp in Germany all this time.*

"Just don't bother driving in if the weather is atrocious. Days like that are slow anyway."

"I'll be sure and remember." Fannie finished tidying her workspace and headed to the back room to collect her coat, gloves, and galoshes, but a cloud had settled over her thoughts. It had been months since they'd heard from Dale. Were the Germans preventing their prisoners from sending letters? Mom wrote to him every few days. Fannie had written to him again last night, and she'd keep on writing no matter what, until she heard something.

Drawing up her wool collar and tucking her face against the gusting wet flakes, Fannie shuffled through a couple of inches of fresh snow to her car. She got inside and shuddered, then glanced at her wristwatch before firing up the engine. The kids would be getting out of school in half an hour. She could swing over past the country schoolhouse on her way home and pick them up so they wouldn't have to walk. She wouldn't have to wait but a little bit. That would give her time to run by the Cameron post office close to home and mail her letter to Dale. Ten minutes later, she dropped off her letter.

The postman looked at her over the rim of his glasses. "Something came in for you today after the carrier left with your regular mail, Miss O'Brien. Want to take it now or wait for it?"

"If it's not inconvenient, I may as well take it now." Her hopes aroused. Did he mean something for her particularly or something more general for her household? Finally news from Dale perhaps?

When he handed her the envelope, her curiosity increased because it was addressed to her, but she didn't recognize the handwriting. She saw that it was postmarked Rhinelander, Wisconsin.

I don't know anyone up there. Then her heart skipped a beat. She tucked the letter into her purse and thanked the postman before hurrying back out to her car. Though eagerness was killing her, she'd wait to read it when she was parked at the school. The car might be a little warmer by then. When she pulled up across the street from the one-room school, she left the engine running and slid her finger under the letter's seal, drawing out a single sheet of paper written on both sides.

The return address in the upper right of the page confirmed her question, and a thrill shot through her.

> *Wolfgang Kloninger*
> *Camp Au Train*
> *Munising, Michigan*
>
> *Dear Fannie,*
> *Though you said I might write, I did hesitate to write you*

this letter, fearing you would rather not hear from me after the mishaps of August past. Yet I write, and I hope my words are well received.

We are well here, me and the men with me. We are sent up from Camp McCoy to cut pulp in this woods that is never-ending. We came by train, and it seemed we had gone forever, and we are told this is nothing. That the woods go all the way to the lakes they call Superior and Michigan and beyond. We have many woods around my city of Heidelberg, but I am not sure they span such a space as yours in Wisconsin and Michigan. There have been men working here all through the year. We are sent only to cut the trees and skid them out for winter. Then we will depart. Whether we are to return to Camp Barron or to other farms to work, time will tell. War dictates to all still.

It is not too cold yet. We have been able to buy socks and gloves with our earnings. We are thankful for good food. Some men in the area hunt for venison. Our guards have given us red cloth to wrap around our arms or hats so that we are not mistaken for deer in the woods as we work. Our guards go hunting too. Last week I was startled when one of them fired his submachine gun to bring down two deer that had roamed close to our work area. The men cheered, for we ate steaks with our potatoes that night.

Rudy is learning to cook. He has been assigned to working in the camp kitchen. He and the other cooks make us something called pasties. Do you know of them? They are like a meat pie with vegetables, folded and pinched closed. We often take them to the woods for our meals.

How is your mother? Have you been able to return to teacher's college? I keep your family in my prayers and wish you Godspeed in all you do.

Wolf

Fannie pressed the letter to her chest and stared into the covering of snow already overlaying her windshield. He'd finally written! She'd not allowed herself to believe that he would. When the weeks passed after their brief conversation at the Barron camp in October and she didn't hear from him, she presumed he'd only spoken in the moment. She'd forced her thoughts away from the prisoners. There was no point. They were Germans, after all. The enemy. They'd probably never see each other again.

Suddenly, the passenger door jerked open, startling her, and she quickly tucked the letter into the envelope. Patsy got into the back, then Jerry yanked the door closed and shook snow from his head, settling into the front seat beside her with a chaotic entrance.

Fannie snapped her purse closed over Wolf's letter. "You found me."

"Thanks for coming to get us."

"I didn't think we'd get snow, as nice as it was this morning."

"The temperature dropped like a rock."

"Can we get going?" Patsy asked from the backseat. "I'm starving, freezing, and I have piles of homework."

"I'm hurrying." Fannie put the car into gear and pulled onto the snowy road. She slid when she came to the first intersection where she had to stop. "It's getting slick."

"Want me to drive?" Jerry sounded like he only half-jested. He was a good driver, and she was tempted to let him take over, but she was a good driver too. Her dad used to tell her so.

"I'll be fine. How was your day?" She wanted him to talk, and Patsy too. Her thoughts were like squirrels storing nuts, jumping from branch to branch and burrowing here and there with nuggets of detail about Wolf's letter and what she would write in reply.

They arrived home without incident ten minutes later, and after kissing her mom on the cheek with a hello, she went straight upstairs to begin.

> *Dear Wolf,*
> *It was a pleasure to get your letter today.*

She erased "today." It gave away her anxiousness in replying.

> *I'm happy to hear that everyone is well and that Rudy*
> *is learning to cook.*

Fannie couldn't write fast enough.

Two weeks later, at the end of a busy week, another letter came. Wolf thanked her for her reply and wrote that he was learning quite a bit about the lumber business from the men he'd spoken to who made it their liveli-hood. He told her they were friendly, even though some of them had loved ones in the war. Most of the other prisoners were younger than Wolf, not more than twenty-three years old. It was hard for these Michigan men to hate such youngsters, one of the older American workers had said. They reminded him of his boys gone off to war.

Fannie penned a reply after chores on Saturday morning, before setting off to help with the laundry.

> *Dear Wolf,*
>
> *I am very happy you wrote. I was not simply being polite that day when I said I would be glad if you did. We were almost to Thanksgiving on the day your letter came and with it our first big snowfall of the season. I suppose you're not very familiar with an American Thanksgiving.*

She proceeded to explain it, trying not to sound too elementary. Then she went on.

> *We're only two weeks out from Christmas now, though we don't plan to do much this year, just go to church and enjoy a family meal. Patsy and Mom and I have been busy knitting socks and putting together packages with some of the other church ladies for the boys. That's the only Christmas gifts we're concerning ourselves with. Jerry brought up a Christmas tree from the woods, and Patsy pulled out the box of ornaments and decorated it last night. I only watched. I miss my dad. I feel I can tell you so and that you will understand. It felt different without him here, though Cal was kind enough to put the star on top in his place.*
>
> *What about you? I'd love to hear about your Christmas traditions. Will you be allowed any celebrations at the camp?*
>
> *Your friend,*
> *Fannie*

Wolf's reply came sooner than she expected it might.

> *December 27, 1944*
> *Dear Friend Fannie,*
> *I am very sorry that you did not have your father with you as you remembered the holy season. You may always tell me how you feel, Fannie. I am grateful you are comfortable in doing so. If I may, allow me to wish you greater joy in the New Year. It is strange, is it not, to think that there might be a chance of happiness in the New Year, even as our two nations are caught in this terrible clash of wills, seeming to come to no end? Will it? Will the world rage until it tears*

itself apart, or can we hope that the New Year will bring peace and hope for all of us once again?

Forgive me if this thought discourages you. I do not mean for it to do so. Just the opposite, in fact. I pray you have heard from your brother. I pray he is well and that your family is also well. But for the absence of loved ones, your Christmas holiday sounds most pleasant. We too enjoyed a day of worship and song. It was good to hear the men singing "Stille Nacht" and "O Tannenbaum," although we had no tree to gather round but those we see outside our camp every day.

In Heidelberg, I went to worship with my parents. I have no siblings, as I was born late in my parents' life. After worship and singing, we would sometimes go to the home of my aunt and uncle and my cousin Elisa. We would share a meal and sing more carols, my mother and her sister taking turns on the piano. Elisa and I would cut out decorations for the tree when we were younger. When we grew older, we would sit and talk about our hopes and dreams and discouragements, as young people do. I have not seen Elisa since her graduation from secondary school a year after mine. She was engaged to be married before the war. Now, I do not know. My mother has written that Elisa's fiancé has not been heard from in some time. We all hope he is all right.

Heidelberg is a lovely city. One of the loveliest in all of Germany, if I do say so. I hope much has not changed during the war. The city is nestled along the Neckar River in a wooded gorge. The ruins of a grand castle are perched above. Some call it a romantic city. I wonder what you would think if you saw it.

Fannie sat on the edge of her bed and lowered the letter as she tried to envision the magnificent old city. She'd already looked it up in a library encyclopedia and knew about the ancient castle, how it had been built as a refuge and place of worship by the Celts on the Heilegenberg, or "Mountain of Saints." The city's famous Heidelberg University had also played a role during the Reformation in the fifteenth and sixteenth centuries. She couldn't remember why it had been left to ruin. Something about the French and lightning, if she recalled. She would ask Wolf more about it.

She couldn't imagine being away from home as long as Wolf had been and wondering what shape things would be in when she returned. Had Cal nursed those kinds of questions after learning about their father's passing? At least he hadn't had to worry that their home might be blown apart by war.

Though it might have been if Leo had had his way.

That was another sad story. So many sad stories would wait to be told in the wake of this war. That was one thing she was sure of.

This time Fannie would wait a few days to write back to Wolf. There was so much to think about and ask him, and she didn't want to forget a thing.

By due course, their letters slowed down as winter settled in tightly around them. About once a month their letters passed each way. Yet Fannie was just as excited each time she found one waiting for her in the mailbox. Once, Wolf's letter included a note from Rudy for Jerry and Patsy. Wolf had asked her to seek her mother's permission before giving it to them. It was harmless though. Just a message "from a friend." The English was poor but understandable. Not nearly as clear as Wolf's, though he admitted that he had been friendly with a guard who helped him correct some of his grammar.

It wasn't until late March that Calvin discovered the exchanges. He'd trudged down to the mailbox himself. Upon his return to the house, an unsealed letter went skidding across the kitchen table in front of Fannie, where she was wiping the surface with a cloth.

"What's tha—" Her word died on her lips when she saw the handwriting and realized that Calvin had looked at the contents. "You opened my letter." She didn't shout, yet the shock of her tone couldn't be contained. That he would do such a thing galled and stunned her.

"I hoped maybe it was from Dale."

"You opened my letter." She said it more strongly this time, and she narrowed her eyes as she picked it up and spun on him.

"Your letter from your German, you mean? I had a right! I deserve to know what my own sister is doing under my roof."

"*Your* roof? This isn't just your roof. This is *our* home, and I have as much right to my privacy as anyone in it." She smoothed the envelope and pressed the seal in place, even though it wouldn't stick again.

"What do you think you're doing, Fannie, writing to him? Nurturing some kind of romance? *Dearest Fannie*," he mimicked.

Had Wolf written that, called her dearest? "No! It's not like that."

"Isn't it? Aren't you just like those women in town who meet up with the prisoners at the fence to—"

"Stop it! Don't you dare." She glared equally hard back at him and stepped nearly toe-to-toe. "How dare you accuse me of something so vulgar!" Her chest heaved with anger that wouldn't be tamped down. She slapped Cal hard across the cheek.

His head jerked, and he said nothing for a long moment, only stared at her. Finally, he sneered. "I guess it doesn't matter since my ears were ringing anyway."

She turned her back and looked down at the letter. Should she feel ashamed? She didn't, in any case. "It's my life, Cal, and this war won't last forever."

"What?"

She turned to him, realizing he genuinely couldn't hear her. "I said, it's *my life*. Leave me alone."

He coughed out a derisive laugh. "You're acting like a fool, Fannie."

"I'm not a fool for wanting peace. I'm not a fool for seeing that these men didn't hurt us. This man saved me!" She held up the letter.

Cal put his hands on his hips and pursed his lips. He gave his head a shake.

"You know I'm right. They did nothing wrong. It was only Leo."

"He'll be going back to Germany when this is all over." His voice was controlled now, gentler. "And no matter what it says in there"—he jabbed his finger toward the letter in her grip—"they're not coming back here to work this summer."

"I know he'll leave. I'm not stupid. But we are going to need workers again, Cal. You know it as well as I do. Mom probably already made up her mind to hire the Germans back. There's still not enough of our own men home."

A little snort escaped him, but Fannie pretended not to care. He started to turn, and Fannie shouted so he'd hear, "You know I'm right!"

Calvin marched back onto the snowy porch, slamming the door and leaving a trail of snow melting in his wake.

Fannie pushed the letter into her apron pocket and went for the mop, glad that Jerry and Patsy were at school and Mom had gone to her quilting group that was busy finishing another quilt to raffle for the war effort. After swiping the mop over the puddles on the floor, she hung it back on the hook by the kitchen door and pulled the letter out of her pocket. With a glance toward the window to be sure Calvin wasn't on his way back in, she drew out the pages.

> *Dearest Fannie,*
>
> *How good it is to have gotten another letter from you. The dark winter days would seem long indeed if not for the bright light you shine into them.*

Fannie crept fingers to the back of her neck then along her jaw, warming at Wolf's words but also seeing them through Calvin's eyes.

> *Yet this time will not last forever. Already the boys are talking about the spring to come. There are rumors we will return to Fort McCoy, and once again we will be sent to work on the farms and in the factories. There is a shortage of guards here, so I am given charge of my own men and ordered to supervise. I urge them to do their work well, for I am optimistic that the acts of one man last summer will not be held against us. I do not know if there is any chance we will be brought to Barron again. I harbor a hope that we will be.*

She placed a hand over her mouth, and tears blurred the rest of the letter. Did he hope—really hope, as she did—that they would see each other again? That if the war dragged on, he would work again in their fields? Was such a thing too impossible to wish for?

Calvin's boots scraped on the porch once again, and Fannie hastily swiped at her tears and tucked the letter into her pocket. Springtime seemed both very near and very far away all at once..

≣CHAPTER 24≣

April 1945

Thanks to Calvin and Jerry, Fannie's family had plenty of firewood to heat their house during the long Wisconsin winter, and her brothers had managed to keep the ice out of the cow tank. Fannie felt almost as if she'd been allowed to return to those unburdened days before her dad died and before Calvin and Dale went away. Now, across soggy fields, the sun warmed the earth, and little evidence of winter remained in the northwestern part of the state beyond the remnant of dirty snowbanks along the roadside and beneath the trees shadowing the creek bank. Would the arrival of spring mean better days ahead? The season had always made Fannie feel like everything could begin anew. But would they ever hear from Dale again?

Oh, how she wished this war would end! *Any day now. . .* she told herself as she stood frying potatoes in a cast-iron skillet on the stove. *Any day!* The news had been pouring in of late. U.S. forces had crossed the Rhine, and hundreds of B-29s firebombed Japan. Every country in the Western Hemisphere had joined the war. Millions of Axis prisoners had been captured on the western front and in Italy, and General Eisenhower demanded Germany's surrender, even while war in the Pacific raged on. And most importantly to those at home, it was said that prison camps were discovered, yet there'd still been no word of Dale.

Fannie salted the potatoes and thought of Jerry, just a boy, but he'd proven himself man enough to step into Dale's shoes and do the work required of him. He'd more than just grown up. He'd grown older in other ways beyond his years. Was it because of losing Dad? Or was it the struggle over all the unknowns about Dale just like those Fannie wrestled with? Sometimes, instead of going out with his friends, Jerry would come home and sit with Cal. They'd play checkers and talk about the farm or reminisce about a fishing or hunting trip or other such occasion from years past. They sounded like a pair of old farmers down at the feed mill.

She turned the burner lower as the scorching scent of potatoes wafted past her nose. At least winter was over, and with those prison camps uncovered in Germany, they must learn something of Dale eventually. In the meantime, they distracted themselves with life's simpler things.

The family talked at dinner last night about seeding and how many acres to put into corn this year. If this war did go on, the demand for supply would only increase. More than ever, her family wanted to do their part to support the boys on the battlefields. To bring home their husbands and sons.

Fannie dropped a handful of onion skins into the scrap bucket and glanced out the front window next to the dining table at the sound of an automobile drawing up into the yard. She didn't recognize it at first. Then, as the motor quit, Cal's girl—or the one who'd once been his girl—stepped out. *Liza Brachman. . . Oh my goodness.* She looked prettier than ever, wearing red lipstick and with her dark hair drawn up. She had on a bright blue coat over her dress and carefully skirted mud on the path in her black leather pumps.

Fannie turned the burner off and tucked a strand of hair behind her ear as she met Liza at the door. She opened it wide before Liza could knock. "Why hi, Liza. It's been forever."

Liza stood demurely. "Hello, Fannie. Is—is Calvin home?"

"Come on inside. He's not here at the moment, but he should be home soon. He went to drop Mom off at the ladies' aid and run to the post office and to do—oh, whatever it is he does when he goes to town. You're welcome to wait for him."

She fidgeted. "I. . .well, yes, maybe I will." She glanced toward the living room as she followed Fannie inside.

"Grab a seat. I just made a pot of tea."

"I'd love some, thanks." Liza pulled off her gloves and unbuttoned her coat. Fannie noted that she wore a pretty dress, red-and-white striped. This was a good sign—she hoped. It must matter to Liza how Cal found her.

Fannie poured her a cup of tea and set it on the table alongside a pitcher of cream. "We have honey. Want some?"

"Oh, that sounds lovely. I used up my sugar card a little early this month."

Fannie had forgotten that Liza lived on her own—or with another young woman. She was Calvin's age, and she'd gone to secretarial school. She supported herself these days. Fannie vaguely remembered that Liza had talked about joining the war effort in some way, but she'd ended up keeping her job.

Fannie set the honey crock on the table and laid a spoon out for Liza. "Help yourself. Mr. Peters keeps bees and raises apple trees, so we usually trade him a couple bushels of corn every year for some honeycomb. Mom separates it and uses the wax to seal jars."

"Oh yes. I remember him and his bees. I didn't know he was still doing that since his wife passed."

"I think it keeps him busy and less lonely."

"How sad. That he's alone, I mean."

Fannie nodded. Many people were alone now, since the war. There'd be widows aplenty and bereaved mothers and fathers, just like her own. She went for a cup next to the stove and poured her own tea. Then she pulled out a chair at the table by Liza. "I'll join you. I've only had one cup." Fannie smiled and added a dollop of honey to her tea. She stirred it slowly until it dissolved. "It's nice you've come to see Calvin. We haven't seen you here since he's gotten back," she said pointedly.

Liza rested her cup on the table. "Yes. . .I know."

"You broke up."

Liza's blue eyes widened at Fannie. "Is that what you think? I never broke up with Cal."

"You didn't?" Fannie's suspicions aroused. "I guess Cal didn't say you had. Not precisely. But he—I mean, you and he haven't been seeing each other, have you?"

Liza sighed. "No. We sure haven't. I've tried. Oh, Fannie, how I've tried. I didn't want to call your house and upset your mother, and of course Cal can't hear well on the telephone. I've sent him notes and letters. I wrote to him often when he was overseas. I was so excited to hear he had come home." She bowed her head. "And so devastated when he didn't contact me." She lifted sad eyes to Fannie. "I've tried talking to him the few times I've seen him out. He says I should forget him and move on."

"Cal said *that*?" That Cal had broken up with Liza and not the other way around shocked her. What in the world was wrong with him anyway?

Liza nodded. "I guess you could say so." She picked up her tea and took a sip as Fannie processed this news. Setting her cup down again, she looked squarely at Fannie. "But I'm not giving up on him. I know he's not seeing anyone else. He might dance with a few of the regular bar floozies to try and make me jealous or mad enough to leave him be, but he doesn't take them seriously, so I don't either. I just don't know what I did to make him lose interest or stop caring. Before he left, we talked about a future. You know what I mean?" Her eyes begged Fannie to understand how serious they'd been. "Now he says he's too broken and can't offer me anything. I don't believe that."

Fannie shook her head. "No. Me either." She stood and paced to the stove where she stared at the potatoes in the pan.

"I'm sorry. I'm keeping you from your dinner."

"No." Fannie turned to face her again. "I just needed to move around. Liza, do you love Cal?"

Liza pinched her lips together and nodded. Tears sprang into her eyes. "Of course I love Cal. I've told him so a thousand times and in all my letters. He said it too. Lots of times. And he said it like he meant it, not like he just wanted kisses." She flushed, then raised her chin. "But now. . ." She turned away and wrestled with her coat pocket until she produced a hankie. She dabbed her eyes and nose. "I don't know how I'll convince him that my feelings haven't changed, but I will. I can't believe that his really have stopped."

Fannie folded her arms and leaned against the kitchen counter. "I agree. If Calvin's broken, it's only in spirit. He has a lot of anger at the things that happened over there. I think it's getting better though. I hope so."

Then Wolf strode through her thoughts, and Fannie had the panicky feeling that Calvin's stubbornness would return with the coming season if they brought the workers back.

"Have you heard anything from Dale?" Liza jerked Fannie's attention away from the PWs.

"No. Nothing. Maybe he's in another camp the army hasn't reached yet."

"They say the condition of the prisoners is terrible."

"Oh no!" Fannie came back to her chair and sat on the edge of it. "I hadn't heard."

"I haven't seen any pictures, but the rumors I heard were that the prisoners are terribly malnourished, and they say that there are many—" She grasped Fannie's hand. "Oh, Fannie. I shouldn't even say what I heard."

"Tell me. Please."

Liza looked at Fannie with tenderness. "Well, they say that many of the prisoners died and were left unburied. Others lie in mass graves that the Nazis didn't bother to fill. They say there were some atrocities, but I don't know much about that. It's only hearsay from the office," she added as Fannie's mouth fell open and her heart stammered.

Not Dale! Dale is coming home! She licked her lips, but when she tried to swallow, the muscles of her throat refused to comply. She shook her head, trying to shake away the shock. "It's all right, Liza. I appreciate you telling me what you heard. I guess we'll know the truth of it soon enough."

"They show the latest news reels at the cinema. I'll go and watch them with you if—if you want to find out."

The sound of an automobile turned their attention to see Cal getting out. He wore a frown when he glanced at Liza's car, but he didn't slow his step.

"I say we take Calvin along too," Fannie said. She squeezed Liza's fingers before releasing her hand.

Calvin shucked off his coat with his back to them. "What are you doing here, Liza?" There was no warmth or welcome in his voice.

Liza straightened. "What do you think? I came to see you, of course." She spoke a little louder than Fannie had ever heard her speak before, and it was apparently enough for Cal to understand.

He cuffed up his shirtsleeves and walked over to peer into the skillet on the stove. "Why's that?"

"Calvin!" The anger in Liza's voice was clear to Fannie, even if it wasn't completely evident to her stone-hearted brother.

He turned and crossed his arms belligerently, then leaned back against the cupboard, crossing his ankles. He didn't even come over to sit with them.

Fannie rose. "I'll leave you two to talk."

Neither acknowledged her, so she slipped from the room. She dodged up the stairs and closed herself in her room, but then she changed her mind and opened the door a few inches. She wouldn't mind knowing if Calvin did anything stupid like stomping off and leaving Liza there on her own as he might be prone to doing. But she needed a distraction too, so she sat down at her desk and pulled out a sheet of paper to write to Wolf. Her pen hovered over the page for a moment. Should she tell him what she'd heard from Liza? He seemed well informed, but likely they told the prisoners at the camps about the American victories sweeping across the European continent. He might even have learned more about the prison camps there in Germany than she knew from Liza.

> *Dear Wolf,*
> *We haven't heard from Dale yet, but I've heard rumors.*
> *I guess I don't yet know if they're true.*

Liza's words strode through her thoughts and brought a burning sensation to her chest. She laid her pen down. *Malnourished. Dead. Mass graves. . .* She pictured Dale out on the battlefield, and suddenly he was in Africa. Wolf and the PWs were shooting at him. Her heart raced at the image, and an anger she hadn't felt in months began spinning tornado-like through her veins. If Dale was dead, every German was partially to blame.

Weren't they?

"Don't you turn away from me again! You cannot run from this, Calvin!" Liza's raised voice shot up the stairwell, and Fannie drew a deep breath.

No. That wasn't true. Dale had to be alive, and as far as she and her family knew, he'd never been sent to Africa. But she couldn't write to Wolf about this.

She focused on the activity downstairs. Hopefully, Liza would give Calvin the full piece of her mind he deserved. Fannie would tell Wolf about the tête-à-tête going on down there once she learned of the outcome. She glanced at her alarm clock on her nightstand. The kids would be home from school soon, and she promised Mom to have their dinner ready.

Cal and Liza's voices bounced back and forth, and Fannie did her best to tune out the words, even as she abandoned her letter and decided to select an outfit for church on Sunday instead. It was good those two were talking. *Having it out*, as her dad would have said. Liza was smart to corner Cal here at home. If he decided to storm off, he'd have to return eventually. Liza seemed like the kind of gal who could wait him out. But Fannie never heard a door open or slam. Their voices eventually softened. Finally, she couldn't hear them anymore, so she pushed back her lace bedroom curtain to see if there was any sign of them outside. Liza's car was still here. So was their own. Had they reconciled? Or were they just sitting there in the kitchen, staring at each other in stony silence?

She turned and tiptoed out the door. Then, with a bit more purposeful noise, she headed down the stairs. She poked her head around the kitchen door, but the room was empty. The smell of cold potatoes still rose from the stove.

"We're in here."

Fannie whirled at Cal's voice from behind. The couple was seated on the couch, and Liza was tucked snugly beneath Cal's arm. She gave Fannie a soft smile. Cal looked a little sheepish, but neither was he cowed enough to be made light of.

"You two look like you've worked some things out."

"You could say that." Liza laid a hand on Cal's chest. "Can I tell her?"

He stroked his free hand down both sides of his mouth with a hint of chagrin. "Might as well."

A broad smile split Liza's face. "We're getting married." She turned and gave Calvin a resounding kiss on the cheek.

"You. . . What? Really?" It seemed impossible, but Fannie's heaviness lifted. "Calvin! I'm so happy!"

"It took a while, but he finally saw the light of day."

Fannie rushed over to them, and with a bit of awkwardness, Calvin stood to his feet and allowed her to hug him. "There's not a thing wrong with any of us that love can't fix," she said as she held him close.

"You *would* say that." He rolled his eyes.

Then Liza stood up, and Fannie hugged her too. "Welcome to the family, Liza."

"Thanks, Fannie."

"Wait until Mom hears. She'll be so glad." The rest of their family skipped through Fannie's mind, and along with them a melancholy over their dad's missing out and, of course, Dale. But he'd be home again soon. He would! She'd not stop praying until he was.

"When will the big event take place?"

"Soon as the war is over and the boys are home. We want to bring a little joy," Liza added.

"And you will."

"Yeah, well, that could be months from now, so don't get too excited," Cal said.

Liza tugged him close. "Don't go thinking you're getting out of this, Calvin O'Brien."

He turned an ear toward her. "What's that? I can't hear you."

"Oh you!" She slapped his shoulder.

Months from now. So much would happen over those months. Lord willing, Dale would return. So would the German prisoners. And if the war did end, what then? Would she ever see Wolf again?

"What do you say we go out and celebrate tonight?" Liza suggested.

"Fannie, why don't you and Jerry come along to the movies."

"I wouldn't miss it." She shared a smile with Liza that was both celebratory and knowing. Together they'd all discover if the rumors were true.

⟩CHAPTER 25⟨

May 1945

Wolf stared at the movie screen, and horror seeped like a cold, damp spring through his bones. Images bounced and flickered through the dark room. Stark images of black mud and emaciated white bodies, men herded like cattle, and women—at least he thought they were women—hunched with shaved heads and sores on their hands and faces. Hollow-eyed. Pathetic.

Then there was the dead. Human beings, bones strung together with the thinnest sheets of flesh, stacked like the cords of logs he and his men cut. Brittle. Broken.

Wolf clutched the arms of his chair with muscles taut and wooden. His mind shattered. How had they done this? What kind of evil lurked in the heart of man to do this to another? Bile soured the back of his throat, but he did not pull his eyes away. He let the newsreel burn them. He watched the staggering steps of other prisoners, once soldiers, muscled and robust, now skeletal frames donning soiled clothing that hung on them like shapeless, oversized rags. He could only imagine the smell. Nevertheless, some of them smiled through rotting teeth. Some cheered. Others nodded. Some wore the dazed look of those too long ill or simply in disbelief. Many had to be carried out on stretchers. Rescue. These had been rescued by Allied soldiers.

Finally, eyes filled with moisture, Wolf hung his head, but his heart rammed repeatedly against his chest, and he wanted to clutch hold of it and make it still, while at the same time he wanted to feel the pain. Surrounding him, the other PWs were equally silent, lost in the stunning reality of what had taken place. This could not be propaganda.

After the newsreel ended and white letters and numbers flashed in gibberish across the blackened screen, the lights came up. The men, nearly as dazed as those who'd been rescued, pushed stiffly to their feet, their shock evident in their stifled movements. They filed silently out the tent door, shuffling not unlike those men in the film, the living ones, if living they could be called.

There was no excuse for what had been done to Germany's prisoners, nor would Wolf make one. Was Fannie's brother one of those sickly, starved men, or were his remains heaped in a pile of bleached bodies? Might he have already descended into a mass grave somewhere under German soil? Would Fannie's flesh and blood be lost to her forever? Wolf had seen boys struck down and buried where they'd fallen in the muck and mire or beneath the hot desert sands. But this. . .this horrific treatment he could not fathom.

He stumbled. Otto lay a hand on his back. "Are you well, Hauptmann?"

Wolf nodded and moved on. He glimpsed the changed stature of the guards on duty. They glared at the prisoners. No one spoke as they trudged back to their own tents. Wolf ducked inside and headed straight to his bunk. Rudy plopped down across from him, his face pale and eyes red.

Horst tossed his cap onto his pillow and lowered himself like an old man with aching joints. "It is true, isn't it?" It wasn't really a question. He scrubbed a hand over his face.

Rudy whispered, "I do not understand such hate. Fear I understand. Justice I understand. But this. . . It is madness."

Wolf raised his head. "Such hatred is a poison, and there is nothing about it that can be understood, Rudy. It is simply to be endured." He sighed and spoke as much to himself as to the younger men gathered around. "Only God can change the heart of man."

"Such poison spreads quickly," Fritz said. "Our taskmasters will hate us more deeply than ever. Now that they have seen with their own eyes what our countrymen have done to theirs."

Murmurs of agreement swept around the room.

"We will do what must be done." Wolf scanned their faces. "We will do our best work, ja? We will not give them cause to inflict punishment on behalf of those who committed such crimes. God alone will be our Judge, just as He will judge men who have done such things."

"I wanted to come back to America after the war ends." Hermann spoke from where he stood in the corner, and the rest swiveled to look his way. "They will not want any of us to come now."

"You want to come back here?" Rudy's face had regained some of its color.

Hermann dipped his chin in a nod. "There will be a future here. I would like to find my cousin's family. Maybe stay with them if they will sponsor me."

Wolf gave him serious study. "You've investigated this possibility."

"Ja, I have. What will be left for us in Germany? The Allies are winning. Leo is no longer here to prevent us from admitting it."

There were more murmurs, and then they each turned to their own thoughts. Wolf lay back and tucked his hands beneath his head. No one argued with Hermann's conclusion, least of all Wolf. The younger man was right. The Allies were a step away from victory in Europe. They all could feel it.

The next morning, they returned to the woods under the guards' watchful eyes, and one week later, they filed out the doorways of their tent barracks at dawn to board a train. Wolf couldn't help recalling the rolling images he'd seen of empty train cars used to haul Jewish and Allied prisoners packed together like hogs to slaughter toward the German concentration camps. And overriding his thoughts were the questions about Fannie and her family. What her mother would think. How angered her brothers would be. How she would feel. He'd not have to wait long to find out. Yet somehow, he already knew. A devastation gripped him at the knowledge of this new chasm that had opened between them. A devastation she would share but for a much different reason. He thought only of how the unfairness separated them more greatly. But Fannie would think of what her brother suffered, and she would need to lay accusation at the feet of someone responsible. Wolf could not blame her if she chose him and his fellow PWs.

That same evening, Wolf dropped his small satchel on a musty-smelling cot in the barracks of the Barron camp. The strange familiarity of the place quickly returned, and he sensed that no matter how far away this time was, years from now the smell of wet dew on canvas, of filthy socks and the latrine not far away, of the soft summer nights. . .such smells would return him to this place, even when he was an old man.

And then there was the farm. The next day, his crew received their assignments. They were returning to the O'Briens' farm. This time Corporal Taft would not accompany them. He had been sent elsewhere during the winter, and another soldier took his place. A private who did not speak German and could not interpret for them. Wolf was thankful for the opportunities he'd had to learn more English and for correspondence with Fannie that had improved his practice. The others too were learning still.

Wolf's heart ticked a familiar rhythm in his rib cage as they bounced down the Wisconsin roads in the back of the transport truck with its canvas sides up and flaps closed, prohibiting their view. But he'd memorized the trip long before. He knew the turns onto each road. His body shifted instinctively as he anticipated each one. His adrenaline rushed as the vehicle braked and dipped into the familiar ruts of the O'Briens' long drive. Every sinew of his body pulsed with wondering what it would be like to see the O'Briens—to see *Fannie* again. Puddles splashed beneath the wheels in the same holes as last year, and in a handful of moments, the truck halted. The men shifted restlessly, and Wolf wondered what they were thinking. A glance between him and Rudy, then to Horst and Richard, and between Fritz, Hermann, and Otto left him with few doubts. Their eyes all held the same question: What would their reception be?

When the guard flung open the back, Horst was the first to descend from the truck. Broad-shouldered Richard followed, then the others. Otto smiled weakly at Wolf, who waited until last. He peered back into the dark space, almost expecting to see Leo there smirking at him from the corner.

The sun momentarily blinded him, but he soon found his focus. Calvin O'Brien was striding toward them. Face-to-face, Wolf braced himself, and Cal also squared up, spreading his legs and folding muscled arms across his middle. It dawned on Wolf that he'd rarely seen Calvin without a gun in his hand or tucked beneath his arm, but today he carried no weapon. Seeing him without one seemed strange and comforting at once.

Yet, as Fannie's brother stepped near enough that Wolf could see the glint of his eyes, he realized that Calvin had not changed much in his view of them, even after Wolf had stopped Leo's attack on Fannie last fall.

Calvin stood only an arm's length from Wolf and gave him a hard look. He spat to the side and raised his chin. "I don't hear real good, but I can still give orders. I know most of you understand me, so all you have to do is listen up and do as I tell you." Even though his words addressed them all, he never veered his gaze from Wolf. "Far as I'm concerned, you're still the enemy. You've done good work for us in the past, and we expect you'll do the same until they send you back to where you came from. We have a lot to do around here, and Uncle Sam says you're the ones to do it." He spat again.

Despite his hard line of instruction, however, everyone's head turned as first one car, then another, and still a third came roaring up the driveway. The lead car's horn blared, which Wolf recognized as the O'Briens' car, and the other two followed suit. Arms waved and shouting came from out the open windows. All three vehicles lurched to a halt in a stirring of dust, and Jerry and Patsy O'Brien jerked their car doors open.

At that same moment, the screen door on the house clattered open, and Fannie stepped onto the porch. Frau O'Brien followed right behind. Wolf forgot the commotion altogether as he fixed his gaze on Fannie. She'd raised a hand to her forehead, shading her eyes from the bright sun, a stance he'd come to think of often when he thought of her.

It was the first time Wolf had laid eyes on her in over six months. In some of the quiet moments during that long cold season when he'd read her letters, Wolf wondered if he'd imagined the smoothness of her skin and the bloom on her cheek, or the way her dark eyes could look quizzical one moment and then a slight dimple would appear the next, revealing a sense of humor she often kept tucked away from casual observers. Today she wasn't dressed in her brother's dungarees for field work. She wore a pink dress with white-and-pink striped trim, and it suited her shape most appealingly.

"Did you hear?" Patsy shouted as she ran toward Fannie and her mother on the porch. She waved a piece of paper.

Jerry jogged toward them with a yell to his brother and the prisoners. "It's over! Victory declared in Europe! The war is over!"

"And there's a telegram from Dale!" Patsy's voice squealed across the lawn.

Their friends in the vehicles behind them laid on the car horns again in a joyous cacophony.

Wolf immediately sought out Fannie's reaction, but when Frau O'Brien swooned, he lurched forward as though he could run to help. He just as quickly regained himself as Fannie grasped her mother, offering support.

Patsy ran up the steps and took her mother's other arm. Together, the sisters helped her to the rocking chair.

Now Calvin too drew back as if in disbelief. Despite his poor hearing, he must've heard enough to understand the gist that something momentous had occurred. "Stay right here." He took long strides until he united with his family, who were poring over the paper Patsy offered.

His mother handed it to him, then she broke down.

"Is it really true?" Fritz mumbled. "The war is over?"

It took Wolf a moment longer to absorb his questions. He glanced at them; at Horst, Fritz, Rudy, Otto, Hermann, and big Richard. "Not the war, but Germany's part in it."

The men shifted, some grasping arms and whispering questions, but there was no denying the relief and even the joy on their faces. Yet it mingled with uncertainty too. Yes, Germany's part in the war had come to an end, but just as quickly Wolf's brain buzzed with the question they all must ask. What did the future hold for them now?

Fannie's family on the porch still talked until Jerry ran back to his friends. In a moment, the cars roared off again, leaving Jerry and Patsy behind, horns and occupants whistling as they careened off in a scrim of dust.

Frau O'Brien went indoors with Patsy, and Calvin turned toward the PWs again. But Fannie stood on the porch, just looking. Wolf stared back, certain her gaze was searching for his, yet she didn't approach, didn't smile, didn't wave. Then she turned on her heel so that her pink skirt flared slightly, and she followed the others inside.

Calvin reached them. "You heard. Germany surrendered. Tomorrow there'll be no work. V-E Day, they're calling it. Victory in Europe. My brother. . ." Calvin looked away as his Adam's apple climbed and lowered jerkily. He cleared his throat. "My brother is alive." He ground his jaw, and now he looked again at Wolf. "They found him in one of those camps." A long silence descended as they all stood there waiting. Then Jerry approached and Calvin turned to him. "Get these guys busy, will you? I thought I could stand the sight of them, but now I'm not so sure." His fingers coiled as he strode away, and Wolf imagined that right then Cal wished he still had his gun.

"Herr O'Brien!" Wolf shouted and took a step. The private moved with him, ready to intervene. Wolf acknowledged him with only a glance.

Cal halted and turned back around. He pulled his shoulders back. "What?"

"I am glad your brother is alive. I hope he is well."

Calvin studied him as if to be sure he heard correctly before turning away again.

Wolf couldn't beg Cal's forgiveness for the sins of others. He could only speak the truth of his own heart. If Cal wanted to pass judgment on all of them for the acts of some, such a thing was out of Wolf's hands.

Ultimately, he and his boys were at God's mercy, not Calvin O'Brien's. He quoted scripture loud enough for only Rudy and Fritz, the two nearest him to hear: "Will not the judge of all the earth deal justly?"

⋛CHAPTER 26⋚

Three weeks after they learned of Dale's rescue, he was on a ship bound for the United States. In that time, V-E celebrations brought Fannie and her family a new buoyancy of heart and spirit. Still, even in her thankfulness and with the busy days of preparation for Dale coming home to distract her, Fannie's feelings toward the Germans among them remained ambiguous. How many ways had Dale and the other newly rescued prisoners been mistreated? Severe illness and starvation would prevent many of them from ever coming home again. Even while she and her family sought to treat the German PWs with kindness—feeding them, seeing that they had rest and refreshment, having herself bandaged an injury a time or two—what had the Germans done for her brother and his fellows? Offered them barely enough gruel to subsist upon? Provided little warmth in winter or warm clothes to cover their bodies? Ignored or punished them when they fell ill? The movie reels and news reports flooded back and galled her.

Dale wrote to them while on a train from New York to Chicago, but he mentioned nothing of his imprisonment. He'd kept his letter to them brief and light, saying in shaky handwriting that he'd lost a little weight, only amending it to say, "well, a lot of weight actually." But he claimed it was nothing his mother's home cooking wouldn't mend. He told them he could almost smell her apple pie. Nevertheless, the army was sending him to a hospital in Chicago for a while.

Mom had gotten a ticket as soon as she could and gone to be with him. Now, finally, she was bringing him home on the noon train. Mom had phoned to say that Dale was weak but gaining strength and that his spirits were good.

So this morning Fannie and Patsy baked three pies just to make his wishes come true. Fannie set them on the table to cool. As steam rose from the slits in the piecrusts, her eyes were drawn out the window where she could see the workers in the field, hoeing shoots of new corn. Her study drew easily to Wolf's tall form and his white-blond hair, and her insides knotted with confusion.

Realistically, she understood Wolf had nothing to do with Dale's condition, but the old anger she'd felt a year ago when learning that their enemy would be coming to their farm surged again, and she didn't know where to place it. She'd prayed for God to take it, and it shrank, but still, the desire to hold on to it lingered just within her grasp. Someone had to take the blame.

Patsy breezed into the kitchen with a book in her hand, and Fannie jerked her gaze from the window.

"Yum! How did they turn out?" Patsy inhaled the apple and cinnamon aroma.

"Good, I think. I'm going to get washed up. It's almost time to go to the station. Is Dale's room freshened up?"

"Windows are open. Bed is made. I even put some flowers on his desk. He'll find it just like he left it."

Fannie rinsed her fingers at the sink and dried them on a flour sack towel. "Run and tell Jerry to make sure he's cleaned up a little bit before we get back, okay?"

"I didn't think I was allowed to go out there." Patsy sounded quizzical.

Fannie removed her apron and hung it in the pantry, avoiding Patsy's inquisitive eyes on her. She forced out a reply. "They aren't our enemies anymore." A month ago, she didn't want them to be. But now? After learning how Germany treated her brother?

"You don't need to tell me. *I* get it. Honestly, Fan, the PWs have been here for a month, and I've not even seen you go out there except to talk to Cal once or twice or ride the tiller with Jerry. You spent the whole winter writing to Captain Kloninger, and now. . ." She gave a protracted sigh. "Have you even spoken to him since he returned?"

"I haven't seen the need. Cal is handling things now." Which was a huge relief.

"I thought you liked him. I mean, *really* liked him."

Patsy was right. With Calvin taking charge, Fannie had done her best to avoid all of the PWs, most especially their captain. "As soon as the Japanese surrender, they'll be getting sent back to Germany, so what's the point?"

Fannie looked up in time to catch Patsy roll her eyes. "Whatever you say, Fan. It just seems rude and not like you, that's all. He did save your life, after all."

Fannie opened her mouth to respond, but before she could figure out just what to answer, her little sister batted open the screen door and stepped out.

Fannie pressed a hand to her forehead, then shook off Patsy's reprimand and left the kitchen. She didn't want to think about this now. Didn't need her emotions about Wolf stirred up any further with Dale coming home—no matter how directly Patsy has struck the bull's-eye.

She'd only just gotten changed out of her work clothes and her hair pinned in place when Cal hollered for her.

"Coming!" She reached for her clutch and trotted down the stairs. "You about set?"

He'd washed up and changed, and Fannie caught the scent of his hair tonic. "I'm ready." At the car, Cal held open the passenger door, and she moved past him. Then he got behind the wheel and started the engine. "You smell nice," she said loudly, turning her head to make sure he heard her.

"Liza will be by later." He gave her a wink.

As they headed down the drive, Fannie couldn't help looking again toward the workers, and this time Wolf caught her glance. Was that a nod of greeting? Patsy's reprimand bit into her, and she felt ashamed.

She snapped her gaze forward. Cal hummed a tune as they turned onto the road and sped off. He'd progressed. When they'd first heard the news about the prisoners in the Nazi concentration camps, and all of her family reeled from sorrow and disgust, Fannie worried about the effect on Cal and whether or not he'd digress. But after seeing the films, reading the papers, and listening to the radio broadcasts, she soon realized that Calvin hadn't been upended by the information the way she was. He said he'd seen enough overseas to believe just about anything of Hitler and his SS and the rest of the Nazis. Fannie suspected that Liza's regard had also gone a long way to ground him again.

Mom focused on being grateful that Dale was returning, even though she didn't hide her tears for the ones who were lost. Fannie didn't ask questions when she saw her laying another one of her cobblestones between the house and barn. Maybe when they got home, Fannie would find a way to mark her thankfulness too. She was relieved, after all, not only for Dale and Calvin but also for the fact that the German PWs had been taken out of the war.

Getting captured might have saved their lives. They didn't know what kind of maniac was leading them. And yet. . .

She suppressed her tangled thoughts and looked at her watch. "We're a little early."

They arrived at the depot with plenty of time to park and stroll to the platform. It wasn't a crowded day. An elderly couple waited on a nearby bench, while a woman kept a sharp watch on two young children, occasionally giving an eager glance down the track. The shriek of the whistle and rumble of wheels came soon enough, and Fannie clutched Cal's arm. "Here it comes."

Her heart pounded faster as the train chugged in and squealed to a stop. She scanned the windows for some sign of her mother and Dale. First a middle-aged man got off the train, then a pair of women roughly her own age, and then an older man with a cane, and finally her mother appeared.

She lurched forward, waiting for Dale to emerge. It was a stark moment before Fannie realized that the limping man with the cane and thin crop of hair was him. Dale! Her breath caught.

"Mom." Her voice came in a short gasp. Had she really spoken? She wanted to cry out, but sight of him sent such a torrent of emotion running through her, all she could do was stutter-step forward, grasping at the fact that the frail fellow looking at her was truly Dale.

His face was thin and his eyes shadowed and hollow, but when he smiled her way, that much hadn't changed. She hurried over.

"Fannie." He held open his skinny arm, and she fell against him gently, but his embrace was solid. "Look at you."

She dared not repeat his words. "I'm so glad you're home." Her eyes blurred, and when she peered through her tears, Dale's eyes reddened for a moment, but he didn't shed a drop.

"My, my," he said several times in between looking her over and reaching to shake Cal's hand. "Been a long time. Longer than I ever thought it would be."

Mom dashed a finger beneath each eye. "Come on, Son. Let's go home. I'm sure Patsy and Jerry are anxious."

"My, my," Dale said again, shaking his head as his glance swept the depot with the white spire of a church rising up behind, the field across the road, the old hometown in the distance. He leaned on his cane as he walked.

"Do you hurt, Dale?" Fannie had to ask. How could her strong, energetic brother possibly be so feeble?

"Not much. Just a little weak yet is all. I'll get better. Don't you worry. I'll be as hale as Calvin before you know it."

Fannie kept her arm in his, offering her shoulder for support should he need it. But he never put his weight on her, slight as it was. They took their time heading to the car while Calvin retrieved their mother's luggage along with Dale's meager duffel bag containing mostly some toiletries he'd received while hospitalized.

"Mom, why don't you sit up front with Calvin." Fannie opened Dale's door and held his cane while he got in the back.

"Thanks. I'll probably not need that thing in a few more days. I feel ten times as good as I did already, just after eating regularly."

She smiled and scooted around the car, but her heart clenched at the thought of how ill he must have been and how many days and nights he might have gone hungry, especially near the end when the Germans were thinking only of getting away. He could've easily died if rescue hadn't come soon. Her throat caught again on a sob, and she had to turn her face toward the window to contain it.

"You can eat as much as you want," Mom said from the front seat while they waited for Cal to stuff her bag in the trunk.

Calvin slammed the lid and got in. As he started the engine, Fannie searched for something bright to say. "You'll get your wish, Dale. I baked you a pie. Three, actually."

Dale chuckled. "Three pies! My, my. Not sure I can eat three pies."

Calvin grinned into the rearview mirror. "Jerry and I can help you out with that."

Fannie felt her breath come a little easier. "Patsy did the crust cutouts for the top. She likes to make designs. Leaves and flowers and things."

"She always was creative."

"You won't believe how tall she's getting. Jerry too. He's as tall as you."

Dale scratched his chin. "Hard to imagine those two growing up. A fella goes away for a couple years and comes home to a new family, practically."

Mom turned her face to Cal. "Calvin, Dale mentioned wanting to visit Dad's grave as soon as could be. Will you be free later, after dinner? We can all go to the churchyard together."

"Sure. Mind if Liza comes along?"

"She'll be family soon," Mom said.

"I heard congratulations are in order," Dale said. He leaned forward and patted Cal's shoulder with his knobby fingers.

As they neared home, Fannie wished she could catch her mother's eye. Had Mom warned Dale about their hired help? Fannie cleared her throat. The driveway was just ahead. Calvin slowed the car for the turn. As they swung in, she quickly spotted the seven men still bending over hoes in the cornfield and their guard standing only a few yards away, watching on.

"Mom?"

Dale reached across the seat and squeezed her hand. "She told me."

Fannie grasped his fingers and met his gaze. He smiled softly then turned his face toward the window.

What did he think or feel about the news? After all he'd been through, like Cal, he had returned and found the enemy here at his home. Even though they labored in their simple work clothes with the stark letters *PW* printed on the backs, did he envision them in their brown Nazi uniforms, tall boots, and narrowed gazes, ordering him about? Did he hear angry words and insults? Did he see his fellows beaten or shot or left lying sick on a flea-ridden pallet?

Her heart charged ahead, and her grip tightened in his, but he only kept his gaze trained thoughtfully on the workers. Then it finally flitted toward other things—the house, the barn, Patsy waving wildly from the porch step, and Jerry trotting down to rush past her.

And Fannie could breathe again.

Being finally together, all of them except their father, felt right and normal. To Fannie's recollection, it was the first moment things had felt that way in more than two long years. As they got out of the car and Dale was swamped in more hugs, the tension slid out of Fannie and relief rushed into its place.

Liza arrived in time for dinner, and together their family relived old stories and shared a mountain of laughter while they ate beef stew. Then they moved to the living room with plates bearing huge wedges of apple pie. Dale wanted to know about everything since he'd been gone. How Jerry's high school football team was looking, whether Patsy had read any good books lately, all about Fannie's work at the library and whether she'd be able to return to school in the fall, if they'd had trouble with potato beetles last year, and when Calvin and Liza planned to tie the knot.

He told them a few stories too, but not the kind she expected him to share. He mostly skirted the frightening, horrible, painful things that

Fannie was positive he stored away inside. He told of brighter moments among his comrades and spoke about men whom he'd grown to feel were family too.

Dale cut into his pie. "There was one fellow in particular. Michael Rosen," he said. "He was about forty years old. A family man. Said he owned a restaurant before the war. Jewish though, so he lost it. A man of greater faith I have never met." Dale took a bite and seemed to drift momentarily while he chewed. They gave him time to think about his friend. Fannie wondered what became of Michael Rosen. "And there was another man too. We were never family, not like Mike and me, but he was a Christian man. Max, his name was, or so I learned. We only called him Herr Meisner." Dale took another bite.

"Why'd you call him that if he was your friend?" Patsy leaned forward, balancing her empty pie plate on her knees.

"He was a German guard." Dale's eyes lifted momentarily and swept past Fannie's. "Not all of them were true Nazis."

Cal grunted as he pressed crumbs onto the back of his fork. "So I've heard."

Fannie frowned. Why'd Cal have to say that? Now she felt compelled to respond, but then Mom spoke up. "The Germans working here have been hard workers and nothing but polite. I don't believe there's a Nazi among them."

"Not anymore," Calvin said.

"Since the surrender, you mean?" Dale asked.

"They never were." The answer leapt from Fannie's lips. "There was one man we couldn't trust." She gave Jerry and Patsy a quick glance. Hopefully, they caught her warning not to mention what Leo had done. "But he was sent back to Fort McCoy."

"Something happen?"

Jerry stretched his long legs and belched. "Nothing worth mentioning."

Mom stood. "Jerry's right. Nothing worth mentioning."

"Some of them are only Fannie's age," Patsy said. "One of them isn't much older than Jerry."

Mom took Dale's empty plate. "Students mostly, and their captain is a teacher, if I understand right. Patsy, let's scrape the dishes, and we can go visit Dad. We'll wash them later. Fannie, there's two whole pies left. Why don't you cut one of them up and take it out to the workers? They've been hoeing all day, and it'll be another hour before they finally get their supper back at camp." She glanced toward the living room window. "I see them coming up to the yard now. Probably getting a drink before they leave."

Fannie stiffened inside, but after what they'd just said about the Germans not being Nazis, she couldn't disobey. Certainly that must be her mom's reason for giving her the task.

Then Dale rose to his feet and reached for his cane. "I need to stretch. I'll come with you, Fannie."

Why not let the boys out there get a good look at what their countrymen had done to her brother? She raised her chin. "All right."

▆CHAPTER 27▆

Wolf doused his head at the water pump then tipped his face beneath the spout to catch draughts of water into his parched throat. Refreshed, he stood and swept his damp hair back from his forehead in time to see Fannie and her brother step off the porch.

Fannie stiffened as their eyes met, and Wolf offered her a small nod, but then she dropped her glance and smiled at Rudy instead. Wolf hadn't seen her smile in a long time. Now, even though it wasn't directed at him, he was glad to see it. Someone said the word *pie*, and he realized what it was she was handing out to each of them.

Wolf waited a little apart from the rest. He'd like it if she came to him. Maybe he could finally speak to her. The guard happily accepted a piece of the dessert and joined the rest of the men to chow it down. The past couple of days he'd finally begun to relax with them.

She looked Wolf's way again and spoke to the thin man who had to be her brother Dale. Now she would have to bring Wolf his serving apart from the others. But it wasn't Fannie who approached him first. Rather, her long-lost brother walked over while Fannie lagged behind. The man looked him over as Fannie finally stepped close enough to stretch her hand out with the pie tin.

"Help yourself," she said, her brown eyes flashing momentarily at him but not alighting long enough.

"Danke, Fannie." He accepted the entire tin since only one piece remained, but he didn't remove the pie.

"I take it you're their ranking officer," the brother said.

"Ja." Wolf shrugged. "I was. Now I will once again be only a teacher. You are the missing brother who was prisoner in Germany."

The man's brow lifted. "I am Dale O'Brien." He tipped his head to Fannie. "Fannie's brother."

"We heard you had come home. I am glad for you and for your family."

"That so?"

"You will find it hard to believe, Herr O'Brien, but I have prayed for your safety as I prayed for the safety of my own friends and family."

Stilted silence filled the space for a moment. "My family tells me you've helped significantly here last summer."

"Ja. We hope so. Your family has treated us well. Much better, I fear, than you were treated at the hands of my countrymen, or so I have come to believe."

Then the American looked at the ground while he seemed to consider Wolf's sincerity. Finally, he cleared his throat and held out his hand. Wolf moved the pan to his left hand. "No hard feelings," O'Brien said.

"Dale," Fannie murmured. Her brow wrinkled.

"I regret your suffering and that of so many others," Wolf said.

"Yes, I do too. But it wasn't your fault."

"Dale," Fannie whispered, "you don't have to say that."

O'Brien looked at his sister. "Don't you think it would be better if we started moving on now?"

"The war isn't even over," she murmured.

"It's over for us. . .and for them." He dipped his head indicating Wolf and the others. "I don't want to keep reliving every moment."

A rush of relief trickled through Wolf, but he tried not to let his feelings become obvious. "I understand if Fannie does not feel the same. She worried for you greatly, and she was often given tasks heavy for her. Much too heavy to bear alone."

"I wasn't alone." Her eyes flashed at him, and to see her come to life before him, even in her anger, made him glad.

"No. Never alone. You had faith in God."

"I had my mother and Jerry and Patsy and then Cal."

"Ja."

"Dale suffered, and it's the Germans' fault. It's. . ." Her face reddened, and she dropped her gaze. "Take your pie. Let's go, Dale." She turned her shoulder away.

Wolf couldn't let her go. "Fannie. Wait. May I speak to her?" he asked her brother.

The man squinted, then nodded.

"Dale."

"Talk to him, Fannie. He isn't asking for much." He limped away with his cane, and Fannie stood before Wolf, flipping back a strand of hair before moving her hands to her apron pockets.

"Go ahead."

Wolf glanced over to the boys resting, quenching their thirst, and talking. He took a step toward the silo at the far end of the barn. The move encouraged her to walk beside him, farther from the others. Walking several slow paces, he finally halted when they were well out of earshot.

Fannie looked back at the others. Her brother stood speaking with the guard, but he didn't glance their way.

"Danke, Fannie. I have hoped to speak to you for a long time, and now that your missing brother is found. . ." He shook his head, unsure how to continue. She seemed ready to bolt, and he didn't want to lose her. "I know you have suffered greatly, and in some ways, we are indeed all to blame. All of us who brought you this war." He searched her face, but she would not look at him steadily. "If I could take the hurt from you and from your family and bear it personally, I would. If I could have prevented you from losing your father or if I could have set your brother free sooner, I would have. If I could have stopped Hitler himself"—he clenched his hand at his side—"I would have done anything in my power to do so."

Her eyes came up now, and they shone with unspent tears. She swiped them away, her aggravation obvious.

"Please forgive us, Fannie. Forgive *me*."

"I want to," she whispered. "But. . ." Her hands gripped her upper arms, clutching her body.

"But you are angry, and just–justified to be so." It took a moment to find the correct English word.

"I am not your judge," she whispered.

He looked to the house, but no one was watching, so he did the unthinkable. He reached up and wiped away a tear that had slipped to her cheek. Her intake of breath shot straight to his heart, and such a pounding began that it took all his willpower not to pull her into an embrace. But to supply comfort or something more?

"Fannie."

She shook her head, but at least she didn't step away.

"I am sorry."

"No." Her voice choked. "You've done nothing wrong. You've always done your best for our family. You even saved me from Leo." She sniffed, and a new shed of tears began. He felt his pockets, but there was nothing he could give her. She lifted the edge of her apron and wiped her eyes. "Come with me." She strode purposely around the side of the silo.

With one backward glance, Wolf followed. Dale O'Brien's glance caught his, squinting again, but he didn't move toward them. Would the man tell Calvin, and would Calvin follow with his gun blazing? It didn't matter. Fannie asked him to follow, and follow he would.

She halted out of sight around the silo and faced him. "I didn't want them all to see me crying." Now she wiped her tears more adamantly into the soggy end of her apron. Then she reached back, untied it, and pulled the whole thing off, using it to towel her face. "There," she said through a final sniff. "That's better." But her voice still sounded clogged.

"Are you all right?"

She nodded. "I'm just so. . .so sorry. And so confused. Dale is here. He's going to be okay. But. . ."

"Ja. I know. I saw the papers and the films. It is terrible what happened to him and all those other men. And the women too. If something like that happened to someone I cared for, I would feel the same."

"Have you heard from your family?" She pushed her hair back, a move that always showed she was in command of her composure.

He nodded. "They tell me things are hard, but they will get better eventually. For some there is not that hope."

"Wolf. . ." Her hand came to his shirt front, but she quickly drew it back. "There is so much to say to you. I've wasted weeks."

"We have time. Perhaps not today, but—"

"Do we?" Her face lifted and her eyes begged for a full answer.

"The war is not over yet. They have not spoken of sending us home for some time still."

"And when you do go, what then?"

He shrugged. "I cannot answer." A thought leapt into his head. It had been there before, creeping in and out as he lay on his bed at night, sometimes while he hoed corn or thought about the pea crop they'd soon be picking. But dare he speak it aloud? He might offer her a lie. Would it be a lie though? What *would* happen once he was sent home? For he would be sent home eventually. "Hermann hopes to emigrate. He would like to come back to Wisconsin someday."

Her eyebrows lifted, and her lips parted in surprise. "He could do that?"

"I do not see why not. He will need to find a sponsor, from what he tells me."

Her breath hitched. "A sponsor?"

"Someone willing to house him and help him until he finds work and is able to become established here."

"Anyone?"

"Possibly." Wolf shrugged. "He thinks perhaps he can find a relative. A cousin."

Her chest rose and fell a little more rapidly, enough for him to notice and to catch the way her pulse jumped in the hollow of her throat. "You would never do so yourself." The way she said it held a question—perhaps one she was afraid to ask. Perhaps one she'd set herself against. Perhaps a question that he himself had allowed to whisper in the recesses of his consciousness.

"I have not fully considered it."

"I see." Her eyelids fluttered.

"Until recently."

She seemed to capture her breath then, allowing him the opportunity to hold her gaze, to study her as he'd long wished to. And he did wish to. He wished to imprint her not only into his mind but into his very being.

The guard's sharp whistle beckoned him. Fannie touched him then, her fingertips grazing his arm, lighting there and sending shock waves through his body. Then she dropped her hand. "I think you would have no trouble finding a sponsor. . .should you decide to return to America. To Wisconsin," she amended.

Wolf smiled and Fannie returned it, however demurely. "We will speak of this further. We will not be sent away for a long while yet. I must return now. I do not want to anger the guard or your brothers," he said.

"No, of course not."

She gave him the correct answer, but her face broadened into a smile that told him that the past was behind them and that her real concerns had been replaced with peace.

≡CHAPTER 28≡

August 1947
Two years later

Peace—flooding her, taking over the world in its topsy-turvy manner.

Though Japan's defeat was a foregone conclusion in the summer of '45, it was September before they surrendered and the war finally ended. Tears were shed again, and Mom laid another cobblestone. Yet all that season long, the Germans still worked for them. Whenever Fannie's schedule allowed, she labored in the field alongside her three brothers and the PWs. Only she didn't think of them as PWs now. She thought of them as the boys. Except for Wolf, though she did think of him. Often.

When they found themselves picking beans beside one another or eating lunch together that her mother provided out on the lawn, they talked of what he would do if he came to America. How he would find work. Where he would live. How long it would take. That had been the hardest part to imagine. Wolf always spoke forthrightly, pointing out that there would likely be a long process and that he had his parents' needs to consider. She could see that the idea of going home to Germany only to leave them again agonized him. So, would he ever come?

That there was something deeply personal growing between them she could not deny, yet never did he try to claim her heart or any other part of her, even though there were times she wanted only to reach out and hold his hand. Sometimes the boys went for a short swim in the creek and came back to the house with wet hair and damp shirts, and Fannie would admire Wolf from a vantage point where he might not notice her staring. Once he did, however, and her skin had heated, but he smiled, and she suspected he might wish for something more too.

Now, nearly two years since V-J Day, Fannie sat on the tractor seat, the setting sun warm on her brow as she drove it across the field toward the lane. She'd been cutting oats while Dale, Calvin, and Jerry bound them into shocks. Then Patsy rang the dinner bell, a brand-new installment since newlyweds Calvin and Liza learned they were going to be parents. With Liza's time coming in only another six weeks or so, Calvin wanted to make sure he could hear if his wife needed him. Liza assured him that even if he didn't hear the bell, someone else would, and they'd be able to fetch him in plenty of time.

As the men headed toward home with their tools, bellyaching about how ready for supper they were, Fannie left them and drove the tractor down the lane to the mailbox. She squinted into the sunset while she inhaled deeply of the earthy smells—of fresh-cut oats, waving green cornfields, and even the smells of dirt and warm skin and old tractor oil. She would miss this when she put her newly acquired teacher's certificate to use and took up her teaching position at the Greenwood School in just a few weeks. She could still help around the farm on the weekends, but now her elder brothers would run the place without the three siblings who'd kept it operating while they were overseas.

Jerry would be off to his second year of Wisconsin State College in River Falls, where he was pursuing agricultural courses, so things would be left solely up to Calvin and Dale. Dale had gained almost the entirety of his strength back, just as he'd assured them he would. Only now and then was he plagued by a little cough and knees that occasionally ached. Even so, he never made much of it. Patsy would be back at school in a couple of weeks too. She was a high school junior this year and would no doubt make the most of the experience.

Fannie parked the tractor at the end of the drive and climbed off the seat to retrieve the day's mail. She flipped open the lid on the rusty box, and her heart skipped a familiar beat when she discovered a letter postmarked Heidelberg, Germany. She would have recognized Wolf's neatly angled handwriting even without the mark or return address. She tore open the envelope.

Over the past year and a half, soldiers came flooding home looking for work again, and just before Cal and Liza's wedding last year, the PWs were sent back to Fort McCoy. Eventually, they were repatriated to Germany. Wolf and his boys weren't finally shipped off until late spring of last year.

During those weeks and months as the world struggled to return to normal, and while Fannie's heart screamed for joy that the killing had ended, she also wondered whether all the things she and Wolf had spoken of during the waning summer and if Wolf's decision to return to Wisconsin someday would change. He had family in Germany. Parents to care for. And surely he would be needed in the role of teacher again, once his country regained its footing.

She'd shed tears numerous times over the months since, keeping them to herself, of course. That is, until Patsy burst in and found her with her damp face pressed into a pillow. Then a strange thing happened. Patsy cried too. Not drastically, but she'd swiped at some tears and let others tumble down, holding Fannie and telling her that she understood. She had no such notions that Rudy would ever come back to America, but she was young. She admitted she would get over him. Already had mostly. It wasn't love. Not like it was for Fannie. Her heart ached for Fannie.

Love! Fannie's head sprang upright. "It isn't that," she told her sister, dabbing a handkerchief to her eyes, but Patsy shushed her and rubbed her back.

"Of course it is. I may be only sixteen, but I'm not blind to what happened between you. Or naive," she added.

And Fannie hugged her sister tightly.

Then Wolf had written. His first letter from Germany was a long one. Longer even than any he'd written to her from the lumber camp. He told her that Germany was in a shambles, though his own city had been largely undamaged. He'd sent her two photographs, one of his parents standing in front of their home and one of himself. It looked like a professional picture, the sort he'd probably had taken for his teaching position. He was a little younger in it. He said it was taken before the war. He looked handsome, but Fannie thought him even handsomer at the age she'd met him. How would he have changed again in two years' time? Too bad he couldn't have sent a more recent photo. She tucked the picture of Wolf into her Bible and prayed for him and his parents. She couldn't imagine leaving her mother and siblings to move to another country—another continent—yet she didn't stop praying that one day he'd come.

She wrote him back right away, and they continued to write letters back and forth, though sometimes the mail was delayed because of the troubles still going on returning life to order back in Germany. In one of those letters, he gave her the heartrending news that he had been released from his teaching position. Having been a prisoner in the United States, his employers considered him contaminated by Western thought.

But did that mean he would not remain in Heidelberg, or that he would simply seek another position?

Eventually, though, the day arrived when he wrote to her mother and asked if the O'Briens would consider a sponsorship. Fannie's heart thrummed with thankfulness as Mama laid a new stone in the walk to the barn and praised God for giving their family a new start, for Calvin and Liza's baby to come, and for those young men who'd been enemies once. And now today. . .

She pulled in a breath as she read the words:

> I will take passage on a merchant ship, working my way to America. I think I have learned what it means to do hard work.

There was humorous chagrin in his words.

> I will also work for my train passage. I hope your family does not change their minds during my travels, or I will have to sleep under the stars when I arrive.

She laughed aloud. He would *not* be sleeping under the stars unless it was on the deck of the ship. She'd fix up a place for him in the barn. Calvin would have his new house ready to move into before long, and then Wolf could have Calvin and Liza's room for as long as he needed it. Wolf hoped to find a teaching position here, but in the meantime, he was not afraid to take any work that might come to him. He would labor happily on the farm to earn his keep from Fannie's mother.

Fannie finished reading his letter, then folded it up, tucked it into its envelope, and held it to her chest while she drove the tractor one-handed back up the drive.

———≈———

It was the first of October when the telephone rang—two short, two long—their ring on the party line they shared with four other farms. Mom answered the call. "Yes, I'll accept the charges." Her chin lifted, and her glance found Fannie. Fannie sat at the kitchen table with a bowl of apples, half-peeled. Her fingers coiled around the paring knife in her hand as her heart quickened. "Yes. . . Hello. . . It's no trouble. . . Why, really?" Mom's voice heightened, and Fannie's heartbeat sped. Mom fixed her gaze on her with a nod. Fannie stood. "Why don't you speak to Fannie? It's all right." She held out the receiver.

Fannie took the heavy black receiver. "Hello?"

"Fannie." She could not mistake Wolf's voice for all the world.

"Where are you calling from?"

"I am at a station in Milwaukee. My train will come through Barron at four p.m."

She wet her lips and gripped the cloth-covered telephone cord. She could hear some kind of announcement echoing over the line. "Four o'clock, you say. Someone will meet you at the station."

"If it is inconvenient, I will walk."

"It's not at all." Where were her senses? Her brain fluttered about without being able to still. "Mom and I will be there or maybe Dale. Someone. Don't worry. We can't wait to have you," she added with a glance at Mom, who stood watching. "Goodbye."

Fannie set the phone in its cradle on the edge of the counter and turned around, her mind still spinning. It was only ten o'clock.

Liza lumbered into the room looking very uncomfortable. She was four days overdue and seemed to have gone from excitement to resignation that the baby might never be born. "I heard our ring. Something important?"

"It was Wolf. He's coming today."

Liza rubbed her lower back. "Today?"

Fannie nodded and turned on the tap. She needed a drink of water, something to do with her hands, a way to steady her thoughts.

"You look nervous. And excited," Liza said with a grin.

Fannie tipped the glass back and drank, but it did nothing to stem the heat rising to her face.

Liza chuckled. "Oh, Fannie. To think you have fallen so hard for someone you hated so deeply."

"I did not hate him."

"I'm sorry. Hate is a strong word."

"I mistrusted him."

Liza lowered her bulk into a kitchen chair, her knees splayed beneath her skirt. "You were right to at first. We all have German friends. What is Wisconsin without her German heritage?"

"And Irish," said Fannie.

"Aye. A-rrighty then, *Miss O'Brien*." Liza imitated a brogue but stopped to add, "And Jewish."

Fannie looked at her. "I never thought about your maiden name before."

"Your niece or nephew will have quite a mix of ancestry. My mother is a mix of German and Scottish descent."

"I suppose if we began to untangle all the roots of our family history, we would find that there is really very little that separates any of us."

"That's the way I look at it."

Liza's kindness etched itself on Fannie's tumbling thoughts. She smiled at her sister-in-law. "Thank you, Liza."

"What for?"

"For being so good to Calvin and to all of us."

Liza waved away Fannie's gushing with a puff of breath as she pushed herself straighter on the chair. "Well, resting here to get comfortable didn't last long. I think I'll walk a little bit. Want to come?"

Fannie shook her head. "No. I think I need to stay busy for the next"—she glanced at the wall clock above the sink—"four or five hours. This is going to be the longest day ever."

"It's already the longest month."

They both laughed, and Liza waddled out the door.

When Fannie had gotten the letter in August telling of Wolf's imminent plans, it was decided that he would not be sleeping in the barn. The weather would turn cold any day now. With Calvin and Liza set to move into their own house by the end of the month and Jerry gone off to school, Dale said that it was only right that Wolf would bunk with him. He brought the subject up himself when she'd come upstairs with a basket of clean laundry.

"Not like I'm not used to having bunkmates," he told her as he lifted a stack of his folded shirts from her basket and put them into his dresser drawer.

Fannie set the basket on Jerry's bed. "Dale, you've never shown a moment of bitterness about Wolf or any of the prisoners. Not even one. Don't you feel it sometimes, after all that happened to you? You told us about the men who were like family to you over there, even that German guard, but what about the cruel men?"

Dale turned to her and sat on the edge of his bed. "Have a seat, Fan."

She sat across from Dale on Jerry's bed so that their knees almost touched. Dale rested his elbows on his legs. "It would be easy to live there in that ugly past, thinking all the time about all the bad things. Truthfully, there have been times I felt them swallowing me. But then I remind myself that it's in the past.

"I'm not saying it's easy. Truth be told, I wake myself up at night sometimes from bad dreams, you know? I cry and I can't remember why." He didn't wait for an answer but straightened his back, planted his palms on his thighs, and went on. "Then I remind myself of what I know. I know that evil men will have their just reward. I can't judge the whole human race or even a small part of it by them. None of us can. You know. . ." Dale looked into her eyes but seemed to see straight into her heart. "There were Americans who did wrong too. I saw some of it with my own eyes. Boys who shot down prisoners who'd surrendered, just because they had the power to do it and they hated them. Just to get even." He bowed his head over his clasped hands for a moment and then lifted his gaze straight at her again. "It was war, and things like that happen in war. Awful things. Things that I hope to God some of those fellows will repent of. But it's war, Fannie. And it's over. Your friend Wolf. . .well, maybe he'll become my friend too."

Tears had already clouded her vision the instant he mentioned giving up the past, and now her tears washed out. "I love you, Dale." She leaned into his arms, and he hugged her.

"I love you too, Fannie." He set her back and straightened with a glance around the room. "My, my. So what do we do with Jerry's model airplanes?"

Now, weeks later, with the memory of their conversation tucked into her heart, she went upstairs and ran a hand over the new quilt they'd laid over their guest's bed. Gone were the war posters and model planes. Jerry's dresser drawers were empty except for a pair of work overalls in the bottom one. Wolf would fill those drawers with his own things. There were hangers available for his slacks and a couple of nicer shirts. Even a hanger for a suit too, if he had one.

She tried to imagine him sitting with them in church next Sunday. Would she be able to stop smiling long enough to hear the sermon?

Finally, the hour arrived for her to leave for the station. Patsy had gotten home from school, and Mom set her to peeling potatoes for their supper. She groaned, complaining that she wanted to go to the station with Fannie, but it had already been decided that Mom would go along.

Then Liza waddled into the room, a stricken expression on her face and her hand holding her lower belly. "I think my water just broke. I mean. . .I know it did. It's. . .Oh no."

Fannie saw what Liza felt. Patsy gaped too. Mom went into action. "Get Cal."

Fannie blinked. "Where is he?"

"I don't know."

"He's at the new house," Liza said.

"Is Dale with him?"

She shrugged. "Probably."

"Let's get you comfortable," Mom said, taking Liza's shoulders. "Patsy, bring us some towels."

Fannie glanced at the clock. Three-fifteen. "Should I ring the bell?"

Mom was as composed as Fannie had ever seen her while she helped Liza to a chair. "Dale will hear it. But maybe you should drive over there either way."

She hustled out the door and rang the bell at least a dozen times. It clanged across the fields. The new house was about a quarter mile away on the southwest edge of the property, not too far from where the creek crossed the road. Pulse jumping, she ran to the car and roared off. Better to be safe and certain he got the message.

She didn't need to say a thing. Cal met her at the door, his expression as urgent as her own. "Dale said he thought he heard the bell. I was about to head over. Liza?"

Fannie nodded.

Hammering echoed through the empty house. "Dale! It's Liza's time. I'm leaving."

The hammering ceased, and Dale appeared in the doorway, a grin stretched across his face. "Don't let him hurt himself, Fannie. I'll keep laying floor down."

She smiled, and together she and Cal raced to the car.

They reached the house to find Liza pacing the kitchen and puffing breaths between Mom and Patsy.

"How's she doing?" Cal rushed to his wife's side, replacing Patsy.

Liza leaned into him with a tiny moan. "Not too badly yet."

Mom was matter-of-fact. "It'll be a while, Cal. It's her first." For Mom to remind her own son that it was their first child was the first crack in her veneer Fannie had seen.

She glanced at the clock again. Three thirty-five. "I've got to get to the station."

"I'll come!" Patsy said.

Mom pointed at the sink. "You stay here and finish peeling potatoes. Put them on to boil so they'll be done when the meat loaf is ready. I'll go to the hospital with Calvin and Liza. I'm not going to miss my first grandchild being born. You help her to the car, Calvin. I'll go fetch her bag." Mom left the room.

Fannie stared as Calvin moved his puffing wife by and Patsy scraped thick potato skins into the sink beneath a scowl. "I'm sorry, Pats. If it matters, I'm sure Wolf will be glad to have something good to eat when he gets here."

Patsy gave a weak smile. "I know someone has to hold down the fort. You'd better get going. You'll miss his train, and he'll think you forgot."

Fannie nodded, but she felt dazed. She hadn't planned on meeting Wolf alone. "I suppose I'd better."

She barely reached the station on time. There were more people waiting this time than when they'd come to meet Dale. Normalcy had returned to her homeland. The sound of steel wheels and a train whistle met her ears before she'd really had time to catch her breath and decide the best place to wait. So she stood on the platform, staring at the oncoming iron beast like a ninny while a flutter built inside her chest. The train stopped, and the passengers began descending. She took a step forward, searching through the crowd, past faces, and then. . .Wolf stepped from the car and turned to the platform. He moved to the step, and her heart seized. A head taller than the gentleman in front of him and broader in the shoulders, he spied her only half a moment later.

He wore a suit. Tweed. His hand went to his hat, pulling it off and clutching it to his chest as he descended from the train. His hair was slightly longer on top now, though neatly trimmed and combed back from his forehead, and his gray-blue eyes creased in the corners as he smiled.

Fannie's breath rushed out, and she moved through the thinning crowd until she came to a stop before him. He set down a worn brown case she hadn't noticed he carried, then dipped his head. "Hello, Fannie."

She blinked, hardly able to conceive that he was real. "You're here." Finally, her senses returned and heat rushed up her spine. "Hello, Wolf. Welcome. Welcome to America."

"Thank you. It is good to be back."

"Oh. . .I meant to say *Willkomen. Willkomen in Wisconsin.*"

He gave a light chuckle and bowed his head. "Danke, Fraülein." He looked at her for another long moment, and it was as they simply stared at one another that Fannie felt the past two years fall away. Many things had happened since. Some she'd written about in her letters. Some had never bothered to find their way onto the page. She was older now, almost twenty-five, and he was thirty-two. The war had changed them all, and time had played its part.

She smiled again. "Are you ready to go? Everyone is waiting." And then she remembered Liza was having a baby. "Well, not everyone. It seems my brother Calvin is going to become a father today. Liza is in labor."

"I apologize for arriving at an inconvenient time." He picked up his case and put his hat back on. She followed his movements, then turned and stepped with him across the platform.

"Your timing could not have been better unless you had come months sooner."

As they reached the edge of the platform, Wolf held his hand up to offer her assistance stepping down. Fannie laid her palm in his. In all their time together, never had they touched so intentionally. Now, as their hands met and his fingers closed over hers, Fannie felt grounded. As her feet touched the earth, she reluctantly let go.

At the car, Wolf stowed his case on the backseat, then slid into the passenger seat beside her. Her heart still hammered at his presence in her life. "How was your trip?" Her question came out airily, but at least she'd thought of something more to say.

"All went without incident. I worked aboard ship and hope to never have to take up that life." His face creased with a smile as he talked, telling her about his tasks on board, about arriving in New York Harbor, and his journey since. She intermittently asked questions, and their conversation relaxed, bringing them home.

"Everything looks familiar," he said, sounding peaceful. "Except. . ."

"That's Cal's new house over there across the field," she said as they turned into the drive. "It's almost finished. They'll be moving in by the end of the month."

"Perhaps there will be something I can help him with."

"That would be kind of you."

"You painted the barn."

She beamed as they drew up the drive toward the house and the bright red building. "Yes, Dale said it needed to be done. Dad would have loved to see it looking so fresh. His father built it."

"I enjoy hearing you speak about your family."

Fannie glanced at the house where things were still very quiet. Not even Patsy came bursting out. "Are you hungry? Patsy has dinner waiting. Or would you like to stretch your legs?"

He chuckled and opened his door. "A walk before dinner would please me. I've spent many hours sitting on that train."

She walked around the car beside him, and for a moment they stood gazing out at the farm, the fields, the buildings, the corn drying on its stalks in the setting sun. Fall colors changed the leaves in the woods edging their land, and at this late time of day, the beauty of it all filled her up—or was it the realization that Wolf had stopped looking at the farm and was looking at her?

"Fannie, I am so grateful that your family has offered to sponsor me. Coming to your country was never my dream before."

"What changed your mind?" Her heart pattered as his fingertips touched hers once again.

"You know the answer."

His hand coiled over hers, and he drew her closer. Their forearms brushed together. His eyes, suddenly so blue, searched hers.

"For me?" The words came out on a breath.

"We have written about many things, but never the thing I wanted to say. Is it wrong of me to hope that your family will one day be more to me than hosts?"

"It is not wrong."

"I have only just arrived, and we have not seen each other in so long a time. Still. . .is it wrong. . ." His Adam's apple pulled upward, and they inched closer. "That I wish to kiss you?"

Her throat went dry. She gave a tiny shake of her head.

Wolf let go of her fingers and moved his hands up her arms. With a caress to her shoulders, he lowered his head. Gently, his lips met hers, growing from greeting to promise. Then he softly drew away, and the deep blue of twilight outlined his features, features she wanted to look at every day forever.

The screen door sang on its hinges into the evening. "Are you going to wait out there all night or come in and get some dinner while it's still warm? Hello, Mr. Kloninger," Patsy called.

Wolf grinned, and Fannie grinned back. "We'll come now," she said. "Any word from the hospital?"

"Nothing yet. I suppose that'll take all night too."

"Must be a boy," Wolf said. "My mother says boys always take their time."

"Does she? I would like to meet your mother."

"One day, I would like that too." He warmed her with another smile and reached for her hand. Together they followed Patsy into the house, where dinner and a new someday awaited.

AUTHOR NOTE

Thank you, dear reader, for allowing me to introduce Fannie and her family and for learning beside me about this fascinating aspect of WWII. So many of my friends have been interested in this story, and I appreciate each and every one who encouraged me to explore the history of the POW camps in my home state.

Growing up in Wisconsin, my school history lessons never taught about the prisoners held here during WWII. In fact, most of the records about those men and events were destroyed in the 1950s. Newspapers seldom printed word about them, and any information about the presence of enemy prisoners working in the Midwest's agricultural industry was heavily censored at the time. If it weren't for the research of author Betty Cowley in her 2002 book *Stalag Wisconsin: Inside WWII Prisoner-of-War Camps*, I might not have been able to write this story.

So why the secrecy and why the German POWs?

WWII was in its third year when the Japanese bombed Pearl Harbor on December 7, 1941. The United States immediately joined the Allies in declaring war. England was greatly relieved, since they had been basically on their own in fending off Hitler's advances across Europe. However, rumors were rampant that Hitler intended to drop weapons to the several hundred thousand German prisoners of war being held in England. This created a panicky concern, so America agreed—somewhat reluctantly—to take any prisoners captured after November 1942 out of England and bring them to the States on empty U.S. Liberty Ships—the transport ships built to carry our soldiers to the fray in Europe and elsewhere.

The prisoners were brought stateside and spread across 156 "base camps" throughout the United States. Before it was over, America was housing over 371,000 Germans, along with 51,000 Italians, and 5,000 Japanese as well as other nationalities. Here in Wisconsin, the prisoners were sent to Fort McCoy, a former CCC camp (Civilian Conservation Corps), and they were called simply PWs.

It wasn't until the prisoners were settled here and in places like Camp Custer (MI), and Camp Sheridan (IL) that the idea grew that the PWs could pay their own keep by helping with the severe labor shortage in the agriculture industry, a result of so many American men fighting overseas. The PWs could not be forced, according to international treaties of war, and they had to be paid in scrip the equivalent of eighty cents a day for their help. Soon "branch camps" were set up to bring the workers to communities where their help was needed. Wisconsin, a state with one-third German population, had thirty-eight of those branch camps. There was one in my hometown of Wisconsin Rapids, though I didn't learn of it until last year.

The camp at Barron was real. Camp Barron was one of the most northern camps in Wisconsin. However, from there, my story is fictionalized, starting with the fact that I brought my PWs there a few weeks earlier than they actually arrived (July instead of August). In another timeline adjustment, while the song "Don't Fence Me In" was indeed a hit among the camps across the country, die-hard '40s music fans might note that Bing Crosby and the Andrews Sisters recorded the song a few months after I had the prisoners singing it in my story. The song was written ten years earlier, but it didn't sweep the national charts in the States until it was resurrected late in 1944 and sung by Roy Rogers in the film *Hollywood Canteen* and was then recorded by Bing Crosby and the Andrews Sisters. Frank Sinatra came out with a popular rendition at the end of the year as well.

While some PWs didn't believe that Germany was losing the war, there were never any reports of attempted sabotage by men at the camp nor of secret Nazi activity, as depicted in my work of fiction. Any prisoners who held true Nazi leanings were not permitted to work outside the camps and, in fact, were retained in special prison camps in other locations in the country. Usually, if a man with Nazi sympathies was in a camp, he was rooted out quickly for stirring up resistance (not unlike Leo in the story). At Barron, the prisoners went on strike twice, but both strikes ended quickly, first when a "no work, no eat" policy was put in place and the second time when tent flaps were lowered in the heat of summer.

Most of the men of the branch camps who were sent to work in the factories and fields were just as I described them—young men and family men, longing for their homes and for the war to end. They were glad to be out of the fight. According to Betty Cowley's research, the men in Barron County alone supplied more than 50,000 man-hours of labor, and they earned over $48,000 for the U.S. government.

Some of the camps reported escapes. However, most escapes were day trips. Men wandered off and were picked up later enjoying an evening on the town or having a bite in a local establishment. Some had set out to meet with local girls, others to locate family members who resided in Wisconsin. Many prisoners did find sponsors and returned to settle in Wisconsin after the war, just as Wolf did.

Despite no real sabotage by German PWs recorded in Wisconsin, word of the camps and workers was kept as low-key as possible, as community feelings were mixed. Propaganda had created enough fear that sabotage was possible, and with so many families having lost sons and husbands to the war, there was enough hatred to go around.

In other historical aspects of the story, I was startled that Hitler actually did declare some Jewish blood "null" in order to keep his war machine operational. I decided to make my nemesis in the story a man who was not happy in his own skin and incorporate some of that unfortunate history. I felt that Leo's story shows how racism can take many forms and is not limited to any particular creed or color.

The real story here is twofold. First, we are one race, the human race, and as Fannie pointed out to Liza, "There is really very little that separates any of us." Second, along with the many women who turned their hands to planting and harvesting and working long shifts in the nation's canneries, we can also credit the German prisoners held on U.S. soil during WWII with helping to save the crops during that final year of the war when America's own men were off fighting in Europe and in the Pacific. In ways that couldn't have been guessed at, they helped the Allies win the war.

For more information on the German PWs in WWII, I encourage you to look at my Pinterest board https://www.pinterest.com/nmusch/season-of-my-enemy/ and enjoy the photos, article links, and inspiration. You'll even see an actual photo of some of the Camp Barron prisoners. If you have any questions or comments, feel free to email me at naomimusch@naomimusch.com, and I also hope you'll keep in touch by stopping by my website and signing up for my newsletter, *Northwoods Faith & Fiction*.

NAOMI MUSCH is an award-winning author who writes from a deer farm in the pristine north woods of Wisconsin,where she and her husband, Jeff, live as epically as God allows near the families of their five adult children. *Season of My Enemy* is her sixteenth novel. When not in the physical act of writing or spending time loving on her passel of grandchildren, she can be found plotting stories as she roams around the farm, snacks out of the garden, and relaxes in her vintage camper. Naomi is a member of the American Christian Fiction Writers; Faith, Hope & Love Christian Writers; and the Lake Superior Writers. She loves engaging with others and can be found all around social media or at naomimusch.com.

⊯ HEROINES OF WWII ⊯

They went above the call of duty and expectations to aid the Allies' war efforts and save the oppressed. Full of intrigue, adventure, and romance, this new series celebrates the unsung heroes—the heroines of WWII.

Mrs. Witherspoon Goes to War
BY MARY DAVIS

Peggy Witherspoon, a widow, mother, and pilot flying for the Women's Airforce Service in 1944, clashes with her new reporting officer. Army Air Corp major Howie Berg was injured in combat and is now stationed at Bolling Field in Washington, DC. Most of Peggy's jobs are safe and predictable, and she can be home each night with her three daughters—until a cargo run to Cuba alerts her to three American soldiers being held captive there, despite Cuba being an "ally." Will Peggy go against orders to help the men—even risk her own life?

Paperback / 978-1-63609-156-3 / $14.99

A Rose for the Resistance
BY ANGELA K. COUCH

With her father in a German POW camp and her home in Sainte-Mère-Église, France, under Nazi occupation, Rosalie Barrieau will do anything to keep her younger brother safe—even from his desire to join the French resistance. Until she falls into the debt of a German soldier—one who delivers a wounded British pilot to her door. Though not sure what to make of her German ally, Rosalie is thrust deep into the heart of the local underground. As tensions build toward the Allied invasion of Normandy, she must decide how much she is willing to risk for freedom.

Paperback / 978-1-63609-207-2 / $14.99

For More Great Fiction Stories
Go to www.barbourbooks.com

BARBOUR
PUBLISHING